THE ANGELS OF KAILASH

THE ANGELS OF KAILASH

Shubira Prasad

Vitasta

Published by
Renu Kaul Verma
Vitasta Publishing Pvt Ltd
2/15, Ansari Road, Daryaganj
New Delhi - 110 002
info@vitastapublishing.com

ISBN: 978-93-90961-27-6
© Shubira Prasad
First Edition 2022
MRP ₹395

All Rights Reserved.
This novel is entirely a work of fiction. Names, characters, events and incidents are entirely imaginary. Reference to real places, actual regions, institutions or community practices has been made in a fictitious manner. Any resemblance to actual persons, living or dead or actual events is purely coincidental.
No part of this publication may be reproduced, stored in a retrieval system, or transmitted in any form, or by any means – electronic, mechanical, photocopying, recording or otherwise – without the prior permission of the publisher.

Edited by Manjula Lal
Typeset & Cover Design by Somesh Kumar Mishra
Printed by Vikas Computer and Printers, New Delhi

To
My father Late Shri Anant Swarup,
from whom I inherited my
insatiable urge for reading
and writing

Acknowledgement

Where do I begin to thank those who helped in the making of this book?

First and foremost, my publisher Renu Kaul Verma who is a dedicated professional. My editor, Manjula Lal, who took her job very seriously and whose inputs greatly helped me. The entire team of Vitasta: Alisha Verma, Somesh Kumar Mishra, Aman Ujjwal, Faiza Yameen, S Saraswathi. Without them, this book would not have shaped up so well.

Then, there are my peer reviewers. Some went overboard in praising the book, each good word keeping me in good humour for many days. Some readers offered constructive criticism, for which too I am grateful. As for a couple of others who criticised just for the sake of doing so, a big thumbs up to you too. At least you turned the pages.

I will be forever indebted to my family which has always been encouraging. My husband, Arun, who kept me on my toes, asking how many words I had written every day. My children, Saurabh and Sarvesh, who took over on the Team

Viewer whenever I faced technical difficulties. I am also grateful to my daughters-in-law Shubhra and Deepika, as well as Aaroh, Myra and Avitraya. You have my heart.

My gratitude for all the support I have received, both personal and professional, to put this book in the hands of readers, knows no bounds.

Thank You!

Preface

This is the second book of my trilogy on the war between demons and human beings, the first being *The Demons of Jaitraya*. The epics say, in the great war of Ramayana, a number of rakshasas escaped. They hid in the bowels of the Earth, in the water and in space and remained dormant for eons. In the 20th century, some of them reappeared in different forms to plague the Earth with wars and illnesses. At the end of his war with Ravana, Rama had asked Hanuman to raise and train a contingent of warriors who would take birth multiple times on Earth, to contain the demons. These warriors were led by the female warrior Aishani, who has been blessed by Ma Durga. She has special powers and so do the other warriors. Together they undergo a quest to make the Earth a better place.

The Demons of Jaitraya described the beginning of the warriors' journey, their special powers and their feats in demolishing the demons. These demons come in all sorts of shapes and sizes, and some have become human-like too. This makes it difficult to segregate demons from humans.

In this, the second book, the protagonist and others have come of age. They are now experienced, ruthless fighters. It describes in episodic fashion how Aishani, Adheesh and their team destroy the demons relentlessly. In a triumph of the good over evil, this is a timeless tale that is worth retelling any number of times.

Contents

Kailash	1
Reaching The Gurukul	21
Library	48
Micro Demons	60
Devnath And The House	74
Uday In Love	98
Demon Values	115
The Half Breeds	131
Two Mothers	146
Soul Exchange	164
Out In The Desert	179
Timingila	192
Drug Demons	206
Pinaki	221
The Brahmin Demons	236
Resurrection	250
Three Coins	262

Amma	283
Tejas And Jara	298
The Mantis	316
Maheesh	332
Postscript	*347*

KAILASH

Adheesh and Aishani looked around. Garuda Devta had dropped them here, how far back in time they didn't know or care. Along with Devnath, they were the three still alive. The others seemed lifeless. Only Devnath could make out that they had a spark of life left in them which would ebb out soon if immediate medical attention was not provided.

He looked at Adheesh, who was still grappling with the trauma but was swiftly coming to his senses. Aishani was sitting very still, in a state of shock. They knew that she, with her knowledge of herbs and plants, could save some of the dying souls. Adheesh went to her and tenderly put his arms around her. She gave no indication that she registered his presence. 'Ash,' he said softly, 'Baby, you have to put your grief on the back burner for some time. People are dying here. They need your immediate attention.

Without your knowledge and care they will die. As it is, they are hanging by a straw, even a strong gust of wind is enough for their life to be snuffed out. Come out of your trance, doll, we will grieve but there is no time now,' he tenderly squeezed her shoulders and waited for her response.

It seemed as if Aishani had not heard him. After a long time, she took a deep shuddering breath and turned to look at him. From a distance, Devnath saw this movement and heaved a sigh of relief.

Taking his hands in hers, Aishani looked around. If she had been in the proper frame of mind, she would have noticed the pure, sweet, pristine air and crowns of tall trees around them. The roots of the trees were at a much lower level but stood tall. Adheesh and Devnath could see some smaller trees and shrubs also, many kinds of different flora that they had never seen. If they had looked at the horizon, they would have seen huge snow-covered mountain peaks. The topography was entirely unfamiliar.

Nearby was some sort of huge cave, a conical or triangular one. A wisp of a thought floated into Adheesh's mind which he automatically dismissed. Were they on Mount Kailash? But how was that possible? As far as he knew, no human had ever been on Mount Kailash. But their circumstances were unusual. Maybe they needed God's protection from the demons, which is why God had sent Garuda Devta himself to bring them here!

Adheesh walked Aishani over to the twenty-odd people lying on the ground. They did not seem to be breathing. Devnath had collected some small stones and shrubs and tried to make some sort of beds for them, a pathetic effort, but something was better than nothing. Aishani drew her breath sharply on seeing them and for a moment forgot about her own anguish and suffering. She looked at Adheesh and Devnath, who were earnestly waiting for her instructions. Devnath had already collected water from a nearby stream and Adheesh had made a fire of sorts. She recognised a few of them. But that didn't matter now. Quickly she got down to work.

Looking around, she espied the tall trees and flowering shrubs. There were blue flowers on long stalks. She had not seen them before but guessed that the blue flowers could be used as pain killers. She had sensed that the bluish or purple flowers were from the Ativisha family, a perennial herb that grows almost anywhere. She knew that the roots of the Ativisha had many medicinal properties including analgesic, anti-inflammatory and astringent properties.

Then there was a shrub on which grew yellow flowers like poppies, which resembled a plant called Amrul, which is not really a shrub but a weed. Its leaves were used as an antidote to poison and its juice could be applied to the whole body for diverse maladies.

These plants could be a modified version of the species Aishani had studied; maybe they were more potent here, as they breathed the pure air of Kailash. She was unsure whether the herbs would help as she had no time to diagnose the sickness of her comatose patients. But she was going to try to save them—or die trying.

She gestured to Adheesh to gather the blue flowers and Devnath to gather the yellow ones. These shrubs or plants were too far away to be brought immediately. But Aishani had shifted from one feverish mode to another. For some time, she had put her grief on hold. Nor did she pay any heed to Adheesh's protestations.

Among the many powers that Adheesh possessed, travelling fast was one. He had never used this power in this life. He nevertheless had to use it now. Closing his eyes, he formed Guruji's image in his mind but what he saw horrified him: He saw Guruji's dead, mutilated body. An intense anger gripped him over which he had no control. He opened his eyes and looked at Aishani and the bodies strewn around. Oh! He could not allow those vicious demons to get the better of them. He, Aishani and their people had taken so many births just to destroy the demons. He could not let anybody die because he could not get the herbs on time. He gestured to Devnath to stay back with Aishani. Despite being fast, Devnath would be no match for Adheesh. Devnath understood and made himself scarce, lest Aishani caught him and scolded him for not going with Adheesh.

Adheesh ran and ran how! His feet were not touching the Himalayan rocks and stones at all, he was skimming over them, almost flying! There was no time to stop and marvel at the resurrection of this superpower. Suddenly he found himself on top of the shrubs. They were sparsely scattered here and there. Adheesh knew that he would find more if he descended a bit lower but collected whatever was available and climbed back. He was gradually gaining confidence in his newly discovered power. In a matter of minutes, he was back on the hill, giving the flowers to Aishani. As far as Devnath was concerned, there was nothing in the world that his Adheesh Bhaiya could not do.

Aishani washed the herbs in water and told Devnath to crush the flowers with his hands. She applied the thick paste on the broken skin of her patients. All three of them worked feverishly, applying the crude paste wherever they could, willing the bodies to show some kind of movement. There was no reaction from anybody. Aishani tore her dupatta, dipped it in water and wet their mouths with a few drops. No reaction. The water just slid away. Nevertheless, they went on applying the paste and wetting their mouths.

The minutes dragged into hours. There was no change in the condition of the victims. In the meantime, Aishani sent Adheesh down twice to get more herbs. Adheesh could make out that Aishani was again slipping into a coma-like despair. Looking after these poor sufferers had diverted her mind from the catastrophe that had befallen them. He desperately wished that he could do something to alleviate everybody's suffering, including their own. He shook his head like a wet puppy; he was not going down that road now. He was a warrior; he knew how to fight and protect. He was neither a doctor nor a nurse.

An image of his uncle Kalpesh and his wife Padmaja flashed in front of his eyes. He had to shake his head again. Thoughts of his family would do nothing but increase his worries and anxieties. He looked around again. The air was so cool, clear, and invigorating. There were so many plants and trees down there. He was positive that each of the plants and trees had some medicinal properties. Aishani knew quite a lot about Ayurveda, but not about the flora and fauna here. This was an emergency of the highest order and they were just twiddling their thumbs. Turning to Aishani he commented,

'I'll go around and see if I can find some more plants and herbs.' Aishani did not respond as she continued her work. Adheesh knew that she had heard and accepted his suggestion. He looked at Devnath who nodded. He was to stay with Aishani and help her. Devnath was mature enough to understand that his master would be more comfortable if he stayed. Being an Aghori, Devnath had stayed in crematorium grounds all his life before joining Adheesh. He had been specially trained by his Guru in Varanasi to look after Adheesh. Adheesh was Devnath's god and Devnath would lay down his life for Adheesh. His training also helped him in recognising the fine nuances of the dead and the undead. It was for this reason that Adheesh wanted him to stay back and assist Aishani.

Adheesh walked for half a mile searching for medicinal flowers. Gradually, he became aware that they were at the base of Mount Kailash, inside a pyramid-like structure. He now wished that he had paid more attention to the theory in the Gurukul. He remembered his guru saying that Mount Kailash comprised of 108 pyramids. Evidently these 108 pyramids made up the huge pyramid which is Mount Kailash. He regretted his inattentiveness now. At that time, he had been preoccupied with other subjects which he thought were more important. He couldn't help marveling at the masters who had created the syllabi of their Gurukuls. There were at least ten lectures on Mount Kailash, of which he had paid attention to only two or three. Most of the classes were about it being the gateway to heaven which did not interest him too much. He knew that the only time he would welcome heaven or Nirvana would be when every demon irrespective of its size, gender or ferocity was eliminated from the face of his beloved Earth. And this was not going to happen in a hurry. They had taken so many births to destroy these demons and the demons were still going strong. He had been engrossed in learning the great martial skills and mastering so many weapons and of course thinking about Aishani that there was no time to pay attention to anything else. Despite the catastrophe which they were facing, Adheesh's knowledge-seeking instincts and adventurous spirit were coming to the fore. Any other time, he could have spent days and even months here just by walking around, seeing things from his own perspective.

As he descended slowly to procure the herbs, he strained his mind to recall the classes which he had so indifferently attended. He had been coming to terms with his emotions and his past lives and destiny. He just had to focus and regurgitate the stored memories of what they had been told about Mount Kailash and Lake Mansarovar.

One concept he found fascinating was that time travelled much faster in this region than in the lower plains of the country. Had Garuda Devta dropped them here in the past, so that by the time everybody healed they would catch up to their present time? He mulled over this possibility. Slowly, the essence of his classes on Kailash Mansarovar began seeping into his conscious mind. His Gurus had lectured that the sacred peak was considered to be the central axis of the world and is known by scientists as the Axis Mundi, sometimes called the World Tree. It is written in the Rig Ved that He has made mountains, trees, hills as pegs to hold the Earth in its place yet fixed them in such a fashion that it still rotates on its axis and revolves around the sun. Four great rivers too have their origin in Mount Kailash: the Brahmaputra, Indus, Sutlej and Karnali. Then there are the two great lakes, Lake Mansarovar and Rakshastal which are situated at the base of Mount Kailash.

Adheesh also recalled that no human being had ever been able to climb Mount Kailash excepting one Buddhist Lama in the thirteenth century. The reason for this was that the track would unexpectedly change, or the climber would suddenly find himself moving in the opposite direction or some other obstacle would loom up. Some people either went back or just disappeared. Maybe God's ganas (minions) made sure that under no circumstance was any human being to be allowed to reach Mount Kailash. Humans were at the lower rungs as far as spirituality was concerned.

Adheesh's head was spinning by now, so he put a stop to his reminiscences. Later, he promised himself, later. Right now, he had to procure the plants and shrubs which he had promised Aishani. Maybe, just maybe, they might be able to save those lost souls.

It was slightly less freezing after a walk of about a kilometre and a half and some plants and shrubs could be seen. He plucked a couple of plants from each species and made a sort of a potpourri. Maybe Aishani would find some useful.

When he returned, he did not find any visible difference in the scenario. Aishani and Devnath were still working on the lifeless victims.

'Bhaiya,' Devnath sounded a bit excited, 'Bhaiya, these people are responding to Bhabhi's treatment.'

Adheesh perked up a bit. Being an Aghori, Devnath knew all about corpses, dead, undead and half dead. Plus, his instincts were much more honed here. After all, Mount Kailash was the abode of Mahadev or Lord Shiva, of whom the Aghoris were impassioned followers. He looked at Devnath, who seemed almost happy, because he saw some improvement in the condition of the victims but mainly because he was at the foot of Mount Kailash. Probably this was the nearest he would ever be to Nirvana. In his wildest imagination, Devnath would not have thought that he would be living so close to his revered deity Mahadev. The circumstances were more than tragic, but he was here!

'I don't find any change Devnath; they still look lifeless to me.'

'Bhaiya, though it's still touch and go for them, life is definitely coming back to them or is being sustained in their bodies. Bhaiya, this atmosphere itself is the purest in the whole universe. Sickness and disease naturally disappear. Our people were totally gone cases, but this purest of the pure air and Bhabhi's knowledge of the flowers and shrubs and their roots have helped them to recover a bit. Bhaiya, I know that the Mansarovar Lake is nearby, if we can somehow get water from the lake, our friends will surely recover.'

Adheesh had enough faith in Devnath to believe his every word. He also knew about the miracles of Lake Manasarover's water. It was said that apart from physically healing a person, it also condoned the sins of his past births. 'Ok, as you say Devnath, I'll go and get the water, you stay with Aishani.'

As much as Devnath wanted to go with Adheesh, he knew

he would be more useful here helping Aishani, looking after their virtually dead.

'Bhaiya, take these containers with you, you can bring the lake's water in them,' Devnath handed two containers to Adheesh, a copper container and a bottle. Adheesh was surprised. Devnath gave him a bag also.

'When did you collect these, Devnath? There was no time in the Gurukul to even think of these things,' Adheesh exclaimed.

'When you were chanting the Garuda mantra with Aishani Bhabhi. I hurriedly collected whatever I could find and whatever I thought would be useful. I put them inside a large bag and brought it along with us.'

Adheesh smiled for the first time since the Gurukul catastrophe, 'Bless you Devnath; the last couple of days would not have been possible without you.'

Devnath preened in pleasure. He lived for praise from Adheesh.

Adheesh looked at Aishani. She was making paste out of the flowers he had just brought. He went to her and said softly, 'Ash, Devnath has noticed some changes in the colour of these people. If we further anoint them with the water of Lake Mansarovar, they may recover faster. Lake Mansarovar is not too far from here. I am going down to collect some water and bring it here. I'll try to return as soon as possible, probably in a day or two,' he embraced her gently, smoothed her hair and left. Aishani did not reply.

Adheesh began his journey down. Devnath had given him a jacket and a muffler to protect him from the bitter cold of the upper Himalayas. Though he did not have a compass or a GPS device with him, he knew that he would have to cover a distance of approximately forty-nine kilometres. Adheesh now had the special ability of walking amazingly fast over rough terrains. He glided over rocks and boulders, almost flying towards his destination. It was nearly night by the time he reached Mansarovar Lake. Even at dusk, the pristine beauty of the placid water took his breath away. The setting sun had thrown a scintillating burst of colours in the sky which were flung over the lake with casual abandon. Adheesh witnessed this display of Divine fireworks impassively. Had he been here under different circumstances with Aishani, they would have been mesmerised.

According to legend, Lake Mansarovar had been made by Brahma, one entity of the holy trinity of Brahma, Vishnu, and Mahesh. He had visualised the lake in his heart and mind and then manifested it. According to Hindu belief, taking a bath in the holy water of Lake Mansarovar washes away the sins of past births. Adheesh knew that to the West was another lake known as Rakshastal. Mansarovar is considered as the holiest lake whereas Rakshastal is known as the devils' lake. The lakes were divided by the river Ganga Chhu.

He folded his hands in obeisance to the lake. He did not want to disturb its waters now. He would collect the water next morning after the celestial beings had had their bath. Again, legend had it that every morning in Brahm Muhurta, that is from 4 am to 6 am, celestial beings come down from heaven to have their bath in Mansarovar Lake. He washed his hands and face in the water of the lake. Small currents passed through him as soon as his hands touched the water. He got up from his sitting position totally refreshed. As he was getting up, he felt something whizz past him. He did not feel or hear anything, it was just a feeling. He knew that it was a small arrow, small but deadly accurate if thrown by the right hand. Adheesh was a warrior, he knew when a weapon was sent to kill and when it was sent just to warn or convey a message. This was a warning. Immediately alert, he whirled around, hands already on his khukhri. Adheesh was never without his broad knife, so much so that people who knew him had accepted it as part of his dress and would have been surprised if they did not see it on his body.

There are many variants of the khukhri which is like a large knife, thick in the middle and turned at an angle of 85 degrees. There are various designs in different parts of the country but in general, it is an all-purpose weapon hung from the waist in a sheath. It is an especially useful weapon for soldiers on field duty as it can be used to hack vegetation and cut vegetables too.

The moment he turned, he saw a man behind a tree who was alert but not really trying to hide. They sized each other up. The man came out from behind the tree and Adheesh was surprised. The man was not Indian. He was very fair with long bleached, almost white hair and piercing grey-blue eyes. He was tall and muscularly built, wearing Bermudas and a T-shirt. Adheesh was not fooled by this man's casual looks. In his hands, he held a bright, fierce-looking sword. On his back were slung some arrows in a quiver and a bow. Adheesh could make out that these were not normal bow and arrows.

He recognised the sword too. He had studied about it in his classes in the Gurukul. It was called the Gram and was one of the strongest swords in Nordic legends, that had slayed and killed dragons.

They looked at each other guardedly. Soon both realised that they were not threats to each other.

'I am sorry; I thought you were one of the demons from Rakshastal come to spoil the water of Mansarovar,' the man spoke in chaste Hindi. His voice was a deep baritone. This time Adheesh was quite surprised, though he did know that warrior students from different Gurukuls all over the world went to different countries to learn their culture and methods of war and demon fighting. It was just that he was not expecting anyone in the Himalayas. He felt an instant rapport with this man. The man continued, 'I am Einar from Sweden. I have been designated to guard the waters of Lake Mansarovar from any devils that might be lurking in the nearby lake.' Adheesh nodded. He knew that sometimes demons tried to contaminate the waters of Lake Mansarovar, which was the highest freshwater lake whereas the Rakshastal comprised of salt water. Both the lakes were in close proximity, but the similarity ended there. The water of Mansarovar was extremely calm and tranquil, whereas the water of Rakshastal was always turbulent and swirling. While fishes and aquatic life abounded in the holy water of Lake Mansarovar, there was no life in Rakshastal and if there was, it was only the negative kind or demon like.

Adheesh held out his hand, 'Adheesh,' he stated simply. Einar nodded and that was that. There was plenty of time for more revelations. For the moment, this was enough.

'State your business and then take rest for the night. You look as if you need the rest and sleep,' Einar observed and commented, 'Let me show you a place where you will be able to relax.'

Adheesh was already nodding with sleep now that his defenses were down. 'I have come to collect some water for my sick colleagues who are somewhere up there. Without this healing water, they might not survive.'

Einar nodded and guided Adheesh to a secluded spot, 'You take rest. I shall guard the lake and you too'. Adheesh nodded, lay down and went to sleep immediately.

The next day Adheesh woke up at the crack of dawn. Einar was already pottering around. He brought him hot breakfast, a gruel of some sort which Adheesh did not immediately recognise. It seemed to be some sort of mildly salted porridge with lots of herbs and dried fruits, not particularly appetising but more than enough to give him a rejuvenating jolt of energy. It was almost six in the morning now. 'I will go and take some water from the lake and continue on my journey. My sick people need this water as soon as possible,' he stated, 'Thank you so much for everything, Einar. The breakfast was quite good. It will last me for the whole day,' he smiled.

Einar walked with him towards the lake, 'When I came here to the Himalayas two years ago, I was allowed to join some mendicants. After my training with them, I was given this job of guarding Mansarovar Lake from the demons of Rakshastal. I have learnt so much here, I have learnt to fight these demons who are so different from my own country. Like they say: A demon is a demon by any other name or feature,' Einar laughed at his own feeble attempt at a joke.

Besides the grave situation on Mount Kailash, Adheesh was now thinking of Lake Mansarovar too. 'There must be other warriors fending off the demons coming from Rakshastal and other places. I don't see them anywhere. For that matter, apart from you, I don't see anybody around here, neither humans nor demons,' Adheesh was perplexed.

'That is because you are in the past, you can see the lake but not the masses near it,' Einar shrugged his shoulders, 'I do not know much about time travel except that I too can sometimes travel in time in extreme conditions,' he stopped as if he had said too much.

Adheesh was taken aback. He thought nobody knew that he and his group had travelled back in time and here was a complete stranger who knew this, was waiting for him and could travel in time too. We are just specks of knowledge in the vast tapestry of the universe, he thought wryly. He wondered how much more Einar knew and who else knew about the plight of his group. I hope not the demons, he mused, otherwise the game would be over before it even began. But he couldn't resist asking, 'Tell me Einar, there are many people around here especially in the tourist season. Any demon can disguise himself as a human being and enter this hallowed place. How do you and the other warriors recognise and fight them?'

Einar smiled, 'There are signs. Adheesh, there are so many signs that you'll be surprised that others don't notice them. For instance, while coming here you must have seen a few assemblages of rocks and stones with engravings on them.

Some of these engravings are painted also. Now most of these engravings are essentially salutations to Lord Shiva. Others have other meanings also. One lead for people like us is these engravings. There are very subtle changes in these engravings. Sometimes there is a minute change in the colours of the engravings or sometimes the direction of the stone changes imperceptibly and you'll be surprised to know that they sometimes sing too. A scientific mind would deduct that the sound comes from the wind going through these stones and rightly so, but there is always a meaning and there is always a message which alerts us. There are many other signs which reveal the presence of demons. We just have to be sharp and sensitive enough to notice them. That and plenty of training,' Einar said laughingly.

'Oh, ok,' Adheesh joined the laughter. 'I will not ask how you deal with the demons. Obviously, you and the other warriors are doing an excellent job; it is because of you that the serenity of the lake has been maintained.'

Einar looked at Adheesh intently. 'I was told by my venerable gurus that my work tenure here would end after some time and an Indian warrior would be sent to escort me to the pyramids of Mount Kailash where I will gain emancipation before I finally leave this world. I shall also witness the gateway to heaven there. I believe that the time and person has come to take me there,' Einar said earnestly.

Adheesh was again taken by surprise. A series of thoughts ran through his mind, but he did not articulate them. The way things were in the Gurukul and with the practically dead people on Mount Kailash, they could use an extra set of hands.

Perhaps it was God's will that had brought both together. He did not understand when Einar said that he would leave the world, but later. There was plenty of time for explanations; right now, he had to reach Mount Kailash as fast as he could to cope with the emergency there. God knows what Aishani and Devnath were enduring. There were so many questions bubbling inside him but there was no time to seek answers to them. The burning need of the hour was to somehow save the victims of the Gurukul.

'Okay Einar, you can come with me, but you'll have to earn your living there. Plus you'll have to catch up with me to reach there. I'm a pretty fast walker.'

Einar laughed. His laughter was joyous and relieved, 'You don't have to worry about me, Adheesh. You go and get the water while I wind up here. The immaculate, pristine beauty of Mansarovar has to be maintained.'

'Another thing, Einar, you have been guarding Mansarovar and now you're leaving it. I'm sure the lake will be protected with or without us. Won't you be handing over the security to someone else before leaving?' Adheesh was curious.

'Of course, all that has taken place earlier,' Einar laughed at Adheesh's surprised expression. Then softly, 'The security of Mansarovar can never be compromised. There are already warriors posted on the outskirts of the lake who will come near as soon as we leave.'

'Oh,' Adheesh was relieved but then again other questions were cropping up in his mind. So, people concerned knew that he was going to come here, and Einar had already handed over his watch to other warriors. It was all pre-planned! When he had time, he would sit with Guruji and ask him all these questions. He felt a jolt again. Guruji had died! He had left them! So, who had planned all this and whose directions were they following or would follow? With a bitter taste in his mouth, Adheesh nodded and went towards the lake. In the bright sunshine, the still blue water of the lake perfectly reflected the mountains that surrounded it. The reflection was so pure that it seemed that there were two dimensions, one above the water and one below. But he was not in the proper frame of mind to appreciate such divine beauty. His heart and his whole being were on fire to reach Mount Kailash to save the lifeless victims.

Einar was true to his word. He was equally fast, if not faster. They did not speak on the way up as that would have broken their momentum. On the way, Adheesh found some more flowers and shrubs. He plucked them in the hope that Aishani might find them useful. They made it to Mount Kailash in record time. Adheesh was desperate to see Aishani. He had slept and rested, but what about her and Devnath and the others? But Aishani and Devnath did not even greet him or even give a cursory glance to Einar. Anybody coming with Adheesh was trustworthy though Devnath unobtrusively did come between Adheesh and Einar. It was as simple as that. They just took the water from his hands, kept it in a safe place before rushing to boil the water which they had collected from a stream. Einar surveyed the scene before him. Too many questions rose in his mind, but all the questions could be answered afterwards, if at all. He was a warrior and had fought and disposed of many unwanted creatures from the world.

Sometimes he had worked alone and sometimes with a team of likeminded people. They had been very badly hurt themselves in locations where there was no medical help. He had learnt to survive with rudimentary tools and herbs. Sickness was not a big deal but the presence of so many comatose people in the lower reaches of Mount Kailash did raise his eyebrows. He knew that the trio were incredibly special human beings with substantial special powers. What he was witnessing had a touch of divinity and he was once again humbled.

He set to work straightway with Adheesh. He helped in cleaning out the dried paste of flowers and herbs from the wounds of ailing persons. He helped in washing them from the water of the stream which Devnath had discovered. Like the other two men, Einar automatically followed Aishani's instructions. It happened so very naturally that Einar didn't even notice it. Initially, he was struck by Aishani's persona. Such a simple looking girl, very worried about the sick and the dying souls. But as he observed her working and supervising them, her stature increased in his eyes and heart. This was no ordinary woman. In fact, she did not seem to be a mere human. The way she was conducting herself reminded him of goddesses in the Nordic culture. He could also guess that Aishani was not only devastated about the sleeping souls in their care but her wounds were too deeply embedded in her heart and soul; the comatose people were just a minuscule part of the larger story. If she was surprised by his agility and willingness in following her instructions, she gave no sign of it. She was working relentlessly to revive the victims. She sponged their bodies with the water from Mansarovar. He witnessed the absolute faith and sincerity with which they were conducting their operation, if it could be called that. Einar knew that something great was going on, otherwise they wouldn't have been here at all. Just the fact that they were allowed here proved that as human beings, they were superior to their brethren.

REACHING THE GURUKUL

No matter how hard they tried, they were unable to revive the comatose patients. One fact was certain: They were alive. Their skin colour had changed for the better, it had started looking fresher. But they were not moving and had not opened their eyes too. Aishani's line of treatment did not change. She sponged them with the water of Lake Mansarovar and applied the paste of flowers and herbs which were available there. Now even this supply was dwindling. After a few days, nothing would be left except spring water. Einar was helping as much as he could—which, in the present circumstances, was not much. The team of four was seated around the comatose patients, each occupied with his or her own thoughts. Periodically, Aishani would get up to check. Devnath was sitting a little distance away.

He would never sit beside Adheesh, even if Adheesh asked him. It was clear in his mind that he was Adheesh's servant and that was it, no arguments. Aishani was quietly sitting beside them but Adheesh knew that now she would be an active participant in their conversations even without speaking. There was a bit of relief that the victims were showing some signs of recuperating.

'Why are you here, Einar?' Adheesh enquired softly. It wouldn't have made any difference if he had spoken loudly. In these hallowed surroundings one tended to speak in whispers, then almost jokingly he added, 'Your culture also has its fair share of demons.'

Einar too smiled, 'Yes there is no dearth of demons in the world or in any culture. I have disposed off quite a few demons in my country. In my spare time, I used to read about the various cultures of the world. Something struck to the core of my heart and mind when I began reading about Indian culture, its history, and its epics. I immediately empathised with whatever Indian mythology I read. I cannot explain it, but I immediately knew that the literature that I was reading was not mythology but had taken place such a long time back that people categorised it as mythology. I knew it was true because I had taken part in many of the conquests.'

Einar stopped, a bit embarrassed, 'That is why I came here to the Himalayas. You know the rest.'

Adheesh and Aishani looked at each other. They knew the feeling. It had happened to them too.

Adheesh patted Einar on the back, 'I knew that there was an esoteric Indian connection. Nobody can come here unless there is a call. You have been allowed here on Mount Kailash. Obviously, you are a very high-ranking warrior and scholar. Welcome to our Gurukul, or whatever is left of it,' he added wistfully.

Einar acknowledged the welcome with a slight nod. He too was curious about their presence here, but he knew instinctively that their wounds were too raw at the moment. They would themselves tell him when the time was right. They sat there for some time idly chitchatting, albeit softly.

Ultimately, Adheesh spoke. 'We just cannot sit here idly, hoping for a miracle. Our friends are not getting worse, but they are not opening their eyes either. I will go down and get some more and proper medicines from Kalpesh and Padma. They are doctors; maybe their medicines will help in reviving these people.'

Aishani looked up sharply at him but Adheesh did not meet her eyes. He knew her unarticulated questions. He himself was in a dilemma. Were any of their family members alive? But he was not going to think of all that, he was not willing to let go of the small strand of hope that he was clutching.

Finally, he looked at Aishani. Something passed between them and he got up to leave. 'Devnath, you have to stay with Aishani. Einar, can I request you to bring some more water from Mansarovar lake as the supply here has almost depleted? In my absence, you are the only one who can fetch the water.'

'Of course, Adheesh, you don't have to request me. I'll do whatever is possible to ease the situation here,' Einar said gravely.

Adheesh left almost immediately. Within seconds, he had

vanished from the horizon. He was using his powers of speed, which was equal to the speed of sound. He increased his speed and suddenly fell. It was as if he had jammed headlong into a huge speed breaker. There was nothing there, but he knew that he had crossed the time barrier and come into the present. Slowing down just a bit, he kept on walking. After some time, he sat in the shade of a tree to catch his breath. He took a sip of the water which Aishani had given him. It was so pure that it rejuvenated him instantly.

A hundred miles more, he surmised. He looked around. There was no change in the flora and fauna, but it sure felt better to be in the present. It would take him approximately forty-five minutes to reach his beloved Gurukul. He couldn't wait to reach but he dreaded the thought of what he would find there. So many catastrophic events had taken place, so many loose ends to be tied that he wouldn't know where to begin. Many people had to be searched out, too many memories revived. His own people were too far away and were not true allies in the scheme of things, so they may have been let off for the time being. But Aishani's family and Ruby's family, they were fully entrenched and committed for the annihilation of the demons and their ilk. What about them, would they be there? If they had survived, where would they be? Surely, they knew about Gurukul's destruction. These and so many other myriad questions plagued him. He fervently prayed and hoped that his side of the family was safe so that he could get proper medicines from his uncle Kalpesh and his wife Padma.

Adheesh had ordered his brain not to think of the most pervasive question of all, but now he would have to face it.

Their guiding light, their mentor, and their patron was gone; they wouldn't know what to do without him. In despair he rubbed his hands over his eyes and was surprised when his hands came out wet. He didn't remember the last time he cried. He was a warrior; he did not have the luxury of indulging in sentiments and emotions. Then did he really cry? Well, he wasn't going to waste time, he decided. He had rested enough and now he started walking towards the Gurukul. It wasn't his normal walk. A normal human being wouldn't have been able to sense him, let alone see him. He was walking so fast that he couldn't be seen.

Soon, he was at one of the entrances of the Gurukul. There was no need to chant any mantras to reach the other side, he had passed that stage. Secondly, the Gurukul was still broken, a pale shadow of its former glory. The pristine verdant forest had been burnt to cinders, all black and brown, rotting, dirty and desolate. This Gurukul, his Gurukul, which used to shine brightly with joie de vivre and was inhabited by handsome men and women, was just an empty shell now, keening and crying for its former glory.

He walked around looking for some sign, any sign no matter how small, of hope. He found it too. Some grass and shrubs were struggling to burst through the burnt ground. There was just a wee bit of green showing through the layers of soot on the earth. Adheesh took it as a good sign. This was the never-say-die attitude of the world and it should be so. Were the hidden chambers like the senior's library still there, or were they also destroyed? This was just a rhetorical question in his mind. His main purpose of coming to the Gurukul was different, something he was dreading. But he and Aishani had decided that he would have to do it. He had come alone as she couldn't risk leaving the sick people alone there.

He had to go to Guruji's cottage and perform a havan and puja for the proper release and peace of Guruji's soul. What kind of puja, he didn't know. Even though he had seen Guruji's mutilated body with his head cut off, Adheesh's mind and heart refused to accept the fact that Guruji was dead. It was impossible. Guruji was immortal, like his Ishta Dev, Lord Hanuman. It was Hanuman ji who had ordered Guruji to establish Gurukuls all over the world and train warriors to destroy demons. These were the demons who had escaped in the great war of Ramayana and hid in Space, Earth and Water. They had gone into hibernation and were coming out now. From the time of Ramayana, Guruji had been training warriors.

Adheesh's legs refused to take him towards the cottage. He stood rooted to a particular spot, wanting to flee in the opposite direction, instead of discharging his duty of going to Guruji's cottage. Finally, with each step as heavy as a rock, he reached Guruji's cottage. The front door had been pulled out of its hinges and was lying broken on the ground. The plants carefully tended by Manoharji had turned into dried shrubs. But Adheesh did not see all this. With his heart in his mouth, he went inside. The cottage was empty. There was nothing there except for a faint lingering perfume that they associated with Guruji. But where was Guruji—rather, where was his body? Oh! The demons had killed Guruji and then taken away his body too! He slumped down on the ground.

His mind stopped working. What about their mission, their destinies, the meaning of their lives? If the demons were so strong that they could kill Guruji and destroy the Ashram, then the destruction of the Earth and indiscriminate killing of the human race would be the next logical step. No, his mind screamed, this is not possible. Guruji could not leave them just like that. There must be a contingency plan. Guruji must have faced such a situation many times in his lifetime. Surely, the Gods must have thought of some alternative. He sat there on the dusty earth for a long time, his logical mind working out various permutations and combinations. Nothing came to his mind. Finally, in extreme despair and weariness, he closed his eyes and waited for some idea or inspiration to come. He didn't know what he was waiting for. Two tears rolled down from the great warrior's eyes. There was no redemption in sight. What was he going to do, what was he going to tell Aishani! He just sat there with his eyes closed for an exceedingly long time.

He must have dozed or fallen asleep, but he got up with a start. For a moment he couldn't see anything. There was a blazing white light pervading the interior of Guruji's hut. It was so bright that Adheesh found it difficult to open his eyes. Gradually, his eyes adjusted to the light and he realized that it was quite a soothing, cool phenomenon. He felt a sense of well-being and waited in anticipation of something good which was about to happen. Sure enough, after a few minutes the light settled down and a figure emerged. Adheesh gasped. His life till now had been full of miracles and magic. He was used to them, but what he encountered just now took his breath away. He couldn't hold himself. He rushed to the figure and embraced him. He wouldn't have dared do it earlier nor would he have the desire to do so earlier. But this was such a startling marvel. The figure was Guruji! The smell which he had unconsciously associated with his Guru was also the same! He was also wearing the same kind of clothes which he always wore, white kurta over a white dhoti. For a moment Adheesh just closed his eyes and gave up to the rapture of holding and touching Guruji. In his heart of hearts, Adheesh thought that he was hallucinating. So what, he thought happily and hugged Guruji some more. Guruji laughed softly.

'Adheesh, you don't have to hold me so tightly. I am here, and I will be here. I am not going anywhere.'

Adheesh knew that he was dreaming now. It was a dream from which he never wanted to wake up.

'Guruji,' Adheesh almost wept with shock and relief. 'I saw you lying here with your head slit and your body cut. The Ashram has been destroyed. Everybody including you is dead. Now you have come back as an angel. I am not letting you go Guruji,' Adheesh babbled.

Guruji put his hands over Adheesh's head, 'Control yourself, beta, I know the ordeal that both of you have undergone. I tried to come earlier, but I could come only when your desire for me would become totally mind and heart consuming.'

Somehow Adheesh controlled himself. Embarrassed he let go of Guruji, but still kept on looking at him hungrily and in trepidation as if Guruji would vanish again or if it was a delusion.

'Adheesh, just like my master I have been either cursed or blessed to be on Earth till eternity or till the time Earth is there.

I am unborn and undead. Beta, in this Kalyug how could I escape the wrath, deceit and cruelty of the demons? I have destroyed innumerable demons and I have also been killed several times. I have always had to come down from the astral world as that is the desire of my Lord Shri Hanuman. We are all made up of various combinations of the Panchbhootas that is the earth, water, fire, air, and space. Whenever I am killed, these Panchbhootas come together in the right combination and I am created again.'

'Why kill you then, Guruji? Your killers must know you cannot be killed!'

'Yes, but the mayhem and chaos which follows my death gives them so much of time and leeway to enjoy torturing all of you and humanity. Though they know that I do not die, still the period between my death and resurrection gives them so much of macabre happiness; even though they almost get wiped off from the face of the earth, they feel that it's still worthwhile. And that is how the drama and illusion of the tapestry of life continues,' Guruji sighed. 'It's all God's will.'

A flicker of understanding went through Adheesh's mind. So this was the game, a cycle which would keep repeating itself, if only to keep the demons happy. But at whose cost and for what? Love and familial ties would be broken, never to be glued properly again. Who would profit from these killings and destruction, if only for a fleeting moment? It would be the demons! Guruji's people were right and unhappy, the demons were wrong but happy. So, what did one want? Happiness or unhappiness? Adheesh shook his head, thoroughly confused. This was unfair. The right people should be happy, not the wrong people. He and Aishani had lost everything, each other, the people they loved, and the very earth under their feet and still their destiny was to kill the happy people. He looked at Guruji.

'It was never stated that fulfilling your destiny would necessarily make you happy, almost never that, but it would make the majority of human beings joyful and comfortable. And that is what we are. Our Nirvana lies in caring for and protecting life on this planet and sometimes beyond it too. We are so vastly different from the demons and in certain respects human beings too. We are the protectors and nurturers of all the living beings on this planet whether it is the humans or animals or plants or insects or birds. Our basic qualities are empathy, faith, courage, boldness, caring and sharing, trust, honesty, integrity, truthfulness, self-control, hard work, perseverance and, above all, love. The demons have the opposite of all these qualities. In short, self-indulgence, cruelty and selfishness at any cost is the core philosophy of the demons and it is this that we have to curb and thwart.'

'Now, to come back to the reality. The ashram must be rebuilt with more than a double layer of security. It was not physical security which was compromised; it was the internal security which led to this massacre. The demons had entered through the bodies of some of the inhabitants of the Gurukul, some of the supposedly weaker ones.'

Adheesh nodded, 'I thought so, Guruji,' he said grimly, 'But before we rebuild the Gurukul we have to find our people and heal those who have escaped death but are totally scarred. Guruji, some of our people are on Mount Kailash. Though their bodies are not showing any signs of decay, they are not showing any signs of life either.'

'Yes, beta, only Garuda Devta is capable of such great feat, carrying all of you so swiftly and giving you refuge in one of the smaller pyramids of Mount Kailash. The pure air and the purest of the herbs could revive them a bit from their death-like coma. Without Garuda Devta's timely help, all our people would have died. They were just hanging by a thread. That and the loving care that the three of you have provided.'

'There is another person there, Guruji, he is also a warrior like us. His experience and help have been invaluable in looking after our sick people.'

Guruji looked questioningly at Adheesh and waited for him to explain. Slowly, Adheesh recounted everything about Einar. Guruji heard him out patiently, slowly nodding his head. Why did Adheesh have the feeling that Guruji was not surprised? Well, he thought philosophically, if Guruji could come back from the dead then Einar too may not be a secret for Guruji.

After a few minutes, Guruji said, 'Einar is going to play an important role in our lives and in the ashram too. He is a great warrior. We must make sure that he is welcome. He will be taking part in all the activities of the Gurukul and in most of your assignments too.'

'Yes, Guruji,' Adheesh agreed immediately. He was happy that Guruji was so welcoming to Einar. He liked Einar himself and was extremely impressed by his prowess, helpful nature, and capacity for hard work. Still, there was a niggling doubt. Why was Guruji so pro-Einar without having even met him? Was he going to get an answer from Guruji? No, of course not!

He smiled wryly to himself.

He continued his account of the suffering people on Mount Kailash.

'They are not reviving Guruji. We just don't know what to do anymore,' he paused. Then in trepidation he turned towards Guruji, 'What about our people: Jayant and Aishani's mother, my parents, my uncles and Geetika and Padma, Ruby and her family. Where are they and how are they?' he dreaded the answer, but maybe, just maybe, someone was alive.

'They are not here,' Guruji said gravely, 'But they are not dead either.'

Adheesh looked joyfully but uncomprehendingly at Guruji. They were alive! But where were they?

Guruji had already anticipated his question. 'As of now we do not know where they are, whether they are together or separated. There has been such mass destruction of the ashram's population that I am at a loss as to where to begin. So many of our teachers, engineers, scientists, spies and specialists are either dead or missing or fatally injured. Each of the sick people at Kailash is an authority on his subject. There were no hangers-on in this Gurukul. Each person was important for the upkeep and conservation of the Gurukul. So, what do we do first?' Guruji mulled. 'Do we search for the missing and hurt people, do we reinvent the Gurukul, or do we go to Kailash to cure the sick souls there?'

'Guruji, we must go to Kailash to cure the sick there,' urged Adheesh. 'With your help, it'll be easier to revive them. You know all about the herbs and lifesaving plants there. Your mere touch will be enough to revive them.'

'Not so fast, Adheesh, I have to stay here in the ashram to reconstruct it somehow. I will have to sit and meditate here to find out how many of us are alive and how many have escaped. I also have to find out how such a great massacre was planned so successfully behind our backs.'

'But Guruji, how do we cure the people at Kailash? We have done everything we could.' Though Adheesh agreed with Guruji's plan, he couldn't figure out how his returning to Kailash would help the comatose people.

'I know, beta, those people are beyond the scope of normal medicines. They need different kinds of medicines now.'

Adheesh waited for Guruji to come up with the right solution and cure. He had a vague idea that Guruji could be at two or more places at the same time. It was a matter of joining the different components of the Panchbhootas in the same combination as Guruji's body. The science was far beyond his comprehension and could be deemed as magic. The thought crossed his mind for a moment, but he brushed it away. Guruji was the best judge of the course of action. If Guruji wanted to go to Kailash, he would have done so. Apparently, his presence was needed here.

As if sensing his dilemma Guruji said, 'Adheesh, we have to work at breakneck speed if these demons have to be throttled. We must get the rest of our people on their feet fast or we become extinct. The Earth will not collapse till the end of Kalyug. So, if these demons get the upper hand, which they have so ably demonstrated in the past few days, we will be nothing but puppets and slaves pandering to their whims and fancies.'

Guruji took out a sort of a stick from his kurta which he was wearing over his dhoti. It was about twelve inches in length and slightly thicker than a pencil. It was coiled broadly like a spring coil with the upper end tapering and the lower end thicker than the rest of the body. Adheesh had heard quite a lot about this diminutive stick known as the Sanjeevani booti or the life-giving stick. Legend had it that when Ram's brother Laxman had gone down fighting the Rakshasas, Hanuman had been sent by the doctors of that time to get the Sanjeevani booti or part of a plant which could save Laxman. Hanuman went to the hill where these plants grew but he could not recognize them. So, he brought the whole hill to the doctors. After Laxman was revived, Hanuman returned the hill to its proper place.

'Yes, Adheesh this is a part of the quadrilateral group of herbs, three of which are already there on the Upper Himalayas. Two of them have already been administered to the sick souls, this is the fourth part, the third part is a bit difficult to find. It is an exceedingly rare plant, generally not found in the Upper Himalayas,' saying this Guruji took out a piece of paper and showed him a sketch. Adheesh looked at it. It was a pretty shrub-like plant with thin leaves and small yellow flowers.

'This is why the sick are not waking up even though they have revived. When all the three herbs are crushed together with the help of this stick and water, they will wake up and become normal, without any loss of strength or vigour.'

Adheesh took the Sanjeevani stick in his hands. Such an innocuous looking stick had the power of playing God. Well not exactly God, but breathing life into an almost dead person. He bowed to Guruji and took his permission to leave. He was raring to go now and wanted to return immediately.

'Guruji, can you tell me which part of Kailash we are in? It seems as if Kailash, though an exceedingly huge structure, is many small parts joined together to make the edifice that we see in front of us.'

'Your observations are exemplary, but then nothing less is expected of you. Kailash is indeed the Axis Mundi or the centre of this Earth. It is made up of 108 smaller pyramids. The place where you landed is a smaller, lower pyramid. That is why no one can see you and no demon can reach you. Plus, the fact that in Kailash you are in the past. No demon has the temerity to reach even the fringes of Mount Kailash. Still Garuda Devta took no chances and took you all back in time. The demons think that all of you are dead. As of now, they are reveling in their orgies for having destroyed our Gurukul.'

Adheesh was a bit confused now, 'And now, Guruji, where are we now? Are we in the past or in the present? It seems like the present,' he observed.

'Good observation, Adheesh.' This was turning out to be a good day. To be praised twice in a day by Guruji was indeed high praise. Maybe things would take a turn for the better.

'And I could come here only because Garuda Devta had empowered Aishani and me, with the one-time boon of time travel, that is, one time coming and going back in time. Once I go back, I don't know how I will come back to the present.'

Guruji looked at him quietly. He was a bit puzzled by Guruji's stare, then it dawned on him. Of course, once they were all healed on Mount Kailash, Garuda Devta would bring them to their present time. He smiled with the assurance that God—and hence Guruji—had worked out everything. They had thought of everything, and he and Aishani were the flesh and blood manifestations of these thoughts. So be it. This was not the time to indulge in self-pity and 'Why me?' or 'Why us?' There was work to do and people to search and save and demons to be killed. He waited for Guruji's instructions.

'You will have to go to the Dronagiri mountains to get the fourth component of the Sanjeevani booti. In local language it is called the Phena Kamal or the Kasturi Kamal. You must be extremely careful, the tribals or the villagers are very possessive about it. They pray to it as God. Even on its own it can heal quite a lot of sicknesses like deep coma, cerebral disorders, broken bones, bodily disorders, and many other diseases. This may not be the right season for it, and you may not be able to recognize it. This plant needs lots of water to bloom and work to its full efficacy. That's the beauty of this great plant. Once it has its fill of water it sustains itself and survives without water even in drought-like conditions. The flowers look like small lotuses and are covered with flimsy layers of cotton. If you get confused, as you will, be on the lookout for such flowers which emit light at night and if you look closely, in the daytime too.'

'Yes Guruji,' he said obediently, as if this was a routine dialogue between a guide and his pupil. Amidst such devastation, they were having a normal conversation. His despair and mortification had lessened a bit after Guruji's materialization, but there were herculean tasks to be performed. How he wanted to rush to Aishani and tell her that all was not lost, that Guruji had come back. He could visualize her relief and joy on hearing the news. But first the Sanjeevani.

'Aishani is not to be told about it at all,' stated Guruji. 'She of all the people around her has suffered the most. She will not be able to bear all the good news at once. It has to be given to her slowly and in small doses till the time she becomes strong enough to withstand the good with the bad.' Adheesh nodded.

'The Dronagiri hills and its valleys are not very far from here—in fact, they are nearby, just about a hundred miles from our ashram.' Guruji looked around. 'Or what's left of it,' he said sadly, 'We do not have any time, so I am sending you there straightaway. Once you get the flowers, inform me telepathically and go straight to Kailash. The sick are all skilled technicians urgently required to repair the Gurukul.'

'Yes, Guruji,' then as an afterthought, 'How could our intelligence be so bad, Guruji?'

'Sometimes they win, sometimes we win, and so it goes on. God keeps on giving them leeway. When the limits are crossed, we have to crush them. A tiny bit of dirt escapes and slowly grows, gradually becomes larger than the world. The cycle continues…'

'Does it ever end, Guruji?

Guruji looked at him enigmatically. Adheesh sighed, touched Guruji's feet and turned to leave.

He looked back at Guruji a moment later, saying, 'There's another thing Guruji, which I completely forgot. It's the reason why I came down here. After seeing you, I forgot everything.'

Guruji waited for him to speak his mind.

'Guruji, I had come here to meet my uncle Kalpesh and

his wife Padma and to take some Ayurvedic medicines from them. We do not have medicines on Kailash, only the herbs and flowers we could find there. Should I go to them now or do I have enough to revive our colleagues?'

'You have everything with you Adheesh,' Guruji said gravely. 'Meeting them would have an adverse effect on all of you and some demons might get a whiff of it too,' saying this Guruji handed over a cloth bag to Adheesh, 'Keep this and give it to Aishani. These are life strengthening herbs. She will find them useful when Prana fully comes back to our lost souls.'

'Yes Guruji,' Adheesh took the bag and left.

The journey to Dronagiri hills was quite uneventful. It was almost like a tourist spot but there were just a straggling lot of tourists there as this was not the season. Adheesh adhered to Guruji's warning and steered clear of any human contact, either tourist or villager. Hiking and being in jungles were in his blood. But here he encountered a problem. He could not find the Sanjeevani booti or the flower. He consoled himself with the thought that when Hanuman ji could not find it; he was just a mere mortal. But unlike Hanuman ji, he did not have the option of uprooting the entire hill and taking it to the Vaidyas who were treating Laxman. He could not be too blatant in searching for it as the tribals considered it their property and did not want to share it with anybody. For this act of his, of taking away the Sanjeevani booti, the inhabitants of this area do not pray to Hanuman ji.

Adheesh fretted for every minute lost. There was no time, his people were dying on one of the pyramids of Kailash. He thought of Aishani and Devnath and how impatiently they must be waiting for him. He fervently prayed that none of the sick suffered further deterioration. He struck gold on the third night, that too by fluke. It was the dry season and most plants had dried up, though they could survive drought-like conditions with ease. It was because most of the flowers were covered by gossamer strands of cotton which had become slightly yellow in color that he could not place them. It was a dark night, and he was working by the method of elimination, combing through every shrub and flower, dried or otherwise. Suddenly, through the corner of his right eye, he thought that he saw a minute blinking light. Must be a firefly, he thought subconsciously, and then stood stock still. Guruji had told him that the flowers emitted light! Slowly and on tenterhooks, he looked around. The ground was covered with these twinkling flowers, though they shone dimly as they were covered by strands of fine cotton. He was surprised. How had he not noticed them earlier? Aishani would have clapped in delight. Heaving a sigh of relief, he carefully plucked the flowers and put them in a cloth bag.

Straightening up he thought, 'Now to go home.' Home for him now was simply where Aishani was.

He sat under a tree and mentally chanted a special mantra which connected him to Guruji.

'Guruji, I am in the possession of the Kasturi Kamal. With your blessings I am now leaving for Kailash.'

'Good job, Adheesh. With the blessings of the Almighty, all of you will come back very soon and the ashram will be rebuilt speedily.'

Adheesh mentally thanked Guruji and set off on his way.

That was a week back. With Garuda Devta's one-time vardan he could reach the lower rungs of Mount Kailash almost immediately. The others were waiting impatiently. He gave them a briefing of what was to be done with all the four ingredients. Without wasting a second, they set about making the medicine—rather, it was Aishani who was making the medicine as he explained how the materials were to be used. If she was curious about the Sanjeevani stick and the Sanjeevani booti flowers, she didn't ask. There was no time to think of these strange things. Their roles had reversed, with Aishani in the driver's seat now and Adheesh, Einar and Devnath acting as her assistants.

Einar had already collected water from the Mansarovar Lake. As usual they meditated and prayed to the stick and the flowers for a short while, then Aishani poured water on the flower with the help of the Sanjeevani stick in a thin steady stream so that not even a drop of water was wasted. They virtually saw the flower unfurling before their eyes. The Sanjeevani stick had started moving of its own volition in a circular motion as soon as it touched the flower. It was as if there was a magnetic attraction between the two. After the flower had thoroughly soaked up the purest of the pure water, a sort of ambrosial, sweet-smelling liquid began seeping out of it. She mixed it with the other flowers. Carefully, they collected this water. Then with the help of a few pieces of cloth, they began to softly massage the comatose bodies with this liquid. Nothing happened for some time, but they still held their breaths and waited for the miracle to happen.

'Adheesh!' It was Aishani whispering to him, 'See.'

Adheesh looked at the person whom Aishani was swabbing with the water from the Sanjeevani flower. There was a pinkish hue on his face and body and his eyelids seemed to flutter. Very soon they opened, and he looked at them dazedly. His name was Satish. He was a biologist, looking after all the flora and fauna of the Gurukul. Satish just sat up as if getting up from normal sleep, as if nothing untoward had happened. There were tears in Aishani's eyes, there were three pairs of moistened eyes too.

'Adheesh, what are you doing here? Wait, let me think. I was tending to my morning chores when this thing came out from a tree, overpowered me, and covered me with a thick black blanket of smoke. I must have passed out,' he looked around. His eyes widened. He looked around puzzled. This was definitely not the Gurukul, but a place much more sublime. But that was not possible. No place could be more pure and more beautiful than the Gurukul. But this... this! Satish could not put his finger on it. He looked at Adheesh for some clarification, but Adheesh had moved away.

Now he could see Aishani beside Adheesh administering some sort of treatment to another. He looked around. Adheesh's bodyguard-cum-assistant Devnath was also there, plus a European, applying a salve of some kind on some people who were lying on beds made of grass and shrubs. On closer look, Satish was shocked to discover that every single person was from their own Gurukul. Three rows of people were in various stages of coma. A couple, like him, had woken up and were looking around dazedly. Devnath was running around with water in a makeshift gourd. Clearly, they were not in a mood for clarifying his doubts.

The four care-givers were now paying attention to those still dead to the world. The others came speedily to their senses as soon as their bodies were sponged by the water flowing through the Sanjeevani booti. Almost all of them came to their senses at the same time. And the miracle was that they felt absolutely fit and healthy. They just didn't know what had happened to them and how. They were also unaware of the fact that their Gurukul had been totally obliterated. Had they known these two facts, they might not have felt so good. They knew that they were in a divine place and were curious to find out why. Only Aishani and Adheesh were in any position to answer their questions. At present they were busy. Devnath, in any case, would not have told them anything, nor would they have asked him. They all considered Devnath a fierce, dangerous bodyguard who got het up at the slightest provocation if Adheesh was involved.

Finally, Adheesh and Aishani found time to meet them. Adheesh came straight to the point: 'We are at the bottom of Mount Kailash. This is also our Gurukul kind of place in the sense that it is hidden from normal human eyes. We had to come here because our Gurukul was attacked by demons. Many of the Gurukul's people escaped wherever they could, many were killed and some like us were sent here,' he said wearily.

There was complete, uncomprehending silence. They all looked at each other for some time then finally one of them spoke. He was Dinesh, plumber, and farmer. 'Where are the rest of our people, Adheesh? How much of the ashram has been destroyed?' Aishani could make out that he was thinking of his own work in resetting the Gurukul and wondering where the rest of his team were, whether they had survived or not.

'How did we come here? Apparently, we were not in a position to come here all by ourselves.' On seeing Adheesh's expression, he stopped.

'Please don't ask too many questions. I too am like you. I won't be able to answer most of your questions as I don't know the answers myself. We are lucky to escape and survive. Let us leave it at that and thank God for his kindness and mercy. We will stay here for a couple of hours to recuperate and then leave for the Gurukul.'

'Yes, Adheesh, I know we are in salubrious surroundings. I'm sure that we had not imagined that we will see Mount Kailash so soon, though I wanted to do so for a very long time, but I want to reach our Gurukul as soon as possible. God knows what destructions those demons have caused there.'

'That's the spirit, Dinesh. When we leave will be decided by our temporary Vaidya Aishani. In the meantime, feel free to roam and drink in the pure air of Mount Kailash. Just don't go too far.'

They nodded and slowly dispersed in various directions. Now only Adheesh and Aishani were left, with Devnath sitting at a respectable distance from them. Einar had also left. Like the others, he knew it was a lifetime opportunity to be allowed to be here on such a scientific and spiritual place. Now that the others were well, he wanted to use this opportunity to explore as much as was allowed.

Adheesh turned to look at Aishani. She smiled wanly at

him. He put his arms around her shoulders and pressed her to him. She sighed.

'Ash.'

'Hmm.'

'Ash, I have to tell you something.'

'Yes Adhee, I know, it's just that I am not very curious at the moment. Maybe after some time, it seems we will keep on losing our loved ones no matter how hard we try to get rid of the demons.'

'Ash baby, I don't think that our personal happiness matters more than happiness and peace on Earth. This too is our personal happiness. We have been sent on this Earth to restore peace on it by destroying these demons. They do their job, and we are doing ours. We have no option but to win. In between, if we snatch some moments of happiness with each other and our loved ones, well, those are bonuses, and we must be grateful for them. Nevertheless, there is something that will lighten your mood and will surely bring a smile to your lips.'

Aishani kept looking down. She was through with smiling and feeling happy. She closed her eyes and waited.

'I met Guruji,' he whispered.

There was no response from her. His magic words did not register in her mind. Adheesh understood and repeated his words. This time she did hear him. She opened her eyes. Adheesh was not the kind to play with her emotions nor was he the kind to make up and falsify facts just to please her. She wondered why he was using this juvenile method to raise her spirits. She pressed his hands to tell him that in his desperation he need not go to such lengths to lessen her grief.

'Ash, Guruji has come back from the dead. He is the avatar of Hanuman ji and like him even our Guruji cannot die. Sure, his body was destroyed but was assembled again by the exact permutation and combination of the Panchbhootas, that is, the elements of Earth, Water, Fire, Air and Space. Even the mild smell of saffron and sandalwood which used to emanate from him is the same,' words tumbled out of his mouth as fast as they could. A moment's hesitation and they might not come out again for fear of shocking Ash. He did not want to give her any more pain, even if it was for her happiness.

Aishani became very still. Then, as if in slow motion, she let go of his hand to face him squarely. There was a bewildered expression on her face and then just a hint of a smile which held so many emotions that he had to smile in return. She kissed him in relief then sat down to assimilate the information. There were many questions. One major part of her heart began mending after this news.

'What about our own people, Adhee? Are they alive? What did Guruji tell you?'

'They have escaped. The demons did not target them in the beginning as the Gurukul was the primary target. That gave our people enough time to escape.'

Aishani was fully awake and attentive now. 'So where are they now?'

'As of now, Guruji just knows that they are in a safe place. He still has to find out where they are and in what condition. Guruji stayed back in the Gurukul to mend and repair the ashram as much as he can do single-handedly.'

Aishani sat on a rock and tried to grasp all the information that Adheesh had shared with her. The past few days were traumatic, to say the least. God took and God was giving back, here in the Upper Himalayas in one of the pyramids of Kailash where no man had ever been, at least not in Kalyug. The purest of the pure air itself was so bracing that given time, the comatose patients from their ashram would have regained consciousness and health even without the Sanjeevani booti. This was the abode of Gods. It was God's will that they come here to recuperate.

'Ash, we cannot divulge all this information to our people here nor can we tell them everything about Guruji or the true extent of the Gurukul's destruction. By the time we go back, Guruji would have restored the Gurukul to a certain extent and then these people can do their work renovating the ashram.'

She nodded, feeling a bit rejuvenated now, and tried to assimilate all the information.

'Yes, Adhee, we cannot tell them that we are a couple of years in the past now. We will all go to the Mansarovar Lake to cleanse ourselves of our sins and then go back to the Gurukul. Oh, Adhee, how do we explain Garuda Devta to them?'

'When we use the celestial weapons, we forget after the exercise. In the same way, their memory of these incidents will also be obliterated. They will just see a rundown Gurukul which they will rush to repair. There will be no time to think of their immediate past.'

'What about us, Adhee? Will we too forget what happened? What do we begin with?'

'No Ash, we are not meant to forget this catastrophe. This time we must totally annihilate the demons who have destroyed us. We must remember each moment of the ordeal that we had to undergo. The memory will give us the necessary impetus and will to obliterate them.'

'Ash, our topmost priority is to revitalise and rehabilitate the Gurukul along with searching for our people. I'm positive that they are also very actively trying to face their adversaries, though we'll have to ascertain who is left and who has perished,' he said sadly.

Tears came to her eyes. She wiped them angrily. 'Everybody is a fighter Adheesh, our team is not so weak that it will break down with a small attack,' she declared.

Adheesh smiled despite himself, 'That's my girl,' he patted her shoulders. 'Let's go.'

LIBRARY

'These are like pinheads, more on a micro-cellular level. They are so small that they are not visible to the naked human eye. We could of course see them, but we were not looking for them in this form. When we visualize a demon or a monster, we think of them as huge ferocious creatures. We sometimes see them as small creatures too. But here we made a mistake, not understanding that they will become so microscopically small, hence invisible, and then join into huge creatures when our backs are turned. We were careless and we have paid heavily for it,' they were sitting cross-legged in Guruji's cottage. A profoundly serious Guruji was looking at them pensively.

At first it was a shock for Aishani when she met Guruji. So much water had flown under the bridge, so to speak.

And here was Guruji all hale and hearty, looking as if nothing had happened. Tears flowed freely and silently from her eyes. When her father Pandit Ram Sharan had died such a horrible death, Aishani had held herself responsible. Life had become a living hell for her. Time stood still. Understanding the dire situation, Guruji had sent her with Adheesh into the past, so that she could reunite with her father and complete her leftover training too. It was Guruji who had got them married when they were in the past. Guruji had become her father and her God. They had taken it for granted that Guruji was Chiranjeevi or immortal. But when she saw him dead with his neck cleanly sliced off from his body, her world had come crashing down. Guruji's death combined with the complete destruction of the Gurukul had completely broken her. She had undergone so much anguish and despair in the past one month that now her pent-up emotions had come to the fore. Aishani wanted to hold Guruji in her arms just like she would have done with her father, but she had to be content just by gazing at him. Both Adheesh and Guruji understood her trauma. They gave her a few moments to curb her emotions.

The ashram was not looking as bad as they had left it, though there were major glaring lapses. One of them was that Manoharji was not pottering around the cottage guarding it. Devnath had been temporarily stationed there. So many important matters would have to be faced and tackled at present.

Einar had returned with them and gone to meet Guruji. Guruji and Einar behaved as if they knew each other from a long time back and were meeting now after a few generations.

Einar touched his feet in the traditional Indian style of wishing an elderly person. Guruji welcomed him cordially and a trifle sadly too. Both Adheesh and Aishani were surprised by Guruji's response. Why was it tinged with sadness? Einar also seemed to reciprocate this feeling. Guruji spoke to Einar, 'You are a bona fide member of our Gurukul now. However, for others to accept you, for them to admit you in their circle, you have to mingle with them, work and laugh with them. You are more capable than the others and your powers are legendary. Every person here has come up the hard way and I am afraid you will have to do the same, though I am more than positive that you will pass all the tests with flying colours. For the moment, I suggest you go out and make yourself useful in the Gurukul.'

'Yes Guruji,' Einar folded his hands in Namaste.

'You are one of the greatest warriors on Earth, but you will still not be given permission to encounter any demon till the time you complete your tests. That has been the rule for every member of this group.'

'I understand, Guruji,' he bowed and went out. Adheesh was puzzled. It was almost as if Guruji was stalling Einar. What for? Was Guruji saving Einar for a greater job? It seemed to Adheesh that even Einar was aware of a greater role for himself in the Gurukul. Adheesh mentally shrugged his shoulders. All in good time. Aishani had not paid much attention to the exchange. She was so enthralled to be sitting in front of her dear Guruji that everything else paled in comparison. She continued with the conversation after Einar had left.

'Are they still here, Guruji?' she asked tentatively.

'Yes, they are everywhere. There are millions and billions

of them, crawling all over the ashram. Why, even now a few of them might be stuck on your bodies and you'll not know, they are so small and weightless.'

Aishani brushed her arms with revulsion. There was nothing on her arms, of course, but the thought itself was repugnant.

Adheesh spoke after a few moments. 'How do we destroy them, Guruji? For that to happen we will first have to see, hear and feel them.'

'Our experts are working on it night and day. Meanwhile both of you go to the senior library and find out as much as possible about these kinds of demons.'

They both looked at Guruji in amazement. The library! Wasn't it destroyed when the annihilation of the Gurukul happened?

As if reading their thoughts Guruji replied, 'There are many places in the Gurukul which are so heavily guarded and invisible that these demons were unable to reach them. Nevertheless, this was the maximum destruction any demon had ever done to any Gurukul and its inhabitants. The library couldn't be destroyed. There had been so many assaults on it in the past that double and triple measures were taken to safeguard it and its precious books. These demons did not have the brains or the knowhow of destroying the library.

'Similarly, there are other places in the Gurukul that the demons could not reach because extra precautions had been taken to safeguard them. These places are invisible to the normal eye and mind. It's only after higher studies and meditation have been achieved that one is able to see these places. Go to the library now, children, find out what is written in our ancient texts about these demons and how we can destroy them.'

'Yes Guruji,' they chorused, reassured, and relieved at the same time. They touched his feet and turned to leave.

'Aishani beta.' She turned and looked mutely at Guruji. She knew that Guruji would talk to her privately now. Adheesh left the cottage and waited for her outside, giving them time to talk privately and emotionally.

'Beta, there is no time to have a long conversation with you now, but most of your people are safe and fighting a winning battle. It will take me some more time to find out about their exact whereabouts. You will be reunited with them after some time. At the moment it is not safe to forcefully bring them here.'

'Yes Guruji,' she whispered. 'Is everybody together?'

'It seems they are for the moment.'

'Guruji,' she couldn't stop herself: 'Will I be able to meet them in the near future?'

'Yes, beta whenever you want, after this operation It won't be practical to go searching for them now.'

She nodded, somewhat relieved, then on an impulse went back and hugged Guruji. Surprised, Guruji put his arms around her shoulders and then patted her head affectionately.

'Oh Guruji,' she was openly sobbing now, 'I too had died along with you. I was a walking dead body. Don't do it to me again, Guruji.'

'I am not immortal, beta, as most of you think. I have died many times, but it's people like you and your love and

Prabhu's maya that I must come back. Moreover, my work in this world is unending. The demons are unending, and they keep on coming back.'

Embarrassed by her own reaction Aishani pulled away from Guruji, bowed her head and just stood there. When her eyes finally met Guruji's, both pairs of eyes were moist, with Aishani conveying her anguish and relief and Guruji conveying that all will always be well. She then turned and followed Adheesh, who was walking towards the senior library. They looked at each other and she gave him a small smile. He too smiled back, relieved that the fog of her despair was finally lifting.

The library looked undisturbed, and a very pleasant surprise awaited them there. Senior librarian Vashisht was there to greet them. Aishani heaved a sigh of relief. Vashisht was in turn overwhelmed to meet them. He greeted them with mingled emotions and there were tears in his eyes.

'I have been waiting for such a long time for both of you. The books are also waiting for both of you. Come, come,' Vashisht almost stumbled in his eagerness to welcome them.

They touched his feet and went inside. The familiarity of the place struck them immediately. They had undergone so much of turmoil and havoc in the past few weeks that now this familiarity seemed strange to them. How can things be the same when their whole world had turned upside down! But the library was the same, the same furniture, the same rows and rows of bookshelves with their intricate and colourful carvings and the same revered and cherished books and manuscripts. There seemed to be a kind of fluttering and sighing from some of the shelves and books, but when they turned towards them there was no sound. The library itself seemed to be in a part of the forest with no walls. The bookshelves were placed amongst the flora and the fauna. This wasn't so earlier. Surprised, they turned towards Vashisht ji.

'After all the mayhem, the library would have been the next target for them. Although invisible, a brick-and-mortar structure would have been quite easy for them to detect. So Guruji gave us instructions to shift the library to this part of the forest. It is totally invisible to outsiders and the surroundings too are salubrious. It would be easier to shift also should the need arise.' They nodded in unison and turned towards the manuscripts.

What a sorry state of affairs. Unlike previous days, there was no joy in Aishani's heart as she approached the books. That the books also did not show their eagerness to be opened by them came as no surprise to her. They were in mourning. A few of their visitors had died in the carnage. Now there was nobody to love and respect them. Yes, Vashisht was there but he did not appreciate the written word as much as the senior interns. They were the ones who after assimilating these readings went outside in the world and followed what was written in them. The manuscripts and the books were so sunk in depression that they did not register that Aishani and Adheesh were in their midst. It was after Aishani and Adheesh folded their hands in namaste and wished the manuscripts that the books came to life. All mayhem broke loose when Aishani touched them. It was only Aishani and Adheesh who understood what was happening. Everything was the same, how could the books move or how could they talk? But they could make out that there was palpable excitement in the air as the manuscripts waited to be taken out. Very slowly, Adheesh and Aishani began to softly caress the books. There was an audible sigh of relief from the books as they recognised their favourite readers' touch. Everything was going to be all right.

Gingerly, Aishani and Adheesh took out one book each. This was done very delicately as the books in their excitement might get torn also. These ancient texts had been preserved very well for such a long time, still they were so timeworn that extra care was always taken in touching them.

After some research, they finally came across a primordial copy in which something was written about minute invisible demons. It was written that the demons were invisible because they were so small. Because of their infinitesimal size, they did not have the strength of a full-sized demon. Hence millions of these tiny demons joined together and became one huge demon to destroy mankind and Earth. Slowly they discovered a couple of more books on these demons. For the moment both Adheesh and Aishani were more interested in finding the ways and means of destroying these demons rather than their history and evolution.

'Adhee see this,' Aishani called out to Adheesh. Adheesh went to where she was hunched up over a manuscript trying to decipher the ancient script. Adheesh was more familiar with this language which was prevalent in the time of the Ramayana. He took some time in reading and then translating it to Aishani.

'Ash, there are billions and trillions of them. They cannot be destroyed in one go or even one day. It would take at least one paksh (fortnight) to get rid of them.'

'That's too long, Adhee; they'll destroy more than half the world in this period.'

'Yes, Ash there must be some way to tackle this. It's taking a lot of time. By the time we get around to finding the perfect antidote, these minuscule demons will have wreaked so much devastation.'

'Adhee, if there is a description of these demons in our ancient scriptures, it means that they must have been active in the ancient times too. I'm positive that the means of destroying them must be here somewhere in these pages. Careful, Adhee, these pages are more than fragile.'

'I know, Ash. In their eagerness, the pages are almost turning themselves. The moment I turn my eyes towards a thought, the pages turn, and I come to the content which I had in mind.' They looked at each other and smiled. This was their world, the books, their forest, and everything around here.

'Guruji wouldn't have sent us here if there were any better methods of eliminating these demons,' she began reading again

'Adheesh, look, come and see this,' she whispered in an excited tone. They spoke in hushed tones so as not to excite the books too much.

Adheesh went to her table. After reading a few lines and figures, he said, 'Ash I think we finally have a breakthrough.'

'What, Adhee?' she spoke a bit loudly, then lowered her voice when she felt some of the books stiffening up.

'It's written that their powers get considerably depleted when any part of their body is destroyed. We know that millions of minuscule demons form to become one or a few huge demons. There is no central brain to these huge demons. If, say, an arm is destroyed, then it stays that way. This is a quantum leap in our discovery of killing the demons. Their powers decrease gradually as we destroy their body parts till the time we finish them off completely.'

'So how to destroy them? Let's find out.' They went back to their reading and research.

'Well, we could drown them, no? Or we could dunk them in alcohol and then kill them. We can shoot them into space—no, we just got rid of the demons in space, we don't want any demons in space again. Or we could burn them. Yes, I think that would be an ideal solution. We burn them. See Ash, these methods are written here.'

'Adheesh, there are millions of them, how do we catch them to burn them?'

'Apparently Ash, like any other run-of-the-mill demon, these too are attracted rabidly to blood. Any living being's blood will do when they are thirsty and hungry, but human flesh and blood is preferable anytime.'

'And how do we get so much blood, Adhee?'

'Wait; let me read some more, have patience. Here it's written that first these demons must be lured by the scent of fresh human blood. Before that, a huge pit has to be constructed with inflammable material like dry wood, twigs, etc. along with large amounts of camphor. The demons will follow the scent of fresh blood and flesh, stumble and fall in the pit which will be lighted in that instant. Since they are so tiny, they will get burnt immediately and perish.'

Aishani took a moment to assimilate this information.

'Let's go to Guruji, Adheesh, and apprise him of our plans.' Adheesh nodded.

Inside the hut, they touched Guruji's feet and sat down. They informed Guruji about their findings in the library. Guruji nodded, asking a few questions here and there.

'Guruji, may I ask a question?' Aishani asked respectfully.

Guruji turned towards her and waited for her question.

'We found out about these micro demons in the library, which means that they must have existed ages back. It seems they do not have any consciousness except to kill and destroy. But somebody must be controlling them, I mean without any consciousness how can they plan and find out things like our location?'

'You are right, Aishani, the story does go back a long time, even before the time of Ramayana. Ages back one Asur (demon) called Arunasur prayed to Brahmaji for centuries. Brahmaji was so pleased with his worship and devotion that he granted more than one boon. Arunasur had amassed so many boons from Brahmaji that he became practically indestructible and more powerful than the devtas too. As is the wont of demons, he began torturing the whole world, including devtas. That is when Maa Durga took the form of millions of bees, hornets, and wasps, covered his body, bit him all over and killed him. From that time onwards, one of the avatars of Maa Durga is prayed to and called Bhramri Devi.

Arunasur was a highly intelligent, powerful, and cunning demon. Even while he was being killed, he tried to duplicate the powerful bees or Bhramaris which were killing him. His bees would have countered Maa Durga's bees, but he died before he could complete the full exercise. The upshot was that though Arunasur died, some of his demoniac bees had come alive. They had been formed with a lust for destroying any person or thing with a touch of the divine. That and the ability to multiply manifold. They had been destroyed in the ancient ages by the devtas. They would come up again and be destroyed again. They have been like the proverbial cockroaches which have survived through the centuries. Obviously, some of these micro bees or demons had been left behind. They grew in numbers. Not much attention was paid to them, because nobody could see them, and they harmed people only sporadically. But they were growing right under our noses. In this century we were the first ones to be attacked. We were totally caught unawares. Our security systems were strong, but these were invisible micro demons. Their next target could be all religious places or even other Gurukuls where there is a strong presence of the divine. So, you see, we have to work expeditiously to destroy them.'

MICRO DEMONS

The pit stank to heavens. It was filled with rotting wood and leaves. They had tried to keep it as dry as possible which was not easy as dead things require moisture to rot. On top of this filth were the carcasses of dead animals and the topmost layer was of rotting grass with animal bones. These were put together to attract the demons. The trench was not full and anyone looking at it would see just a stretch of grass and shrubbery. Guruji had created this optical illusion so that the demons would get the smell of food, walk over the pit, and fall into it. This was their standby plan just in case their main plan did not work out.

Aishani's heart would come to her mouth whenever she thought of the main bait for luring these demons to the pit.

That was the scent of fresh human blood and flesh. No way were they going to ask for any volunteers from the survivors of the Gurukul nor was Adheesh going to allow Aishani to become bait. Einar had sensed something and had volunteered to help, but Guruji and Adheesh too had waved aside his offer on the pretext that he had to compete in all the tests first and had to help in repairing and restoring the Gurukul. As for Adheesh, he felt that killing these demons was their own personal matter, but he was slightly puzzled by Guruji's reaction. It seemed to him that Guruji was saving Einar for some other critical and valuable assignment. Now it was Aishani he was worried about. She was besides herself with distress and anxiety that Adheesh had chosen to be the bait and Guruji had concurred. She wanted to find some other way to destroy these demons, but Adheesh would not hear of it.

'No way has it been ordained that yours will be the finishing killer stroke, so to say. You don't have to lure the demons here. You have to make sure that after they fall in the dump, you and the others swiftly ignite the fire balls and throw them in the pit so that they get burnt immediately.' Looking at Aishani's distressed, distraught face, he took her in his arms. 'Nothing will happen to me, doll. How can anything happen to me when you, Guruji and Devnath are there to protect me?'

She looked at Devnath hovering just outside the door and was somewhat reassured. But this was Adheesh. She had lost him so many times in their past births. Would she lose him in this birth again? First Baba, now this! Even Guruji had left them when the nano demons had destroyed the Gurukul and killed Guruji. But though Guruji had come back because he was Hanuman ji's avatar, no other human would ever be allowed to breach the statute of returning to this world in the same form after death. The only way to come back was to take new birth and begin the whole rigmarole again. There were just too many permutations and combinations. It was best that they stayed together as much as possible in the present and reveled in each other's company. Adheesh stroked her hair softly and kept quiet, giving her time to come to terms with the situation.

She didn't know where her immediate family was. Amma, Jayant, Ruby, Uday, Tejas, Adheesh's family. If Guruji had said that they were safe then it was so, but she would not have anybody to share her worry and anxiety. How could she let go of Adheesh in this so perilous and treacherous mission? She shuddered, tears stung her eyes and she clung to Adheesh. They were sitting on the banks of the Gurukul's river. It was hardly a river now, having vanished completely during the onslaught on the Gurukul. It was slowly coming out bit by bit, reassured by the presence of Adheesh, Aishani and some other inhabitants of the Gurukul. It felt lonely and exposed without the usual flora and fauna around it. They knew that one day the river would come out with full force. All its pent-up water would devour the nearby banks too. But for now, it was scared, and its waters were just popping up now and then.

It was written in the ancient texts that since these minuscule demons were in such huge numbers, they could not be killed in one go. It would take more than a week to dispose of these creatures. As there would not be more than one muhurta (auspicious time) in one week, they would have to burn and kill these demons in the Abhijit muhurta, which is approximately one hour at mid-day everyday – half an hour before 12 o'clock and half an hour after it. Indubitably, every day's Abhijit muhurta was calculated, and it was roughly around this time only. Working at this time would give them more impetus, vigour, and strength to destroy the demons.

Aishani stayed in his embrace for some more time. Then she extricated herself from his arms with her chin up in the air. There would be no going back now. This time nobody was going to take her Adheesh away from her. Absolutely not! They were going to kill the demons and that was that. They had already chosen four team members from the straggling set of people who had earlier survived the onslaught of the demons. These four were as motivated as they themselves. They had seen the destruction of the Gurukul and their loved ones. They did not need any motivation apart from a great burning desire to destroy the demons. They had with them sacks of inflammable material. This was not the normal ignitable paraphernalia; it was made up of all kinds of Vedic and tantric ingredients, which have been used since time immemorial in exorcising demons. In this case there were more flammable materials like camphor which in itself was not enough to burn the demons but was an excellent facilitator in burning other ingredients.

'Our Gurukul is still infested with millions of these demons. They are like invisible termites. They assemble and go for the kill in a very stealthy, planned manner. There is only one way when they fall out of pattern, that is, when they smell fresh blood and flesh. They relish any living being's flesh and blood, but a human's blood is irresistible, especially if it has been freshly cut and dripping. Then they become mad with lust and greed and their meticulous attack goes up in the air,' Guruji informed them.

Three pits had been made for this purpose, to burn the demons on three consecutive days. They were oval and were hidden in the shrubberies of the jungle of the Gurukul. They were at a distance of five hundred metres from each other. On Guruji's instructions, Devnath and a couple of other workers had made a makeshift cottage for Adheesh and themselves. Adheesh's cottage had all the medical paraphernalia which they could recover from the Gurukul's Vaidyashala. They had plenty of towels and gauze and arrangements for hot water. Apart from the medicines which the Vaidyas had kept there, Guruji had given them some more herbs. The Vaidyas were not fully familiar with the herbs, but they did know that these herbs increased blood in a noticeably short span of time. The two doctors of the Gurukul had a rough idea of Adheesh's requirements. Hence, they had planned the medicines and supplies. The four people who were selected for this job would be hiding in the four corners of the pit waiting for the demon(s) to fall into it. A place under a tree half a mile from the pit would be the rendezvous point of the bait with the demons.

'Guruji, I will be there tomorrow at 11:20. The Abhijit muhurta will begin at 11.45. I will have ten minutes to open up myself in two places in my body, my muscles and one of my nerves so that the demons get a whiff of blood and flesh both. Once they start assembling and begin forming into a large one, I'll begin my run towards the pit.'

'Right Adheesh,' Guruji concurred, then turning towards Aishani he said, 'I shall be at the south end of the pit chanting the Bagalamukhi mantra and you will be at the west end chanting the Bhramari mantra which we will anyway be chanting the whole night tonight.'

'Yes Guruji,' her voice was unwavering and steadfast. Adheesh looked at her. If he was worried about anyone at this point, it was her. He knew that she had placed her immense fear and anxiety for him in a corner of her heart and sealed it. He also knew that this fear would not be unlocked till the demons were destroyed. All this flashed in his mind for a moment. He, too, was a warrior and he had to prepare for one of the greatest battles of his life, which was tomorrow. He was going to use himself as the bait. Nobody could take his place as, one, there was nobody to spare and two, he had to lead and set an example, and three, his reflexes and his running speed were the fastest in the Gurukul.

Aishani and Guruji spent the whole night sitting in front of the Bagulamukhi Yantra and the Bhramari Yantra and chanted their mantras till 11 a.m., after which they went to the south and west of the pit and kept on chanting. The Bagalamukhi mantra was chanted and Maa Bagulamukhi was invoked to destroy enemies and demons. The Bhramari mantra was being chanted to weaken the nano demons. Guruji was not going to spare anything or anyone in the process of destroying these demons who had just one thought: to destroy human beings and their habitat, Mother Earth.

Adheesh was under the Peepal tree at 11:20. He looked around but couldn't see or hear or even feel any malevolent presence near him. But they were present, he knew. Guruji had said that these demons somehow knew that there was superior blood here. That is why they were congregating here and not in any common area. They just had to be crazily attracted to something to assemble and join to become the huge entity that they were. Taking a deep breath, he took out a sharp knife and then took off his upper clothes. He was now naked from the waist up. Very deliberately but surely, he made a slash on his upper arm muscles and a cut on one of his arteries. He had to do it very carefully as he had to repeat the same procedure a few times more. Blood immediately spurted out from his vein. He had cut a thick muscle also. He was sure that the demons must have smelled and sensed his flesh and blood. Sure enough, after a wait of about five minutes, he could see a dark smoky form rising in front of him. Very soon it turned into a huge black entity which seemed to be running or gliding towards him. Without waiting for the demon to fully form itself Adheesh began running. The demon(s), surprised at this behavior of the human, also turned and began the chase. No way was the demon going to let go of this opportunity of fresh flesh and blood. Adheesh was now running at the speed of lightning. Even so, a thought entered his mind that this huge demon did not seem to have a mind of its own. It was as if each of the minuscule demons had been fed with only one data or thought: to kill and plunder humans and drink their blood and eat their flesh. They would cling to a human body in thousands or in lakhs and eat and drink him in a matter of minutes. After some time, nothing would be left of the living being, not even the skeleton. Not waiting for this thought to grow, he increased his pace. He zigzagged between the huge burnt trees and boulders which had been placed strategically to distract and disorient the demon. The demon too was roaring now and running after him. In this chase sometimes a part of its arm would be left behind or even a part of its head. The demon did not have enough time to bind itself fully. But it did know that its priority was to kill and eat human flesh. This was fed in their data. It had almost reached Adheesh, but only because Adheesh had slowed down a bit so that the demon could come near him. They had now reached the pit when Adheesh sat down suddenly. With a roar the demon jumped over Adheesh, but Adheesh was not there, he had slid out from under the demon and the demon fell headlong into the pit. Everyone was waiting for it. The four men had their sacks open and ready. They immediately started throwing shovels of the tantric ash on the monster in the pit. A roaring blaze of flames and smoke went up in the air. The entire pit was a conflagration of red, yellow and orange, the cries of the micro demons screeching like broken violin strings sometimes together, sometimes separately depending which body part broke or burnt. There was a continuous put-put sound as each of the nano demon sizzled in the fire and burst. The acrid tendrils of smoke desperately rose towards the sky hysterically trying to escape the blazing inferno and the screaming demons also trying to escape with it. The smoke fumes got into Adheesh's eyes and throat, making him cough. His eyes watered, preventing him from seeing the gory scene in front of him, but he still exulted at the sight. 'You plucked my insides and that of my loved ones, you stole my soul and theirs too, we were nothing to you. I hope you rot in hell till eternity. We are both in pain now, just different kinds of pain, your pain is the pain of death, my pain is the pain of hope.' Adheesh thought all this in the moments that he was a spectator in front of the burning pit.

The monster(s) howled and tried to climb the burning abyss, but the moment it tried to hold onto something, that part of the hand or leg would fall off in the burning pit, making it more challenging and painful for him to climb out of the blazing hellfire. Adheesh knew that the fire, once invoked, would have no pity, no mind, and no culture. It would happily and violently consume whatever came in its way and reduce it to ashes or any kind of melted liquid, without bothering about consequences.

Gradually the asur (nano demon) became weaker and weaker. Its loud bellows turned into shrieks and squeals. The more it tried to climb up, the more it slipped, giving the four people around the pit more time to shovel the tantric ash over it. Then there was the loud chanting by Guruji and Aishani. Everything together was the death knell of the creature. Adheesh did not stay there to witness the gory scene. His arm was cut up and his artery was still bleeding. The demon in a desperate bid might jump out of the pit and latch onto him. Devnath was waiting for him just at the periphery of the pit. Adheesh had ordered Devnath to keep himself fully covered, lest the nano demons espied and shifted towards him. If there was one person more desperately worried about Adheesh than Aishani, it was Devnath. At the moment he was probably more desperate than Aishani. He swiftly tied a tourniquet on Adheesh's arm then quickly bundled him up in a huge soft and hot blanket, threw him on his shoulders and ran. He wanted to put as much distance as possible between the demons and Adheesh. That and the fact that Adheesh required immediate medical attention.

They would be doing this again tomorrow and maybe after that too. It had to be done, for the ashram to be totally cauterised and purged of the demons. Thankfully, there were a couple of doctors amongst the survivors, even though the medical supplies were meagre. But Adheesh was an extremely healthy man with the strength of a bull. He just needed some antibiotic medicines, creams and plenty of clean cotton and gauge and he would be fit in no time. The Vaidyas were waiting for him. They began their work straightaway.

Adheesh and Aishani did not meet that evening or that night. Adheesh did not go to meet Guruji too. He had to preserve every ounce of his strength. Devnath was looking after him, feeding him proteins and herbal juices and ensuring he got plenty of rest, except that there was no time to recoup. The Gurukul Vaidya was there with them supervising his recovery. Devnath applied the Ayurvedic herbs and lotions which Guruji and the Gurukul doctors had given him and had instructed him on how to use them. Adheesh could not have asked for a better and more committed nurse and caretaker than Devnath. His loyalty and caring instincts for Adheesh were incomparable.

Adheesh could not have met Aishani and Guruji even if he wanted to. They were totally involved in praying to Ma Bagulamukhi and Bhramari Devi, especially at night when they were the strongest. Not even a second had to be wasted.

All this had been thought of and decided earlier. Guruji and Aishani had stationed themselves near the pits where Adheesh was luring the demons. These pits were made in the interior jungles of the Gurukul, where there were less chances of people accidently arriving and getting the scare of their lives. Not that there were many people left in the Gurukul after the massacre. Even in the Gurukul, only the most secret places had been left by the nano demons. Even so, Guruji had covered the entire area with an invisible mantle. There were invisible demons here and two Goddesses were being invoked. They could not take a chance of any of the entities being disturbed. Those who were present in this part of the jungle knew exactly what they had to do to keep the whole operation under wraps. So great was their loss that they would do anything to destroy the demons who had demolished their Gurukul and killed their loved ones.

Two more pits had been dug, almost on the outskirts of the Gurukul. They had read in the ancient texts that to purge the Earth of these nano demons, there had to be three combustible onslaughts on them. The first onslaught itself would destroy most of them and the second the rest of them. The third would be just an extra precaution in case a few stragglers were left. Nobody in the ashram wanted to take any chances or leave even one microscopic demon alive, hence the third pit. Adheesh also knew that later a few of the occupants of the Gurukul would nick their body parts to make their blood flow and then go around with a burning torch in their hands. He sighed. They had all become paranoid.

Next day, the same exercise was repeated with the same

consequences. Adheesh had slashed an arm and an artery of the other hand. Blood spurted out from the slash and the artery. Today the demons took a bit longer, assembling to make a small demon, much smaller than the earlier one but still sizeable, a sure sign that the majority of the demons had been annihilated in the first day's fire. It was exactly as it was written in the books of the senior library. That meant that tomorrow there would be no such demons, but nobody was willing to take this risk. Devnath was beside himself with worry. Adheesh had two deep wounds and he had lost much blood as after cutting his vein, he had to run for about fifteen minutes towards the pit with the blood flowing through his hand. There was no way he could have got a blood transfusion in this battered and ravaged Gurukul. There was simply no one to give him blood, forget about the right equipment. Devnath desperately wished that he could take Adheesh to his father's hospital where he would be looked after so well, just like Aishani was cared when she had ingested the demon Raktabeej's blood. But nobody knew where they were, whether they were dead or alive. Even then Adheesh couldn't have gone and stayed in his father's hospital. Three consecutive exercises from a faraway place would just not have been possible. Devnath shook his head; he had more important things to think about.

Adheesh developed a mild fever the day after the second episode. True, he was one of the strongest warriors, but he had to allow his blood to flow profusely, so that the demons could easily smell it. In two days, he had become very weak and there was still the third day to go. There was no way that Adheesh could be stopped, the ancient text had said three times to remove even the faintest trace of the demon particle. Nobody would have stopped him, even if they wanted. The repercussions were too gruesome and heartbreaking, to say the least. Everybody concerned was worried about Adheesh and desperately trying not to think about him, instead they focused only on getting rid of the demons. They knew that even the smallest stray thought would break up their concentration and hinder the execution of their exercise.

Devnath was the worst hit of the lot. To see his master in such a condition and not being able to do anything about it was breaking him from inside. His God may or may not die. This was too big a price to pay. Finally, on the third day when Adheesh cut himself during the Abhijit muhurta, no shadows were formed. Adheesh heaved a sigh of relief but still waited longer than usual, just in case. He then ran, almost stumbled, towards the pit where Guruji and Aishani were chanting the Bagulamukhi mantra and the four men waiting on the four corners of the pit with their sacks of combustible ingredients. Adheesh looked at Guruji. He kept on chanting his mantra for some more time then stopped and gestured to the four men. They immediately poured the mixture of the sacks into the pit. Fire immediately rose with a roar, searching and wanting to consume its victims, but there were no victims now. The fire would be allowed to burn till it abated and petered out on its own.

With a sigh of relief, Guruji gestured to Devnath, who was hovering around waiting for Guruji's orders. Without a word and with alacrity, he picked up Adheesh and tenderly threw him over his shoulders. He then ran towards the cottage where the doctors were waiting. Adheesh had passed out.

Aishani came much later. She and Guruji had stayed back chanting the mantra, in order to wind up any invisible microscopic demon, after which they went back to tender their gratitude to Ma Bagulamukhi and Bhramari Devi for helping them out of this calamity and requesting them to return to their abode in the heavens. That itself took almost a whole day. Everything had to be done meticulously. If these deities felt even an iota of dissatisfaction, they would either retaliate against them or not come when invoked again. This was a risk which neither Guruji nor Aishani could take. Aishani had willed herself not to think about Adheesh at all, lest her concentration wavered.

When she finally went to Adheesh in the makeshift cottage, where Devnath and the two Vaidyas were looking after him, Adheesh was sleeping. He was pale from the loss of blood and it seemed to her as if he had shrunk in the last three days. He was a hollow caricature of the man she had parted with four days back. Tears came to her eyes. She was so proud of him— her partner, her world, and her husband. He had sacrificed himself so that the others could live safely but nobody would ever know about it apart from the few people who had taken part in the exercise. She sat down beside him and gently took his hand in hers. He didn't move but she knew that he knew. She closed her eyes and began praying to Ma Durga.

DEVNATH AND THE HOUSE

It was the greatest relief for Devnath when Aishani rushed inside the cottage with her bags of herbs and medicines. But it was more than herbs and medicines. Devnath had seen the kind of love and chemistry his master and mistress shared. Though Adheesh's mutilations were mainly physical, he knew that with Aishani's no-nonsense meticulous dressings and loads of tender loving care, she would speed up his master's recovery. There was nothing for him to do there except to sit outside and guard the cottage. Not that he minded it, not at all. He just pottered around the cottage-cum-hospital, much like Manohar ji used to do in the past in front of Guruji's cottage. He surveyed his surroundings and saw only a devastated land. He also saw that the Gurukul was being renovated very swiftly.

He could not but marvel at the hard work Einar was putting in to bring the Gurukul to its former glory–if not more. Devnath also knew that there were many places in the Gurukul that the demons had not been able to penetrate. They crushed only the physical things that came in front of them. There were many areas which were hidden from the normal human eye as well as the demoniac eye. He himself had not been to many of these places but he had seen Adheesh and some others entering them.

A few days passed like this, Adheesh was recouping albeit a bit slowly. The remaining denizens of the ashram were working at breakneck speed to repair and restore the ashram under Guruji's expert guidance. Though he wanted to join them, he could not dream of leaving Adheesh alone, especially when he was so unwell.

It was Adheesh who called Devnath to him after a couple of days, 'Devnath, I am recouping but it will take me some more time to fully recover. The ashram is also being reshaped and reconstructed at a very satisfactory speed. But there are some more very important works which Aishani and I have to do. Aishani is a law onto herself. She will not leave me even if I begged her. She will not listen to me at all. You are the only person who will understand the depth of what I am asking, you know so much about me and Aishani that I won't have to prompt you for the next step.'

'Yes, Bhaiya tell me, you know I can lay down my life for you,' Devnath answered promptly.

Adheesh thought for a minute then said, 'You know both of us are very worried about our people, so worried that we become sick just by thinking about them. My people may not have been so badly attacked by the demons as none of them are intrinsic demon killers, even though they now have an inkling of what we do. Of course my parents know everything. But it is Aishani's people that I am most worried about. Her mother and brother both are demon fighters, though passive ones. Ruby and her brothers are active demon fighters. Are they alive, if so then where are they? You will have to go and find out Devnath,' Adheesh said emphatically.

Devnath nodded. He too had been thinking about their families. The past couple of months had been so stressful and breathtaking that they could only look after the immediate precipitating factors. Now that the situation was under control, they had to search for their families. Aishani and Adheesh could not leave the Gurukul, so it was up to him to find out about their families. He was a bit reluctant but it was his master's desire which was an order for him.

'Devnath, go to Aishani's house first,' Devnath acknowledged.

'You may not find anything there, maybe not even the house or only the shell of the house,' Adheesh coughed and winced in pain, 'Wait there and meditate. You are an expert at meditating and waiting. You'll start hearing sounds and odd supernatural flow of energy, don't get alarmed and don't attack. This will be the house itself trying to communicate with you, if at all it recognizes you. It will communicate with you only when it begins to trust you. So be soft and gentle; the house is an entity in itself and it can give you quite a lot of inputs.'

For a minute Devnath just stared at Adheesh, then shook his

head. They had gone through so many hazards and adventures, still his master did not fail to surprise him. So be it. He touched Adheesh's feet and went out. Like Adheesh, he could now easily enter and leave the Gurukul whenever he wanted.

Aishani's house was not very far off. When he entered the town, everything was the same. The townspeople were not aware of any untoward happenings in the nearby forest. In any case, they could not see the Gurukul nor were they aware of it. He began to slowly notice the signs of ravage as he neared Aishani's house. He kept walking till he stood before it. He put his hands on his hips and stared. Only the skeletal remains of the house could be seen. It was a crumbling ruin, charred black. The wind passed desolately through its broken doors and windows sighing and keening. Devnath knew that it was not only the air but the house lamenting. Slowly, he went up the broken stairs. The house slowly becoming aware of an intruder in its midst began closing its doors and windows, but there were no doors and windows. After a while, it just gave up.

Devnath, who could commune with spirits, sat in the middle of the hall, closed his eyes and began aligning himself with the spirit of the house. As expected there was absolutely no response. It was as if the house was ridiculing him and asking if a brick-and-mortar structure could ever have feelings. Undeterred, Devnath kept on concentrating, trying to connect with the house. Finally, after some time, the aggressive sounds faded away and there was complete silence. Even the wind slowed down as if eavesdropping on the conversation.

Slowly, as though in a dream, Devnath thought he heard a question. He knew now that it was not just in his head, he actually heard a question from the house. The desolate sound had all the pain and bewilderment of recent bereavements. In spite of his harsh, cruel experiences, Devnath's heart softened. The house was inconsolable like a ravaged pet which had been abandoned by his masters.

'I am Devnath, Adheesh Bhaiya's assistant,' he said proudly.

There was a long silence. The house was trying to absorb the meaning of these words. At last it remembered and understood. It began blabbering—or so it seemed to Devnath. It was a building, not a human being with a language. It had acquired an intellect and feelings because there was magic in this household. Gently, Devnath steered it towards his own questions.

'Where is everybody, big brother?' he asked mentally. The house ingested and liked this appellate. It began blabbering again. Devnath sighed. He had to sift information from these ramblings. Who could speak normally under these extreme circumstances, least of all a house? He smiled wryly at his own humour. From the great dramatic sighs and banging of broken doors and windows, he deduced that Aishani's and Ruby's families had gone beyond the mountains and taken refuge near the Ganga river. He could make out from the sketchy direction that they had gone in the north-east direction.

'What happened big brother? Can you tell me?' Devnath had started getting the hang of the house's jargon which was a series of sighing, banging of doors, going completely silent and then allowing the wind in and out at its will. It took all his will power and concentration to understand what the house was trying to tell him. Devnath had to sift through all the house's garbling and deduce the picture. What the house told him put his hair on edge.

It seemed that Jayant, Tejas and Uday were in the backyard making a tiered frame with wheels for Madhu to perch her potted herbs so that they could get sunlight from all sides. There was an atmosphere of revelry and camaraderie. Jayant went to the edge of the courtyard to get some more wooden planks. Casually, he glanced at the small jungle outside the courtyard. This was the same jungle where they all used to play when they were children. He noticed something unnatural in the scenario. Nonchalantly he stood there for a moment to confirm that everything was normal. Jayant had fluoroscopic x-ray vision. This was a skill or diksha given to him by his father on one of his birthdays. What he saw just now stopped him in his tracks. Oh no! It couldn't be happening, but it was happening. He rushed screaming back to his friends.

'They are coming, they are coming, they are too small but too many in numbers almost like flying insects!'

Nobody needed any more prompting. They were so used to all this that their senses were on high alert all the time even when they were sleeping. Ruby who was inside the house with Madhu also came out running. Uday immediately took over.

'Tejas run home and fetch Ma and Papa here,' he ordered. Tejas was faster than any creature in the world, but he stopped and looked quizzically at Uday as if asking: 'Why you are calling them in danger when they should be running away?'

'Go,' Uday ordered again, his pupils were turning black. Tejas turned swiftly and ran towards his house. Uday and Jayant looked at each other for a moment and understood exactly what was happening,

'Jayant, get me as much kerosene oil as you can and

whatever inflammable things you can find; Ruby, gather as many important things which you can find in the house for survival, take Aunty and wait outside the house for Ma and Papa. Jayant and I will join you after sometime,' his words came out like the staccato of bullets. They ran inside.

Jayant rushed outside with cans of kerosene oil. How there were so many cans of kerosene oil in his house he did not know nor did he pause to think about it. Quickly they poured huge amounts of kerosene oil in a large circle around the house leaving just a bit bare and open on the North side just for one person to squeeze in or out. The insect demons were coming from the South side. Jayant stared at the horizon for some time then whispered softly, 'Uday, there is more than one kind of creature. There are bigger demons following these mini insect demons.'

Uday paused, 'What kind of demons, Jayant? And how many?' His pupils had already turned jet black. Was there a shadow of a smile on his face? Jayant also knew his friend. If there was a smile on Uday's face then it was in anticipation of the kill. This was his forte, this ruthless and merciless killer of animals and demons. Jayant knew that such a brutal, cold-blooded warrior was required in their midst. But now was not the time to think of these things or even be grateful that Uday was there. Now was the time to face the demons.

'I don't know Uday they seem like hybrid ferocious animals, each creature a cross between many animals and equally savage and ravenous. These are so much bigger that they will be able to cross our circle of fire, from here they seem to be uncountable but they could be anything between fifty to eighty,' Jayant was slightly worried now.

'No problems Jayant, you take care of the insect demons, make sure that they do not cross the fire circle, I'll take care of the rest,' saying this he took out a heavy axe-like weapon except that it wasn't an axe. Uday lovingly called it his Pashu. He had named it after the divine axe of Lord Parshuram who was the sixth avatar of Bhagwan Vishnu. It was made of a long heavy shaft probably made up of wood and iron together. At the top end was a big, rounded axe almost like a scythe, its outer side sharp as a blade, its inner side was serrated. It was as deadly as it looked. Uday sometimes used it with one hand and sometimes with both hands, depending on the situation. By this time Ruby and Madhu had collected the items which they thought would be useful in this scenario. This wasn't too much of a challenge as Madhu was always ready for such a contingency. There were always two bags packed with all the necessary items in case they had to temporarily rehabilitate. She went with Ruby on the northern side of her house where a part of the fire circle had been left for them to cross to the other side.

'Ruby beta you stay here and wait for your parents and Tejas. I'll go inside and see how I can help them.'

'Aunty please stay here,' Ruby implored her. She was bewildered. How could Aunty even think of going inside the house again? If anything, Jayant and Uday would be distracted by her very presence. Ruby didn't know about Madhu being a warrior. Madhu did not reply to Ruby's alarmed cry. She just went inside. There was no time to waste. There were lots of containers in the kitchen store containing oils and alcohol, kept there only for this sort of contingency. Madhu knew that very small demons could be demolished either by burning or by drowning them in alcohol or in alcohol mixed with water. There was a large store room filled with these liquids. Jayant and Uday were too busy to help her with those huge containers, but Madhu was a warrior and had been one for ages. She took a deep breath and began pushing the barrels out in the backyard where Jayant could use them. She gave a sidelong glance to the scene in the backyard where a full-fledged war and mayhem was going on.

In the meantime, Tejas had come back with his parents. Handing them over to Ruby, he rushed inside the house where Madhu was struggling with the huge barrels of oil and alcohol.

The demons were on their heads now. The insect demons could not cross the fire. They just jumped into the fire, were burnt to a crisp and died. Jayant was making sure that the fire did not get extinguished anywhere. He kept on lighting fire and pouring oil in the circle. After some time, Tejas also joined him. But it was Uday who was fighting the toughest battle. The bigger hybrid demons or animals though not very large were still strong enough to jump over the fire. Uday was in his element. Holding the Pash with both his hands he swung around like a dervish cutting the deformed hybrids in pieces. There was blood, crushed bones, animal parts spread all over the backyard and the side of the house. Uday was whirling around so fast that now Jayant and Tejas had difficulty in locating him in the gory melee of body parts and strange inhuman screaming and screeching.

Uday must have destroyed about a hundred of them but

they still kept coming. Jayant knew that they were fighting a losing battle. They had to escape anyhow now.

And then it happened. Nobody could ever cross Uday's axe or the Pash and live, but here it was somehow different now. Any demon which came near Uday was slaughtered mercilessly, but they were so many and Uday was only one. Jayant and Tejas were busy in keeping the fires aflame and sizzling when a couple of the hybrid demons found some leeway and entered the house. Tejas and Madhu ji ran after them. They did not have any weapon with them, they were going to be torn and killed by the demons, but they hardly thought about it. Their protective instincts were so strong that they just rushed inside to confront these animal demons. Tejas was still holding a blazing torch in his hand and Madhu had a jug of alcohol in her hands. The moment the hybrid demons saw them, they ran towards them growling and snarling and swiped at both of them. They fell down, the alcohol spilled on the ground and the torch fell on top of it. The alcohol caught fire immediately and so did a part of the house. They watched helplessly as the fire spread immediately. But even in this chaos Madhu noticed that the demons had ceased their shenanigans and were sort of standing in one place and growling. Jayant had also come after them and he also noticed the same thing. A jumble of thoughts entered his head but he realized they could think about the reasons for this temporary truce later if they were alive. He rushed outside and somehow managed to catch Uday's attention. Uday, covered with blood, flesh and gore was still going strong though now there were perceptibly lesser number of the hybrid demons. Jayant urgently told him about the scenario inside the house. The whole house had caught fire and the fire was on the way to become an inferno and devour the whole house.

'We must escape now,' Jayant desperately insisted, 'They might come out of their inertness anytime.'

Uday nodded. He also understood that probably these demons' destination was to enter this house which they had—now they didn't know what to do. Taking advantage of this temporary truce, he signaled the others and all of them ran out to the North side where Ruby and her parents were impatiently waiting for them. Ruby had taken the car out and it was already running. They all jumped into it but not before Jayant closed the fire circle on this side. Ruby drove fast. It was already night and they had to get very far as soon as possible. Madhu looked back. Her beloved house was going up in a blaze of fire and there was nothing they could do about it. Jayant understood her feelings and tenderly put his arms around his mother.

All this while Devnath had listened to the house with rapt attention and empathy. He looked around. The house was just a shell now; it was just a black caricature of a once majestic and proud building. But its soul was still intact and it was pining for its inhabitants.

He folded his hands in Namaste to the house, 'Thank you so much. I promise you that I will bring everybody back safely.'

The house shook with happiness. As he was getting out of the hall into the verandah, the house shook and a few pieces of the broken ceiling fell in front of him. Devnath tried to circumvent the falling piece of mortar but another piece fell in front of him. It seemed as if the house did not want him to go or maybe it wanted to tell him something more. He could not sit and chat anymore. He looked up at the house and said, 'I can't stay anymore now. It's getting very late. You know I am going to bring them.'

In response the house shook some more and a piece of crumpled paper fell in front of him. A small golden key also fell on top of the paper. Devnath picked up both. The paper seemed to be a rough map of some sort. He did not understand.

'What do I do with it? Do I have to give it to somebody?'

The house banged its window. Slowly through much banging and shaking Devnath realized that the paper was a map of the direction which Aishani's and Ruby's people had taken in their bid to escape the demons. What a time saver! He also realized that the house wanted him to take the key as well. He did not know for what purpose as yet.

'Oh, thank you so much. Now I'll come with them much earlier.'

The house sighed happily and then allowed Devnath to leave.

A cold dark gust of air enveloped him as soon as he came out of the house. He looked around. Was the house deterring him again? It did not seem so. The wind blew around him again, dark and sinister. He understood. These were the negative supernatural forces swirling their macabre dance around the house and its surroundings. Devnath smiled. This was like more in his alley. He had been reared up with similar forces surrounding him. With them it was either kill or be killed. He opened his cloth bag and took out a few things.

These were two large human bones, a human skull and a small two headed pellet drum known as damru. He sat down in front of the house closed his eyes and chanted a few mantras in an alien language. Then he poured some sort of a liquid in the skull, shallowly cut his left palm with a sharp knife and let this blood flow into the skull. Dark dense smoke came out of the skull. Devnath took the bones in his hands and wrapped himself in the smoke and then began dancing with the bones and the damru. It was a ghoulish dance with Devnath clanking the bones and shaking the damru, all the time chanting and twirling and going around the house in a frenzied manner. The liquid in the skull was boiling now almost spilling over. There was rabid and distraught screaming all around the house and inside it too. There was a match going on between Devnath and his forces and the dark forces which had enveloped the house, both not very different from each other. The only difference that one was under the control of Devnath and the other was without any control with unchanneled negative energies. He did not give up; he knew how to get rid of them. He continued with his dancing, dipping the bone with the liquid in the skull and banging against each other. Each clanging brought out fresh blood curling screams. Slowly the screams faded, the liquid stopped boiling and returned to its light red color. Devnath stopped his dance when he was completely sure that the evil spirits had been completely exorcised. He cleaned and packed his items and started on his journey. He looked back at the house. He did not expect any thankfulness but maybe he expected some sort of acknowledgement. But the house was absolutely quiet, no sound not a peep. Considering it was so garrulous some time back Devnath found it just a bit strange. Then it struck him. Of course! The house had been so ravaged in the last couple of weeks by the evil spirits torturing it that now it was sleeping like a baby after he had chased away all the evil spirits. So be it. Devnath saluted the house and began his journey.

Devnath followed the map. It was a hurriedly made map not to scale, though it did not matter too much as Devnath was familiar with the place where the families had escaped. The map was hastily scribbled by either Jayant or Uday and hid in one of the cornices of the hall in the hope that one of them would find it. They had gone somewhere in the Gangotri and were probably still there. Devnath simply took a bus to Haridwar and from there took another bus to Gangotri in Uttar Kashi. Gangotri is the origin of the holy river Ganga, one of the most pious of places where demons would dread to go. It was all so very scenic and very cold too. Devnath was oblivious to all this. He just wanted to rehabilitate these people and rush back to his master Adheesh.

Once he reached Gangotri, the map became a bit sketchy and after that the trail ran cold. Probably family themselves didn't know where they were going. He camped near the Gangotri temple and spent the whole day searching for them. He wasn't very familiar with their faces. He wasn't sure that he would be able to recognise them if they were going around in disguise. There were no passwords or code words between them. Devnath recognised and categorised them by his instincts. Among this group he knew that Uday was the most dangerous one. He would not have even an iota of mercy for his enemies. If someone brushed past him carelessly and Uday did not like it, then that person might have a broken arm or leg in the next minute or so. Devnath was sure that even the demons thought twice before taking chances with Uday. But Devnath had a small niggling doubt about Uday. He was pretty sure that there was a soft side to Uday's personality, a fact which Uday hid very successfully. The next in line of dangerous warriors in this group was Aishani Bhabhi's mother Madhu. Devnath was surprised, rather shocked by his own observation. Aishani's mother was just a housewife, quite content in looking after her home and family. She never seemed to long for anything else. The vibes which Devnath got from Madhu was that she was a very experienced warrior who would not hesitate even for a second to kill someone if the requirement arose. What a ridiculous assessment, Devnath thought to himself. He kept his thoughts about Madhu in a corner of his mind to mull over them some other time. He had his opinion about Ruby, Jayant and Tejas too, but he would think about them later.

Devnath just kept on roaming in the streets and jungles of Gangotri hoping against hope to find them. He put his hands inside his pockets in despair thinking about what to do. There was something in his pocket. Curiously he took it out. It was the key which the house had given him. He stared at it thinking. Yes this was it! This was the key to finding them! He went to a slightly crowded lane and attached the key to the bark of a tree which was on the road but facing a bit away from it. And waited. Nothing happened. A few passersby crossed the tree without being aware of the key. Disappointed but still full of hope, he took off the key and fixed it to another tree in another lane. This happened two times more. It was getting dark. He took off the key and began searching for a place to spend the night. Maybe a dhaba owner would allow him to sleep near his kitchen. He started walking towards a couple of dhabas that he had seen on the way. Tomorrow he would begin again. It was getting dark and there was an eerie silence about the whole place. It did not deter Devnath as he had lived in eerie and unnatural silences for most part of his life. But amidst all the silence there was another sound, a wary and stealthy sound as if somebody was following him furtively and quietly under the cover of trees. Immediately alert, Devnath went on walking nonchalantly as if he didn't know that he was being followed. Devnath was very intuitive. He knew that he was not being followed by a demon. They were very rare in this part of the world. There was sacredness and piousness in this part of the world, the atmosphere was not conducive for demons at all. He was not going to take any chances. Gangotri was the abode of Gods and devtas. A demon would not dare enter such a pious place. The water of the river Ganga only was enough to burn a demon. But he could not make out whether the person following him was a friend or foe. Sheer cruelty was emanating from the aura behind him. Devnath's hair rose. But again it was not a malefic aura. Devnath was confused. The person behind him sensed this confusion and in a flash had Devnath's head in his hands from behind. Not to be outdone, Devnath's khukhri was out even before that person could fully lock his hands around his throat. They wrestled with each other for a few minutes only by which time

Devnath managed to have a glimpse of the man's face.

'Uday,' he said in a muffled tone as the grip on his throat tightened, 'I am Devnath,' he croaked. The grip didn't loosen though the pressure did not increase. Devnath had met his match as far as strength was concerned. There was no ambiguity that Uday would break his neck in a trice if he so much as suspected Devnath to be a spy or a demon. Finally, after what seemed hours but were only a few seconds, Uday loosened his grip, just enough so that he could see Devnath's face. He stared at Devnath for some time and when he was convinced that it was actually Devnath he loosened his grip.

'What are you doing with this key?' they went and sat on a ridge near the road. It was totally dark now. The only light was from the petromax lamp from one of the dhabas.

'Adheesh Bhaiya sent me to search for all of you. I went to Bhabhi's house where I got the key and the map,' Devnath answered simply. By Bhabhi he meant Aishani.

'Where are they?' Uday asked, 'Are they…...' he could not formulate the sentence.

'They are alright and in the ashram, waiting for all of you.' No way was Devnath going to tell him anything more than that. Their life was such that nobody could be trusted and secondly, it was not his place to divulge their whole story. It was Adheesh and Aishani's job to tell them whatever they found fit.

'Where is everybody?'

'Come, let's go to them,' Uday got up.

They went behind the Gangotri temple. Half a kilometre from the temple there were huge trees. Devnath followed Uday behind the trees till the time they came upon a cottage. They were all there, Aishani's mother, Jayant, Ruby, her parents and Tejas. It was a reunion of sorts, except that they weren't very friendly with Devnath. They knew that Devnath was Adheesh's most trusted aide and if the house too had trusted him then he was trustworthy. Everybody wanted to know about Adheesh and Aishani. Devnath gave them only sketchy details. It was not his position to tell them anything. They did not ask about Guruji because they did not fully know what had happened in the ashram. Devnath was relieved when finally they did not ask any more questions. They had rightly presumed that he was uncomfortable in answering all their questions as either he did not know or did not want to.

'I have come to take you back. The demons have been destroyed; there is no danger there now.'

'Yes, we'll leave in the morning. It's quite late, it won't be safe to leave now,' Madhu said simply. Everybody concurred, first because they respected her and second because she was always right. She served the simple food to everybody, thick chapattis with chunky pieces of homemade butter on them with cauliflower and potato curry. Everybody ate it with relish, most of all Devnath for whom it was like manna from heaven. He was not used to homemade food where love is poured into it in copious amounts making it incomparable to any other kind of food.

'Uday Bhaiya had killed two of them,' Tejas chortled, 'But there were so many of them that we had to come here,' he said plainly as if that explained everything.

Devnath looked at them quietly and awkwardly.

Everybody was demon ravaged, but also raring to go. Madhu ji quietly beckoned Devnath in a corner.

'Where is Aishani?' she asked softly.

Equally softly Devnath answered, 'Bhabhi is fine, she is with Adheesh Bhaiya.'

Madhu searched Devnath's deadpan face and read it. After sometime she seemed to be satisfied. She went towards others and began preparing to go home. It took them one full day to reach home. Madhu ji drew in a sharp breath when she saw her home in that dilapidated condition. The others were also awestruck. After sitting in the verandah for some time, Devnath took their leave. Now he had to look for Adheesh Bhaiya's family.

Adheesh's home was about a mile from Aishani's home. Devnath dreaded going there. God knows what he would find there. His legs became lead after some time. They wouldn't go any further. His hands on his cotton bag tightened, caressing the bones. He might need them here too. How could he face Adheesh if things were not good here?

Somehow he dragged himself to the turn which went towards Adheesh's house. The road was as it was. A bit surprised he walked some more. Again the same familiar landscape. Somewhat encouraged he walked some more till the time he was standing in front of Vidyadhar ji's house. He was thunderstruck. This house and its surroundings were exactly as they were earlier. Devnath was confused now. Did the demons not attack this place? No, that was not possible. They had destroyed everything and everyone dear to them. How could the demons leave this place! Even though he dreaded the next step he decided to go inside. He knew he would find dead bodies inside, but this was a chore which he had to do even if it was an abhorrent one. He slowly dragged himself inside and was astounded. He stood there holding his breath. Anytime the scene was going to change. But nothing changed. There was a mild hustle-bustle all around. People were going about their work normally and nobody paid any attention to him. He was an employee of this household with slightly extra privileges. That was all.

'Oh Devnath!' he whirled around. It was Vidyadhar ji, Adheesh's father. He went and touched his feet.

'Okay, now that you are here, Adheesh must have also come back, isn't it?' Vidyadhar ji asked him jovially.

In his shock and stupefaction, Devnath could not say anything. He just stood rooted to the spot not quite able to articulate the words. Vidyadhar ji was a bit puzzled now. He looked closely at Devnath and gave a gasp as if he understood that all was not well with Adheesh and Aishani. Quietly he gestured Devnath to an adjacent room and closed the door. Devnath stood there silently. Even here he would answer only in monosyllables. Vidyadhar ji knew better than to prod him for answers. He cleared his throat and asked the most dreaded question in his vocabulary, 'Is Adheesh alive?'

Devnath gave Vidyadhar ji a fleeting amazed look as if it was preposterous to think that anything would happen when he was with him. He nodded. Vidyadhar ji let out his breath slowly, 'And Aishani?'

Devnath nodded again.

Vidyadhar ji somehow held his relief. He knew there were

other very serious and devastating things involved, but later. One thing at a time, the most important would be tackled the first.

'They are hurt, are they in a position to be brought here?'

Devnath nodded in the affirmative.

'Great,' Vidyadhar ji was all business now. 'How do we bring them here? I cannot send the ambulance there for obvious reasons. Nor can we take anyone there. I will take the car. Only you and I will go there. Once they come here things will automatically turn for the better. Or will they?' he looked at Devnath searchingly. But Devnath was not up to such sophisticated questioning. He merely nodded again.

Vidyadhar ji called his younger brother Kedar on the telephone and gave him a few instructions. Kedar understood and immediately swung into action. Next Vidyadhar ji went to his wife Anuja who was giving instructions to one of the gardeners. Anuja straightened up when her husband said something to her. She put her hand on the chair in front of her to support herself. A bystander looking at her would see a woman looking at her beautiful garden in quiet contemplation.

Within an hour Adheesh and Aishani were in Vidyadhar ji's hospital. Kedar was fully in control. Adheesh was brought from a back door. The less people knew about it the better it was. A team of doctors began working on Adheesh. When things settled down a bit, Kedar went and sat beside his Bhabhi Aishani. She was distraught with worry. Adheesh had lost so much of blood that he was still almost in a comatose stage. Blood was being transferred in his body and his wounds were being attended to. Kedar looked at her, 'I know I should not be asking too many questions, but just out of curiosity what kind of demon would cut or bite him in such strategic places. A demon like a wild animal would just attack and tear out the flesh of its victim from any random place in the body. But these wounds have been inflicted very thoughtfully. Do demons give themselves that much of time?'

Aishani gave a shuddering sob and seemed undecided for a moment. But it was Kedar, Adheesh's uncle and now his doctor also. He had a right to know, if not everything then at least some part of it, 'A demon did not attack him, Chacha. He inflicted those wounds on himself.'

Kedar was thunderstruck for a moment. Questions clamored in his mind and he opened his mouth to ask some of them. One look at Aishani's woebegone face and he kept quiet. He, as well as his younger brother, had a very fair idea about the destiny that Adheesh and Aishani shared. It was better not to ask too many questions. At least now he knew that these wounds were not made by an animal or a demon, but by Adheesh himself, thereby reducing the chances of infection. Still, he was not going to take any chances. After he came out of the ICU, his younger brother Kalpesh who was an Ayurvedic doctor would take over and his allopathic medicines would also continue. At present Adheesh was sleeping most of the time. It was the effect of the sedatives that had been administered to him.

For one week Aishani and Devnath did not leave Adheesh alone with anybody. Aishani would be beside him sitting on a sofa while Devnath would either sit or pace restlessly in front of his room. Adheesh had recovered quite well by now. He cajoled and forced Aishani to go home and take some rest.

After much cajoling she reluctantly went, not before giving specific instructions to Devnath who understood exactly what she wanted. If Adheesh was not so much in love with Aishani he would have rolled his eyes in exasperation.

After Aishani had left, Adheesh called Devnath inside his room.

'Come Devnath come and sit here,' he pointed to a chair near his bed. But Devnath never sat in front of Adheesh.

'Now tell me everything, Devnath. Where and how are Aishani's people? Are they as comfortable as people are here? It seems that the demons struck only the Gurukuls.'

'No Bhaiya, they are or were not well,' he stopped and tried to put his words together. Devnath was a doer, not a talker. Even a simple conversation made him uncomfortable.

Adheesh was expecting to hear something like this. When he saw his own people in a normal condition, he began hoping that no harm would have come to Aishani's family also. Now it seemed that was too much to ask for. A smile flickered on his face when Devnath told him about his bone dance. He had seen Devnath doing it earlier and he looked utterly ridiculous shouting and chanting and twirling this way and that with the bones doing their clickety-clack dance like two knitting needles.

'Then?' he became serious again.

'I secured the house with my spells. No demon would be able to stay there now. Bhaiya, the house was talking to me. How is that possible? How can a house talk?'

Adheesh laughed again at Devnath's naivety. He had spent his life amongst ghouls and demons but could not get over the idea of a talking house. Gently, he channelised Devnath's thoughts again towards Aishani and Ruby's families and their plight. After Devnath told him everything, he asked Adheesh, 'Bhaiya it's very nice that this house and your family were not attacked by the demons, but why not, considering you and Bhabhi are their biggest enemies?'

'I have been thinking about it, Devnath. I think it is because my people are normal average human beings. Aishani and I were not there. They would have come here after destroying the Gurukul but we were not around. Their primary directive was to destroy the Gurukul, us and Guruji, which they did successfully. They missed us by a whisker in the Gurukul and when they did not find us here, they must have gone to Aishani's place. Thinking we were there, they destroyed that house. Uday and Jayant must have given them a run for their money, but they still had to flee,' Adheesh ended lamely, 'Or that is what I think.'

Devnath nodded, not totally convinced, and they left it at that.

UDAY IN LOVE

Uday was in a dilemma. He couldn't get the girl off his mind. Her name was Prisha. The name meant 'a talent given by God' or God's gift. He had met her while strolling on the banks of the river Gangotri early one morning. The air was cold and pristine. There were huge boulders on the banks of the river and inside the river too where the water was shallow. It was so bitingly cold that there were no people around. Ice crystals had formed in the water, on the boulders and on the mountains around.

It was so quiet and beautiful that Uday, who never much paid attention to Nature's beauty, was mesmerised. He sat on a rock and drank in the tranquility around him. In another hour or so, locals and tourists would start coming out of their homes and hotels and there would be noise everywhere.

The spell would be broken by these human sounds. Before that happened, Uday would try to soak as much of the breathtaking beauty as possible. At this point, the holy river Ganga had a strength of its own. It flowed with confidence, its billions of drops joining and moving together. The reflection of the tall trees and the taller mountains in its waters was so perfect that it looked like pure stained glass.

Uday's contemplations were like meditations. From the vantage place where he sat and surveyed the panorama in front of him, he could see beautiful birds flitting and twittering on the river front. The melodious chorus greeted him every day, always with new notes. Songs tumbled from the trees akin to the jeweled water cascading down. It was almost like two rivers calming the eyes and the ears.

It was on one of his sojourns that he saw her. At first, he thought she was a nymph dancing on the waters of the river, but as she came nearer, he realised that she was a girl, a slim and extraordinarily beautiful girl. He stood still, his nerves on edge. There was danger looming around. An extraordinary urge to protect her entered his heart and mind. He looked around sharply but couldn't see any dangers from which to protect her. Uday was seasoned enough to know that evil lurked everywhere, whether one perceived it or not. The girl was unaware of her surroundings and just kept jumping from one rock to another over the river. Her movements flowed with such dazzling grace that they took his breath away. She did not notice Uday at all, probably because he was so still that he seemed to become part of the flora and fauna. Suddenly, she disappeared. Uday was surprised. He looked all around but she was nowhere to be seen. People had also begun coming out, though the sun was still reddish. She must be very shy, he reasoned, probably that is why she left so suddenly.

Next morning, in the wee hours of dawn, Uday was back in his usual place. He walked a bit but his heart was not in it. He fretted and waited for her. Very soon, the crowd would begin coming in. He knew she would not be there then. He had no option but to wait. Suddenly the hair on his arms stood on end as if there was great danger in the vicinity. Uday ignored it. He was ecstatic. She had come dancing and pirouetting on the flowing waters. She was like a fairy. The petite girl danced around the trees and the boulders and stones of the river, weaving ribbons which brought multihued colours to the rather whitewashed, pristine area. Uday stood very still and then slowly sat down so as not to disturb her. She danced only for a short while and Uday sat and just watched her, she was so beautiful tip-toeing from this wave to that and from one rock to another. He had never seen or imagined such a beautiful, ethereal dance by any human being. And here she was, enthralling him with her graceful, lithe movements.

This scenario repeated itself over a week and then one day, Uday moved a bit and she saw him. She stood bolt upright on a small rock, not knowing what to do. Slowly, she turned to look at him as if she had been caught stealing, then drawing herself together she jumped blithely on the rocks and disappeared before Uday could make another move. Terribly disappointed, Uday went back and feverishly began waiting for the next morning.

She did come the next day but did not dance; she walked

softly on the small boulders and waves while surreptitiously looking at Uday from the corner of her eyes. She smiled tremulously when their eyes met and then immediately looked away. On the third day, she approached him, and they spoke. Uday did not know what they talked about, nor could he recollect later on. But the outcome was that they immediately became friends. And lovers. They would spend whole days and sometimes nights also in the throes of their new-found love. Once when they were sitting below the trees bundled in each other's arms, they heard the sounds of scratching, as if a beast was rubbing or scratching against a tree. Uday tried to ignore the sound but it persisted. Prisha moved as if to leave, she seemed to be scared of everything, raising Uday's protective instincts to the fore. She was almost shaking with fear.

'I have to go now, I can't stay here anymore,' she whispered, disturbed by the sounds.

'No, wait,' Uday said desperately, 'You cannot go now, there is still some time left. Just wait here for five minutes, I'll get rid of whoever is making this hideous sound. You'll wait here, won't you?' he almost begged her. His eyes had already started changing colour from brown to jet black.

'Okay,' she demurred reluctantly. Uday kissed her again and then left. Soon there were some screeching and angry blood-curling screams, enough to freeze a normal human's blood in fear. However, nothing happened to the girl—rather, there was a small smile on her face which she hid very carefully lest Uday came back earlier than expected. Soon Uday was back. He took some leaves from the nearby trees and wiped himself. There were blood splatters on his face and body. The leaves were full of moisture so he did not need water to wipe off the blood.

'Uday,' Prisha almost screamed, if that was possible for her, 'There is blood on you, did the animal catch you? Are you hurt? What was it?' she almost sobbed.

'Nothing, my darling, it was just a bear,' he tried taking her in his arms again, but she pushed him back. 'A bear?' she squeaked, 'You fought a bear? Has it hurt you or did you chase it away?' her voice seemed a bit disappointed, but Uday brushed it off as anxiety. For him, disposing of a mountain bear was a routine thing. Nothing came in his way; he was the mighty, invincible Uday who could slay any beast or demon with just a flick of his powerful hand. Nobody could be allowed to disturb him when he was with the only woman he had ever loved in his life. His romance with Prisha was the purest form of love.

'Now, where were we?' he began nuzzling up to her again, but she softly pushed him away. 'It's morning now Uday, I have to leave.'

'Stay for some more time,' he entreated but she seemed to be in a hurry to leave, almost as if wanting to go urgently. Uday didn't want to force himself on her. Reluctantly, he agreed and she left hastily. Uday also left for his temporary home. As soon as he turned on the gravel road and could not be seen anymore, Prisha came out from her hiding place and ran towards where Uday had killed the mountain bear. It was a clean blow, Uday was an expert warrior and there was very little blood. Prisha was ecstatic; she sat down and made a clear, sweet sound of a bird. She then sat down beside the bear, tore his stomach without any effort and started eating it. Soon there were other birds swooping down on the ground beside her. On touching the ground, they morphed into slim creatures just like her, sat on the corpse of the bear beside her and began enjoying the raw fresh bear meat.

Uday's people were used to his disappearances and his dark brooding nature, hence nobody found it amiss when he did not speak to anybody or was out for nights in a row and sometimes days also. But Ruby noticed. Whenever Uday sat in the small cottage with them, his broodings did not seem to be as dark as they were earlier, in fact on one occasion she saw him smiling too. Ruby was startled. Uday smiling was indeed a matter to be looked into. There were only two things which would give him pleasure: one was falling in love and the other was killing demons and animals. Demons were out of the question, as this was Gangotri where no demon would dare intrude. He would also not kill animals without any provocation. In any case, practically every animal and bird here was on the endangered species list and Uday would not kill any of them. So, what was it? Ruby wondered. Uday falling in love was preposterous! Besides there was no girl here, apart from a few tourists who came and went away in a day or two.

Now Ruby was on full alert. Uday being almost cheerful was not normal; therefore, it had to be scrutinised. She thought of following him but that would just not do. With no alternative available, she had to bank upon Tejas, who was faster and quieter than anybody when the need arose. Moreover, if Uday caught Tejas snooping on him, he would just give him a big smack on his head and that would be that.

'I know where Uday Bhaiya goes,' Tejas said loftily.

'Where?' Ruby was very curious. Despite Uday being happy, Ruby had a premonition that there was trouble afoot. Not that things were always right in their lives, but this seemed a bit different. Earlier, in any situation they would all be together working towards a single cause, but this time Uday was acting in a most secretive manner and was happy about it too.

'He goes to the upper part of Gangotri, sits and looks around for hours.'

'And does what? Did you ever see him talking to somebody?' Tejas nodded adversely and then rolled his eyes.

'Tejas, now listen to me carefully, it's very important that we know what Uday does there.'

'Why, do you think he's made friends with demons?'

'How is that possible, Teju. But a demon might ensnare him! This is what you will do,' Ruby made him memorise a few points for the next morning.

Tejas was too frisky a boy to sit still in one place for a long time. But now he was also agog with curiosity. The place was cramping his style as there was nothing to do here. Tejas was used to an exciting life, which was generally running here and there, showing off by stretching his body, being a pest and maybe killing a small demon or two. After so many days of boredom, Ruby had given him work which involved some excitement and of course mystery and risk too—the risk that if Uday caught him then he would get the smacking of his life and mystery because nobody till now knew what Uday did or where he went.

Ruby woke him up very early the next morning. In fact, it was still night but Tejas was up with just a slight nudge from Ruby. They gave Uday a head start and then Tejas followed. Ruby had given him two bars of chocolates as one never knew how long Uday would be on his sojourns. Tejas did not follow Uday on foot. That way, he was sure to get caught. Uday's senses were always more than alert. Tejas followed him from the top of the branches of the tall trees that dotted the landscape of the region. If one tree was far from the other, he just stretched his body into a thick rope and then caught the higher branches of the other tree. Tejas had become an expert in elongating and contracting his body. He always carried a bottle of water because water helped his body in recovering and reverting to his original size. Apart from the fact that Tejas could spy easily on Uday from the treetops, he had a vantage 360-degree view of the area.

Today was different. There was somebody already waiting for Uday, sitting restively on a boulder on the riverbank. Uday was rushing up to her. Tejas perched on the last tree and peered through its foliage. What he saw fascinated and disgusted him. The person waiting for him was obviously a girl. They embraced and kissed each other passionately and stayed in that position for such a long time that Tejas started getting cramps. But he was very interested too. He had never thought that his grim, humourless elder brother could be so romantic.

Suddenly, they went behind a grove of trees and Tejas could not see them anymore. If he climbed down, he would be exposed, and he did not want to take that chance with Uday. This was so boring and uncomfortable. Tejas sat in that uncomfortable position for almost one and a half hours, constantly on the lookout. Tejas did not have much of an eye for this kind of beauty, but he did have a photographic memory. He was so bored that nothing was happening around him. All he saw was a river flowing, some animals grazing and peculiar species of birds flying or strutting around. At last, Uday came out of the grove of trees. The girl was not with him. Uday's eyes had turned the usual black when he was on a killing mission. Tejas was alarmed. Had Uday Bhaiya discovered him spying on him? No, it was something else. Uday did not even look in his direction. He went straight towards a bear which was scratching itself against a tree trunk. The huge bear didn't have a chance against Uday. With one strong stroke of his Pash, the bear's life was snuffed out and it lay dead. Calmly, Uday cleaned his Pash and went back towards the grove of trees. Tejas' heartbeats slowly started returning to normal. He shifted his position and continued spying. Soon Uday came out with the girl, they kissed again, then both went on their ways, Uday towards his temporary home and the girl to wherever she had to go. Tejas stayed aloft the tree for some more time to give himself some leeway before he went after Uday. Tejas did not know that it was the second bear that Uday had killed in that region.

It was then that he noticed the strangest thing. The girl hid behind a tree waiting for Uday to turn around a corner then ran straight towards the carcass of the bear. She sat down beside the bear and let out a cry, the sweet but deep penetrating cry of a Himalayan bird. It was such a natural cry that nobody would have paid any attention to it. But very soon some more people like the girl joined her. Clearly, they were all excited. Without wasting a moment, they dug into the bear, tore into its skin and hair like it was parchment and began eating the flesh and chewing the bones. Tejas forgot about Uday. He sat stock still and stared at the gory scene in front of him. These beautiful people were eating the bear! How was this possible? There were no demons in Gangotri. Tejas waited for some time, then swiftly went back the way he had come.

On reaching home, he went straight to Ruby who was sitting with Madhhu ji. Tejas sat there quietly waiting for Madhu to leave, clearly agitated. Both the women noticed this. Finally, Ruby said, 'Tejas, Madhhu ji knows everything, you can tell both of us about what you have seen.'

Tejas hesitated only for a minute as he totally trusted Madhhu ji. His words tumbling out, he quickly narrated what he had seen, adding some smart aleck comments of his own. The women heard him with rapt attention. Like him, they knew that Gangotri was one of the safest places on Earth. Ruby was thinking hard: Uday meets a beautiful girl, they fall in love, Uday kills a bear that is disturbing them, then the girl and her ilk eat up the bear behind Uday's back. Why did they not kill the animal themselves? Why ensnare Uday and then make him kill the animal? That they were demons, there was no doubt, but what kind of demons? The actual part of killing was not executed by them, they made somebody else do it in a very adroit manner.

Ruby had no choice but to take the matter in her own hands. For two days, she stalked the girl but did not get a chance to get hold of her because of Uday. Frustrated, she shared her dilemma with Madhu. It was possible for Madhu to make Uday do almost anything as he always felt responsible for her when Aishani and Adheesh were not around.

'Uday beta, can you take me to the mandir tomorrow, I cannot go there on my own. These knees of mine don't allow me to walk on these rocky uneven roads.'

Uday naturally did not want to go; he would miss his date with Prisha.

'Sure Aunty, whenever you say,' he replied.

'Thanks beta, we'll go early in the morning as the crowd will be less. Later, we may have to stand in a long line.'

When they left the next morning, Ruby immediately headed in the opposite direction. She knew where she had to go. Tejas had given her a full briefing. She reached the place soon enough, but she was now treading softly for she did not know what kind of demon this was, whether it was a shape shifter or a genuinely small female demon. She waited behind a clump of shrubs. So engrossed was Ruby in her quest, she could not pay attention to all the beauty surrounding her. She camouflaged herself in the colours of the hills and water and stones and sat very still. It would have been very difficult to segregate her from her surroundings. Soon the girl came in sight and Ruby held her breath. She could understand now why Uday was so smitten. She was ethereal, dancing so lightly from one rock to another. She was wearing small anklets with rings attached to them. The sound of her anklets combined with the tinkling of the flowing water were making heady music. The moonlight still shone on some of the rocks, white and silver crisscrossing the other. It looked as if a fairy was dancing with abandonment and thoroughly enjoying herself.

Even Ruby, an apsara, wanted to keep looking at her.

She shook herself out of her trance. She had not come here for this. This was a female demon out to entice her simple brother. Yes, she knew that Uday could be very cruel when he wanted to be or when the occasion required him to be so, but at heart he was a simple, gullible person. Anybody could take advantage of Uday provided they crossed his armour first. Though Ruby was an apsara, she was enough of a warrior to handle smaller demons. Whether she would be able to handle this demon was yet to be seen. She always had a sharp curved knife hidden in the folds of her clothing. By now the she-demon had started coming coquettishly towards the edge of the river, probably to meet Uday. With one big swing she held the girl from behind her throat and placed her curved knife on her neck. The girl screamed, rather tittered in fear and then froze with terror.

'Who are you and why have you made friends with Uday?' Ruby spoke in a gruff voice though it did not come out as threatening as she wanted, but the girl was suitably scared. For some time, she could not speak out of fear. When she got her breath back, she realised that Ruby may spare her life, she wheezed and said shakily, 'Please, free me, I'll tell you everything.'

There was something in her voice that made Ruby trust her. Slowly she lowered her hand, carefully keeping her knife ready. The girl held her neck with her hand and began coughing.

Slowly she began, 'We are the descendants of the noble Jarita, a great revered bird in ancient times. We have been scholars and teachers from that time onwards. Our father was the great saint Mandapala who because he did not have any progeny, took the form of a huge bird and married our mother. They had many children together. But he later abandoned her. Jarita hid in the Khandva forests and reared her children. A couple of her children turned rogue and married Rakshasis. Together they killed and ate any living thing that came in their way when they were hungry. But they were essentially good people. They soon tired of their shenanigans and wanted to lead a peaceful life. They went into prolonged penance and ultimately wrangled forgiveness for themselves. But the taste of blood remained with them. They again asked for a boon to stay away from their craving for blood by staying in a pure place where no blood would be split, nor could they kill anybody to whet their appetites. We were allowed to stay near Gangotri so that our progeny could become pure again. With its pristine purity, Gangotri was sure to cleanse us of all our sins. But as is the case with so many boons, there is almost always a rider attached to it. We have been unable to get over our craving for blood and raw flesh. We do not kill anyone or anything but sometimes we instigate somebody else to do the killing for us so that we can fulfill our avarice for fresh blood and flesh. The rider here is that to become pure again, we have to be killed in such a way that every drop of our blood flows out. An adjunct to this is that we have to be killed by a warrior who had been in Bhagwan Ram's army.'

'Hence Uday,' Ruby mused.

'Yes,' Prisha said miserably. 'But I really love him, it's just that when I touch him, I am reminded of flesh and blood and I cannot stop myself. I know this also that I will attain Nirvana when somebody kills me in the same way. I will then be released from this awful curse.' She put her hands together and implored, 'Please help me and please help us in attaining moksha.'

Ruby was slowly getting convinced by the girl's story. She did vaguely remember something about a great bird Jarita from one of the history classes in the Gurukul.

'Let me see if I can convince people to help you attain moksha. You're aware it requires quite a lot of will power?'

The girl acquiesced and kept her head down. Ruby sighed, 'Be here tomorrow early morning along with your people. We'll see if helping you is possible.'

Ruby went home. Madhu was impatiently waiting for her. Ruby sat down beside her and told her everything. She looked anxiously at Madhu. 'Uday will be heartbroken, who will tell him?'

Madhu too looked worried. Ruby had not involved her parents as Madhu was acting as the surrogate but practical parent. Somebody had to tell Uday. Whether he agrees to kill them or not depended on his feelings for Prisha. Madhu made up her mind.

Uday returned in the evening with a smile on his face. He acknowledged Madhu and she nodded back. Ruby had already made sure that nobody was around and that they had complete privacy. Madhu came to the point straightway. There was no beating around the bush. Uday listened attentively with his head down. Not once did he raise his head or eyes and look at her disbelievingly.

'Beta, to help another living being attain moksha is one of the greatest services to mankind. God tests us in many ways, some of His ways are so cruel and heartbreaking that it seems impossible to perform them. You are a warrior of Bhagwan Ram's army. You know all about mental, emotional and physical games. You know that your destiny is straightforward. Kill the demons. If in that process some demons attain moksha, that's all for the better.'

Uday kept sitting in that position long after Madhu had completed her story. She sat with him sharing his agony and silence. Finally Uday got up, picked up his Pash and made to go out. He bent down to touch her feet. Their eyes met when he straightened up. They had turned absolutely black. Madhu knew what was going to happen. She was sad yet proud; this was the stuff legends were made of. He was going to sacrifice his love.

Uday returned the next morning with no change in his behaviour. He was his usual taciturn self, the difference was that now there was no smile on his face and if one knew him, one would have noticed him washing his Pash over and over again. Everyone knew that what was done was the right thing, then why did they feel contrite as if they had committed a crime? Uday informed them that he was going out for a couple of days. They understood and agreed immediately, though they were still wary of him carrying his Pash.

Uday walked aimlessly around Gangotri. His mind was a blank. The saddest part was that he believed it when she said that she loved him. She had begged him to kill her in such a way that all her blood would flow out. She had entreated him to kill her colleagues too in the same manner. His hair rose whenever the scene came in front of his eyes. This is when Uday met Devnath, who had come in search of them. In his despair, he had not noticed Devnath trying to fit the small keys in different places. When he espied Devnath conducting this strange act, he thought it was another demon.

The next day, they left for Rishikesh by bus. From there they took another bus to Haridwar and finally a taxi home. Madhu's heart was beating fast. She put her head on Jayant's shoulders. Jayant put his right arm around her and pressed her shoulders softly. He knew exactly what his mother had lost and what she was thinking.

The house knew that they had returned. If it had been a dog, it would have rushed up to them and pranced all around. But it was tied to the earth; it could just bang its walls and make piteous sounds. Madhu rushed to it and embraced the verandah wall—whatever was left of it. The house continued its piteous wailing for some time, with Madhu crying along with it. Ruby and her parents waited quietly. They knew what she was undergoing. The boys went around the house assessing the damage.

After a few minutes, Devnath requested Madhu's permission to leave. He touched her feet and left.

'Bhabhi,' Badrinath said softly, 'Please stay with us for a day or two. We shall begin the repairs from tomorrow early morning.'

'Bhaiya, I cannot leave my home now that we have come back to it,' Madhu was crying silently. Ruby's mother Ajita embraced Madhu, 'We understand Bhabhi, this is only for a day or two. The moment there is some semblance of repair, we ourselves will bring you here,' she reassured Madhu.

They were not sure if their own home was in a habitable condition or whether the demons had attacked it. Reluctantly,

Madhu agreed. Thankfully, Ruby's house had not been attacked by the demons.

There was a frenzy of activity in Madhu's house from the next day. Guruji sent two engineers from the Gurukul, who were of great help. Madhu didn't really want their misfortune to become the talk of the town. There would have been too many uncomfortable questions. The engineers from the Gurukul had a magic touch. The house was as good as new in a week's time.

DEMON VALUES

In just a couple of months, Einar had become an integral part of the Gurukul. He single-handedly did the work of more than ten people in rebuilding and revitalising the Gurukul, being in more than two places at the same time. The few people left in the Gurukul were working round the clock to bring it back to its former glory. They had to adjust to the idea of such a different though very handsome man mingling so freely with them and treating the Gurukul as his own. He even spoke their language Hindi fluently, with a few chaste Sanskrit words thrown in casually. This is what happens when you learn a new language late in life and there are not many people around to converse with.

Guruji knew who Einar was, where he was and how he would come to them. Apart from Einar being a warrior,

Guruji also knew about some of his personal traits or extra powers. One of these traits was recognising any demon in any form, no matter how well camouflaged it was, be it a human being, an animal or even an inanimate object. This was a huge plus point for the Gurukul and its inhabitants, even though they had no clue about it.

Only a few senior students were allowed in the Gurukul during its renovation for obvious reasons. Though Tejas was not a senior, he somehow scraped through, probably because he would have been more of a pest outside than inside. Adheesh and Aishani had become Einar's good friends. They had started liking each other from Kailash itself and now their friendship had been blossoming daily. Uday was still a bit wary of Einar, but that was Uday's essential personality. He never trusted anyone apart from one or two truly close friends. There was not much interaction between Einar and Ruby. Einar was strong and handsome; Ruby was smart and exceptionally beautiful. Both were young and would have made a very handsome couple. Ruby seemed to be engrossed in some private problem of her own. Aishani noticed it and meant to ask her at some opportune moment but somehow nowadays she never got a chance to be alone with Ruby. The reconstituting of the Gurukul was going on at an amazingly fast pace, with everybody doing their bit to the best of their capabilities. It did not require Einar to make any special effort with Tejas, who with his sunny personality became friends with everybody immediately.

There was a community centre in the city which everyone liked to visit. It had shops, two cinema halls and a theatre where plays were staged at regular intervals. There was a children's playground also. All in all, a good place for people to spend their leisure hours. And a fertile place for the demons, who constantly strived to be here. Where would they get such a wide variety of humans to hunt and tease, to kill and eat?

The Gurukul inmates also went there as it catered to almost all kinds of aptitudes. On top of that, it was supposed to be a safe venue also. Even if there were demons here, they had mingled so well with the humans that they had imbibed qualities like compassion, kindness, caring and sharing. All this made them virtually harmless. It was here that they would meet their neighbours and other citizens and exchange pleasantries with them. Earlier, their parents used to partake in these societal niceties but now the youngsters followed suit. It kept them grounded, so to say.

Like everybody else, Adheesh and his group also went to the community centre whenever they could find the time. This time Einar was also with them. They were laughing over something when suddenly Einar stiffened. Only Adheesh noticed it. A special bond had developed between Adheesh and Einar ever since their Kailash days. He noticed Einar's discomfiture and immediately grasped it had somehow to do with the presence of a demon. But how could a demon be here, this was a clean place and was periodically scanned by their supervisors for demons. Hence as soon as he got a chance, he spoke to Einar.

'Quit worrying Einar, there are no demons here. This is one of the very few places where we can come and go as we please because it's clean.'

'Adheesh, I can see demons in any form, whatever their camouflage. Pardon me, but you have become just a bit detached hence, are unable to see the obvious.'

Had it been any other person, Adheesh would have felt slighted, but this was Einar, who had in such a short period become such a great friend of his. Maybe there was some kismet connection, he didn't know. To begin with, Einar never talked for the sake of talking and his observations were never made lightly. Maybe he had slipped slightly, Adheesh thought guiltily. Well, he was going to pull up his socks in a jiffy.

Einar continued, 'That distinguished-looking old man and his wife have been demons from centuries.'

Adheesh slowly turned around. No, that was not possible! That was Mehta Uncle and his wife Mrinalini Aunty. Uncle had retired from the civil services a long time back and Aunty was a very efficient, sophisticated housewife. They were the stalwarts of their society, always leading from the front and taking part in all the happenings of their town, either good or bad. They had been in this sleepy town for ages. Their grown-up children and grandchildren would visit them from time to time. Those times were really the high points for the Mehtas. There would be family outings and picnics and parties in which almost half of the townspeople were invited.

For a moment, Adheesh was shaken with doubt. It was not possible. Maybe Einar had received mixed signals or misinterpreted them. But Einar never made mistakes, he thought morosely. He looked so sad that despite the gravity of the situation, Einar smiled momentarily. But he sobered up immediately.

'It's not the senior Mehtas who are the threats, it's their grandchildren. Probably that is why you all did not suspect them.'

'You're right, Einar. I did notice that one of their grandsons avoided looking at me. I thought it was just one of those random things and did not pay much attention to it. We'll have to look into it immediately.'

They stayed in the community centre for some more time. Adheesh could not enjoy the sports and the gaiety any more. They watched Aishani, Ruby and Tejas taking part in many of the inane frivolities being offered and thoroughly enjoying themselves, while Uday sat alone brooding in a corner. After some time, they all went back, the rest to the Gurukul and Adheesh and Aishani to Adheesh's home. Midway, Adheesh turned to Aishani, 'Ash, Guruji had told me to meet him. I will not go inside; I may get stuck there. You go; I'll come back in an hour or so.'

'What's the matter, Adheesh? You weren't your usual self in the community centre also. Why, did you notice anybody or anything?' Aishani took his hands in hers and looked at him anxiously.

He sighed. He had never hidden anything from Aishani, nor was he going to now. But he wasn't going to commit anything on presumption.

'No doll, not really, but I have to discuss this with Guruji before I tell you anything,' he stroked her hair. 'Don't worry, it may be nothing serious.'

'Okay,' Aishani said dubiously, 'Take care and come soon.'

'I will,' he smiled and left for the Gurukul.

Aishani stared after him for a long time.

'Bhabhi, come it's getting late, Bhaiya is going to be alright,' it was Devnath speaking softly. After Kailash, Adheesh had designated Devnath to be with Aishani most of the time. In the beginning, Devnath did not like the idea much but being with Aishani and working with her gave him a glimpse of her massive powers and the conclusion that she had to be protected at all costs.

Guruji was meditating when Adheesh reached his cottage. He knew when Guruji would get up from his evening meditation, so he just waited. He pottered softly around Guruji's cottage much like Manohar used to do. He shifted his thoughts from Manohar. That area was still too raw to delve into. So many close friends and colleagues had been lost in their last altercation with the demons; they still had to come to terms with that. Manohar was an old and valued member of the Gurukul. Nobody knew what happened to him or where he was, but they surmised that he had been killed by the micro demons. Somebody had been looking after the flora and fauna outside Guruji's cottage, that much was evident from the cleanliness and the well laid out beds with healthy plants springing up from the soil. But Manohar's aesthetic touch was missing. Maybe Guruji did it himself with a flash of his hands; he smiled to himself, provided Guruji thought of it.

Finally, Guruji came out of his cottage after half an hour. He looked at Adheesh without surprise. Adheesh also knew that Guruji knew why he was there. Guruji beckoned him inside the cottage. He went inside and sat on the cotton mat on the floor. Guruji waited for Adheesh to speak.

'Einar has stated that Mehta Uncle and his family are demons, though of a mild variety. Years of mingling with the humans has almost turned them into humans, though the demon strain can never be removed. Mehtas have been the stalwarts of the society participating in all the activities of the town. What do we do, Guruji?' he asked gloomily.

'Nothing Adheesh, we do nothing, at least not here,' Adheesh looked up sharply. So Guruji did have a plan to dispose of these demons. They were demons, so they could not be harmless, he reasoned to himself. He was friendly with Mehta's two grandsons Atul and Karan who were approximately his age. He had gone for a hiking trip with them and enjoyed it too. He shook his head. Atul and Karan were demons? Adheesh looked at Guruji appealingly, who looked backed at him impassively.

'Mrinalini Mehta wants her grandsons to know who they are. She wants them to exist as human beings but be aware of their roots too. Rakshasas have been great scholars and they have great strength and valour. It is these traits that Mrs. Mehta wants them to be aware of. What she forgets or doesn't want to remember is that along with these good qualities are the most prominent traits of demons that is lust: lust for all that is bad and harmful. If you invoke the good qualities, then you arouse all the bad qualities too. The Mehtas have already begun the initiation of these two boys. In the beginning, there was bewilderment and confusion, but now the boys have rather begun enjoying the powers that they will attain after a few more sessions. That will be the time we move in and nip the bud,' Guruji said simply.

Adheesh nodded, a bit sad. A plan was already being formulated in his mind when Guruji interrupted his thoughts. 'Another thing, Adheesh…'

'Yes, Guruji?'

'You will plan the whole operation, but the actual execution will be carried out by Einar.'

'Yes, Guruji,' Adheesh agreed readily though he was a bit puzzled. Personally, he was always happy to work with Einar at his side, but this decision was a bit mystifying.

'Apart from the fact that Einar is a sort of a guest in our Gurukul, he is also our student and your friend. He has been tested and he has crossed every test with flying colours. People like Einar cannot sit still, they have to be on the go all the time, that is their relaxation. That is how he came to the Himalayas and learnt so many things. We owe a lot to him. What he has done for us and what he will do for us will be unprecedented in the history of mankind. He will keep on giving even from beyond the grave. We can give back only by offering him things which he likes to do. The most dangerous and viperous rakshasas can be executed only by Aishani or by you and Aishani together. Einar does not have much time. He must destroy as many demons as possible in this short time. That is his destiny, and we have to fulfill it.'

'Yes, of course, Guruji,' Adheesh readily agreed, though by now he was even more perplexed, 'Guruji I didn't understand. Does Einar have less time with us, or does he have less time here on Earth?'

'Everything is in God's hand, Adheesh. Either way, he will be leaving us,' Guruji was obscure and enigmatic. Adheesh knew that he would not get anymore revelations from Guruji, but alarm bells had begun ringing in his mind and heart.

'Adheesh,' Guruji seemed to be mulling over a point.

'Yes, Guruji?' he turned back.

'Sometimes the human strain becomes so prominent in these hybrid demons that their DNA itself changes. In such a case we do not destroy those demons, rather we take them under our wing and send them for higher meditation. There is a separate unit for them where they attend special classes so they can mingle unobtrusively with humans.'

Adheesh was startled. At the back of his mind was always the thought that demons never change, no matter what. They may camouflage themselves, but never change. And here Guruji was talking about harbouring them!

Guruji smiled at Adheesh's startled expression, 'He is beyond kind,' Guruji looked up at the sky. 'He makes us, gives us free will and then again gives us a chance to follow the right path and truth.'

Adheesh nodded, touched Guruji's feet and left for home.

Next day, Adheesh and Einar got together to chalk out their strategy. They went to the community centre again. It was the holiday season, and outdoor trips were planned by different groups for both young and old. They kept a surreptitious eye on which activities Atul and Karan would join. As expected, both of the Mehtas' grandsons volunteered for trekking in the hills and jungles surrounding their town and village. Adheesh and Einar volunteered for the same. Altogether, there were twelve men and boys for the trekking trip. The senior Mehtas were also going to join the trek, probably to guide them in recognising their true self and find their true destiny, Adheesh mused.

They had to leave early the next morning. Both Adheesh and Einar were expert trekkers and hikers, their occupation had taught them more than enough. Both knew that something would happen on this trip, they would have to keep their senses alert all the time.

The two boys were clearly inexperienced and anxious. On one hand, they did not want to kill, on the other hand, they wanted to experience the kill because they were demons. What a dilemma!

'We will begin from here, go straight for about 700 yards; there will be three trails, two on the right side and one on the left side. Group A will take the second trail on the right side and group B will take the left trail. Group A will follow me, and group B will follow Uday.' This was the guide Subramaniam giving instructions. He was popularly called Subbu. He was an expert mountaineer now living a retired life in this community, volunteering as a guide whenever any such group was made. Adheesh and Einar were in different groups but thankfully both the boys were in Adheesh's group. The senior Mehtas were in Einar's group.

'Just short of the peak, which is our destination, there are two small huts where we will assemble in three hours. The trail is relatively safe but rough and rocky. The higher you go, the denser it becomes with sharp shrubs and trees. Be careful that you don't trip on broken branches and jagged rocks,' Subbu warned them. All the group members nodded solemnly, Boy Scout style. Einar and Adheesh nodded at each other. They had already fixed the points where they would meet if anything untoward happened. They did not have their main weapons with them which were Adheesh's sword and Einar's Gram—that would have attracted too much attention, but they were warriors and never unarmed. Both had smaller weapons which they concealed expertly.

The two groups went their respective ways with much bonhomie, backslapping and chattering. Slowly the trail turned steep and jagged. The chatter had subsided. There was a trace of huffing and puffing in the older lot, but the younger ones were quite excited, and were following Adheesh enthusiastically. Adheesh was keeping a sharp eye on Atul and Karan. No untoward incident took place. At every turn, Adheesh expected some violence, any kind of violence, but nothing happened. Had Einar misconstrued his hunch, he thought, a bit puzzled. No, he could not doubt Einar, it was he himself who had become soft, he brooded.

Soon, they arrived at their rendezvous. The other group arrived after fifteen minutes. Adheesh looked at Einar, who shrugged his shoulders.

By and large, the path was still wide and smooth which meant that it was frequently used by villagers. Some good Samaritans had even put garbage bins along the way. Adheesh smiled, then wiped his neck. It was hot and the sun was still shining brightly. Adheesh knew from experience that the much-needed respite from the heat would come at night as they go up in the tracks. Sure enough, in about half an hour, the sun started setting and the forest began reasserting itself. The paths became narrower and rockier as they snaked around the huge trees. The roots of these trees were gnarled and crisscrossed. The path became uneven and steep with sharp rocks jutting out. As dusk fell, the area had already begun to look spooky. Nostalgically, Adheesh remembered his hikes with his uncles Kedar and Kalpesh.

They kept walking, keeping an eye on the Mehtas and their children. After some time, they reached a clearing. Subbu called out to them. If there was one person who enjoyed himself more than the others it was Subbu. Such opportunities of managing, controlling and guiding came to him only once or twice a year and he wanted to make the most of it.

'We will camp here for the night. Most of you have brought essentials with you. There are provisions in these two huts too. You can go inside and see if you need anything from the huts. We will take some refreshments and then we will make our tents and turn in for the night.'

The refreshments were more like tea and dinner rolled together. After the long hike, everybody was naturally hungry and ate with great gusto. It was then that both Adheesh and Einar noticed an unusual thing. Everybody was eating after the strenuous trek except the Mehtas, the parents as well as the two teenagers, Atul and Karan. There was an air of palpable excitement around the two boys, though the senior Mehtas were behaving nonchalantly. Alarm bells began ringing in both their brains. They sat with their respective groups, ate and behaved jovially while keeping a sharp eye on all the Mehtas. After some time, they noticed the older couple casually strolling towards the jungle. The twins got up to follow them, but Mrinalini gestured to them to stay back which they did, albeit reluctantly. Einar also casually sauntered towards the jungle. Einar just stood, apparently enjoying the beauty of the jungle and the setting of the sun. Amongst his gifts was the gift of sharp hearing. From where he stood, he could make out the Mehtas whispering to each other.

'Not now,' Mehta whispered.

'The kids are very hungry,' Mrinalini whispered back, 'They've had a grueling day and good food is the only thing they want just now.'

'Don't you see,' he muttered angrily, 'If they eat now their stomachs will be satiated and the impetus to reach out for their real food will be that much less. In fact, Atul may not even go for it,' Mehta looked around to see if anybody was listening to them, but nobody was there except for the foreigner Einar, who didn't understand their language and was far away examining fruit on the trees. The Mehtas talked some more and then went back.

Einar lingered for some more time then went back and stood near Adheesh. Einar looked and nodded his head at Adheesh. There were some more revelries in the camp after which Subbu called it a day. They had already pitched their tents. After some more talking and friendly banter, everybody retired for the night. Subbu's tent was a little far from the rest. Those who had some experience with Subbu's sojourns were greatly relieved as his snores were enough to blow away the roofs of their tents. Soon all was quiet, and everybody was sleeping. Or so it seemed. Adheesh and Einar were obviously alert and awake. They had gone into their tents but had come out after ten minutes or so. There was some movement in a few tents, but this too petered out. Subbu's obnoxious snores had settled into a rhythmic pattern like a steam engine chugging atop a mountain slope and then sliding down with various kinds of whistles.

Adheesh and Einar were sitting on opposite sides of the clearing. There was no trace of sleep in their eyes. If anything, their senses were coiled like snaky springs ready to jump at the slightest provocation. Nothing so far. They waited patiently, knowing that something was going to happen tonight—exactly what and where, they did not know. The wind had begun picking up. It wound between the huge surrounding trees whistling and roaring. Soon, even Subbu's snores were no match for the thundering and ear-splitting clamour of the wind. Adheesh and Einar became even more alert. Gradually the wind died down and an ominous silence settled on the camp.

Adheesh circled the entire camp without noticing anything untoward. He signaled to Einar that all was well. But somehow Einar was not convinced. His sixth sense told him just the opposite. They both looked at each other and jumped. The camp was so quiet because Subbu's snoring had stopped. They looked at Subbu's tent. It was eerily quiet. Then Einar pointed to the ground in front of Subbu's cottage. Adheesh looked down and almost choked in shock. There was a trail of blood coming out of the tent, a thin trickle from where they stood, gradually becoming thicker at the door of the cottage.

Silently, they ran towards Subbu's tent, opened the flap, went inside, and froze. Subbu's body had been hacked and split open and some people were gorging on his flesh and gnawing at the bones. However, one person was standing away from them watching them silently. He was tall, thin, and pale like the full moon, dark shadows under his sunken eyes, staring at the horror in front of him, his mouth open in a silent scream.

The group stopped their activities on seeing Adheesh and Einar. They were human beings, but they looked more like gorillas with hair covering their face and bodies. Angry at being disturbed, two of them lunged at Einar and Adheesh. Einar was waiting for them, he had two serrated knives in each hand. He plunged his weapons deep inside the stomach of these gorilla-looking humans and forcefully turned the knives in their stomachs. There was no chance that they would survive this counter-offensive. Adheesh had also taken out his knives but he controlled himself at the last minute. Guruji's words rang in his ears that Einar would make the first move, then if required Adheesh would make his move. Both the human gorillas slumped under Einar's ferocious attack. There was a loud wail from the apparently female gorilla who was also feeding off Subbu's body. The fourth person was still staring and standing in the corner shocked and frightened beyond his wits. Adheesh and Einar stood there for a minute when the transformation of the gorillas began. Sure, enough as expected they metamorphosed in their former selves, the Mehtas. Karan was the boy standing and shaking in the corner.

'Why did you kill them?' shrieked Mrinalini, sobbing hysterically.

'Ma'am, I think you are the one who has to give the explanations,' Adheesh interjected, 'The three of you killed Subbu. He did not harm you in any way. He was acting superbly as a guide and was kind and encouraging to everybody.'

'We had to do this,' wailed Mrinalini, 'The children had to be made aware of who they are and what their legacy is. We come from a long line of erudite demons, very well read, deeply knowledgeable and cerebral. The children must know their values and traditions. So much of mingling with the humans through the ages has made them soft and mushy. We were just showing them where their true legacy lies,' she cried through her hiccups.

'But what you showed them or tried to teach them were not the right values, rather you were teaching them quite the opposite,' Einar calmly retaliated. 'They had to be stopped, they had already done so much harm.'

'This is a part of their destiny. To go up in life, they have to sustain themselves like this, there is no other way,' Mrinalini moaned again.

'I'm sorry, this just cannot be allowed, not in the present age and context,' Adheesh said firmly. He then turned to look at the other twin Karan who was still staring horrified at the scene being enacted in front of him. So, this was what Guruji was talking about. Karan was the demon with more human traits than demons. He was the one who had to be rehabilitated! There had always been good and bad demons. The good became devtas, guiding and healing with a loving hand. The bad demons turned into a force that delighted in destruction and pain, through greed and hate.

He sighed. Now to make up a plausible story and wrap up everything before the others awoke.

THE HALF BREEDS

'When the demons escaped during the time of the Ramayana, all of you know that they escaped in myriad places and come out according to their own fixed times which could be in any century. It could be this century or four centuries earlier or maybe even two centuries later. You have fought these demons through the ages and each of you is very well versed in fighting and annihilating them. But then there are exceptions to any stories and many histories too.'

They were sitting in the shade of the banyan tree behind the main building. The ashram had slowly begun to look like the old Gurukul albeit with a few changes; changes which Aishani thought made it look even better.

The flora and fauna were picking up very well, though the larger trees still had to grow to their full height and breadth.

The Botany department was working round the clock to speed up the growth of these trees. With a little nudge from Guruji, the larger trees had begun looking as if they had been there for ages. Everybody had worked tirelessly to clean up the streams and the tributaries of the river and the waters of these watercourses had slowly started singing now, after the great devastation. Though it was not springtime, every tree and every flower bud seemed new, and so they were. Smaller birds had started making nests in these trees and their trilling and warbling had begun waking up the inhabitants of the Gurukul early in the morning, though the bigger birds had yet to gather the courage to roost here. All in all, happiness and optimism were creeping back into the Gurukul.

Any passerby watching them would see Guruji giving a discourse to some students and teachers too. This time the Gurukul had been reconstructed in such a way that whenever two or more people sat together to discuss something or just talk, an invisible protective aura would surround them, and no outsider would be able to make out what was happening there or what was being said. The topic under discussion was indeed very serious. Guruji's core team of Adheesh, Aishani, Jayant, Ruby, Uday, Tejas and now Einar too, were present.

Tejas was the fidgety one. He could not sit still in one place. Usually, whenever there was a meeting among his own people, he would be jumping around or if it was outside, he would be hanging from a branch of a tree. It was true that he was the youngest and everyone gave him this much leeway. But he had a genuine issue. To maintain his body's suppleness, he had discovered that he had to drink lots of liquid and move about so that the water was fully absorbed in his body. Water is an elixir for every human but more so for Tejas as it kept his special power intact. One of the reasons that people did not take him very seriously was his fidgeting. He was attending Guruji's meeting for the first time. Tejas was feeling immensely proud of himself and was full of a sense of self-importance. He was finally being taken seriously and was not going to let anything spoil it. He sat very quietly without moving a hair on his body, though after some time his body had started screaming for movement and water.

Guruji was apprising them of a situation which was steadily coming to the fore and had to be nipped in the bud before any real damage could be inflicted.

'Many of these demons came out of hibernation in between the centuries, transformed themselves into humans and surreptitiously mixed with the human race. They marry humans, mate with them, and have offspring. These children look like humans, behave most of the time like humans, through generations. And after more intermingling they became more human than demon by nature too. But demon blood cannot be written off so easily. Occasionally it manifests its nature in some individuals and that is the time when things take a very severe turn.

'These throwbacks are the most dangerous of all. They know all about human feelings and emotions because they are human. But their demon nature is also there in the core of their being. It becomes all the more pronounced when they inadvertently get a taste of human blood. Centuries-old memories flood their psyche. Some of them are unable to process this phenomenon and take the easy way out by killing themselves. It is the others we have to worry about, those humans or demons who after the initial battle with themselves allow the demon part of their nature to become predominant. It has become impossible to weed out these demons from normal human beings as they are now more intelligent and more cunning too. Many of them have the capability of transforming into human or demon at will.'

Guruji paused and looked at the assembly in front of him.

'Guruji, these people have now become super intelligent,' Adheesh concurred. 'The demons have always been undeniably very intelligent. The memory of that cruel and cunning intelligence combined with their normal human intelligence makes them extremely dangerous and equally difficult to pin down.'

The others were quiet as they paid full attention to the discussion. Their minds had already started the various permutations and combinations of ferreting out these disguised and sophisticated demons, but probably Guruji had slightly different plans.

'Our spies and intelligence teams have found out many disturbing things about these demons. Quite a number of them have discovered each other and are in contact with each other. They are highly placed individuals in society. Some of them, after discovering who they are, have become shattered by the revelations. These individuals have a much more pronounced human side than purebred demons and are sometimes more prone to becoming violent and going berserk. In any case, both kinds are dangerous to the human race. One breed is the one which wants to go back to its roots and the other desperately wants to stay human, but once in a while, still wants to drink blood and harbour other such negative and contradictory desires, more on the lines of Dr Jekyll and Mr Hyde.'

Everyone smiled inwardly. It was funny for Guruji to use such an illustration to explain a point. There was a sharp intake of breath from the young warriors seated in front of Guruji. Tejas desperately wanted to run somewhere. Guruji eyed them seriously.

'Remember this, children, every action has an equal reaction. In this case also there is some good for us in the face of such adversity. These are the particularly good human beings who after getting shattered by the knowledge that they are demons, have gone to the other extreme in philanthropy. All this is very good but they do become demons inexplicably and kill without any awareness that they have actually killed human beings and other forms of life too. When they regain their humanity, they don't remember their demoniac nature. They go on with life as if nothing has happened but leave a bloody trail behind. They do not hide their tracks because they have no idea that they have killed or harmed anybody. It is these demons that have to be destroyed before the others, who know what they are and accept it as such.'

'Uday and Einar will be leading this charge along with Ruby, Jayant and Tejas,' Guruji stated nonchalantly. They all nodded their acquiescence. Adheesh and Aishani were taken aback. Not that they had any objections to the others leading, what was surprising was that Guruji had not included them in this exercise. Maybe Guruji was preparing them for some other operation. Well, he must have his reasons, Adheesh mused. He mentally sent a message to Aishani and received a reply in the affirmative. Reassured now, he gave a cursory glance at the group. With the exception of Einar, everybody was clearly puzzled. Guruji dismissed the class and they went their ways. So, there was not going to be any explanation as to why Adheesh and Aishani were not included.

Once everyone had dispersed, Adheesh and Aishani received a telepathic message from Guruji beckoning them back. They looked at each other, smiled and walked back towards the banyan tree. Guruji looked at them benevolently, 'Both of you are exempted from your duties for some time. For the past six months, you have been subjected to all kinds of suffering, excruciating distress and pain. You have superpowers but are still human beings. There is a limit to your endurance. Both of you have to recoup mentally, physically and emotionally too. Aishani has still been able to vent out some of her emotions, but not Adheesh. I want both of you to take a total break. Go somewhere or stay at home with your people or whatever,' Guruji was at a loss for words. He had never taken a break himself, hence he fumbled in giving them many options. They smiled in spite of themselves.

'But Guruji…' Adheesh had not even voiced his protest when Guruji put up his hands and stopped him. 'No buts, Adheesh, both of you are not to come to the Gurukul at all.' Then seeing the shocked look on Aishani's face he relented, 'Ok, you can come to the Gurukul for a short while every day but no mixing with the others and no work. Just relax, go around and be happy, my children,' he said gruffly. Aishani's eyes had become moist. They touched his feet and left.

Uday and Einar went to the Vishnusthana where administration and politics was taught. By this time, Einar had passed all the exams of the Gurukul with flying colours and was part of the inner circle. It was just a formality but mandatory nevertheless. Einar was one of the greatest warriors they had come across. His knowledge of the demons of his part of the country now coupled with the powers and knowledge of the Indian warriors made him a formidable enemy.

The Vishnusthana was also the place where the gathered intelligence was brought and deciphered. Based on the inputs given to them in this department, they would make their strategy and then throw down the gauntlet. What they found here was not very surprising as Guruji had told them almost everything. An unexpected discovery was that almost all these good Samaritans were geographically quite near to each other, so it would not be very difficult to ferret them out. They gathered intelligence from the experts or teachers or warriors in the Vishnusthana and then sat together in the library to discuss their strategy. The absence of Adheesh and Aishani was a bit strange, but they had undergone stranger experiences.

Ruby had taken lots of water for Tejas, without which he would have become restive. They were in the junior library as they were not qualified as yet to be in the senior library. Uday had recently qualified, but he sat with his group as that was more convenient for all. In any case, the books in the senior library would have eavesdropped on every word of their conversation which wouldn't have been very safe as there were still some powers capable enough to rip secrets from the books.

Armed with the intelligence which they had received from the spies of Vishnusthana, they made a foolproof plan. Each of them had an important role to play in the new scheme of things. The whole operation would begin with sector reconnaissance by Tejas who could climb any structure, slide through the smallest aperture and get a rough idea of the people and their habits and the places they visited frequently. Jayant would not be far behind. With his x-ray vision, he could see even the most hidden places and people. They had all been briefed that these pseudo-demons or pseudo-humans were the most tortured people at the moment. By far, it was self-inflicted torture. The shock and guilt of being a demon had wreaked havoc with their psyche. They were all good beings, they wanted to be good and so they were most of the time. They behaved like model citizens of society, but every once in a while, a trigger would go off in their brains forcing them to do something drastic like killing and eating humans. Later on, they would have no recollection of any of their misdeeds.

This is where Ruby came. When these so-called normal people transformed into demons, they would begin lusting after women. They would become like putty in her hands. She would bring them one by one to houses next to each other. After that it would be child's play for Uday and Einar to dispose off these half-breeds. Uday with his Pash and Einar with his Gram—there would be no match for anyone with these two.

Was it because of this that Guruji had entrusted this task to Uday and Einar? Ruby mulled this thought. Adheesh and Aishani had won and lost too many battles, emotional as well as physical, in the last couple of months. Maybe they would have hesitated a bit when the innocent half-breeds or the human demons cried and pleaded for their lives. This wouldn't be the case with Uday at all. Once Uday was convinced that these human demons were a menace to society and the orders were sanctioned, Uday was virtually unstoppable. He would kill without any mercy or compassion. Ruby suspected that the same was the case with Einar. Another thing that Ruby noticed about Einar was that no matter how hard he fought and how severely injured he was, he always seemed to be fully recovered by morning. This was probably one of his gifts.

Ruby sighed. They were all so gifted and powerful that nothing surprised her anymore. Or maybe Guruji wanted to give some real rest to Adheesh and Aishani. Poor things, she thought affectionately, so recently married but with no time for love. She sighed again. She never compared herself to Aishani who was her leader and she was one of Aishani's defender. They were all Aishani's sentinels. But sometimes, though very rarely, her heart pinched. She had to pay a very heavy price for protecting Aishani. Not that she ever resented it. Given a choice, she would have chosen the same path again. Like any other woman, she too had longed for a man to love and cherish her. Ruby shook her head. To work now. No more reminiscences.

Ruby didn't exactly know if any catastrophe had taken place in the Gurukul or if Adheesh and Aishani had faced any major setbacks and obstacles. She and her family and Aishani's family had to face so many issues of their own. First there were the microscopic demons which somehow, they could not defeat because they were beyond numbers. Then Madhu's home catching fire and the demons raiding the house and destroying it every which way. Then they had to flee to Haridwar and stay there and to top it all Uday's liaison with the demon Prisha. Ruby knew that Uday had never really loved any girl. Once she suspected that Uday had been attracted to Aishani. But that seemed to have ended abruptly even before Adheesh had entered the scene. Ruby could not know the reason nor was she very interested. Coming back to the present, Ruby could feel it in her bones that the same micro demons had attacked the Gurukul and its inhabitants. There were many signs of new beginnings in the Gurukul which a visitor would not notice but for Ruby, the Gurukul was more home than her own home. She would know even if a small branch of a tree broke in the Gurukul. The trees, plants, birds and even their study centres were the same, but the larger birds were not there, the ancient trees were missing. Ruby knew that these trees had just come up—how, she did not know. She knew that she could ask Aishani any time and Aishani wouldn't have hidden anything from her. But these days Aishani did not seem to have any time. She was always involved in one thing or the other. Of course, it was mainly about demons, but Aishani had become involved in other things also. Exactly what, Ruby could not pinpoint. Aishani had taken to looking after and talking to the other members of the Gurukul. She would give them medicines and converse with them a bit more freely than earlier. Though Aishani was aware of all staff members of the Gurukul, she had always been a reserved person. At the back of her mind, Ruby knew that Aishani's personality had not changed, something in her life must have changed permanently. Maybe it was a new maturity.

Then there was the case of the missing staff members of the Gurukul and new members joining, the latest and most surprising being Einar, a bona fide class 1 Swedish warrior. Only one thing was clear: Aishani and Adheesh had gone together somewhere, and they returned with Einar. A few other questions had cropped up in her mind. Ruby couldn't help wondering that when Aishani's home was being burnt, why didn't Aishani and Adheesh come to the rescue? Were they battling some demons of their own? Why had the Gurukul changed? Sometimes the 'No questions' policy of the Gurukul became quite exasperating.

She shook her head. She was going to concentrate on the job at hand. It was easier for Ruby to ensnare humans rather than demons. Her assignment would be to entrap these human demons and try to assemble as many of them in one or more places.

She sighed. Another day, another beginning.

Intelligence reports had revealed that the half-breed demons had made a few groups and mostly stayed together to protect themselves, share their misfortune and share their glee too when they transformed into demons. What the intelligence of the Gurukul did not inform them was that these were a faction of tortured souls. They had imbibed the positive traits of humans and were now more than three-quarters human than demons. They had almost forgotten that they had been demons at some age in some long-gone century. They desperately wanted to be humans, but inadvertently when there was an extreme emergency, their demoniac nature came to the fore and made them crazy enough to perform diabolical acts of killing, torturing, eating, and drinking human blood and flesh. Later they wouldn't even remember what gruesome acts they had carried out. If any of them even dimly remembered what they had done, they were so appalled by their behaviour, that they would just run away and hide themselves in a remote corner of their world and stay there for days, weeks or even months. They were totally and sincerely repentant and didn't know how to desist.

The team was aware of the wretched and conscience-stricken feelings of these individuals, but Guruji said that mercy could not be shown to these half-breeds as they were more dangerous than full-blown demons. These half-breeds would mingle with the main population and would strike when there was least suspicion.

This time the operation began with Ruby. They did not know how Ruby lured so many so-called demons to this place, nor did they care. Uday and the others felt just slightly uncomfortable knowing about Ruby's potential risk as she was their human sister. They instructed her to lure these demons to a couple of condominiums, where they would be waiting. Ruby did as she was told. Einar and Uday had zeroed in on the condominium where Ruby had lured them, but Ruby could not tell them with surety as to which houses they were in because she had bewitched them and brought them here in the thick of night when she couldn't see the house numbers. But she did remember some of the topography and of course she could describe the features and the build of most of the half-breeds. Jayant had taken over after that, and based on Ruby's description, he could with his extraordinary vision exactly pinpoint which apartment and even which room they were in. It seemed most of them were scattered in the apartments of two condominiums.

After that it was child's play for Uday and Einar, although it was going to be a long, rough night. Jayant led them to an unpretentious apartment which seemed to be the larger one. They were fully armed with their weapons. They knocked on the door behind which they could hear some sounds. After the knock, there was complete silence. They waited, then knocked on the door again. There was now the sound of scuffling feet as if people were trying to run away. Einar and Uday looked at each other, then broke open the doors. The half-breed humans and demons were taken aback. There were around ten people there, both male and female.

'What is the meaning of this? How dare you come in inside like this?' one of the men questioned them angrily. He had a deep, attractive and sophisticated voice. Had it not been for their iron-clad intelligence report, they would have wavered for a moment. The others were also well dressed and suave looking. It seemed they were having a party of sorts and so were suitably affronted. Uday looked at them closely. Sure enough, there were tell-tale signs of hastily wiped blood on their hands and the corner of their mouths. Uday roughly pushed the man who had confronted them and went inside. Einar too went inside. They staggered and gagged when they surveyed the scenario in the inner room. There were two naked bodies laid on the rather large table. One of the bodies was half eaten and the other seemed to have just been killed. There were four more demons around the bodies, their mouths filled with the flesh they had torn from the bodies lying there.

The demons recovered quickly from the shock of having two strangers barge in on their feast. In an instant, they had taken out their weapons and turned to attacking mode. But they didn't stand a chance with these warriors. Uday and Einar slashed and crushed them with their respective weapons. Uday had the equivalent of Lord Parshuram's machete and Einar's Gram had killed dragons too. The whole operation was conducted so swiftly that the half-breeds could not even scream. The only sound was the ripping of flesh and the cracking of bones. There was blood everywhere, but Uday and Einar hardly noticed. Their operation had just begun. The half-breeds were strewn in other houses here. They had to do all this tonight itself because if some of the demons escaped, it would be difficult to find them.

As far as hiding the evidence was concerned, Uday and Einar did not have to worry about that. A cleaners' team would always accompany the warriors whenever they were on an assignment, especially in crowded places. These so-called cleaners had a very important role to play in the scheme of things as there would be total chaos and panic in human society if so many dead bodies were found, some of them not even human. These cleaners worked very efficiently, quietly and swiftly. It would not be out of place to surmise that the cleaners too had some power that made them clean the gory mess so swiftly and quietly. By the time they wound up their operations, there would be no trace that any untoward incident had taken place. It was better for everybody: Demons were destroyed and the humans did not get to know about it.

Einar and Uday quickly rushed to the next spot they had been told to go by Ruby and Jayant. Ruby had been instrumental in getting so many of the half-breeds in one place and Jayant was giving a running commentary about where they were and whether they were hiding or not. After that, it was child's play for the two warriors. But by the time they reached the end of their destruction, somehow, a few of the half-demons had got a whiff that humans were killing them. In fear and desperation, they tried to run and hide, but Jayant and Tejas followed them everywhere with Uday and Einar close behind. They were so terror-stricken and distressed that some of them literally turned into demons which was their original form. But they had been humans for so many generations that now they were unable to adapt themselves. The moment they realised that they had turned into demons, their better side would turn them back into humans. As Guruji had said, it was a Dr Jekyll and Mr Hyde situation for them, except that the transformation was moving at a faster pace than they could control. Some could not withstand the alarmingly fast transitions. They just gave up and died.

Even then, the only people they could kill were small defenceless children. They had killed and eaten human babies earlier too. That was when they inadvertently without any reason turned into demons. They were no match for Uday and Einar, who slaughtered them swiftly in one go.

Even so, a couple of demons did manage to escape in the melee. Ruby noticed after some time but by then it was too late.

TWO MOTHERS

It was all over the news channels and newspapers. Babies were being stolen from all over the country and not a single child had been found yet. Distraught parents were laying siege of police stations, the district administration's office, any place where they felt they could get help for locating their infants. Chief Ministers and even the Prime Minister had reassured the parents that no stone would be left unturned in finding the children.

'Who are these people if not demons?' Aishani was getting incensed by the minute. They were sitting at Aishani's place. Everybody was there: Ruby, Uday and Tejas also. This was a sort of get-together to give a proper introduction to Einar, who they explained was a warrior just like them, but from Sweden.

Adheesh and Aishani narrated how they had met Einar when they were convalescing in the Himalayas along with the sick and the injured of the Gurukul. His country too was infested with demons of different kinds. Einar had single-handedly demolished many demons and derived pleasure out of it too. He always felt that his killing of the demons was his small contribution in keeping his society safe and secure. But Einar had always felt restless. He had always felt that his soul was missing something, though he had no idea what it was. Along with this feeling there was an urgency to set out on some kind of quest. Einar had this ability that whenever he fought a demon, no matter how hurt and broken he was, he always recuperated at night and was fresh and raring to go in the morning. But he was also aware of the fact that he was an old soul and that his end on this Earth was near. Hence the restlessness.

Adheesh and Einar had hit it off straightaway. Einar had helped them quite a lot, though Aishani was so busy that she had hardly noticed. There, in the Himalayas, she constantly needed large amounts of hot water and all sorts of herbs which she always wanted yesterday, no questions asked. Both Adheesh and Devnath knew better than to counter Aishani. They knew what she was doing, working frantically against time and of course they didn't want to face her wrath. But they did become harried and overwrought. The herbs were not easily available; they had to sift through whatever was available. They did not have large utensils to boil water, so somebody had to be there to boil water all the time and chop wood without a proper axe. At such a time, a third hand was more than welcome. Though

Einar could not comprehend why there were so many sick and battered people, he understood the scene immediately and got to work right away. Later, when the patients began showing signs of recovery, Aishani noticed Einar. It surprised her that a person who was just like them but from another country was helping around as if they were his own brethren. On his part, Einar had never seen any woman like Aishani in his life. There was no dearth of brave and beautiful women in his country. There was a sheer aura of strength and power emanating from her of which she herself was unaware.

Now here he was after about a month or so. Today was his introduction to Aishani's family, not only her immediate family, but everyone in their group. Instinctively, he knew about the great upheavals that had taken place in this house. They in turn were surprised by Adheesh's choice of friend. He was so different from them, at least physically. Einar had prominent Nordic features. He was tall with rugged features, blonde almost white bleached hair, blue penetrating eyes, large capable hands and feet. It was his handsomeness and his aloofness that made him so attractive to girls and women too. But Einar hardly noticed the female attention, he was so engrossed in his own explorations. Climbing and trekking in the Himalayas did give him some peace. In fact, this was the only place where he found some semblance of homecoming. He had stayed in the Himalayas with a couple of mendicants who taught him several things about spirituality and about his own past births. He did not share all this information with anybody for obvious reasons. He did not have any friends; he was a loner and he liked to keep it that way. Besides no one would have believed him even if he had told them of his experiences.

Initially, Einar had felt lonely because there was no one like him or even remotely like him. It was only when he met Adheesh and Aishani that he had this glimmer of a revelation that there could be more people like him in the world. He was blown away by Aishani's dedication to the patients at Kailash. He did not know her background, but he knew that she had suffered great losses and was still grieving. Despite that, her wholehearted devotion and care towards the victims was awe-inspiring. They kept on working tirelessly for days caring for the crushed and broken bodies. The wounds of these people were healing at a sure and steady pace now. Sometimes, one or two of them could go out to have a look at the majestic surroundings and marvel at its beauty. There was ice and snow everywhere, but they did not feel the cold so much. Devnath informed them loftily that it was God's abode, and the temperature was controlled to suit everybody who stayed here. They smiled at his logic but in their heart of hearts they knew it was a worthy theory. Each of them believed they could spend the rest of their lives here with full contentment and bliss. But God, of course, had other plans for them which was to make the rest of the Earth as beautiful and as pure as Kailash.

It was like a homecoming for Einar when he met Aishani's family along with Ruby, Uday and Tejas. He was overwhelmed with surprise and happiness. To think that there were other people like him in the world on the same level, with the same mindset. He was no longer an anomaly. These were a set of people exactly like him in his thinking and action too, with the promise of more to come. Everybody here believed in the supernatural. He had heard and read about India being a very spiritual country but this! This was totally beyond belief. His years of loneliness were erased just like that. He wasn't even aware that he was lonely. It was only when he met this 'normal' family that he realised that he was lonely because he couldn't talk to anybody about his feelings and beliefs. They were not superheroes or heroines, just people with special powers. Another feeling he had was that every person who was there was somehow rallying around Aishani. He could not pinpoint this feeling; he just knew that it was so. It seemed to him that even Aishani was unaware of this aura around her. There were such strong people around her, everybody embodied with special powers.

Gradually, he began developing a deferential feeling for Aishani. It was as if she were the one who would finally kill each and every demon and the others would be there to facilitate her in her endeavours.

When they returned to their homes and the Gurukul, Einar went back to stay with the hermits who would complete his indoctrination. After it was done, the ascetics informed him that he had come back to his family and this is where he would spend the rest of his life. This was exactly what Einar wanted to hear. After being in the Himalayas and meeting Adheesh and Aishani, he too felt that now he was among his own people. The urge to search was diminishing fast. Of course, he had much to learn about these wonderful people but that would come later. For now, he just wanted to enjoy himself, be in the moment, so to say.

Adheesh and Aishani both were aware that Einar could travel in time though he had confessed to them that he could not travel too far, just a couple of years back and forth. In the meantime, so much had happened here in the Gurukul and in Aishani's home. Einar was unaware of all this, nor was there any need to tell him. What Einar saw and met was a loving family with their own quirks and fancies and what he could make out was the firm iron-like bond between them. There was this subconscious thought in his mind that these were all old souls bound together by innumerable past births. He thought the Gurukul was one of the most enchanting, beautiful places he had ever seen. He knew that there were many spots in the Gurukul that he would never come across as they were hidden from the normal eye and he would have to pass through many exams before seeing a few of them. But he was going to take things easy and let things come to him as and when ordained.

He met Guruji, the portly grandfatherly type of druid. Einar was not fooled by his appearance. Guruji's sharp, twinkling eyes told a different story altogether. Just like Aishani, he also felt sort of a pull when his eyes met Guruji's. It was as if he had known Guruji for a long time, much before he was born. He touched Guruji's feet as he had been taught by his hermit guides in the Himalayas. Guruji blessed him.

'You are us; you belong here, you have been brought here for a reason.'

Einar nodded. He knew that his meeting with his foster family was not a coincidence. One of the sayings in Hindu philosophy is, 'You don't get anything more than your destiny and you don't get it before the right time.' Einar too had started believing in this.

'We are facing a crisis. This time our orders have come from a more human source. He is nevertheless a particularly strong person, in fact the strongest in the government machinery.'

The three of them stretched forward to hear Guruji's words clearly.

'Though they are all humans, they are still different from average human beings. There is really no need for you to know their identity. It's enough that we have been promised all help if any such requirement arises,' Guruji informed them.

They waited.

'There has been a spate of child kidnappings in the last few months. All of them are unsolved. In some cases, a couple of babies have been discovered dead and blue. The cause of death is a very deadly poison. There are no signs of struggle or even puncture marks. All the babies range from the ages of six months to eighteen months. It seems that they have not been kidnapped to be sold off. They are just kidnapped to feed a she-demon's maternal instinct to suckle a baby,' Guruji continued without mincing words.

They listened patiently. Nothing fazed them now. Anything was possible, however bizarre. By now they knew that every demon had its own agenda and its own axe to grind. Ultimately, the result was the destruction of the human race one way or the other. The present crisis was just a bit surprising for them. They had not heard of demons having maternal instincts. What they knew about the demons was that in extreme hunger they ate their young ones without any compunction. This particular she-demon seemed to have such strong maternal instincts that it wanted to feed even a human child without bothering about the consequences.

'Apparently, this she-demon's baby was killed in one of the skirmishes with a female human warrior while it was still lactating. The demon baby had crawled away from its mother. A female warrior saw it and didn't know what to do. All babies are cute and innocent, and this one was no exception. She took the baby with the intention of leaving it in a safe place where its mother would find it. Unfortunately, when the she-demon felt the need to feed its baby, she discovered that the baby was missing. It went into a rage, went in search of her baby and found it with a human. Without thinking, it attacked the female warrior. After a fierce altercation, both the protagonists survived but unfortunately the baby demon died. Demons do not have any significant maternal instincts; whatever instinct is there is only till the baby is suckling. Since the she-demon could not find gratification for this instinct, the desire somehow became entrenched.

'After that incident, it was always on the lookout for babies. It would change into a beautiful female and mingle freely with humans. At an opportune moment, the she-demon would steal a small human baby and rush to the jungle to feed it. But it was a demon's poisonous milk. There was no escape, the babies had to die, and they did.'

Guruji continued, 'Not only is this demon to be destroyed, but its death ritual will also have to be of an uncustomary kind. Its bones and hair must be burnt and the flesh, especially the breasts, have to be slashed and buried. Only then this rabid maternal instinct will not be transferred onto another she-demon,' Guruji stated emphatically.

The three of them sat quietly at Guruji's feet with deadpan faces, not allowing their thoughts and emotions to reflect on their faces. It was one matter to cleanly kill a demon or demons. It became gory when you had to break the body into different parts and then cremate and bury it at the same time. How gruesome that would be. Guruji looked at them and understood. He was not their Guru for nothing, 'You do not have to bother about the disposal of the demon's body. This will be done by the undertakers who will go along with you in this venture. You will just have to kill the she-demon.'

Though their faces were still deadpan, Guruji could feel the relief in them. They were his star pupils, meant for much greater things than burials and cremations.

'It will be better if you have Ruby as a team member with you,' Guruji instructed them. They nodded in unison. Aishani gave a sigh of relief. There had really been no time to have a heart-to-heart conversation with Ruby, especially after the demolition of the Gurukul. Ruby too had many experiences to share with her. Even now, Aishani did not know whether they would have any private time for themselves, but she cherished Ruby's company and was happy that Ruby was going to be with them. Adheesh was comfortable with Ruby and Einar was smitten with Ruby's beauty. There was no dearth of beautiful women in his country, but Ruby's ethereal beauty could not be surpassed by anybody on Earth. Her personality changed subtly around the men whom she came in contact with, drove them crazy, making them want to be with her all the time.

Einar was not fully aware of Ruby's powers, but he was aware that she was not fully an Earth creature.

Adheesh, Aishani and Einar had stationed themselves in this town. Guruji had sent them here. They had received the information that the she-demon was somewhere in the periphery of this town. When they went around, they realised why this she-demon had been here for a long time. On the outskirts of the town was a dense jungle which suited the she-demon just fine. She would snatch a baby, rush to the jungle, feed it and after the human baby died, throw it back in the town's premises. Along with Devnath, two undertakers from the Gurukul were also accompanying them. Devnath was not going to let go of such a great chance to prove his valour and expertise in this field. Not that it was required: Adheesh was fully aware of Devnath's prowess. Probably Devnath wanted to prove something to himself. Interacting with the dead and their bodies was his forte. Adheesh too accepted that Devnath would be a great help in this mission.

The five of them sat together and discussed their strategy. They could not anticipate when the demon would kidnap a child. It was difficult to differentiate between the she-demon and a human female because this demon would be disguised as a human female. Only Devnath would be able to identify demons because of their peculiar smell. In its human shape, the she-demon would be so shrouded with human smells that nobody would be able to tell her apart. The two undertakers were also sitting at a respectable distance from them. Their names were Chhaya and Mukund. They were the invisible people of the Gurukul, seen but not noticed. Like everybody else in the Gurukul they were also warriors, but they knew just the rudiments of warfare—just enough to save themselves from a small demon or stall one. They had more or less understood why they were with this elite group. Chhaya was an expert in burying anyone or anything deep inside the Earth without anybody suspecting anything. Similarly, Mukund could burn anything and if required the fire or the resultant smoke would not be detected even by the most sophisticated machines.

'Well, we just cannot wait here twiddling our thumbs, hoping for the she-demon to make its appearance and kidnap a baby,' said Adheesh impatiently, 'Time is running out.'

'Adheesh, if we have a bait then we can lure this she-demon towards the jungle and kill her,' it was Einar.

'That is an excellent idea, Einar, but where do we get the bait from? In this case the bait can only be a baby. We don't have a baby and no mother would give her baby to lure the demon. Though we will naturally do our best, we cannot guarantee the survival of the baby.'

Ruby who was listening to their discussion very attentively suddenly quipped in, 'I can get you a human baby,' she declared.

They all turned to look at her unbelievingly.

'Ruby, where will you get a baby from? Don't be ridiculous! Who will give you their baby? We just cannot snatch it away from someone,' Aishani was vexed.

'Don't ask too many questions but I assure you that the parents will willingly hand over the baby to us for this good cause and I know that with such great people around me, no harm will come to the baby.'

Aishani looked at Ruby closely, but she refused to look Aishani in the eye. Drawing a sharp breath, Aishani did keep quiet, with a sneaking suspicion that there was much more to the story than what Ruby would tell them. She sighed. She would have to sit with Ruby in a quiet place with lots of time to extract the truth from her, perhaps tell her a couple of her own truths in exchange for the real story. Even then, Ruby might not confess or tell her anything. But there was no time now for these musings. She looked at Adheesh. He looked at her impassively, unperturbed. That was the thing with men, she thought. What was such a big deal for women was just a non-issue for them. Well, she'll just have to deal with both of them later. Now they needed the bait or the baby.

Ruby turned to them, 'I'll bring the baby in the afternoon tomorrow. Then we'll go to the market. It's a busy place. Women go there to buy household goods. Some of them would be around with their babies and children. Hopefully, the she-demon will also be there. We won't be able to make out but Devnath will know. When he gestures, I will deliberately leave the baby in a chair or something on the pretext of buying knickknacks. Seeing an unattended baby, the demon will pick it up hurriedly but quietly and will rush towards the jungle to feed it,' Ruby closed her eyes for a moment. Again, Aishani had the niggling feeling that Ruby was hiding something. It suddenly seemed as if the tables had been turned. Ruby had always been a follower and a protector, never a leader. Though Adheesh and Aishani never openly recognised it, in their heart of hearts they knew that each person would gladly and voluntarily give their lives for their leaders. The role reversal, even momentary, was quite surprising though not entirely unpleasant. They sat down together to discuss their strategy this time along with the two undertakers Mukund and Chhaya.

Adheesh and Einar scoured the market to find the spots where women were most likely to do their shopping. The entire team would be there but it was Devnath who would smell out the she-demon. It was his moment, and he did strut for a few minutes before the crowd began assembling in the market. Ruby would also be among the shoppers along with the baby. Ruby entered the market just before its peak time. They were sure that the demon would go there earlier so that it could find a baby to suckle her breasts. They roamed aimlessly in the market, senses on alert, but no signal came from Devnath. It was late afternoon now. The hustle-bustle of the market was at its peak. Adheesh's party was getting desperate. Evening would set in after some time, and crowds would start thinning out. Very soon it would be time to make dinner and prepare babies for bed. If the she-demon were to strike, it would be now or there may not be any kidnapping.

'Who would have thought that we would actually want a baby to be kidnapped, that too Ruby's,' Aishani whispered to Adheesh and immediately covered her mouth with mortification. What was she saying! Ruby was just bringing a friend's baby and they had to save the baby and give it back to Ruby to return it to his parents. Adheesh was looking at her impassively. My God, he knew! Or he had also guessed the same thing! But what had he guessed? They both turned to look at Ruby and the way she was holding the baby. For the first time she noticed the tension on Ruby's face. The baby was totally at ease in Ruby's arms. There could be other reasons for this, such as her familiarity with the baby. But if the baby were hers, this was the biggest sacrifice she would ever make in her life. As Adheesh and Aishani looked at each other, their eyes said everything. Their eyes pledged to each other that they would not let anything happen to the baby.

In the meantime, Ruby had placed the baby in his pram and had busied herself with some bangles and bracelets in the shop. Einar was on full alert. In fact, his senses were always a notch sharper than the others. He had practised and meditated extremely hard to be where he was today. From the corner of his eye, he saw Devnath make a very subtle gesture. It was a ladies' shop and they had placed themselves at some distance from it. There were several women surrounding the shopkeeper demanding to see one thing or the other. Some of them did have children but they seemed to be in the age group of two to four years, not really in the breast-feeding stage. Only the child with Ruby was about eight months old. Devnath's gesture was a very casual one, like swatting a fly, but Einar instantly became alert. He couldn't go too near the shop, because of his colour and features. But even from a distance, he could make out the she-demon now. She was so beautiful with deep kohl-lined eyes, a perfumed body, immaculately worn sari and thick long hair. By now the she-demon had started hovering around Ruby and the baby. Even if Ruby was aware of any danger near the baby, she did not give any indication but coolly went on choosing the bangles. Before any person in the team could catch on, the she-demon had pulled the baby from the pram in one go, hid it inside her sari pallu and almost flown towards the jungle.

Immediately, they all turned and ran after the she-demon. They ran from different directions and ran almost at the speed of lightning. Speed was the crucial factor here. The she-demon could not be allowed to sit and breast-feed the baby. By now the she-demon must be desperately looking for a quiet, secluded place where she could suckle and love the baby even if it were a human baby whom she could easily eat. It was a quirk of fate, but she must have kept on lactating even after her child's death. Her maternal instincts had peaked to gargantuan levels. The hitch was that any child just could not digest her blood as it was poisonous for human babies.

While rushing after the demon, Aishani had a glimpse of Ruby's face. Ruby's hands were on her chest, her eyes were closed, and her face was slate white. Aishani had no time to think but that image stayed in her mind. She rushed with the others after the she-demon, who thankfully was still searching for a secluded place. By now the baby had also started fretting, giving the demon more incentive to feed it. At last, she found a place in a grove of trees. Adheesh and Einar were ready with their weapons. Adheesh had his special bow and arrow, one that could maim and kill demons but he would have to use this very judiciously as the baby was in between. Same was the case with Einar. He had a sword known as the Gram. The Gram had been used to kill dragons in Nordic mythology. But the hurdle was the same. The baby had to be protected at any cost.

Adheesh looked at Einar. An understanding passed between

them. Einar ran towards the she-demon with his sword while Adheesh aimed his arrow from where he was. So engrossed was the she-demon that she sensed and saw them a moment too late, and a moment was all Adheesh and Einar required. Adheesh aimed at her legs and Einar struck her shoulders. The demon was sitting on a tree stump. It did not fall—rather, it just slumped onto the ground. The baby fell on the ground and started crying.

The she-demon was now desperate to feed the baby. It did not feel the pain of its arms and legs being cut off. It was now or never. If it could not feed the baby now, it would be dead before she could fulfill her heart's desire. With a roar which was an amalgamation of pain, anger, and love, it fell on top of the baby and tried to feed it. Aishani was watching all these theatrics from a distance. Another minute and the baby would find the she-demon's teats, would start suckling on them and die. This could not be allowed! She thought desperately. Only one thought came to her mind in this frenzy. She pulled her arrow from the bow and with one clean stroke cut off the demon's breasts. For a moment, nobody understood what had happened, least of all the she-demon. Then with a howl of rage, pain, and frustration it turned towards its enemies. Adheesh and Einar had sized up the situation immediately and since Einar was nearer, he kept slashing at the demon till it died. Adheesh was instantly at her side and so were the undertakers.

'Good work, Einar!' Adheesh and Einar did a sort of high five. Einar smiled modestly. 'All in a day's work,' he said quietly. They left the carcass of the demon with the undertakers Chhaya and Mukund.

Aishani tenderly picked up the infant in her arms and tried to wipe its blood-spattered face with her hands. The baby had again started crying. It was hungry and it did not like so much of movement, including falling. Aishani and Adheesh rushed towards the market with the baby. Einar followed them a bit slowly. Somewhere near the market, Adheesh stopped Aishani, 'Ash, I know we are in a hurry to deliver the baby to its parents, God knows what stress they must be undergoing. Don't you think it would be better if we clean up the baby a bit? It's almost covered with demon blood. The parents will panic even more if they see the baby like this.'

She hurriedly cleaned the baby. Not liking this too, the baby bawled loudly, bringing a smile to their faces. Aishani paused. It made sense. Again, Ruby's grey face flashed in front of her eyes. Einar had caught up with them. 'I have a bottle of water with me,' he gave the bottle to Aishani, who quickly washed the baby's face.

By this time, they had reached the outskirts of the market. Ruby was desperately waiting for them there. She plucked the baby from Aishani's arms and rushed with it behind one of the shops which had closed by now. Aishani tried to rush after her but Adheesh held her hand.

'Wait for some time, then go to her,' he said softly, 'Give her time to become whole again.'

Dumbfounded, Aishani stared at Adheesh. Here she was still guessing and Adheesh had understood. Einar had also understood, though he did not know their earlier story. Aishani waited for some time, then went behind the shop where Ruby was sitting with the baby. The baby had stopped crying and was now contentedly sucking at her breast. Ruby's eyes were closed. She opened them when she sensed Aishani nearby. Aishani went and sat beside her. Ruby put her head on Aishani's shoulder and closed her eyes again. A few tears escaped from her closed eyes.

Softly she said, 'Ash, I wanted to tell you but somehow you were not available whenever I wanted to talk to you,' a sob broke through her lips.

'Shh..Ruby...shh, don't say anything, plenty of time for revelations. Let the relief sink in and love your baby. We'll talk about it when you're completely relaxed.'

Soul Exchange

They were all moving together: Adheesh and Einar in front, Aishani and Ruby next, Uday and Jayant following behind. Tejas was also part of the team, but he preferred to accompany them jumping from tree to tree. Devnath was everywhere. These two would be roped in only if there was a serious situation. Then Tejas and Devnath would have to toe the line. They were on a relaxed routine surveillance in another jungle, one of the many which dot the lower Himalayan range. They had not been informed of any demons in this part of the jungle. It was almost like a vacation, and they were not as alert as they would have been in an operation to hunt and kill demons. 'Adheesh, I see some hazy figures around the trees and the shrubs,' Jayant told Adheesh.

'Is that so? Let's go near them and see them,' so saying, he followed Jayant towards a grove of trees.

'There! I see a large moving shadow near that tree.'

'Ok,' Adheesh went to that tree and swung his huge sword at the spot Jayant had indicated, but no demon emerged, and his sword just whooshed through thin air.

'There's nothing here, Jayant, maybe the light of dusk played tricks on you,' Adheesh smiled, 'Come on Jayant, don't feel bad, it's happened to you earlier too. You see things.'

'Ok Adheesh if you say so,' Jayant replied, clearly not convinced by Adheesh's logic. It was his job to see the unknown and unseen. He was sure that there were unseen creatures, but they quickly changed shape or just vanished into thin air as soon as any human went near them. Through the years, Jayant had honed his skills to such an extent that he could intuitively feel the presence of a negative being, almost as if he could read their thoughts. He did not like it at all when he saw Adheesh and the others walking nonchalantly through the jungle. He looked over his shoulder. Aishani and Ruby were giggling over some silly secret. In front, Adheesh and Einar were ambling along chatting. Uday was just a bit behind them, not taking part in the conversation—that was Uday, always a loner.

To say that they were caught unawares would be an understatement. They were slightly less careful, and this cost them the lives of the two most important members of their group.

After the Gurukul attack, the demons had become confident, cocky and risk-prone. Demons, in any case, were never disciplined and at the present moment were flush with arrogance and bravado; they would take any chances now, no matter how slim or asinine. That is exactly what happened to Adheesh and Einar, apart from the fact that they were not on high alert.

Adheesh and Einar were reminiscing about their Mansarovar and Kailash days. Uday couldn't help overhearing. He was stunned as he heard the story. Here he was thinking that he had undergone the most dangerous ordeal of his life! But his nightmare was nothing compared to the calamity faced by Adheesh and Aishani. Normally, Uday would never have eavesdropped on anybody, leave alone Adheesh and Einar, but this was so mind-boggling that he inched just a bit closer.

A huge demon suddenly jumped in front of them. It looked like a thickset old man, but though its silhouette was that of a human, it had the face of a lion with a huge scorpion tail which was spraying arrow-like bullets. These darts or arrows were filled with an extraordinarily strong poison. The poisonous darts stung them all over their bodies. Einar was slightly in front of Adheesh, and he was got very badly stung by the creature's poisonous darts. Adheesh tried to save Einar by coming in front of him and confront the creature. As a result, he bore the brunt of the arrows and fell.

In an instant, Einar sized up the situation. This was the shape-shifting demon that killed Einar and mauled Adheesh like a rag doll. This particular demon was a Manticore. Einar was familiar with the Manticore. He knew that it would now sit and devour Adheesh while shooting his poisonous darts all around so that nobody would disturb him during his meal. Something had to be done swiftly. In a flash Einar swung his sword, the Gram, and with a clean swipe, cut the Manticore's scorpion tail which was ejecting the poisonous darts.

With a howl, the Manticore fell to the ground. His scream was like the sound of a trumpet. It knew that it was beaten and had the animal cunning to retreat. Somehow it got up on its haunches, spread its wings and rapidly flew away before Einar could hit it a second time. Einar had to let it go, even though he wanted to chase the Manticore and kill it. He was gravely wounded and fell near Adheesh. Uday saw the whole ordeal with horror. He saw Einar slashing the tail of the creature and he saw the monster howling loudly and flying into the jungle. Unsheathing his sword, he ran after the demon, which was flying at a low level, probably because its tail was hacked and severed. Uday soon vanished behind the creature.

Ruby and Aishani were stunned by the drama which unfolded before them and was over in an instant. They rushed towards the two warriors, but it was too late. Jayant, Tejas and Devnath too rushed to the spot. It all happened so fast that they couldn't even begin to fathom what had happened.

'No, Nooo!' Aishani screamed unable to hold her anguish and desperation. She was like a demon herself, fighting like a tigress in rage to protect her cubs. Except that now there was nobody to protect. The two people who were with her were no more with her. The others were just a moment behind. Adheesh and Einar were lying on the ground dead and frozen. Adheesh's body was covered with stab wounds, no way could he have survived these attacks; Einar did not have too many stab wounds, but he had also succumbed and now they both lay dead at her feet. The others arrived a little too late. They were slashing their weapons left, right and centre ineffectually.

Dazed, Aishani sat down beside Adheesh and took his hands in hers. Uday returned after a few minutes, having failed to locate the demon. His anxiety about Adheesh and Einar made him give up the chase. He and Jayant had now taken position and were shooting at a dizzyingly fast pace. Tejas and Ruby too, even though not bona fide warriors, were shooting in all directions. But the whole exercise was in vain. The killers after achieving their targets had vanished and the others were clutching at straws. Giving up, Ruby turned towards Aishani, who was totally stunned, oblivious of the mayhem around her. She had a stony expression on her face and was looking fixedly at Adheesh.

Ruby could understand her dear friend's grief and despair and disbelief. Ruby just sat beside her, not knowing what to do. She herself was in pain. How could this happen? They had been sent on such an unimportant mission and now nothing was left. Through a haze of pain, she saw Devnath going to Adheesh's side. She saw Devnath touching Adheesh, then he touched Einar. Very slowly Devnath, turned towards Ruby and whispered, 'They are still alive, barely so, moving them even an inch will bring their deaths. We have to do something extremely fast and very slowly too.'

Then very softly so that only Ruby could hear him, 'Einar is about to depart anytime now.'

At first the words did not register. When she finally comprehended Devnath's meaning, Ruby was too afraid to move even, lest something happened. What could they do? They were far from the nearest hospital, and they could not be moved. Ruby thought hard, then she softly and gingerly went and settled in a corner behind a tree and sat down to meditate and communicate with Guruji. She fervently prayed that Guruji would hear her. In her hand was the special rosary which Guruji had given her for such contingencies. She willed herself to hold her agitation and began chanting the Durga mantra on her Rudraksha beads. In folklore, Rudraksha beads are supposed to be the tears of Lord Shiva when his wife Sati died. Rudraksha trees can be found in the Upper Himalayas where Bhagwan Shiva resides.

Ruby chanted the mantra with utter humility and desperation, willing the Goddess to send Guruji to her. She didn't know how; it was just blind faith. She desperately wanted both Adheesh and Einar to survive and become well. Such was the apsara Ruby's power that Guruji heard her prayers and appeared in front of her. Believing and disbelieving, Ruby didn't know how to react. Silent tears flowing down her eyes she fell at Guruji's feet. Guruji surveyed the whole scene in front of him, the two bodies lying there and the bewildered team standing there unable to get over their shock. Quickly, Guruji walked towards Adheesh and Einar. Guruji touched both the bodies, looked at Aishani and the others and then decided something. Guruji turned to Uday and Devnath and said, 'Einar has just died, Adheesh too is on the verge of dying. I have to do something immediately, otherwise we will lose both of them.'

Saying this, Guruji instructed them to make a broad circle of sorts around the three of them and face the outer side. They would be able to detect renewed threats and not be witness to

Guruji's rituals. The warriors were too shocked to say anything or even react. Zombie-like, they followed Guruji's instructions and turned outwards. Only Aishani was inside the circle, but she was too far gone to comprehend the goings on. She was in a state of shock, with no idea of her whereabouts or what was happening around her.

Guruji always knew that such a day would come, but there were still so many obstacles to be removed. The Shakti or the power of both Adheesh and Aishani together was required to thwart the demons now coming out of hibernation in droves. This particular era and century were very conducive for demons as humanity was swiftly sliding towards depravity and immorality. Guruji sighed. What had to be done would be done and it had to be done very swiftly. The forest was equally quiet, waiting with bated breath and in anticipation to see Guruji perform his miracles. But what was done, was done, and could not be undone. He could not bring the departed soul back, but he could transfer one soul from a battered body to another healthy body.

Einar's soul had already begun fading. If it fully departed, then the process of physical decomposition of his body would begin. The ritual would have to be fast but at a measured pace too. Guruji sat in the lotus position between Adheesh and Einar, placed his hands on their heads and began chanting a vastly different mantra. The outside circle could hear the unfamiliar chanting, but they could not make out the words, if at all they were words. Nor were they interested. They had full faith in Guruji. They hoped against hope that Guruji would bring both of them to life.

After some time, Guruji took out a few things from his bag and laid them on the ground. He then proceeded to make a makeshift havan kund, lighted a fire and began his havan. The air around them grew heavy. They were in a sort of a clearing inside the jungle. Guruji was throwing unknown and unrecognisable things in the kund. Slowly the air lightened around them and covered their area of the forest. It was like an invisible cloak. Guruji did not want any disturbance. The large bright circle covered all of them and it kept on getting brighter. Very soon it became difficult for them to look straight into the light. They became even more alert. Inside the circle, Guruji was like a conduit between the two bodies.

A knowledgeable tantric would have known what Guruji was doing. He was transferring Adheesh's soul into Einar's body. It was not a straight procedure but a three-way process. First Adheesh's soul had to come out of his body. Then it had to enter Guruji's body. From Guruji's body, Adheesh would get the impetus to enter Einar's body. It had to be done this way as Adheesh's soul would have been directionless, not knowing what to do. It could have either remained on Earth without a body or it could have jumped and joined his Maker. It had to be done very expeditiously, as now Adheesh's body was without a soul and had to be transported to the Gurukul hospital without delay, as decay begins almost immediately. If the others could see, they would have been astonished to see slight movements in Einar's body. Very soon, Einar's body began showing signs of life though he was dead. He turned from grey to white and now there was a pinkish pallor creeping into his skin. Adheesh did not show any signs of recovering. He was just lying there.

Guruji soon wound up his chanting and ritual and signaled to the others to face him.

'We have to take them back to the ashram.'

Devnath opened his mouth to say something but closed it again without articulating anything. His sixth sense was telling him that something stupendous had taken place behind their backs. Exactly what, he did not know. In awe of what Guruji had done or not done, he along with the others quickly made makeshift beds and carried the two barely alive bodies to the Gurukul.

Adheesh was now in Einar's body. The first two days when they took the bodies of Adheesh and Einar to the Gurukul, Guruji and his doctors were extremely busy with them in the Gurukul's Vaidyashala or the hospital. On the third day, Guruji summoned Aishani to his cottage. Sick with grief, Aishani went and sat in front of Guruji.

Guruji told Aishani that the creature which had created such sickening, heart-rending havoc was a Manticore. A Manticore is a creature from Persian mythology though it is sometimes mentioned in Indian mythology too. Guruji also told her that sometimes demons or creatures from other regions are summoned when their own numbers are exhausted and when they are in fear of total annihilation. This along with the shape-shifting demons had brought such great disaster to them. They were more or less always prepared for the shape-shifting demons which were quite common in this part of the subcontinent. But even the elders were not prepared for the Manticore. In Indian mythology, it basically means a man-eater (Manti or Mard or man and Core or Khor or 'to eat'). They had not been able to fully view the Manticore as it destroyed them before they could fully comprehend it. Later, when he came to his senses, Adheesh had a hazy memory of an old man with the body of a lion and the tail of a scorpion throwing sharp arrows at a very high speed. He was told that some of them had huge wings also. Even though it had a human face, it had three sets of sharp upper teeth and another three sets of sharp lower teeth, enough to tear a man with one thrust of its huge jaws.

'Beta, Einar died in the skirmish in the jungle.'

Aishani nodded. She was expecting this. The shape-shifting demons had very cunningly outwitted them.

'Einar's time had come. He had to go…' Guruji paused, then went on, 'Adheesh was so badly hurt that moving him even slightly would have killed him. Adheesh's time has not come. So, I did what was the most practical thing to do under the circumstances. I have temporarily shifted Adheesh's soul into Einar's body, only till the time Adheesh's body fully recovers. I have performed a small ritual for Einar and his soul. Once Adheesh's soul returns to his own body, Einar will be given a full cremation according to the laws of his land and according to his wishes.'

For a few minutes, Aishani did not comprehend the full import of Guruji's words. Then her eyes widened. Adheesh was alive! And kicking also! Literally! She began crying softly. Gradually her crying turned into uncontrollable sobs. Guruji patted her head tenderly. So powerful yet so sensitive and delicate. Guruji was Lord Hanuman's disciple. Like his Lord, Guruji was also a Brahmchari. Despite having centuries of life's experiences, Guruji did not have much idea of a woman's psyche. But because of his proximity to Aishani through the ages, he could feel her despair and agony. Guruji had reached that level of Nirvana where he was not attached to anything in the world, but if he had an iota of feelings and emotions towards anybody, it would be Aishani. If anybody's happiness made him happy, it was Aishani's. If Guruji had personally ever wanted to protect and care for anybody in this world it was Aishani.

Aishani looked at Guruji through her tears, 'Can I see him?'

'Yes of course you can, but at present you won't be able to make out that it is Adheesh, till the time he speaks to you. He will regain consciousness in a few days. In the beginning, he won't even be able to recognise himself. We will all have to help him to adapt to his new body. Many people will still not know the truth, just a handful of us.'

'And what about Adheesh's real body?' Aishani whispered. She was fast getting used to this idea.

'That will take a long time, beta. His soul is not there in his body. When the soul is there in the body, it connects with the universe and to everything around it, be it people or medicine. The body heals itself very quickly. As of now, Adheesh's body is just a shell, a totally broken shell. It will have to heal from the outside with herbs, mantras and even tantra. We cannot send him to your father-in-law's hospital for obvious reasons. We do not want to divulge this secret to even the nearest and most trustworthy persons. Another point is that Shri Vidyadhar ji's hospital, though one of the best in the country with state-of-the-art machinery and the best doctors, is still a hospital for humans with sicknesses and diseases that usually beset humans. What has happened here is not a sickness; it is the transference of one soul to another person's body. This can be done in the Gurukul, nowhere else.'

Three months passed. Adheesh adjusted to his new body, albeit slowly. Einar's body had suffered wounds that took time to heal. Einar was from a very cold country. He had to be treated differently, but the Vaidyas of the Gurukul soon came across medicines which suited his body. Then there was Adheesh's soul with its own embedded habits and patterns. Though Einar had lived in the Himalayas for a significant number of years, his body's basic physiology was Nordic. When his soul was there, he and his body could adjust to the Indian way of living. His soul was in sync with his body. But now Adheesh's soul was in his body. Einar's body baulked at the very idea of so much vegetarian food with a smorgasbord of spices, whereas Adheesh's soul wanted simple, spicy vegetarian food. There were so many other differences that it seemed that there were two independent personalities in one body. One was the soul of Adheesh and the other was Einar's body.

Then there was the emotional angle. The niggling guilt that he was responsible for Einar's death would just not leave him. Adheesh knew and the others in his immediate circle knew and had experienced that flash of a moment when it became imperative for a warrior's instinct to protect, which was what made Einar come in front of Adheesh, for which he had to pay dearly with his life.

So, this is what Guruji had referred to once when he said that they owed a great deal to Einar. Even Einar had once told him in the Himalayas that he did not have much time to live and that his journey to Kailash would be his last journey. Everything was pre-planned, Adheesh mused. Einar knew he was going to die, Guruji knew that Einar would leave his body on Earth and Adheesh would occupy it. Adheesh sighed. Life was so complicated. Far better to be a warrior and live a simple life. He knew that there would be complications again when he went back to his own body, as by that time his soul would have adjusted to Einar's body.

They were sitting in their usual place under the two huge banyan trees behind the Gurukul. Nobody knew how old the trees were but their presence itself was comforting. Nobody paid much attention to them, for one they were almost on the periphery of the Gurukul and secondly, they were like any other flora and fauna of the Gurukul. Just the right place for Adheesh and Aishani to have some moments of solitude and privacy. These days Adheesh was wary of touching Aishani. He made sure that he sat at a respectable distance from her. As for Aishani, even though she knew that the person sitting beside her was Adheesh, she could barely look at him now.

'Ash.'

'Hmm.'

'I know I shouldn't be saying this, but sometimes I get these strong urges to eat non-vegetarian food. I really would love to have some luscious meatballs with lingonberries.'

Aishani shifted away a bit. She had discovered that if she did not directly look at the person sitting beside her, then she could talk to him like she would talk to Adheesh. She still had to adapt herself to this physically different looking person. Initially she could just not accept him as Adheesh as even his voice was that of Einar. In course of time, Einar had become a very dear friend. Both Adheesh and Aishani found that they could talk with Einar on many familiar and strange topics. Though their backgrounds were different, their goals and destinies were the same, which was removing all kinds of scum from the face of the Earth.

'I know, Adheesh; it's Einar's body wanting these foods.'

'Yes, Ash I know, but I can't help it. I am myself surprised by this and so many other things which this body demands. May Einar's soul rest in peace. The sooner I go to my body, the sooner we will be able to cremate this body,' Adheesh said almost wistfully.

Aishani understood. Adheesh was getting a bit attached to this new body of his. She had seen this sort of thing happening earlier also, albeit with demons. The demons which entered a body were very reluctant to leave it. True, in the case of demons as many of them did not have a proper body to live in and secondly, it was like a comfortable house which anyone would be loath to leave. It was the same with Adheesh, not only did he have a friendly body, now he had some extra powers too. In this scenario, it was a boon that Adheesh had imbibed some powers of Einar's body as they would need immense surges of power to ferret out the shape-shifters and kill them. Though Aishani too had adjusted to Adheesh inhabiting the body of Einar, nevertheless there was just this flicker of withdrawal whenever their powers had to merge with each other to destroy the major demons. This was a major setback for the elders of the Gurukuls. The demons had not got wind of it yet. The older and the more knowledgeable of them were still wary of the Adheesh-Aishani combination and were keeping themselves out of harm's reach, at least for the time being. But they knew that it was just a temporary reprieve. Guruji was aware of this fact. He and his doctors were working overtime to bring Adheesh's body to some semblance of normalcy. But there was a limit to hurrying up the process, without a soul a body cannot rejuvenate itself.

It was only because of Guruji's superpowers that Adheesh's body was being preserved and healed at the same time. Time was running out.

OUT IN THE DESERT

'There is a great deal of activity going on in the regions near the great Thar Desert.' Adheesh and Aishani were sitting in Guruji's cottage. Adheesh's soul was still in Einar's body. His own body was still recovering in the Vaidyashala of the Gurukul. The primary members of the group knew that Adheesh's soul was in Einar's body. They had to be told otherwise there would have been confusion in the group itself. If they had not been told about this transference of Adheesh's soul in Einar's body, they would have thought that after Adheesh's hospitalisation and in his coma-like state, Aishani had shifted her friendship (for want of a better word) to Einar. That would just not jell. Hence, to avoid the embarrassing situation, Guruji had divulged the truth to the immediate group.

Guruji could make out that things were not totally hunky-dory between Adheesh and Aishani. Of course, there were a few rough edges, like getting used to the various movements of Einar's body, whether external or internal. Einar favoured one shoulder while Adheesh the other. And so on. Then there were the foods which Einar's Nordic body craved. Adheesh's soul baulked at the thought of those non-vegetarian dishes. The saddest fact was that both Adheesh and Aishani knew that their dear friend was no longer with them and had passed on to the Universe and to the Almighty.

Einar and even Guruji earlier had hinted many times that Einar was on this Earth for a short time, but though Adheesh was always puzzled, he never really caught on to the subtle hints. Now Einar was dead and Adheesh was living in his body. Was Einar sent to the Himalayas for this purpose, Adheesh thought many times—but there were no answers, only heaviness in his heart. He wanted to cry and howl for Einar, but he could do that only after he emigrated to his own body.

Then there was Aishani. When Adheesh himself found it difficult to adapt to this body, how could Aishani be expected to fully accept him in Einar's body? They were human beings, darn it! They were used to trusting their eyes even when they knew that the truth was something and somewhere else. Aishani, who was so self-assured, who was the strongest of all, who had been blessed by Maa Durga herself, even she was facing difficulties in accepting Adheesh in Einar's body. Another heart-wrenching fact was that the moment Adheesh's soul went back to his own body, the present body of their dear friend Einar would have to be cremated.

Guruji was aware of this interplay of feelings and emotions in his protégés' minds. He was well aware that if he sent them on a mission in which both their powers were required together, Aishani may not be able to optimise her powers if she did not have Adheesh's powers to fall back upon. Therefore, Guruji chose an assignment in which Aishani had a much greater role to play. Of course, Adheesh would be there to annihilate the demons but he would be working quietly and separately from Aishani.

'These are desert demons; they have occupied a part of the Thar desert and are creating so much chaos and destruction that we cannot overlook it anymore. They are destroying the flora and the fauna, killing, eating, and now targeting human beings too. Earlier these incidents were few and far between, but now their frequency has arisen to alarming proportions. The government is taking many appropriate, strict measures to rein in these rising crime levels, though it is not helping much. Human beings cannot fight supernatural, abnormal creatures. Apparently, a couple of people had survived these attacks of the demons and lived to tell the tale. Both men lost a limb in these attacks: one his arm and the other his right leg. They were with a group of people who had gone to the desert fully armed with weapons. Nobody returned except these two. Their tales were gorier every time and now even army soldiers were unwilling to go inside the desert. Those who did go did not return. As a result, people were withdrawing from these border villages and migrating to other places. Migration is not that big a deal, but the resultant factor is that the border area is becoming deserted, which if not curbed, will become a complication of epic proportions.'

'How many demons are there Guruji, and what kind of weapons should be used to destroy them?' asked Adheesh.

'Quite a number of them, Adheesh,' Guruji thought for a moment. 'Maybe about ten mature, large ones and an equal number of smaller ones who are still learning the tricks of the trade. The number of smaller ones will only increase with time. Disposing them is not all that challenging if one has the right knowledge, means and tools.'

Both were listening attentively to Guruji. They instinctively knew that there was a catch here. Killing any demon was an excruciatingly painful process. Hence if the process were not difficult then it meant that there would be some divine intervention. Guruji looked at them and understood their thoughts.

'These are demons of the desert and have survived in the desert for ages. When there is no victim, they become one with the desert and nobody knows the difference even if one was in their midst. They lie low and wait for a victim to approach them. It's only in recent decades that humans became bolder and began venturing into the desert to settle there with their animals. Gradually, these demons too have become audacious and brazen enough to venture out in these semi-green areas and kill humans and animals. They just fly out of the desert like a mini-tornado, catch hold of their prey and fly back to the middle of the desert to devour them.'

'These demons are mortally scared of water and the greenery which water produces. Just like a fish dies when it is taken out of water, in the same manner these demons die when they are taken out of the desert,' Guruji continued.

They waited as usual. Guruji was leading them somewhere.

'There has to be copious amounts of water in the desert for the demons to drown and die. There has to be large amounts of vegetation too so that when these desert demons run away from the water in terror, they get entangled in the vegetation and are then drowned in the water.'

'But Guruji that would require excessive and superfluous amounts of water, which the country can ill afford!' Aishani exclaimed.

'Yes Aishani, you are correct. It's all God's maya, beta. Man proposes, God disposes. One door closes, another opens. God always keeps a door open. Recently these desert demons have become so bold that after the humans ran away in terror, they began staying in their bhungas only. That way they were in the desert and in vicinity of their victims too, either humans or animals.'

'Bhungas?' both Adheesh and Aishani looked up questioningly.

'They are small mud houses with thatched roofs prevalent near the borders of the desert. It's a good thing that some of the demons have laid siege to these bhungas, for this just makes it a bit easier to destroy them. Once they try to run from the water, they get entangled in the tendrils of the plants and vegetation and then drown in water.'

It still sounded impractical and preposterous to them. They also knew that in their line of work nothing was impossible. Still, they could not fathom how lush vegetation and thousands of gallons of water could be procured in the jungle. Guruji eyed them and understood their doubts.

'Both of you have guessed correctly. There is going to be divine intervention. In the case of these desert demons, Mata Shakumbhari will come to our rescue. As both of you know, Mata Shakumbhari is one of the incarnations of Durga Ma and Aishani has been personally blessed by Ma Durga.'

They nodded. The picture was getting clearer and things were falling into place. According to the legend, when there was a thousand-year drought on Earth, the sages prayed to Ma Durga. In response to their prayers, Ma Durga sent Mata Shakumbhari to end the drought and provide food to the people of this Earth. Guruji nodded then looking at Aishani he said, 'You have to take the blessings of Mata Shakambhari, one of the personifications of Maa Durga.'

Guruji was all businesslike now. These were his sharpest, most capable, and experienced warriors. They would understand these instructions in the blink of an eye.

'First go to Udaipur; from there catch a bus for Sikar. There you will reach Mata Shakumbhari's temple. Do your usual prayers and wait for me to introduce you to the priest. Adheesh, you will be there with Aishani throughout in the pursuit of this mission.' Guruji looked at Adheesh. 'We cannot draw attention to ourselves. Adheesh, I think it would be better if you disguise yourself as an Indian. At the moment, you look too much of a European and that will attract attention.'

'Yes Guruji,' it would have been funny had it not been tragic. Here he was in his friend's body, the friend who had already left the world. He, despite being Indian, had to camouflage himself to look like an Indian. They nodded, touched Guruji's feet and left.

They were sitting in the bus on the way to Sikar.

'Adheesh?'

'Hmm,' he was half asleep.

'We are Hanuman ji's warriors and Ma Durga has blessed us, and we have special powers too.'

Adheesh was awake now, 'Yes Ash, what do you want to say?' he was smiling. He could anticipate her next question. He had coloured his hair dark brown and wore dark brown contact lenses. Dressed like a local, he looked quite Indian. He waited for Aishani to speak.

'Then why are we sitting on this rickety bus and not flying to Mata's mandir?'

Adheesh laughed out loud. This was a running joke between them. There were such few instances of humour between them that whenever an opportunity to laugh came their way, they grasped at it. Laughter was precious.

'Well, let me guess, we are half and half you know. Half special and half human. This is our human half.'

Aishani laughed, apparently satisfied with the answer. They held hands and looked out of the window at the arid landscape.

They reached Mata Shakumbhari's mandir in the evening. Guruji was already there. Other visitors to this temple would have thought Aishani and Adheesh were like any other pilgrims coming to receive the blessings of Mata Shakumbhari. Guruji was waiting there with the head priest, wizened old man who seemed to be sleeping all the time. Guruji had already briefed him of some facts regarding their visit. They knew that Guruji was a very taciturn man and he would have told the head priest truly little, only the bare details. However, that very little was more than enough to give the strongest jolt to the priest. His sleepy eyes opened in awe. He fawned in front of Aishani and almost made as if to touch her feet. A discreet cough from Guruji made him straighten up in embarrassment. A quick look at Adheesh and his eyes opened wide again. He could look through Adheesh's disguise. Why was a foreigner in disguise here, his eyes asked Guruji. But Guruji ignored the question and asked the head priest to proceed.

The priest took them to a room on the first floor. This room was also like a mandir. There was a statue of Mata Shakumbhari with other goddesses, on a platform with some basic puja materials kept beside them. The priest bowed again and left. Guruji turned towards them, 'Go and freshen up children, while I do the preparations.' They went out. A priest was waiting for them. He guided them towards the washroom and then left. Adheesh and Aishani could make out the palpable tension in both the priests and that both wanted to linger but because of Guruji's instructions, left reluctantly.

Both Adheesh and Aishani were now pros in invoking the powers that be. It was all done under the guidance of Guruji. They were just carriers and caretakers of the powers for a very brief period. After their work was accomplished, the powers returned to their original entities. The memories of these powers were always obliterated from their minds, as their human minds and bodies were not geared for such great power and capacity.

Adheesh did not have much to do here except to sit with Aishani and share the puja, mantras and havan with her. Guruji began with his incantation of invoking the deity. Aishani and Adheesh followed. The chantings and the incantations went on throughout the night. They made sure that they chanted in low volume as a high volume would have alarmed the priests and the other pilgrims too. At around midnight, Adheesh felt the temperature change in the room, it became hot then cold. This went on for some time and then the weather became very pleasant. Adheesh knew that the deity had heard their invocations and would soon come to them. Rightly so.

It was around six o'clock in the morning that he noticed a radical change in Aishani. He turned to look at her and was shocked: She had turned almost green. Her eyes were dripping water but Adheesh knew that she was not crying. The hair on her head and arms had grown and become similar to the curled tendrils of plants. Adheesh knew that Aishani was not aware of them anymore. She had become the deity herself or at least a semblance of the deity. Guruji stopped his invocations because Mata Shakumbhari had entered Aishani's body; he continued his chanting.

There was no time to be wasted. Guruji and Adheesh paid homage to Mata Shakumbhari. After some time, Guruji gestured to Adheesh, who immediately went out to call the head priest. He was sitting downstairs in the main temple waiting for them. He quickly followed Adheesh to the room where Aishani was. His eyes widened in disbelief when he saw Aishani. For a couple of minutes, he stared at Aishani then fell down at her feet sobbing. He had seen many miracles in his life but there were none to beat this one. This was Mata Shakumbhari herself! He was besides himself. Guruji nudged him into action.

'Take us to those bhungas where the demons have laid siege. We do not know how long Mata will stay with us. She may stay with us for a week or she may leave in a few hours, we don't know. So, there is absolutely no time to waste, you understand?'

The head priest nodded. How he longed to stay at Mata's feet and pray and just be there. But Mata had been invoked for an extremely specific purpose. Reluctantly, he led them through a secret passageway which led to the borders of the desert. The sun had just started coming up. The arid dry desert spread out before them, miles and miles of sand which was getting hotter by the minute. This was the time for desert demons to prepare for the kill. As the temperature climbed, some innocent traveler would come and take shelter in these abandoned dry huts. The demons would be waiting in the huts to pounce on these innocent people and drag them deep inside the desert, kill them there, eat their flesh and drink their blood. Sometimes they would catch an unsuspecting cow, goat, or other animal. That was how they functioned. They were one with the heat and the burning sands of the desert. Coolness, greenery, and water were anathema to them. This is how the desert was increasing inch by inch, day by day because the villagers were running away, some even leaving their livestock in their panic to flee.

When the party of four reached this border of the desert, Aishani through Maa Shakumbhari set to work immediately.

Copious amounts of water began flowing from her body; she targeted the empty bhungas first because that was where the desert demons would be hiding, waiting for unsuspecting travelers.

Aishani positioned herself in such a way that her back was to the desert, and she was facing those huts where the desert demons were lurking. So great were her powers that the first few huts were flooded with water. The water flowing out of her body could have just flowed down and got sucked by the dry Earth, but it cascaded over the bhungas, giving the demons no choice but to rush howling and screaming out of the huts. Some of them had already begun dissolving and dribbling on the ground. They were not like what a traditional demon would look like with horns and tails and talons and red eyes hissing fire. They were thick gusts of sand held together loosely. Adheesh and Guruji with their experience could make out the face and body of the demon while the head priest when he was not swooning with shock and wonder, could just see sandstorms flying out of the bhungas.

As soon as the water touched these demons, they began disintegrating. Some of them did hold themselves for a few seconds, screaming and beseeching the entity to spare them. But the goddess was in no mood for mercy. Enough leeway had been given to them with the clear understanding that they would never cross their territory, that is, the middle of the desert. They had broken the pact, disrupted the harmony of nature. Hence, they would have to pay the price.

Soon after flooding the first few huts and destroying the demons there, Aishani went towards the other huts and began flooding them too. Another miraculously bizarre thing which was happening was that instant thick dense vegetation was sprouting and spreading at an astonishing speed and was speedily covering the earlier bhungas, thus sealing the fate of the desert demons. There was no way they could go back into these huts even if one of them survived. The whole operation went on till late afternoon by which all the desert demons had been annihilated.

An additional surprising phenomenon was that after the destruction of the desert demon of each hut, the water would naturally dry up so that only greenery was left. By evening, this part of the desert was free of the demons. Mata Shakambhari slowed down and ultimately stopped. She made as if to go back but she waited for a sign from the head priest, who was still looking goggle-eyed at the proceedings. Guruji gave him a gentle nudge. He woke with a start, realising where he was. He folded his hands in supplication to the deity and led them back to the temple through the same secret passageway. Aishani was still dripping water; she was still green with small, soft tendrils coming out of her body. Adheesh was anxious and very worried now. He knew how sick Aishani was going to be once the deity left her body and she became a normal human being. From past experience, Adheesh also knew that even though her mind may not remember anything, her body would take a long time to forget, recuperate and adjust to normal shape. One relieving factor was that now she could be admitted in his father's hospital for recuperation, with round-the-clock care and the best treatment.

Back in the room, Guruji gestured to the head priest to

leave, which he did expeditiously. He was the most respected and experienced head priest, but he knew when he was beaten. Today's happenings were beyond his comprehension. Before he left the room, Guruji asked him to arrange a car for them. He would have done anything for this exalted group. Apart from the miracles which he had just witnessed, what had occurred was a tremendous gift for mankind. The desert would stop growing and people would begin living on its fringes again.

TIMINGILA

Try as she might, Aishani was not fully comfortable with Adheesh in Einar's body. He was her Adheesh, he was not Einar at all, she knew all that very well, she could see and hear their hearts beating together. She could never thank her stars enough for keeping Adheesh alive after the Manticore's fatal attack. Every day, she would religiously thank God for giving her Adheesh, no matter in what form he was. And she also fervently thanked Einar's soul for allowing Adheesh's soul to be housed in his body till the time his own body was healthy enough to accept him back. Despite knowing and accepting everything and being totally grateful for it, there was just this tiny nanosecond of hesitation whenever she looked at Adheesh.

Guruji was worried. A huge earthquake had taken place in one of the neighbouring countries.

The aftershock of the earthquake was a Tsunami in the Indian Ocean which was devastating South Asian and Southeast Asian countries. Guruji's sources had reported that a humongous demon had been reported coming out of the ocean waters. It was a fish really, one of the hugest creatures which the world would ever see and experience. It was called the Timingila, a colourful luminescent creature that had survived from the time of the Vedas. In the Ramayana, the Timingila and other sea creatures have been said to be inhabiting the waters between Lanka and the South of India where Rama had made the Ramsetu or the bridge between India and Lanka to fight the demon king Ravan. It could swallow fish as large as a hundred feet in length, including whales and sharks, in one gulp. So, it was difficult to imagine the size of the Timingila.

No one had seen the Timingila, but people had heard rumours that it was so huge and powerful that it could jump from the ocean to the sky and swallow a huge airplane in one big gulp and then just slide back into the water without any problem whatsoever. The adult Timingilas are around a hundred metres in length with a matching girth. Though seemingly docile as per the ancient texts, the very act of swallowing huge whales, sharks, ships, or anything that came in its way to satiate its hunger would make it extremely dangerous. Reports were coming from scientists of the Gurukul that a huge Tsunami was going to ravage the southern part of India. It would come out from the deepest part of the Indian Ocean and would be of such gigantic proportions that the entire ocean and the aquatic creatures inhabiting it would be swept from the water world to the surface of the Earth.

On its way, it would unknowingly gobble up all large aquatic creatures, thus destroying the ecological balance of the ocean waters. Though it could not be categorised as a demon, it was clubbed with demons for all the harm that it did while feeding itself and the destruction it would cause if it came anywhere near the coastal areas. It had to be eliminated to save the lives and flora and fauna of the ocean and the land if it was thrown out by the Tsunami.

Under normal circumstances, Adheesh and Aishani were the ideal candidates for this operation. Their powers when they were together would proliferate to such an extent that destroying this Timingila wouldn't have been too much of an effort. They would have disposed it in the high seas itself before it came out. They would have gained some experience in underwater exercises too. They had earlier destroyed quite a number of underwater demons, and this would have been an exceptional experience. But this was not going to happen, at least not this time. Guruji sighed. The Timingila was too mammoth an entity to be killed by only one of them. Aishani was just not hundred per cent comfortable whenever she saw Adheesh's soul in Einar's body. There was an imperceptible hesitation, though only for a moment. And this made all the difference. Their powers would not become one and multiply. There was nobody else who could take on this herculean assignment. To save humanity and aquatic life, the Timingila had to be eliminated.

The matter was decided. These warriors would go with him. This would be a learning exercise for them. Guruji mentally summoned them to the Yagyashala. They came with alacrity. Guruji generally called them to his cottage. This was unprecedented, but in their world, nothing was out of the blue or strange. Aishani rightly guessed that this was an emergency and Guruji immediately wanted to embark on it, beginning with a huge, all-pervasive havan. But there was nobody here. There was silence in the Yagyashala. This was not unusual. Nobody spoke in the Yagyashala unless spoken to. But this was silence of the absence of people. There were only three of them there: Aishani, Adheesh and Guruji.

Guruji looked at them gravely, 'We are going to have the havan after some time. I have called you earlier to apprise you of the developments that are going to take place in a few days' time. I have decided that I will demolish this behemoth before it reaches the surface of the ocean.'

This came as a complete surprise to both Adheesh and Aishani. They looked at Guruji in confusion. All their lives they had looked upon Guruji as their guide, friend, and philosopher. They knew that after the holy trinity of Brahma, Vishnu, and Mahesh, Guruji was the most powerful entity in all the three worlds. But they had never visualised Guruji actively and physically taking part in any operation. Guruji meditated and controlled everything with the power of his mind. And he had his teams of warriors spread all over the world.

'Both of you will be with me, albeit at a distance. You will not interfere unless I give you the go signal. This is a chance for both of you to brush up your under-water skills and combat training. On second thoughts, I may allow both of you to enter into the attack in the latter part of the clash.'

They nodded, questions bubbling inside them, but Guruji's words were not to be trifled with. Together they had encountered and overpowered fiercer and stronger demons than this mammoth of a fish. Granted that the strongest force was required to destroy the Timingila, but they had the power. Or did they? The shocking truth struck both at the same time. Adheesh was stunned and Aishani was mortified. It had to do with her hesitation in accepting Adheesh in Einar's body. It was only for a nanosecond, but it was enough to divide them as separate entities. This was because as separate entities, they may or may not have the power to destroy the Timingila. Nobody else in the Gurukul or anywhere else in the world had the capacity to destroy the Timingila.

So, this is why Guruji had to personally take the matters in his own hands. Aishani could not help it. She knew her beloved Adheesh was with her all the time, and they were just biding their time till Adheesh's own body would be fit enough to house his soul again.

Soon the pundits began arriving in the Yagyashala. Guruji wanted to embark on this mission immediately, hence the yagna. As a rule, they never proceeded on an exercise without a havan. The havan took about one hour after which they followed Guruji to his cottage. Some other rituals were performed by Guruji in his cottage. Adheesh and Aishani were now experienced enough to anticipate that they were being prepared to be teleported to the southern part of the country where the Tsunami was foretold to occur.

Guruji placed his hands on their heads and chanted some more mantras. Their eyes closed automatically, and they lost track of time. After a while, it could be minutes or it could be hours, they didn't know, they opened their eyes. They were not in Guruji's cottage any more, though Guruji was still chanting mantras with his hands over their heads. They waited patiently. After some time Guruji removed his hands and they stood up and looked around. They knew that they were down in the South of India and were now on a beach near the ocean. The ocean was very calm and peaceful, but both Adheesh and Aishani knew that it was the lull before the storm. Guruji looked around and then spoke, 'It will be better if both of you familiarise yourself with this part of the shore. You will have to come back here to be teleported to the Gurukul.' They nodded and began walking along the ocean shore. They did not speak to each other as they were lost in their own thoughts. The rocks beneath their feet echoed their thoughts and at every step tested their agility and sense of balance. The imbalance of nature had already begun. The sky above was light blue and soft, the stones were sharp, and fluffy clouds rode on the waves. The lacy waves echoed her heartbeats and all this while the birds flew in an arc and screeched, their gut instinct telling them that something was happening. The shore was like a gateway, a meeting place of the aquatic and terrestrial worlds. The turquoise waves lapped up on the seashore, kissed their feet and retreated, leaving a foamy trail. The waves welcomed the two warriors, they knew exactly who and why they were there. They kept on softly touching and erasing their footprints in the sand.

'Ash, we have to stop our contemplations and join Guruji now.'

'Oh Adhee, sometimes I really pine for the normal. How I wish there were no Tsunami and there was no Timingila to confront and...' She stopped before going any further.

'I know baby,' he said softly, careful not to touch her lest the magic fizzled out. He was her Adheesh, he knew that she knew that, but he had Einar's body. Einar was an exceptionally good friend, the best that they had had, but she could never see Einar in that way.

'Let's brace up and go to Guruji now.'

They reached Guruji in five minutes and waited for instructions. Gone were the deep sighs and pining, instead, standing in front of Guruji were two strong, focused warriors who had nothing on their mind other than disposing the monster Timingila.

Guruji flicked his hands and three pairs of divers' suits appeared in front of them. Donning them quickly, they stood at attention waiting for Guruji's orders.

Guruji spoke, 'These are special suits. They will protect you from any predators of the sea. These will protect you and free you in case you get entangled in the sea weeds or any other dangerous and threatening aquatic or plant life.' They nodded. They were familiar with these suits, having worn them earlier, though when exactly, they didn't remember. Was it in this life or another? There was no time to think of that now.

'First I will go in the water and try to deflect the Timingila from its trajectory. It is so huge that it will be difficult to deflect from its course. It is highly disturbed too. It has been caught up in the Tsunami and is now being pushed to the shore. That cannot be allowed. The Timingila has to be stopped somewhere deep in the ocean and not near the shore. If my efforts to send it back fail, then I'm afraid I will have to destroy it. This is the case with the other large fish too; they don't like to be ousted from their familiar surroundings. No living being does.'

They could make out that Guruji was not happy with the situation but would do it for the protection of mankind and its preservation. Guruji looked at them and chanted some more mantras. They felt just a bit uncomfortable and hot around their jaw lines. Adheesh put his hand to his jaw. There was a kind of growth on his jawline. Within seconds, his jaw had sprouted slivers of slimy flesh. He looked at Aishani. She too had sprouted these slivers on her jaw.

She spoke to him mentally. 'Adhee, you have sprouted a beard!'

'Yes, so have you!' he guffawed mentally.

Mortified, Aishani touched her jaw. 'O my God!' She too had sprouted a thick beard.

They both looked at Guruji, who smiled.

'Well, didn't you want to go with me in the middle of the ocean? Those are gills to make you breathe in the water. I have given you special covering for your eyes too, so they won't sting too much in the salt water. Apart from that, you are on your own. Try to save as many creatures as you can and try to keep them in the ocean itself. No matter what happens, save yourselves first. Observe everything and stay close to me.' Saying this, Guruji went inside the water and disappeared. They stared after Guruji, then looked at the water. It was a crystal-clear cerulean blue. The salty waves rode silently and expansively. Staring straight ahead, they were unable to distinguish between the salty blue ocean and the dusky horizon. It was so peaceful that nobody could imagine the volcanic storm which had built up in the ocean and would destroy many parts of the Earth too.

Amazed by the turn of events and at a loss for words, they held hands and waded into the water. They walked about half a mile, their gills helping them to breathe. Initially, they encountered a couple of species of turtles, some of them small and some huge and green in colour. They looked up from inside the ocean. The sun glowed like a soft diffused disc. The sunlight inside the water was blue not gold and the more they went down, the darker the rays became. The rocks were just shadows now. A fish here or a turtle there glided past them, seemingly unconcerned. The water pressure increased, and the water seemed to become thick like soup. It was truly a three-dimensional world.

As the water pressure grew, their suits propelled them deep into the midst of the Indian Ocean. The ocean floor shone in all its beauty. They were amazed by the flora and fauna. They had never seen such beauty earlier, so delightful, fascinating, and divergent, some standing still and preening in their beauty, some floating like delicate silken waves. They could make out the different colours. Now they could see the aquatic creatures too, most of them fish. Aishani wished she could stay here for some more time to enjoy the ocean's bounty. As they waded deeper into the water, they left the dolphins behind and began seeing the more dangerous creatures of the ocean. Suddenly, Aishani thought she saw a blue whale. In her excitement, she wanted to hold Adheesh's hand to share this sighting, but the moment she turned towards him she saw Einar and the moment was gone. Adheesh was beside her. He noticed her gesture and understood. Together both stared at the brilliantly blue whale. It was so huge that they had to swim for a full five minutes before they could fully fathom its size. It was not alone, it had a partner too, they didn't know whether it was its partner or child. Both looked the same size. With regret they passed them and swam towards where they thought Guruji would be.

There were signs of panic in the saline water. After adjusting to the pressure and flow of the water, they gradually began noticing other things as well. The water was not moving in a wavy fashion, rather it seemed to move in one direction only and that was up and only up. They began seeing schools of fishes going up with the rising water. Soon they espied a killer shark going up, then another and then another. Very soon there was a rush of fishes going up. They could also make out that they were going up with the gushing water which was becoming a gargantuan wave. The scales of the fish resembled silver armour plating as they were unwillingly thrown up by the water. There was nothing natural or soft about it. The water of the ocean swept not gently but with the power of a nuclear blast shockwave.

There was no end or beginning to the wave, they tried to swim away as far as possible to avoid it. Was it the Tsunami? They didn't wait to find out. The chaos was absolute, it was so great as to be totally mesmerising. Drums of war were pounding inside the water.

They had to reach Guruji as quickly as possible. The beauties of the ocean would have to wait to be appreciated. Even the ocean was in no mood to welcome the visitors. Its inhabitants were themselves being evicted forcefully and the ocean was in no mood to entertain any visitors. After seeing the size of the mammoth sharks being thrown out of the sea by the indescribable colossal wave, the urgency to be with Guruji became more imperative. Not that they lacked faith in Guruji's ability to tackle the situation—Guruji was their God, he could make anything and destroy everything, but they were warriors, they loved to be in the field to destroy their enemies. Aishani was again smitten by guilt. This was her job along with Adheesh. Guruji had to tackle this situation because there was nobody else more qualified to do it.

Their powers in the water propelled them into the ocean speedily towards Guruji. Within minutes, Adheesh's tracker intimated that they had reached Guruji, but they could not see him, probably because they were on the other side of the wreckage of a huge ship. Adheesh signaled to Aishani that to reach Guruji they would swim to the other side. Guruji had told them specifically not to interfere, so they wouldn't. They would move in only after Guruji permitted them. They tried to swim towards the other side of the ship. They kept on swimming, but the side of the ship was so protracted that they were finding it difficult to reach the other side where they presumed Guruji was. Something was wrong. Because of their special powers, they were swimming at an extremely fast pace, but the end was nowhere in sight. They stopped. They looked at each other and then at the ship, the hull looked smoother than it should have been. They looked up and down the ship. It seemed to be as huge as its length. Realisation dawned on them at the same time. This was not the remains of a shipwreck, it was the Timingila itself! They looked at each other in shock and anticipation, their warrior instinct immediately coming to the fore. A fish this size would destroy a few coastal towns without even trying. They did not doubt Guruji's capacity to destroy it; they wanted to see how Guruji would do it. But first they had to cross it. After their shocking discovery, they began their journey again and this time they did reach Guruji. The Timingila was so huge that it may not be aware of their presence. But it was definitely disturbed. Great sounds were coming out of its belly; it sounded like the word 'bloop', which is made when someone gulps or swallows noisily. It was probably the only sound it knew, as that is what it must have done throughout its life. They pushed back a little, to have a proper view of the mighty creature and were surprised to see that it was multi-coloured. Some parts of it were emitting fluorescent green, yellow and red lights. The fluorescent colours might be helping it to navigate the ocean.

Finally, they saw Guruji. He acknowledged them with his eyes, but he was looking above them now. They followed the direction of Guruji's eyes and their own nearly popped out. There was another gigantic creature coming towards them which seemed a bit familiar. They desperately tried to search for it in their memory banks. Suddenly it clicked in Adheesh's brain. It was the great white shark, one of the deadliest fishes in the ocean. It was huge and was coming rapidly towards them. He looked at Aishani. She had already taken out her bow and arrow, the same which would throw multiple serrated arrows of ice and fire. He also took out his innocuous-looking sword which with the click of a button would open into five huge swords. But before either of them could make any offensive move, the great shark almost disappeared from view, vanished in front of their eyes with a huge trumpet-like sound. Where did it go? They looked around with alacrity, but the gigantic white shark had just disappeared. After a few moments they realised that the huge shark had been swallowed by the Timingila and the trumpeting sound was the Timingila gulping it down. Shocked and amazed by the drama and sheer size of the aquatic creatures, they just stood there awaiting Guruji's instructions. Though the Timingila too was moving slowly, it did not make any difference to them. It was so huge that they felt that they were just floating by its side. At the same time, even they were being caught up in the vortex of the Tsunami and were being pushed out. They looked desperately at Guruji.

Guruji's eyes were closed, he looked calm. Every ten seconds or so, Guruji would swallow some water, close his eyes, mentally chant some mantra, and then forcefully spit the water on the Timingila. This went on for a few minutes. Nothing happened except that the colossal fish seemed to have stopped and was standing still. They were so small compared to the Timingila that it probably wasn't even aware of their presence. Adheesh and Aishani were getting desperate. All of them were being jettisoned out of the water at an extremely fast pace, but they had full faith in their Guruji. After some time, the Timingila had also started moving up. And gradually they did notice a change, a change so stupendous that they had to deliberately pause and make sure of it. Guruji continued spitting magical water from his mouth at the Timingila. The Timingila had become a bit shorter in length and in breadth too, though it was by far still too, too large for its modification to have any positive effect. They waited while Guruji continued with his spewing of the chant-filled water. Gradually and imperceptibly, the Timingila's size reduced to the size of a large whale. As Guruji continued, it shrank to the size of a small whale. Guruji stopped after this and they all heaved a sigh of relief. A small whale on the coast could be handled. Suddenly they were thrown out on the ocean front. The Timingila was also thrown out, though now it did not seem to be so intimidating. It lay on the coast thrashing because of lack of water. Guruji ran up to it, but by the time they reached it, its thrashing had stopped, and it had become still.

'It's dead,' Guruji said sadly. 'It could have coped for some more time without water, but it could not cope with the sudden shrinking of its body. I wish I could have done something to save it. It's all in Prabhu's hands,' Guruji folded his hands and said a small prayer. Aishani and Adheesh too prayed for the Timingila and the other sea inhabitants which were being thrown out of the ocean.

DRUG DEMONS

"Dada, is it wrong for drug addicts to die? I mean they are hard core addicts; they can do anything to acquire their daily dose of whatever poison they are ingesting. I'm sure they must have killed too to get any small amount of money to buy their dosage of drugs."

Uday nodded. He was sitting with his younger brother Tejas in one of the empty classrooms of the Gurukul. He was surprised to hear Tejas speaking so maturely. He looked at Tejas again and was stupefied to see him grow so much. And why not. Tejas had become a senior in the Gurukul now. He had grown tall and lanky and there was a maturity in his demeanor. But Uday had never really seen him like this. For him Tejas, was like a puppy who yapped around him in circles, always causing a disturbance.

But the bond of love was always there between them. It's just that Tejas was never taken seriously by anybody, he was the cute youngest member of both the families, theirs and Aishani's. And here he was speaking so maturely about drug addicts.

'I agree with you Tejas, nothing can be done about these hard-core druggies. They can never be rehabilitated. But they are human beings, and they are being killed unnaturally. It is our sacred duty as protectors of Aishani and thereby of mankind to protect all human beings, no matter how depraved and despicable they are.'

After some time Adheesh, Aishani and Ruby also joined them. Jayant was also with them. Generally, Jayant stayed away from group meetings unless specifically called by Guruji. Like the others, he knew his duties very well and performed them with all seriousness. As such, he was always on the lookout for any crisis or instability in the environment as and when they appeared. The power of his x-ray vision enabled him to see things which the normal eye could not see. He knew that the Gurukul and they themselves were always under constant threat and his special vision had helped the Gurukul more than once. In any spare time, which was rare, he would just fool around. Sometimes Tejas would tag along with him and with his elongating powers, he had proved to be an unbelievably valuable ally.

'Before we go to Guruji and get instructions,' Jayant began, 'Let me tell you that Tejas and I have discovered who the killers of these druggies are.'

They all turned to Jayant and Tejas in amazement. Tejas

spoke swiftly to Uday, 'Dada we got to know about it only yesterday and I felt that it was only fair that Jayant tells you about it. He was the one who saw the whole operation with his extraordinary vision.'

Aishani and Adheesh were listening very intently. This was getting serious.

Ruby asked, 'What did you see, Jayant?'

Jayant looked at all of them. They were anxiously waiting for his reply, 'Well, the killers are demons, blood-sucking demons.'

They did not fully comprehend the meaning of his sentence though they did get the gist of it. They waited for some more revelations.

'These are blood-sucking demons who are also drug addicts. So great is their need for the drugs that they kill their victims to get them.'

'Not that demons need any reason to kill and plunder. The easy method of going out to buy the drugs would not have suited them,' Aishani commented dryly, 'They could have just snatched the drugs from the junkies without any effort.'

'Exactly! But that's not the point,' Jayant exclaimed.

'What's your point then?' Ruby was getting bored; she had witnessed so many demon killings and vice versa that this was not catching her attention.

'The point is that these demon junkies are cursed in a way that they cannot eat flesh and bones. They can only drink blood and since they are drug addicts, they have to kill and drink the blood of other blood addicts. This is Dracula with a difference.'

The others almost smiled.

When they finally went to Guruji, he promptly dispatched them to the library; Adheesh, Aishani and now Uday also went to the senior library. The location of the senior library had changed after the destruction of the Gurukul. Both the libraries were left intact, mainly because the demons were not looking for them, secondly the nano demons could not find them as they were so well hidden. Another good thing was that on the day of the destruction, there was no human being present, even the librarian Vashisht had taken off. It was just one of those things, the demons could not smell any humans in that direction. Hence a major disaster was averted. Nevertheless, the location of the senior library had been changed. It was now more in the open and it did not have walls, floors or even a ceiling. A couple of seniors had found it very strange and even queried about it. Apparently, there was now a three-layered invisible security surrounding the library and all the bookshelves were given their own emergency alarm codes. If the security of the library was foolproof earlier, it was now much more so. One good thing was they always felt as if they were in the lap of Nature reading one of their favourite books.

Ruby, Jayant and Tejas would go to the regular library which in any case was no less, the difference was that the senior library had more ancient texts and hence slightly more information and solutions. There was full information about the tertiary level and mid-level demons here. Many a times, the regular library was more than enough for their requirements plus more books were in contemporary languages, hence easier to decipher. Guruji had called them the next day. Blood-sucking demons were common enough. There was loads of information on them. But weed junkies were not so common. The search was not yielding sufficient results. Tejas was also trying to help Ruby and Jayant, but basically, he was just pottering around. Reading was not his greatest preference.

It was only when Jayant spotted a book that could be helpful to their cause that Tejas brightened up. At last! Stretching his body, he took out the books which Jayant was pointing at, hidden behind the other books on top of the bookshelf. Jayant had extraordinary vision, so he could see through the first row of books. There were not too many books on this subject and gradually they had gotten relegated to this corner. Invariably all the demons were addicts one way or the other, but their addictions were different from human drug addiction: they were addicted to murder, greed, torture, sloth, anger, and other such vices. They were above vices of imbibing weeds like marijuana or heroin. Their debasement went much beyond that. The warriors sat in the library for hours poring over the books and finally arrived at some conclusions.

On their way to Guruji's cottage, they met Adheesh, Aishani and Uday, who had probably come to the same conclusion. Guruji had just finished his evening meditation when they arrived. Guruji gestured to them to sit. They spread out their mats and sat on the ground in a semi-circle around Guruji.

'So,' Guruji inquired, 'What conclusion have you arrived at?'

They looked at each other, then Jayant spoke, 'Guruji, the only way these demons can be killed is through poison, that too the strongest kind of poison. We will have to find out the poisons that will kill these demons without harming human drug addicts. Then we will pinpoint the demon or demons who have been killing the drug addicts. We must somehow make the demon(s) believe that they are drinking the blood of the drug addicts, but they will be drinking the strongest of the poison.'

'That's good research, Jayant,' Guruji praised him. Jayant smiled self-consciously. Coming from Guruji this was high praise indeed. 'So have you thought of a strategy of making the demons drink the poison?'

They kept quiet and looked down. They knew the answer but were uncomfortable vocalising it. Guruji understood.

'Well now that we have arrived at this conclusion, we have to implement this.' Turning to Ruby, Guruji said, 'There is no one better than you to execute this plan.' Ruby was startled for a minute, the others were also a bit surprised. But only for a moment. They were relieved too. All this was part and parcel of their life as warriors and protectors.

'Yes, Guruji,' Ruby bowed her head in acquiescence.

'All of you will have to sit together and work out a strategy. Poison will be provided to you as and when you ask for it.'

They didn't question that part of it as they knew that if Guruji wanted, more than enough poison would be made available in the Gurukul itself. Touching Guruji's feet, they left his cottage. Aishani gestured to Adheesh. He understood and took the boys in another direction to discuss their strategy. Aishani and Ruby went in the opposite direction and sat near the stream under a tree.

Aishani was all business now. She knew that Ruby was just a bit nervous.

'Ruby, I know that you have been out of practice in the last couple of months. But you are a determined and resilient girl. Nothing can keep you down. It's just that you have become a bit complacent. I think I know the reason too,' Aishani said softly and held her hand tenderly.

'I cannot keep any secrets from you Ash, but now is not the time, we'll talk about it some other time when we are fully relaxed. Right now, we have to formulate a plan to kill the demon junkies.'

'I know, Ruby, this is not the time. I don't know when we will be completely relaxed. We will have to steal time from our exacting schedules to talk and share our lives with each other like it was in earlier times.'

Ruby smiled tremulously. 'Let's get down to business, Ash. The boys will find out the hideouts of these human drug addicts and the places where the demon junkies visit them. We will procure blood from the blood banks and mix drugs like marijuana and heroin in them. The demons will find it easier and better to drink from bottles and packets. In the process I will ensnare them too. Once they have complete faith in me, I will give the poison-laced blood which will put an end to them immediately.'

Aishani nodded, 'Good strategy, Ruby. Let's find the boys and discuss the strategy with them,' she looked at Ruby and hesitated.

'Don't worry Ash,' Ruby too held her hand. 'There is nothing to worry about. My secret is our secret, and we shall discuss it as soon as we settle this matter.' Aishani was not assured, she wanted to talk some more, but the boys were coming towards them now.

Adheesh and the boys were all praises for Ruby's gameplan.

'Most of these human druggies are found on the outskirts of railway stations where they act as beggars. When they get money from people, they immediately go and buy their drugs.'

'This has to be done quickly, as these druggies are getting killed almost every other day,' Adheesh interjected.

'Don't worry, Adheesh; Ruby is fully capable of successfully executing her side of the exercise.'

They all kept quiet after that. Even though they now knew that Ruby was an apsara, a celestial nymph, they were uncomfortable with her human form doing this kind of work: seducing and entrapping the demons.

Aishani spoke out in the midst of the awkward silence, 'Uday, you will procure the drug-infused blood, which Ruby will pass on to the demons after making friends with them. Jayant, you will find out when and where these demons normally visit the drug addicts. Then on the final day, Uday will mix the poison in the blood bottles and Ruby will make sure that the demons drink it.'

Aishani had automatically taken on the role of their leader, and everybody accepted it as such. They knew that Aishani was their leader.

There was a lull in the activities of the Gurukul. Its former glory had been restored and it shone more than ever. There was no trace of the destruction and travails that the ashram had endured but the old-timers knew and exulted at its resurrection.

They felt their home had been renovated and had become better than its earlier avatar. One of the reasons could be that the true value of something is realised only after it is lost and then regained after much toil and hardship. Of course, young people like Adheesh and Aishani could not stop comparing the old with the new. Sometimes, in some places, the new was better designed and better placed than the old, but the new had yet to acquire the comfort level of the old. For instance, the huge trees which dotted the Gurukul were probably older than the Gurukul itself. Some of them had reached the end of their lives, but their dried-up physical forms were still there. Some of the trees had become gnarled and that was their beauty. The fauna was also the same. Guruji had used his powers to bring back almost all the animals and insects and birds burnt in the great fire.

Whenever they were free, Aishani and Adheesh would walk around the Gurukul and revel in its beauty and natural simplicity. They knew that despite the demons' total destruction of the ashram, there were some places which were so well protected that the demons were not even aware of their existence. Plus, these places were invisible.

They knew exactly how much hard work and planning had gone into restructuring the Gurukul and how the engineers, architects, biologists and so many others had painstakingly worked to rebuild it. Of course, all this could not have come to fruition without some stardust and without some divine help from Guruji. But all's well that ends well, they thought happily and contentedly. 'Till now', a voice whispered in Aishani's ears. She did not brush it aside as she knew what their destiny was and how they would spend the rest of their lives. She wouldn't have it any other way. The Gurukul was just a minute example of the determination and tenacity of man. Just as they had got rid of the demons inside the Gurukul, so they would get rid of the demons of this world and make it as pristine and blissful as it was in the Satya Yug. Or die trying.

Instinctively, they knew that a big crisis was brewing somewhere, they just didn't know where. They were not worried either. They had learned to enjoy themselves in the midst of danger. They did think about their past and planned for their future too, but willed themselves to enjoy every bit of their present. Guruji had blessed them with special meditative powers, which detached them from oncoming threats, giving them precious time to bask in each other's love and tenderness. They were fully aware that they had been using divine weapons too. While they did have a distinct memory of the smaller divine weapons and how they had used them, their memories were obliterated after they had used the more powerful and more destructive weapons. Their minds did not remember but in their bodies lingered memories of their assaults; it had taken quite a bit of time to adjust to their human bodies again. So be it.

Their instincts were right this time too.

After a couple of days, they got a message that Guruji had summoned them, not in his cottage but in the seniors' library. This was something new as Guruji always gave them instructions in his cottage. They guessed that these demons must be from very ancient times, and they would have to search for information about them in ancient texts.

The following day, the two reached the library half an hour early. They loved to browse here and the ancient texts returned their gesture. They went through some of the books, then went and sat on one of the corner tables favoured by Guruji.

As usual, Guruji did not waste any time when he reached the library. They touched his feet in reverence. Guruji blessed them and came straight to the point, 'There are some very disturbing intelligence reports which are not totally clear. Apparently, some demons have joined together and are planning a massive offensive on the Earth, one that could ultimately destroy the Earth itself. Now I know that both of you must be thinking, 'What's new about this? We have been fighting these demons from time immemorial'. Well the difference is that these demons are not from the time of Ramayana. Rather they are from a time much before that when Gods used to freely walk on Earth. There were great demons at that time also. Some of them used to pray to their deities for thousands of years to please their gods. Their god would then grant them boons or give them whatever their heart desired.

In this case, three brothers Tarakaksha, Vidyunmali and Kamalaksha who sort of wrangled this boon from Brahma, one of the holy trinity of Gods of our universe, that they will have three everlasting impregnable fortresses. They were the sons of the demon Tarakasura who had been killed by Lord Shiva's son Kartikeya. His three sons prayed to Brahma for 1,000 years standing on one leg. Impressed by their prayers and devotion, Brahma wanted to grant them a boon. They asked for immortality. After Brahma told them that nothing is everlasting on this Earth, they asked for three fortresses which could only be destroyed by a single arrow. They were great devotees of Lord Shiva and knew fully well that only Mahadev was capable of such a feat. In their overconfidence and pomposity, they thought that Lord Shiva would never harm them. Brahma granted them this boon. These cities were also of indubitable categories. They were constructed by the celestial demon Mayasur, who was also a great Shiva devotee. The lowest fortress had walls of iron and was located on Earth, the middle one had walls of silver and was in the sky and the third fortress had walls of gold and was located in heaven. These cities had the power to rove and so they never came in a single straight line and thus could not be destroyed by a single arrow. Only once in 1,000 years would they align in a single straight line when the Pushya Nakshatra would conjoin with the moon for a few moments. Pushya Nakshatra is the most auspicious time to perform any great task.

For some time, they stayed out of mischief but soon their inherently cruel demon character began resurfacing and they started torturing and killing humans and sages, even devtas. They destroyed the peace of all the worlds. The devtas were naturally very disturbed. They, along with their king Indra went to Brahma and beseeched him to take back his boon. Brahma refused but told them to go to Lord Shiva to help them. Mahadev heard them out and agreed to help. The devtas returned happily and amassed a great army to assist Mahadev. They began the war with the demons. However, the demons proved to have the upper hand, as they used all their magic powers which were stronger'.

Then one day the cities aligned, and Lord Shiva came on his chariot and stood in front of the demon army. Greatly relieved, the devtas watched breathlessly. But he just smiled, and all the three great cities or fortresses were destroyed simultaneously. Everybody was shocked; they knew that Mahadev was powerful, but they couldn't assimilate the thought that Mahadev destroyed the triple cities without even touching his bow and arrow. Then Brahma requested Mahadev to at least use his bow and arrow and show the world that he had won the battle fairly and squarely. Mahadev agreed and shot his arrow from the bow over the still burning cities. From that day onwards, Mahadev is also known as Tripurantkari or the destroyers of three cities. To cut a long story short, ultimately Lord Shiva did destroy these fortresses and the demons too in the process.'

Aishani and Adheesh were fascinated by the story. They waited long after Guruji had completed his story.

'So now Guruji, these demons or their descendants have come up again and we have to destroy them,' Aishani concluded.

'Not so fast, Aishani,' Guruji almost smiled. They also looked at each other and smiled. If the situation had been so clearcut, Guruji wouldn't have called them to this part of the library.

Guruji continued, 'These demons are not the runaway demons of the Ramayana. They are from times earlier than that. They had been demolished by Lord Shiva. But some blood descendants remained, biding their time, and strengthening themselves through the ages. In this interim period, the devtas and gods had already left the Earth and now the demons' only victims are hapless humans. So great is their desire for revenge that they are now planning to destroy Mother Earth herself. But God closes one window and opens another.'

After giving them the preliminary information, Guruji was all business now. 'Hopefully we have some time before they actually begin their annihilations', he said. 'Both of you will do some research on these three brothers and their antecedents. Adheesh, you are the only one who can read or at least understand a bit of these ancient languages. After thorough research, we will have to work out a strategy.'

'At present their descendants are quite well placed in society. One is a rich arms dealer, another is an architect and the third, though of the same blood, is an ascetic. Rumours are that he is a great tantric. Their names are Taranjit, Virendra and Vidya Bhushan.'

Guruji left them after giving this sketchy information. They looked at each other puzzled, not knowing where to start. But start they did. They worked feverishly for the next five days. By now, even the books had a fair idea of the time period of their research. So, whenever they crossed a bookshelf, the ancient texts of that period shone with a luminous beauty. They discovered that there was much more to the story than what Guruji had told them. The holy trinity of Brahma, Vishnu and Mahesh were involved in the destruction of the three cities or the fortresses and it was ultimately Shiva who destroyed all three along with the demons with only a smile. The devtas and the sages understood that the whole Universe was Mahadev's creation and that he could destroy it whenever he wished. They researched the whole day and night collecting information. The next day they presented their findings to Guruji.

Guruji nodded pensively, 'There is this problem that we will always have to face. These demons are the direct descendants of Tarakasura, though many times removed. The blood may have been diluted in the preceding centuries, but it is still the same demon blood, with cruel magic in it. Whereas you and your team, though blessed with special powers, at the end of the day, are still human beings.'

'Nevertheless Guruji, we have managed to kill innumerable demons.'

PINAKI

'These drug demons have to be destroyed immediately, before they kill any more human beings. All four of you have to be fully prepared mentally and physically before approaching them. In their intoxicated states they can be more than dangerous.' Tejas was listening to Aishani with rapt attention, 'You won't be there, Didi? And Adheesh Bhaiya too?'

Aishani smiled and ruffled his hair. 'No Tejas, we won't be there. All these three are more than capable of getting rid of the druggist demons, of course with lots of help from you. Without your paving the way for them, the work may become a bit tedious.' Tejas preened and the others smiled discreetly.

There was no need for Aishani and Adheesh to inform them of their whereabouts nor did it cross their minds to ask.

But Aishani and Adheesh were going on a sort of a retreat with Guruji. He was going to take them to a separate and sacred part of the forest where they would stay for a few days. It would be a sort of refresher course for them conducted by Guruji. Totally battered and emotionally broken, this was just the right time for them to recuperate. Guruji would fortify their faith in themselves, apart from teaching them a few more advanced mantras. Guruji reiterated the necessity of cleaning the mind of all thoughts, whether positive or negative, and turn it into a blank slate again. So imbedded was this strong sense of duty and responsibility that they always kept their personal life on the backburner. Guruji knew this that their powers would proliferate only when they were truly together. Not being a family man, rather being a brahmchari, Guruji did not pay much heed to the fact that a husband and wife had to have quality time with each other. This was brought to his notice by Aishani's mother Madhu who had visited Guruji a few days earlier. Guruji met her outside his cottage as he did not encourage women to meet him.

Madhu folded her hands in a Pranam. Guruji blessed her. She was an ex-warrior and was the wife of his most important pandit and faculty member, now deceased. But the paramount fact was that she was Aishani's mother. Madhu came straight to the point. Guruji was sitting on a bench outside his cottage, Madhu sat on a mat in front of him. This was the Guru-Shishya parampara. A shishya or pupil never sat above or at the same level with his guru, no matter who he or she was. Madhu was not a bona fide shishya, she was the wife of the senior most member of the faculty and Aishani's mother, but as far as hierarchy went, she was junior to Guruji.

'The children have gone through grueling times ever since they got married. I know some of them and I don't want to know about their other operations as that would make me more desperate to help them somehow,' Madhu said to Guruji.

'There is no one more superior to Aishani and Adheesh in this whole world,' Guruji concurred. 'So humble and so focused and blessed by Gods, we are indeed incredibly lucky to have them with us.'

'Yes Guruji, but there's a serious matter I wanted to discuss. In the course of their duties, both Adheesh and Ash have been hurt and scarred very badly physically, mentally, and emotionally. There has been no reprieve for them in the last so many months. Granted that they are blessed by Gods, and they have special powers, they are still human beings. They need rest, succour and caring, especially from each other. This is a fact which they themselves are not aware of and if there is any person they will listen to, it is you Guruji,' Madhu implored, teary-eyed.

If it was possible for Guruji to be shocked, then he was shocked. He had been directed by his Ishta Dev to rid the Earth of the menace of demons and through the centuries Guruji and his warriors had been judiciously doing their duty. But once in a while Guruji forgot that his warriors were humans, no matter how blessed they were. They needed love, soothing, emotional and physical respite. Of all his warriors, it was his best warriors Adheesh and Aishani who had gone through the most harrowing times. They needed rest much more than the others. Guruji nodded to Madhu, 'I am sorry

Madhu, please be assured that I will make it mandatory for them to take a break. I shall not send them for the next two missions too.'

Madhu folded her hands and made a gesture of touching Guruji's feet. No female was allowed to touch his feet. Guruji blessed her and she went home happy in the knowledge that her children will have some respite now.

That same evening, Ruby walked down an alley that led to the railway station. The station was accessible not just from the main roads, there were a couple of alleys too. She walked through one of the longer alleys, so narrow that she could stretch her arms and touch the walls on both the sides. The sound of the trains and various forms of public transport leading to the railway station ricocheted from one side of the wall to the other and light from a running train would reflect on the grey dirty walls festooned with splatters of paan and betel juice. There was darkness everywhere, but it was not pitch dark. There was some light coming from the two lamp posts casting their shadow. The alley smelt of garbage and urine.

These alleys were used by daily commuters as a short cut. They threw coins at these beggars or drug addicts sitting there. The drugs had taken over their minds, driving their bodies to unconscionable acts of depravity, forcing them to do anything to attain their next hit. They were almost melting into the darkness and stood around like walking corpses.

There was privacy here as compared to the main roads where it would have been difficult for both the drug addicts and the demons to lurk. Ruby was wearing simple clothes, but her beauty and sensuousness could not be disguised. The human junkies were too far gone to notice this; they spread out their hands like they did in front of every other passenger. Ruby gave them coins too. She walked towards the railway station and came back after ten minutes. Jayant and Uday were also sitting there dressed like beggars. Suddenly Jayant gestured to Ruby with his eyes. Ruby looked in that direction. A tall, dark and slim man had just entered the alley. He walked slowly towards the beggars and began throwing money at them casually. The human junkies were obviously in their drug-induced stupor but still had a small iota of awareness left to recognise that money would give them their nirvana again. The man looked around cautiously. In the present century, even a demon could not be careful enough. If caught, a frenzied crowd could very quickly kill them also or at least batter them badly. His eyes met Ruby's and she smiled sweetly at him.

Even the great sages had been unable to resist apsaras, then who was this lowly demon whose life was guided by lust and drugs. For a minute he forgot why he was there. He stood straighter and stared at Ruby. As he looked into her eyes, he knew that all the beauty in the universe could not compete with this beautiful flower in front of him. Passion had turned her eyes into orbs of red fire and in them he read camaraderie and lust.

Uday and Jayant were hiding behind pillars ready to attack if any harm came to Ruby. Uday's eyes had turned black, signifying that he was ready to kill. Jayant motioned him to be still and quiet. Ruby was not in danger. The demon was beginning to fall into her trap. Ruby passed the demon and sat down on a stool nearby. The demon caught a whiff of her fragrance and was immediately intoxicated. Following her like a lost puppy, he went and sat on a broken drum lying near her. Ruby took out something from her tote and showed it to the demon. It was a dirty bottle filled with blood. She unscrewed the cap. The heady smell of strong marijuana wafted to his nostrils. The demon was on fire and indisputably in seventh heaven. A beautiful woman throwing musk at him and marijuana-infused blood literally at his disposal. He looked at the junkies, then looked at Ruby, his eyes asking a question. She held up the bottle and nodded.

'Why wrestle out the blood from these junkies with the fear of being caught when I have it here,' Ruby spat in disgust at the druggies. She took a long swig of the drug-infused blood and passed it on to the demon. Almost shaking with eager anticipation, the demon nearly snatched the bottle from Ruby's hand and took long gulps from the bottle, then very reluctantly gave the bottle back to Ruby. He shuffled nearer to her.

'What is your name?' Ruby asked, throwing some more rakshasi odour towards him and handing him the bottle again.

'Somasur,' he croaked in a whisper. The heady mixture of the marijuana and Ruby's essence had made him incapable of any sound or movement. Ruby sat with him for some time, then started to leave when the bottle of blood was depleted. She had been very cleverly taking a large swig of the blood and immediately let it flow back in the bottle without the demon noticing it. She had practised it many times before. Nevertheless, she knew that she would have to drink a part of the putrid concoction to allay the demon's suspicion.

'I will come tomorrow again at this time,' she whispered, reassuring him when he protested. Ruby left. Uday and Jayant came out of their hiding place and went after Ruby. Uday's pupils were still black, filled with rage and hatred. The demon Somasur was too far gone to protest any more. The strong dose of marijuana would last him for almost fourteen hours, after which he would begin remembering the incidents of the previous night. His craving for drug-infused blood and hankering for the beautiful Ruby would overpower him again and he would again rush towards the railway station alley.

Next day, there was another demon with him. Ruby had anticipated this and had brought two bottles of drug-infused blood. She was looking more beautiful than last time. This was repeated the next two days. The demons had totally fallen for her and were completely under her spell. The fourth day was the most crucial day. Uday gave her two bottles, one had blood and marijuana and the other had blood, marijuana, and the poison. They were told to be extra careful as this was one of the strongest poisons in the world, as strong as polonium, the deadliest toxin on Earth. Ruby was calm and composed. She had dealt with more alarming situations earlier and was ready to meet this one head on.

As usual, the demon Somasur was eagerly waiting for Ruby after hurriedly throwing coins at the human beggar junkies for otherwise they would have created a shindig. He then went and sat beside Ruby and inhaled her special perfume. Ruby took out two bottles of blood and gave one to Somasur and the second bottle of blood to the other demon. Her body smelled of musk and roses. There was no reason for the demons to be suspicious, for she always drank with them. Uday and Jayant tensed up.

Smiling, the unsuspecting Somasur and his friend each took a big gulp of the blood, then they quickly drank half the bottle. Ruby was ready. She snatched the bottle from their hands before it could drop on the ground and closed it immediately. Uday and Jayant were there in a flash. They watched the fallen demons on the ground, holding their throats, gurgling, and writhing in myriad shades of agony. They now held their hearts too, there was the sound of their ribs cracking like twigs. Blood came out of their eyes and they vomited their guts out. The human junkies were too far gone to notice anything, as yet. Throwing up was a commonplace occurrence here. In a matter of minutes, the demons' convulsions stopped, and they became still. Uday herded his team together and they left immediately. Nobody was any the wiser. Most of them were junkies anyway. One or two other people who had entered the alley from the railway station did not notice anything amiss. They just saw a few commuters going towards the railway station and a few drug addicts lying on the ground in intoxicated states.

'Adheesh, you are a human. Humans do not have the physical or mental strength or power to use any celestial weapon. But since Gods and devtas have left the Earth, many malevolent and dangerous demons with supernatural powers have been left behind. The onus is on human beings to fight the demons and save the Earth. The most important thing here is to not fall into the trap of complacency. Every new demon must be faced with new eyes and a new way of destroying it. You have discovered that the descendants of Tarakaksha, Vidyunmali and Kamalaksha can be killed only by the bow and arrow of Bhagwan Shiva, even that at a certain time.'

Aishani and Adheesh had returned from their much-required vacation. They didn't want to go anywhere. Being in the Gurukul gave them most peace and happiness. But Guruji was adamant, so they went to a nearby resort. Guruji was right, as always. Away from all their travails and tensions, they could relax in each other's company. Though things were not exactly the same. They were together, but Adheesh was in Einar's body and Aishani was finding it difficult to accept him in this persona. They rested, but after a few days, they went back. They were not as comfortable with each other as earlier.

Guruji had welcomed them and sent them straight to the seniors' library to research on the demon Tarkasur's progeny. Fortunately, there was plenty of material on the deceased demon and his descendants.

'Guruji,' Aishani could not hold her excitement anymore. Adheesh too wanted to inform Guruji about the great revelation, but he allowed Aishani to take centre stage. Guruji looked questioningly at Aishani. She almost blurted out, 'Guruji, the three structures can be destroyed only when they come in a straight line when Pushya Nakshatra aligns itself with the moon. We know now that this happens only in about 1,000 years, that too for a split second. This alignment will take in a month's time from now.' She was thrilled and agitated at the same time. 'Adheesh was destined to kill and annihilate these demons and their citadels!' she declared loftily.

'Yes, beta and Adheesh has been praying and reciting the

Shiva mantras without a break since the last three months. Lord Shiva is also known as Bholenath or one who is easily persuaded and grants boons, otherwise even lifetimes are not enough to reach even the lowest levels of Lord Shiva's enlightenment. You have been praying alongside Adheesh to boost his powers. Without you giving your powers to Adheesh, killing these demons will not be possible.'

'Yes Guruji,' Aishani kept her head down. Though their superpowers were finely demarcated, for Aishani there was no difference. She knew that it was the same for Adheesh.

'It is their middle brother, Virendra the architect, who has conceptualised and built the three mansions or rather fortresses in three different locations. These mansions have been constructed in such a way over a huge fulcrum that they keep moving slowly on their own axis twenty-four hours. They are much more than state-of-the-art complexes. They rotate 360 degrees and sway from left to right and right to left all at the same time. Our intelligence report says that there could be huge labs and secret chambers in these complexes, though this is not fully confirmed. These citadels are so far away from the main cities that the locals are not aware of these mansions.' Adheesh apprised Guruji and Aishani of this phenomenon.

Whatever little time Adheesh had after his pujas and rituals, he would spend with the intelligence experts of the ashram, gathering and sifting through all these reports. Of course, there could be no gap in the puja, even for the smallest period. Whenever Adheesh was occupied in research with the experts, Aishani compensated by meditating and reciting mantras on behalf of Adheesh. She was more blessed for it too.

And when both of them had to be away for a short period, there was a senior pundit to carry on the rituals. This senior pundit had no idea of the sheer magnitude of the operation. For him, it was just a routine prayer for Mahadev or Lord Shiva on behalf of Adheesh, which was carried out in the Gurukul from time to time.

'Where are these complexes, Adheesh?' Aishani enquired.

'That again is a fascinating fact,' Adheesh remarked, 'These three brothers have their fiefdoms in different parts of the country. This fact in itself is not remarkable. What is remarkable is that even though they are in different states, these fortresses are in a straight line. They are in three states of the country. The lowest is in Tamilnadu, the middle one is in Madhya Pradesh and the highest one is between the mountains of Kashmir.'

The discussion was taking place in Guruji's cottage. Time was running out. Hurriedly, Adheesh gave a brief on all the smaller observations and their conclusions. There was not much left to discuss now except for the burning question. These three descendants of the demons Tarakaksha, Vidyunmali and Kamalaksha carried the boons of their ancestors in their blood till date. Even with their watered-down genetic code, they had enough power to destroy more than the Earth. They waited for Guruji to elaborate his strategy.

After mulling for a couple of minutes Guruji declared, 'These demons' ancestors had been destroyed by the mighty bow Pinaki or the Shiv Dhanush of Lord Shiva. So, will it be this time too.'

They were stupefied, staring at Guruji in awe and

wonderment. They had read all about the divine bow of Lord Shiva and they also knew that it no longer existed on Earth as it had been lifted and broken by Bhagwan Ram before his swayamvar or marriage to Sita. The name of the bow was Pinaki and it was so heavy that no humans could lift it. Some legends claimed its weight to be 21,000 kilograms. It was made by the celestial architect Vishwakarma with the densest material in the universe, the Neutron star.

'Guruji, even if Lord Shiva were to permit its one-time use, it cannot be done as the bow has already been broken by Bhagwan Ram. Notwithstanding that, even if the great Pinaki was here on Earth, we together with all our supernatural strength will not be able to pick it up, forget about using it,' Adheesh said worriedly. 'There has to be another way.'

'There is a great misconception that Bhagwan Ram broke the Pinaki. It is Mahadev's Trishul which he used all the time. It is indestructible. The bow given to Raja Janak, Sita's father, was not the Pinaki, but it was a Shiv Dhanush, which again was one of the strongest bow and arrow in the Universe.'

Though they were quite surprised by this revelation, they were not shocked. The explanation made sense. The next few days, Guruji took Adheesh to task which Adheesh underwent willingly. The mantras which he chanted were now changing him physically and visibly. Adheesh had become very dark and grown much taller and more muscular in the last one month. His hair and nails had grown very rapidly. Aishani would trim them every day. Guruji had cast an invisible shroud over Adheesh so that nobody was able to see him. Even here in the Gurukul, where everybody saw and assimilated the supernatural phenomena which happened so regularly, people would have been shocked by the changes in Adheesh's appearance. Innocent people would have talked, and the story could have reached the demons.

They had been teleported to this part of Tamilnadu three days earlier. Guruji was also with them. All three of them had to familiarise themselves with the place and Guruji had pinpointed the exact place from where Adheesh would fire the destroyer arrow. It was not the Pinaki, but it was not just any bow and arrow of this world. It was huge but not so huge that it would attract too much attention. It was made of an undefined and unrecognised metal. It shone with a dull coppery glaze. There weren't many embellishments on it. More or less, it looked like any common bow and arrow which a drama company would use. A layman could not even begin to imagine the mayhem which it was going to unleash in the next couple of hours. But Guruji, Adheesh and Aishani knew.

Aishani looked at Adheesh with consternation and with pride also. Pride, because he was the only warrior in centuries to be bestowed with the honour of using a Shiv Dhanush on the lines of the great Pinaki, and consternation because there would be a heavy price to pay for this blessing and his transformation into something other than a human being, a higher self. Aishani knew that it would take him months to revert to his human self. That would be an extremely sick period for Adheesh. She also knew from past experience that both of them would never have it any other way. Their mission was to remove demons from the face of the Earth, and they would gladly do it again and again.

They were standing behind Adheesh. They were on a sort of hillock covered with shrubs and small trees. Good for them, as they didn't want to attract any attention. Another fact in their favour was that it was almost midnight and there was nobody around. Adheesh wasn't aware of their existence. He didn't look human at all. Nor did he look like God. He was somewhere in between and at the moment totally focused on the work before him. In a few minutes, the Pushya Nakshatra was going to align itself with the moon for a few seconds. At this time, these mansions would come in a straight line. Adheesh had the bow and arrow which was blessed by Mahadev. Which was more than enough for Adheesh, the human warrior.

Both Aishani and Adheesh had toiled very hard to reach this stage, though this time it would be Adheesh and his bow which would bring about the ultimate destruction. On Guruji's instructions they had prayed together and many of Aishani's shaktis or powers had shifted to Adheesh temporarily.

Through the ages even the powers of the demons had dissipated quite a bit. So it was almost a fair match as far as powers were concerned. Intelligence experts of the Gurukul were already stationed in Madhya Pradesh and Jammu and Kashmir with their equipment to monitor the demolition of these complex structures. Now the only thing left was to pull the arrow from the bow.

It would be any moment now. Adheesh was waiting with a steely focus and patience. There was no sign of any anxiety or stress. Seconds before the Pushya nakshatra was to align with the moon, Guruji gave the signal to Adheesh. Aishani was a very strong woman but still her heart was in her mouth.

Very calmly, Adheesh picked up the huge bow, strung it with his arrow and pulled. Within seconds there was a roar of fire which could be seen for miles around. They could hear the sounds of carnage and destruction from where they were standing. They knew that some people around that area must have seen or heard the sound of the explosion. But by the time they recovered from the shock, the whole structure had disappeared, and they would be left wondering if they had imagined or if it was just a hair-raising, horrifying dream. There was nothing left to do now but wait for news of the other two structures.

They turned towards Guruji, who was in deep meditation under a tree. They knew that he was in telepathic communication with the intelligence people in the other two states. Guruji did not open his eyes or speak for a long time. They waited, though according to their calculations, they should have got the news of the annihilations immediately. Aishani was getting worried for Adheesh now. The process of reverting back to being a human would take a heavy toll, both of them knew that. They had to reach the Gurukul as fast as they could. They had to return the powers of the bow and arrow before the memory of this phenomenon was wiped out from their consciousness. Adheesh had to return the powers in this consciousness itself.

Finally, Guruji opened his eyes, looked at them and nodded. Heaving a sigh of relief, they began preparing to go back.

The Brahmin Demons

Adheesh was still recuperating from the Pinaki episode. His body was gradually returning to normal. Now that he had become human again, the episode had been completely obliterated from his mind, but his body remembered its larger-than-life size and the vast amount of adrenaline flowing through it. Suddenly it seemed hollow, like a shell. There was no adrenaline, his body was shrinking in spurts and the pain was crushing. Aishani had become his shadow; in fact, she was like a fixture in his room in the Vaidyashala. Guruji and Aishani were the only two people who knew what Adheesh had accomplished and what he was going through. But demons and time do not wait for anybody. Very pressing issues had started building up again but it was impossible to shake Aishani from Adheesh's side.

Guruji sighed. Not being a married and domesticated man, he did not really understand this chemistry and love between two individuals, but he always gave in where this pair was concerned. This time when he visited Adheesh in the Vaidyashala, he took along some books from the senior library and gave them to Aishani. She was surprised and touched by this gesture.

'Both of you can read these books whenever you feel like it,' Guruji stated.

'Yes, Guruji,' Aishani answered gratefully. There were times when she did feel a bit lonely when Adheesh was resting or sleeping. Adheesh was not allowed to talk too much.

'I'll read to Adheesh, maybe he'll perk up a bit,' she articulated softly. Both of them knew that at this stage his brain could not bear too much excitement. His brain was too muddled at the moment.

'These books are mainly for you, beta,' Guruji said quietly, 'Negative forces have begun building up again. Adheesh is not fully in his senses as yet, hence I had to send Uday to Pushkar.'

'Okay Guruji, but why has Uday gone there?'

'Initially, Adheesh was supposed to go to Pushkar but now that is out of the question. Hence, I had to send the next best warrior. Time was of crucial importance. Our warrior had to be there on Kartik Purnima.

'Read these books beta, you will understand everything,' Guruji instructed, then as an afterthought he added, 'Adheesh doesn't need to be involved in this, you will be able to execute this stint on your own.'

Aishani was curious but did not ask Guruji any questions. If he wanted to tell her anything more, he would have done so earlier. She seated herself on the chair beside Adheesh's bed. Devnath had tried to make her as comfortable as possible. Besides the three of them, it was only Devnath who had an inkling of Adheesh's afflictions and sufferings. He was not allowed in this part of the Vaidyashala, but he pestered Aishani so much that she put in a word for Devnath to Guruji, who in turn spoke to the Vaidyas, who very reluctantly allowed Devnath to visit Adheesh every alternate day for half an hour. Aishani sighed. Dear Devnath, since he was banned from doing anything for Adheesh, he tried to make himself useful by looking after Aishani in the short time that he was there. He placed a comfortable single-seater sofa for her near Adheesh's bed along with a lamp on a small table. He made arrangement for her herbal tea. Thankfully there was an electric connection there, to be used only in dire emergencies.

She settled down on the sofa and listlessly began turning the pages of the books which Guruji had brought for her. Adheesh was asleep. He would sleep for more than twenty-two hours of the day, getting up only when woken up for medicines or eating or ablutions.

These books were about some demons who liked to eat the brains of children and weak people, then drink the blood from their skulls and finally wear their intestines around their neck and flaunt these in a macabre dance. She shuddered. Years of killing innumerable number of demons had still not made her immune to the abhorrent and gruesome preferences of the demons.

She picked up one of the newspapers that Devnath would religiously bring for her. Listlessly, she went through it. The papers too consistently presented a gory picture of the country and the world at large. Lately, she had begun following the story of an endemic which had struck one of the Indian states in the East. Children had started falling sick. Doctors were working round the clock but could not cure the children. In the beginning it was not a cause for alarm, but gradually uneasiness began setting in as children began dying and the numbers kept increasing. The whole country was in an uproar. In a poor hamlet in one of the states, infants and children had begun dying. In the beginning it was not alarming, as sometimes young children do succumb to various diseases. But the death rate surged at an alarming pace and in a matter of weeks things went totally out of hand. The government was alarmed. The opposition was leaving no stone unturned in holding the government responsible and maligning it. There were so many deaths that the single lone hospital could not face the onslaught of so many gruesome killings and seemingly natural deaths. Babies and children were just dying of what the doctors claimed was Brain Fever. Bereft and distraught parents and relatives of the dead children were still in shock and flocked to the hospital. The administration knew that very soon the grief would turn into rage and then retaliations would begin. There would be mayhem and chaos in the village. The hospital and its staff would become their victims. Not knowing how to channel their anguish, the grief-stricken villagers had begun thinking of attacking the hospital staff. Sensing this, two of the doctors had made themselves scarce. Of course, the government sent immediate replacements, but the situation had escalated to alarming proportions.

Aishani gasped as a realisation hit her. Undoubtedly, Guruji would not just give her any book on any subject. There was never any coincidence with Guruji. She could join the dots now. So, these children were dying because demons called Brahmrakshasas were killing and eating them. They would eat their brains first, she surmised and shuddered at the thought. God knows what else they did to the bodies after that. They wouldn't have been able to do everything which was written in the ancient texts as it was not possible in the present time and context. But enough harm had been done. One thing was certain now, these demons were devouring the brains of the children, if not the rest of the body.

Guruji had given her this responsibility and she had to immediately put a halt to the morbid and repulsive activities. She buried her head in the pages of the books, this time with full concentration. She learnt that there were chants to ward off the Brahmrakshasas. They were not very unfamiliar to Aishani. She had learned similar chants to ward off other evil beings. But there were a few catches here. The Brahmrakshasas were highly intelligent and aware beings. In the ancient ages before they became Brahmrakshasas, they used to be erudite Brahmin scholars who became avaricious and began exploiting even the lowest of the lower classes in the most inhuman ways. They were cursed universally and consequently they became Brahmrakshasas (Brahmins who became Rakshasas). Thus, they became more treacherous and malicious. But they retained one quality: their scholarly brain and their sharp ability to grasp any text or mantra within seconds. They could imbibe and memorise any mantra or verse spoken by another person. Hence any mantra to ward off these Brahmrakshasas became redundant because after hearing these mantras, they would chant them loudly in such a knowledgeable but garbled manner that the chanter would get confused and forget his own verses. Aishani sat up the whole night reading the ancient text on the Brahmrakshasas. She spent the next two days reading the books and memorising the Brahmrakshasas' mantras.

Uday returned from Pushkar on the third day. Torn between looking after Adheesh and going out to destroy the Brahmrakshasas, Aishani nevertheless left Adheesh in Guruji's and Devnath's care.

'Bhabhi,' Devnath addressed her when he saw her distress on leaving Adheesh, 'You know I will care and protect him with my life. Bhaiya will not come to any harm. The Vaidyas here are the best and Guruji is here. He will recover slowly and surely.' Aishani felt a pang of guilt, she had seen Devnath at work when their Gurukul was destroyed and then his painstaking work on Kailash. In many ways he could be a better nurse than her, except for Adheesh and Aishani's natural chemistry. She sighed, 'I know Devnath, it's just that I don't want to leave him. I have made a list of the chores that you have to do while looking after Adheesh. Please follow it to the dot.'

'Yes, Bhabhi,' Devnath was equally serious. Even the most trifling point in Adheesh's care was taken as an order written on stone. The rest was done by the Vaidyas and Guruji.

Aishani and Uday first went to Guruji's cottage to take his blessings and some more briefing. They travelled by train and reached the said village the next morning. Uday had his weapons in a strong shoulder bag, otherwise they were travelling light.

No one on seeing them would have been able to fathom the vast powers which the weapons possessed. Instead, they just saw an average-looking man and woman, the man with a grim expression on his face and the woman anxious to reach their destination. In any case, the villagers were not interested in any comings or goings, they were too distraught with their own grief and misfortunes. There was no place in the only lodge in the village, it was too full of the relatives of the villagers who had lost their children. Undaunted, Aishani and Uday went around the village and then sat under the shade of a tree. It was like a haunted village. They had heard of haunted houses but this was a full haunted village. There were sounds of crying and wailing from almost every second house of the village. They tried to approach a few villagers, but nobody could tell them anything except that the children died after a mild fever, either at home or in the hospital. They went to the hospital after some time. That too did not yield any results or give them any clue of the whereabouts of the Brahmrakshasas. The children had died either inside their houses or while playing outside in the meandering lanes of the village or in the lone hospital. They left the hospital and sat under a tree.

'Why did you go to Pushkar, Uday?' Aishani asked. Guruji had told her that Uday had been sent there for a specific reason.

'These Brahmrakshasas are so intelligent and so unnaturally strong that mantras have no effect on them. They were highly knowledgeable Brahmins in their past births. As such they have full knowledge of all the mantras of the world and also how to defile them or make them powerless. When you recognise them and begin chanting the mantras, they will do everything in their power to make them redundant. In that case we won't be able to destroy them. The trick here is that you chant your mantras in such a way that they do not emulate you and your mantras weaken them. I come in the picture after this. I immediately destroy them with my special weapons,' Uday informed her.

'What are these weapons, Uday? I didn't get a chance to see them, they must be pretty special if they can kill Brahmrakshasas. Are they divine weapons?' Aishani was curious.

'No Ash, no way are these celestial weapons. I have not been blessed to use celestial weapons, at least in this birth. These are traditional weapons of war, but they have been imbued with special powers. Guruji had sent me to Pushkar for this purpose. If you remember, Kartik Purnima was just a few days back. With some special chants on the night of Kartik Purnima, these weapons are dipped in the waters of the Pushkar lake and left there for the night. By next morning, their powers will have magnified to such an extent that no demon can withstand them.'

'So, what's the catch, Uday?' Aishani was the more experienced one of the two.

Uday could not suppress his smile, 'Yes of course Ash, there has to be a catch: Once you begin using a certain kind of weapon, you will have to keep on using it. The moment you pause, the powers diminish, and the weapon becomes an ordinary weapon and hence powerless against the Brahmrakshasas. The weapon becomes strong again, but it has to be prayed to for some time. It's like charging an electronic device. But by the time the weapon gets charged, it would be too late, and the game would be over.'

Aishani nodded, 'That is why you have a number of weapons with you. If you have to give breathing space to one weapon then you can use another fully charged one,' Uday acknowledged with a nod of his head.

'First we will have to search for the places where these Brahmrakshasas have made their base. It was written in the books that after becoming Brahmrakshasas from human beings, they cannot rest anywhere in the normal way. Hence, they themselves devised a means to relax and rest in a place after their gory orgies. They began taking refuge in trees on the outskirts of villages and towns. Since they could not lie down under the trees, they took to hanging upside down like bats from the branches of trees. They don't have noses too. We'll begin our search from there only and we have to do it very quickly too,' Aishani stated emphatically.

'Does not having noses signify anything, Aishani?' queried Uday.

'I don't know Uday, I think the Brahmrakshasas cannot chant through their noses because they don't have noses.'

Uday was a bit perplexed by this answer, but he decided not to pursue it, 'Anyway, I don't think there are any more children to feed upon, maybe just a handful are left. The Brahmrakshasas may decide to leave this village for fresher pastures. We have to expedite our search.'

They started walking towards the periphery of the village. It was a dusty settlement made dirtier by neglect and indifference. The brain sickness which everybody had started calling it or the Brahmrakshasas did not spare any caste or creed. And often, it was the lower classes' children who were caught, because both the parents would go to work leaving the children behind unattended or in the charge of a slightly older sibling. With no adult to look after them, these children would come out of their houses and play in the bylanes of the village. Many of the Brahmrakshasas' victims were unattended children. Now their parents had gone berserk with grief and were either thronging the hospital or just sitting around listlessly. Since the cleaners had stopped work, the whole village had become filthy, especially the outskirts of the village where most of the garbage was dumped. The village seemed to be surrounded by an open garbage pit, it stank so much.

Uday covered his nose in distaste, 'Just the right place for a demon to be. They are filth and would love to stay in filth.'

'No Uday, remember they were erudite scholars and Brahmins in their previous births. Even though they have become Brahmrakshasas because of their greed and avarice, they still perform their morning ablutions with absolute cleanliness. We won't find them in these garbage dumps.'

'So, do we go back inside the village and search for them?'

'No Uday, we will find them somewhere here only. They cannot sleep on the ground. They will find trees with large branches to hang onto for sleeping. They are cursed to sleep upside down like bats. Even I am not very sure of where to look for them. Maybe if we cross the outskirts of the village we might come across large trees.'

Uday nodded. Snooping and searching were not his strong points. His job was just destroying the evil and protecting his leader Aishani.

Sure enough, there were many large trees approximately a mile from the village which had grown to banyan tree proportions. An immense bulky tree stood in front of them. They could not recognise the species. It had huge branches with dangling green slimy mossy vines. Its massive trunk was gnarled and twisted. There were many other such trees but this one stood out menacingly and ominously, its vines beckoning them.

'Yes,' Aishani whispered. 'I'm sure they are here, I can feel their presence, though we cannot see them as yet nor can I make out how many of them are there in these trees.'

'Okay,' Uday whispered back. 'You begin your mantras, I'll guard you.'

If Aishani was missing Adheesh, she did not show her feelings, but Uday knew and sadness enveloped him for a moment. He had always loved Aishani, though Aishani was not even aware of his existence in that sense—her world began and ended with Adheesh. Uday knew this very well and he never crossed this boundary, nor did he ever let Aishani know of his love for her. Only two people knew of this unrequited love: one was Guruji and the other was his sister Ruby.

The next instant he was all business, scanning the trees for demons. Aishani unrolled her Kusha grass mat and sat on it. She sprinkled the area around her with Gangajal and sprinkled the holy water on herself. Settling down, she began chanting the Narsimha mantra. The Narsimha mantra had been specially formulated by the great sages to get rid of Brahmrakshasas and evil Yakshas. When she began chanting the mantra, her voice was a whisper and then it gradually rose. So much so that very soon the area around her was filled with her crystal-clear voice. This sound was barely registering on Uday as he was completely focused on his lookout for the Brahmrakshasas and protecting Aishani. But after some time, he noticed an imperceptible change in Aishani's intonation of the mantras. He did not pay much attention because he knew that Aishani was the best and knew exactly what she was doing. But he gradually came to realise that Aishani was having some difficulty in chanting. He looked at her with concern. The mantras seemed to be garbled, incomprehensible. With his knowledge of mantras, he could see that what she was chanting was not a pure mantra. The mantras were somehow getting distorted. Distinctly disturbed now, Aishani opened her eyes. Uday now knew positively that the Brahmrakshasas were here or nearby. His eyes met Aishani's. She gestured him to keep quiet and continue with his guarding.

Uday knew that the Brahmrakshasas were familiar with the Narsimha mantra. If they allowed Aishani to successfully chant the mantra, then they would be deprived of their powers and would soon die of hunger. Hence, they were disturbing her in their own way by copying her chant and repeating it loudly in a garbled manner. Though the mantras were the same, a flick here and a flick there in the intonation and accent was totally distorting the strength and meaning of the mantra. He was getting worried and anxious. Very soon Aishani's voice completely changed. She was chanting her mantras in a sing-song way. They did not seem to be coming out from her mouth. Concerned, he turned back and looked at her. Her mouth was closed but she was clearly chanting the mantras. He was confused but only for a minute. Realisation dawned on him. Aishani was chanting from her nose.

The sounds were truly clear and pure, except that there was a nasal twang emanating from the sounds. He smiled in admiration. Speaking from the nose was no ordinary feat. It required years of hard practice to speak through the nose, but this was Aishani who could do anything if she put her mind to it. He beamed with pride. The sounds of the chanting were noticeably clear now because the Brahmrakshasas could not imitate and replicate her anymore. It was so simple that he had to smile. The Brahmrakshasas did not have noses. This was their curse and they had paid for it in other places and other ages also.

Suddenly, he heard a thud as if a body had fallen on the ground. Immediately, more bodies fell on the ground. Uday whirled around. His eyes widened. Huge, horrible, and fierce-looking demons had fallen on the ground because of their weakened state. The Narsimha mantra had greatly weakened them; nevertheless, they were still strong enough to kill human beings. They had a boon that they could not be killed by ordinary weapons. They could only be killed by weapons which were dipped in the holy water of Pushkar lake on Kartik Purnima. But they dared not go near Aishani. If she could speak through her nose, then God knows what else she could do.

There was no one more cold-blooded killer than Uday. The sanctified and supercharged weapons were in both his hands. Without waiting for a moment, Uday began slashing out any which way. Though the strength of the Brahmrakshasas had depleted considerably, they were game enough to fight a good battle. But in their weakened stage they were no match for Uday and his mystical weapons. In a matter of minutes, the whole area under the tree was a gory mass of limbs, flesh, blood and bones. There was no fear in the Brahmrakshasas, they wanted to fight but in their weakened state they could just totter and weakly swipe at Uday and get killed. If there was even a momentary pause, the weapon lost its power. Dropping the old weapon, Uday would exchange it with a new weapon with the speed of lightning and continue with the slaughter and carnage.

Silence descended suddenly. No more bodies fell from the trees. The number of the Brahmrakshasas residing in that tree were too many to be counted on fingertips. But Uday was ready with another set of weapons in his hands and Aishani too continued with the chants. Only when they were completely sure that there were no Brahmrakshasas alive did Uday keep the weapons in his bag and Aishani stopped chanting.

They picked up their belongings and left for the railway station. Aishani had again reverted to being an anxious and worried wife. She wanted to reach the Gurukul as soon as possible and be beside Adheesh. She fretted that they had to wait for one hour for the train. Uday noticed everything. With a deadpan expression, he sat beside her on the train and then dropped her to the Gurukul.

Within two days it began coming out in the newspapers that the doctors and the government had been successful in controlling the fatal disease and completely obliterating it. Aishani and Uday had executed the whole operation silently with the country none the wiser.

RESURRECTION

Aishani had been waiting for months for Adheesh's body to recuperate. Finally, the day came when Guruji called Aishani to his cottage. Her heart palpitating, she sat in front of Guruji. They all knew that Guruji was an ascetic and indifferent to human emotions. But sometimes the circumstances were so overwhelming that even a stoic like Guruji became involved. She waited for Guruji to say something. She knew it was about the soul exchange between Adheesh's and Einar's bodies. 'Please Mata,' she mentally prayed to Maa Durga, 'Please make the transfer successful.'

For the first time, she felt that Guruji was at a loss for words, but she brushed the thought aside. Finally, Guruji spoke, 'We have done all that we could have done for Adheesh's body and we have been successful too.

His body has healed very well even though there was no soul to nurture it. The real test will be day after tomorrow when the transfer of souls will take place.'

Her heart missed a beat again. 'What test? He was Guruji. Guruji cannot make any mistakes!' She looked down lest Guruji see the terror and turmoil in her eyes.

'Does he know?' she blurted unthinkingly.

'Who? Adheesh?' Guruji asked, not really approving of her question. Aishani couldn't help herself. She knew very well that Adheesh's soul was in Einar's body, and she had been trained to recognise souls, but a part of her brain had always resisted Adheesh in Einar's body. She kept quiet.

'Yes beta, he knows,' Guruji said softly, 'He has to know, the whole exercise involves him and only him. He probably did not share with you as you no longer look at him with the same eyes. Anyway, your tension and anxiety will be over now. You will get your partner back but you will again lose an exceptionally good friend.'

She had tears in her eyes, 'Yes Guruji,' she said hoarsely, 'Nobody can replace Einar. We never had a more committed warrior than him. It seems that he came here specially to sacrifice his life for Adheesh.'

Guruji nodded, 'So be it, this is all Prabhu's maya; mere human beings are incapable of understanding it.'

Aishani had an inkling that Guruji knew more than he was telling her, but that was Guruji's way. He would tell her when the time came.

Next day, she reached the hospice of the Gurukul, a series of long low buildings around manicured lawns. Very few people in the Gurukul were aware of its existence as it was surrounded by an invisible wall. This was where the highest levels of Yagnas were performed and many other Tantric and Vedic rituals too. The soul transference would also take place here. The hospice was beside the Gurukul river—they called it their river because it was visible only inside the Gurukul. Nobody knew where it came from and where it went. Initially, some people did show curiosity, but questions were not encouraged, so they left it at that. Anyway, the river was part of the magic of the whole Gurukul. The greenery around here was looked after by efficient gardeners and biologists. It was not allowed to grow of its own free will. This was a hospice, everything had to be spick and span, even the air seemed to be cleaner and sweeter than the rest of the Gurukul. Peace and quiet prevailed.

There were only a few people in the room: Guruji, Aishani and a few highly qualified Vaidyas and Pandits. Adheesh's body was lying on a bed and now Einar was lying on the next bed. Only the extremely close circle knew what was going to happen. Aishani had mixed emotions. There was extreme happiness that after months of medication and treatments along with Guruji's tantric rituals and yagnas, Adheesh's body had finally recovered. It was a herculean task even for Guruji. Adheesh's soul was not in his body, there was nothing to hold on to the treatments, the body on its own just could not respond to medication or it would at best become a zombie-like creature known as Betaal. But that was not the purpose. The purpose was to make his body fully intact and perfect, in other words inhabitable again. And today the soul repossession would take place.

Both Adheesh and Aishani were understandably disconcerted and sad. They were elated that Adheesh would get his body back now, but they were grieving that their dear friend Einar would be gone forever. True, Einar had died when the Manticore had so viciously struck him. His soul had passed but at least his body was with them, fully functional. What a dilemma. With Adheesh's soul leaving his body, it would just be a non-functional shell and would have to be cremated. They didn't want that, but they wanted it too.

With these conflicting thoughts, Aishani sat in a corner of the room trying to be as unobtrusive as possible. Guruji began his ritual with the havan. This was quite a different havan with special offerings. Instead of ghee or clarified butter, a mixture of various oils was used, and the chants were different. The other two pundits were chanting with Guruji. The chanting began as a low hum and gradually built up into a crescendo. Adheesh's soul which was in Einar's body could hear everything clearly. That was the purpose too. Gradually his eyes started closing and his body became heavy. Soon his soul lost all consciousness, and he went into a coma-like state. Sitting tense, in her corner of the room, Aishani could just hear the loud chanting of the three people: Guruji and the two pundits. She could not see any changes in the demeanor of either Adheesh or Einar. Not that she was expecting any significant changes, but if anything had happened, she could not see it.

After some time one of the Vaidyas got up and approached Adheesh. He began removing the medicated bandages from Adheesh's body. Aishani's heart was in her mouth. She knew that there were two reasons for the bandages being removed. The first was that Adheesh's body had healed to such an extent that strong medication was not required now. The second reason she surmised was that for a clear and effortless entry in his own body, all impediments were being removed so that the soul could lie down easily over his own body without any hindrances. Vaidyaji had taken off all of Einar's clothes and covered him with a thin cloth. Guruji and the other priests continued with their chanting and the havan. Aishani was dimly aware that all three of them were chanting different kinds of chants. When one priest was almost on the verge of finishing his mantra, the other would pick it up from there and begin a different incantation. After this mantra was complete, Guruji would pick up from there and generate another unusual chant. All these impressions were taking place at the back of her mind, she wasn't conscious of them. But some memories were being made and maybe she would think about them later, if at all. At the moment her memories were only of the good times that they shared. Their peace and contentment in life stemmed from their love, which always connected them. Though his soul was in Einar's body, before coming to this hospital, he had held her hand and whispered, 'You hold my heart as if it were a precious gem. You are the only doctor I need. Keep in mind that though I am here for the soul and body exchange, it is you who keeps me alive and you who keeps me strong.'

Aishani closed her eyes tightly, not allowing her tears to escape. She tried paying attention to the chanting of the mantras which were going on, but try as she might, she could not let go of her sense of dread and uneasiness. All this went on for a long time. Aishani found her attention diverting again. Her thoughts slipped on to the time when she first became aware of Adheesh. Involuntarily, she smiled at the memory. During her first year in the Gurukul, when she was performing the havan along with the other students, her elbow touched Adheesh's hand and sparks flew. Her memories were a kaleidoscope, some sad and some so joyful. Every facet of her life was so fascinating and thought provoking. She had plunged into depths of despair and reached the heights of ecstasy. She wouldn't change it for anything in the world. But at the moment she was in despair and she was hopeful too, both at the same time. Ecstatic because she was finally going to see Adheesh in his own body and hopeless because they were finally going to lose Einar. They had already lost their dear friend but now they would have to say goodbye to his body too.

Gradually, she became aware that the chantings had petered down and Guruji and the other priests were in the last stages of their ritual. She shook her head and promptly brought herself to the present. What happened? Was it over? She looked at Adheesh with trepidation. There was no change in his demeanor and no sign of any movement. She looked at Einar, there was no movement. Confused, she looked at Guruji. Guruji nodded in the affirmative. Aishani heaved a sigh of relief. Tears came to her eyes, but she held them. She would not let them fall.

'It will take some time for his body to accommodate and finetune his soul to his body. Even after that it will take some time for his body and soul to re-adapt to each other. You will have to be very patient with him and provide TLC till the time he fully recuperates.' Had it been some other time Aishani would have smiled at Guruji's use of TLC, but now she was brimming with emotion.

She looked questioningly at Guruji.

'Yes beta, you can go to him, but he will remain in this condition for some time to come, you have to be patient. The best of our medical staff is here to oversee his recovery.' She nodded and tentatively went towards Adheesh. Not daring to touch, she just looked at him. He was so still, maybe there was some colour on his cheeks, she could not tell. She looked at Einar. He too was still. Tears came to her eyes. 'Dear dear Einar, who are you, why did you come here? I think you came her specially to give life to Adheesh. It must be some long-lost debt that you have paid off in this birth. Now you have gone, and we will never be able to shake off our feeling of guilt and anguish.'

Once the anxiety and suspense of Adheesh and his soul re-entering his body was over, she went into mourning for Einar. Not only had Einar saved Adheesh, he had also given his body to Adheesh. It was like he had been sent to them especially for the purpose of helping and healing them. They were forever in his debt and they didn't know how and when to repay him.

'Aishani, Adheesh will take some time to fully recover and come to his senses. The emergency at this time is the funeral or cremation of Einar,' Guruji was very somber. Aishani nodded.

'Do we inform his people, Guruji? Einar must be having some family members,' her eyes dimmed as she looked at Einar's body, now just a shell. It had housed two souls and now it was deprived of two souls in this lifetime. How normal and alive he looked, as if he would just wake up.

Guruji shook his head, 'His parents died in an accident when he was very young, a couple of relatives did keep him for some time, but they became very uneasy when sometimes they saw his powers. Ultimately, he was shunted from one orphanage to another where again people were wary of him. These experiences taught him to be a loner. In a nutshell, his years in the Himalayas honed his skills and made him what he was. He had all the qualities of a Nordic warrior and later the qualities of an Indian warrior too. He knew he would die like this fighting with the demons. Once when he was talking to me about his Himalayan odyssey, he had told me about his desire to be cremated,' Guruji divulged, 'His last wish has to be fulfilled at all costs.'

Aishani nodded her head in absolute agreement. Apart from being a very dear friend, he had blessed her by giving her life and her reason for living, which was Adheesh. She was forever indebted to Einar. And there was no way she could ever repay this debt.

A few days later, they went to Varanasi's Manikarnika Ghat beside the holy Ganga to cremate Einar. A few chosen teachers of the Gurukul had gone with them, along with Uday and Tejas. Adheesh could not travel as he was still reeling from the effects of the soul exchange. Women are not allowed at Manikarnika Ghat but one word from Guruji put an end to any objections, enabling Aishani's participation. Guruji and the priests of the Gurukul performed all the rituals of the cremation themselves, instead of hiring local pundits to perform the last rites.

Varanasi or Benares is considered to be the holiest city of the Hindus. It is said that Varanasi is the most favoured city of Lord Shiva and whoever dies here and is cremated here, attains immediate Moksha, the sins of all his past births being wiped out. So strong is this belief that Hindu devotees from all over the world come here to die. As such, there is always a long line of people waiting to cremate their loved ones and dissolve their material bodies in the Panchbhootas or the five great physical elements of earth, water, air, fire, and space. Consequently, Manikarnika Ghat is always overcrowded. The priests who perform the last rites are less in number and so are caretakers and sweepers. As a result, the ghat was chaotic and presented a messy, filthy sight. Nevertheless, it is most revered. Einar's soul had already left his body. This way at least there was some consolation that his soul would achieve salvation. They all paid their last homage to Einar and came back with heavy hearts full of memories. Einar had given his weapon Gram to Uday to be given to Adheesh, since Adheesh was himself not available to receive this revered weapon.

'My beloved Gram will belong to both of you now. I am at peace now knowing that it will be in good and honest hands and will only be used to destroy demons and the scum of the Earth.'

Uday had nodded his acceptance in the affirmative, then queried. This was before they had encountered the Manticore, 'Why, are you going anywhere?'

'I think so,' Einar had answered.

After returning from Varanasi, they were in an extreme state of mourning. Though most of the Gurukul was sorrowful, they were more or less reconciled to the fact that

Einar was no more with them. Loss of warriors was an accepted fact in the Gurukul. It was the training centre for warriors who had to fight demons, black magic and a plethora of unimaginable negative energies and horrors. It was inevitable that a few warriors would die or succumb to their injuries. The inhabitants of the Gurukul had adapted themselves to this fact. But the core team of Adheesh and Aishani was heartbroken. They just could not reconcile themselves to the fact that Einar was not there. He was the best friend Adheesh ever had. Adheesh and Uday were senior members of the team and together they worked like two well-oiled cogs of a wheel. They instinctively understood each other, but Adheesh and Einar had developed a special bonhomie with each other. So much so, that Einar had given his life for Adheesh and then even housed his soul in his body.

'How I wish that I had met him before the cremation,' Adheesh almost lamented. They were sitting under their favourite banyan tree behind the Gurukul. It was dusk. The sun had almost set, night was still far away, though it had sensed that it had already set in the hearts of the two people sitting under the tree. They owed their lives to him and how! Now with his passing away, they wouldn't be able to return the favour.

Aishani tried to console him, 'You had met him Adhee, in fact you were him for so many months,' her emotions were in tatters. Their whole lives they had been doing things for others and now somebody had sacrificed his life for them. They were life givers and Einar gave them his life. The worst part was that there was no way to say thank you or show their gratitude. They sat in despair, each engrossed in his/her own melancholic thoughts. They heard feet walking towards them. They stiffened, but relaxed when they saw Uday. He was holding something in a long bag. He came and stood in front of them. They looked at each other somberly.

'Come Uday, sit down,' Aishani invited him, but Uday kept standing. Even in the dusk they could see that his pupils had turned black. They knew that this happened only when Uday was under great stress, which he was at present.

'I have brought something for both of you,' he said gruffly. Surprised, they looked at him. This was not a time for gifts. Surely Uday would not do such a thing. They looked at him expectantly. Slowly Uday opened the bag and took out something long from it. They gasped. It was Einar's magical and powerful sword, the Gram. They knew that it was one of its kind and was one of the strongest swords in the world. They had been so preoccupied lately, that they had not given any thought to Einar's belongings. The sword was all which Einar had. They looked at Uday in shock. It was an emotional moment for all three of them.

'How did you get it?' Adheesh questioned him.

'Einar had initiated me to it and had instructed me to take it and give it to you at an appropriate time.'

Adheesh was at a loss for words, 'But…how…It was with him when he was fighting the Manticore?'

'This conversation had taken place before that. I had not paid much attention at the time as he had told me to take the Gram when he died. I thought he was talking of a much later stage, but he was talking of the present. Einar probably knew that he would die in the skirmish with the Manticore.'

'Yes Uday, I always knew that Einar knew much more. When I met him for the first time at Lake Mansarovar, he was waiting for me. He was one of the rakshaks (guardians) of the lake. He was with us at Kailash too. It was due to his help that we could return to the Gurukul much earlier.'

Uday kept quiet. He was in the dark about that episode of their lives. He did not ask, that was not the wont of the Gurukul warriors. If they felt the need to tell him, they would; there was no hurry.

The three of them sat together quietly in the darkening night for a long time, paying homage to their dear friend one last time.

THREE COINS

The demons now knew that they were beaten and if they didn't make a run for it, they would be dead. Before Adheesh and party could do anything, the demons vanished before their eyes. From experience they knew that the demons could be there itself, they had just become invisible. Hence Aishani and Uday kept on slashing the air in the hope that they would connect with the demons. But no. The demons had vanished. There was no way they could catch them now.

Dejected, they turned towards Adheesh who had blown up the safe and pocketed the two coins in the safe; one was already with them. There were other demon artifacts also. Adheesh tried to fit as much of them as he could in his bag, who knew what supernatural and evil things these were.

The less the demons had these things with them the better it was for humanity. All three of them came together and rushed towards where Ruby and Tejas along with Swami Muktananda alias Tito, were waiting. Tito had arranged a car for them along with first aid. He could see that they were hurt. There were signs of struggle on their bodies, what kind of struggle Tito could not even imagine.

'We could not catch two of them,' Aishani informed him.

Tito nodded glumly, 'They will come for me now, they will not leave their informer.'

The others looked at each other. It was true. Tito would die a torturous death anytime. Adheesh made up his mind, 'Come with us to the ashram, Tito. You have been a great help to us. We would never have found the coins without your help. Meet our Guruji, who will decide how you can live safely from now on.'

Tito nodded. There was no other choice. They left. Adheesh wanted to hand over the coins as well as the demon talismans and artifacts to Guruji as soon as possible. He knew that they would now be kept in the Gurukul's museum under lock and key, under strict security. The others were quiet in their own thoughts. They had failed in not destroying all the demons here. This would rankle for a long time to come.

The operation began almost a month back. They were sitting in one of the havan halls.

'There are reports that a holy man and a preacher has garnered an unprecedented number of followers. That is not a matter for raised eyebrows. However, what is surprising is the kind of followers that have flocked around him. His followers have become a cult. Their adulation for him knows no bounds. A bit of digging has thrown light on the fact that he has achieved all this in just a matter of a few years.'

'That's nothing new. Godmen keep on cropping in our country like mushrooms. They rise like shining stars, stay there for some time, get caught and vanish from the horizon. These conmen have become so common that I have stopped paying attention to them.'

'Hmm, but this godman is different and very dangerous.'

'How so, Bhaiya?'

'Well, we all know that these fake godmen have a cult following and their followers do whatever their Guru or so-called God desires. They are blind to their spiritual guru's shortcomings. Behind the scenes are the criminal activities of the henchmen of these gurus. All sorts of crimes are committed in the name of religion and spirituality, be it drug trafficking or human trafficking or organ export, you name an atrocity and it's there. Our principal concern is not this. The government agencies are always on to such people. Our focus will always be on demons.'

'You mean to say that this Guru or his cohorts are demons?'

'I'm afraid so,' Adheesh responded grimly, 'There are many of them, they have blended so well into human culture that they now completely understand the psyche of the people of our country. Sometimes they look and behave more human than humans.'

Tejas and Jayant were paying full attention now, though Tejas was hanging upside down from the rod between two pillars in the room. They had all got used to Tejas' antics so they hardly paid any attention to these shenanigans. They knew that Tejas needed to do these acrobatics to relieve the extra energy from his system. Tejas' brain was as sharp as any of them, it was because of his activities that he did not seem to be present in the moment.

'He calls himself Swami Muktananda. There are still four more junior swamis there, all of them demons. Theirs is a huge state-of-the-art ashram where devotees are given all the material comforts. When a devotee enrolls, he is not found wanting for anything, he gets to pray to his favorite deities, listens to mind-boggling sermons, excellent food—though vegetarian and all his needs being met most efficiently. Behind these prayer halls and rooms for the devotees in this resort-like ashram are the laboratories which are called chikitsalayas. It is here that the demons make merry. There are divisions for drug trafficking, human trafficking and an organ removal unit too.'

Uday's eyes were getting darker and darker. Left to himself, he would have just barged into Swami Muktananda's ashram and killed him straightaway with his Pash and he would have killed the other demons too. Adheesh and Jayant looked at each other. Adheesh put up his hand, 'Wait, the main part is yet to come. Under ordinary circumstances these fake gurus fade out themselves or the government catches them one way or the other. But this group is way different. For one they are too intelligent, more intelligent than an average human being. They think and cover their tracks four steps ahead. There has been no whiff of a scandal, even the government agencies are a bit soft on them.'

'So how do we get to know about them?' Jayant asked.

'Because our research is conducted from totally different angles. We are not looking for human criminals, that is a separate field with which we have little or no connection. Our researches are based on searching for entities with the basest qualities. No doubt human beings in this age are almost at par with demons, but there are still many base qualities that separate humans from demons. Our spies have zeroed in on this Ashram with these four head priests or head demons. In the day they give sermons and later behind the scenes there are orgies, demon orgies. Human beings are kidnapped, tortured and killed in the most brutal manner possible, their blood is drunk, flesh is eaten. Some inner organs are saved to be exported to hospitals and medical clinics. Sometimes people are eaten alive too.'

Tejas shuddered, 'Bhaiya, no devotee ever smells anything?'

'No Tejas, nothing. First of all, there is such blind adulation and faith, no doubt derived from some sort of hypnotism and mesmerism which holds them in thrall, and they are blind to any sinister goings-on in the ashram. In any case, Swami Muktananda and his cohorts are too cunning and clever to leave any suspicious imprint behind. We must go about this operation very carefully, because if their devotees get wind of our operation, then we will have to face their onslaught too. Muktananda is their God and anybody who is against their God is their enemy.'

Adheesh continued, 'There is more to the story than merely this. Apparently, this person who calls himself Swami Muktananda began his life as a petty criminal, stealing here and there whatever and wherever he could filch anything.

He didn't know what his parents had named him. His life began in an orphanage where he was called Tito. To survive in the orphanage, he imbibed all sorts of vices. After leaving the orphanage his aspirations grew to great proportions and he met real criminals and killers, people who killed for the lust of it, people who enjoyed killing. Though their modus operandi was exceedingly difficult and gross, the fruits of these operations were also too great. Without having any moral compass and no education Tito thought that this was life. People liked him because of his cute smiling face with curly hair, ever willing to do everyone's bidding, and then filching their money and running away. This was how he had survived in the orphanage. When he came across these killers, Tito thought his life was made. His task was just to lure the hapless victim to the killers who then gave him his cut. That was it though Tito had a rough idea of what happened to the victims. His intrinsic humanity would always come to the fore whenever he saw the gruesome murders. But he kept to himself, firstly because he was getting good money and secondly, he was afraid of his partners. These were demons who would have no qualms in making a meal of Tito if he so much as squeaked against them.'

'But gradually the number of victims dwindled. Even the demons understood that Tito had reached his limits in procuring more victims for them. They were cunning and intelligent enough to not make a meal of Tito. Instead, they gave one of their three ancient magical coins to Tito.'

This got everybody's attention. Even Tejas came down from the ceiling and sat down with Jayant and Uday.

'Are they the same coins to which Guruji refers to time to time, the elixir of the demons?' Uday mused.

'Exactly,' Adheesh rebutted, 'Though demons are demons by their own unique attributes, these coins enhance their barbaric qualities manifold.'

'How so, Bhaiya?' Tejas quipped. He was all ears now.

'Each coin performs a different role. It makes one super confident of himself, one can have a literal fan following of millions of people just like that and the blind adulation will be so much that people will happily die for you. These coins attracted massive amounts of money too. There has always been a tussle between humans and demons to have these coins in their possession. Centuries back, these coins were with some human beings who later became so flushed with arrogance and overconfidence that they became careless. They began thinking that they were so successful and prosperous by their own merits and stopped giving credit to the coins. This was a fertile ground for the demons who immediately stole the ancient coins from these careless, foolish humans. Ever since then the demons have been creating more havoc than was ever thought possible.'

'Which coin was given to Tito? Wait, let me guess,' Jayant said, 'It was the coin which mesmerised people to adore Tito.'

'Hence an ashram was constructed from the donations given by Tito's followers who ranged from the poor to the ultra-rich. Both were required as the disappearance of a millionaire would have raised many eyebrows and questions,' Uday said grimly.

'Yes, the other two coins were not given to Tito because

the demons wanted Tito to be under their control. Overnight Tito became Swami Muktananda. When Tito realised his fan following, his ego puffed up and to prove himself more he began studying to give his sermons. The adulation was so much that his fans would have adored him even if he sang ditties. It was a win- win situation for both the demons and Tito. Matters reached such a head that that there was a killing almost every day. Tito or Swami Muktananda's only job was to lure the unsuspecting followers to the Satsang hall and that was it. The predator demons did the rest of the work without anybody being the wiser. But despite no ethical values, Tito, or Swami Muktananda was still a human being. Somewhere his moral radar was getting repulsed by these gory happenings in this ashram. Now that his basic needs had been met, his mind began digressing towards other things in life. He began getting repulsed by his masters' cannibalism and lust for power and torture. Bit by bit he concluded that he did not want to live this life anymore. He was also under the misconception that his fan following was the result of his own studies and hard work. In course of time, he had almost forgotten about the powers of the coin, but he wore it like a locket because he feared the demons.

'Hmm, it seems that first we have to penetrate their ashram, mingle as devotees, gain everybody's trust, get all the four demons together and try to catch them red-handed and then kill them. Quite a tall order, eh Adheesh?' Uday remarked. Adheesh patted Uday on the back, 'Yes Uday, we'll give ourselves two days' time, mark it, no more than that, you never know how many people will be killed, tortured and eaten in these two days.'

Uday nodded and left with Tejas following him. Jayant hung around for some more time. Adheesh looked at him questioningly.

'Jijaji,' Jayant addressed Adheesh this way only in private, that too when he was very disturbed, 'Jijaji, we will have to take the help of Didi and Ruby also. We will take on one demon each. Ruby and Tejas will enter the ashram and we will follow them gradually in the next week. We are not to know each other; we must not be seen talking to each other at all.'

'Jijaji I will look after Aishani di. You keep an eye on the others and guide them too. Aishani will be alright with me around her.'

'I know Jayant. We will meet Guruji in the evening. You brief Ruby and I will appraise Ash about the facts.'

The next day they made their plans and went to Guruji. He tweaked a couple of points here and there and then gave them the go-ahead. Guruji's trusted lieutenants Aishani and Adheesh were there to lead the group. Guruji knew that they were mature enough to control the rest of this core committee from getting emotionally involved and doing anything irrational or out of turn. Before leaving Guruji gave Aishani and Adheesh one small booklet each, 'This will take care of all your contingencies and weapons. These are your weapons, and they will come to you when you call for them. Look at them and familiarise yourself with them. Always keep this booklet with you.'

They nodded, touched Guruji's feet. Guruji blessed them and they left, heading for their favourite tree, under which they opened the booklets. There were six pages each in the booklets, including the front and back cover. On each page there were innocuous-looking pictures without any meaning whatsoever. They looked at the pictures and then at each other in puzzlement. What did Guruji mean? While they were mulling over the possible options, they noticed a subtle change in the pictures. They looked closely. Sure enough, now the pictures had changed into pictures of weapons. Astonished, they looked at the pictures of the weapons. They were all pictures of weapons which had been used from time to time against demons. There were pictures of some weapons which they had not used yet but could use them easily enough. They understood Guruji's allusion now. These were not pictures; these were actual weapons which they could activate by mentally chanting their respective mantras to invoke them. It was like nano chips were imbedded in these pictures. As realisation dawned, the pictures changed again into pretty flowers and hills. Only Aishani and Adheesh had the power to invoke these weapons almost by will power. Trust Guruji to think of everything. They smiled at each other and practiced their mantras for the next two hours.

It took them one day to reach Swami Muktananda's ashram. Jayant had written to the ashram a day earlier and they had immediately got a positive response. There was a vehicle waiting at the railway station to escort them to the ashram. Once there, they were welcomed in the reception area by personnel wearing immaculate uniforms: saffron kurtas and white pajamas. Everything was immaculate, spick and span. Their names were quickly registered, each of them was given an itinerary for the next one week. They were then escorted to their rooms. They were free for the rest of the day. Each of them had a separate room though the management of the ashram knew that Adheesh and Aishani were married. The rooms were spartan, though with all modern facilities. This time was crucial for all of them. They had a week's time to complete their operation: to destroy the demons and collect the three ancient coins which the demons were misusing to their hearts' content.

The initiative had to be taken by Ruby as planned. By the time she came out of her room, it was evening. People were roaming around in the salubrious surroundings. There was greenery everywhere, lush verdant lawns, trees, disciplined beds of beautiful flowers and shrubs, various kinds of tittering birds. Almost like paradise, she thought. Slowly she noticed two groups of people walking on the same path but opposite directions. There were separate buildings in front of her. One group went in one building and the other group went in the next building. One was the yoga room, and a sermon was taking place in the other room. Ruby went inside. She recognised Swami Muktananda from his photographs. What a soothing and melodious voice! Ruby sat down on one of the chairs at the back. Her brief was to tackle this person first. It was getting dark. Soon the sermon was over, and people began filing out slowly. A few people gathered around Swami Muktananda as usual. When people are very troubled, they tend to gather around the person who they know will help them. Ruby patiently sat through all this. When everybody had left, Swami Muktananda also prepared for leaving. A current passed through him as soon as he crossed Ruby. He stood there rock still and stunned. Since there was not enough time, Ruby was using all her powers to entice him. And who was Swami Muktananda, a mere human posing as a godman. He was no competition. Ruby was the direct descendent of the celestial beauties, the apsaras. He sat down beside her. Ruby took his hands in hers. There was no need for any conversation. He was hers without any conditions. He wanted to hold her in his arms, he wanted to close his eyes and lie down in her lap, he wanted to dance with her, he wanted to begin a never ending conversation with her and he wanted to be with her always in this life and beyond it too.

'Let's go somewhere in privacy, we have so much to talk about,' Ruby whispered. Swami Muktananda or Tito just nodded; he was so overwhelmed with love that he could have died for her, there and then.

'Where should we go?' Ruby asked him softly. Tito looked at her uncomprehendingly, then he finally understood. She was asking him to take her to a hidden, secluded place where they could love each other and talk forever. He quickly led her to quiet spot, and they sat there for an exceedingly long time. Never in his wildest imaginations had Tito ever visualised that such an exceptionally beautiful woman could ever fall in love with him! Without saying anything she understood his plight, though she did ask him a few questions, to which he replied readily and happily. It was as if a heavy weight had been lifted from his heart now that he had found his soul mate. He was no match for the apsara Ruby. He emptied his heart, life, and soul to her, cried and laughed at the same time.

Meanwhile, the others had gone in different directions searching for clues. Tejas was the fastest of all, flitting from one tree to another, stretching like a thick rope whenever there was some distance between two trees. He wore camouflaged clothing so that even if anyone became suspicious, they would not be able to place him. By the time they thought of giving him a second look, Tejas would be too far away and they would think that it was just an optical illusion. Jayant had the gift of seeing through animate and inanimate objects. He began by looking through each and every building and structure and trees of the ashram. Uday just wandered around. To any other person, it would look as if a guest were just dawdling around getting used to the ashram and its surroundings. Uday was totally ready with his Paash which was hidden and invisible, but nevertheless very much part of his body. Aishani and Adheesh explored the grounds together, ever ready with their weapons. The check-in security had been quite tight at the reception, but they were no match for this motley group. They were masters in their art and had been so for the last few ages. If Guruji had wanted, they could have demolished the ashram there and then only, but that wouldn't have been fair to the other innocent souls residing there even if they had been party to the demons' shenanigans, either knowingly or unknowingly.

There were other new members also roaming about trying to get a feel of the ashram. It was all so beautiful and peaceful and disciplined, though the landscaping was artificial.

'Oh Adhee, it's all so charming and tranquil, I could stay here all my life,' Aishani sighed wistfully, holding his hand.

'Control Ash, control, we are here for a job and

unfortunately we will be the ones to kill and shed blood here. This place may not be so alluring then. Start preparing yourself mentally, things will begin very soon,' Adheesh pressed her hand with empathy. He understood her desire for a peaceful life. He also knew that given an option Aishani would never hesitate to choose her present life to rid the world of all the demons on Earth. There was simply no other alternative. This was their life and so be it. Aishani put her handkerchief to her nose as they walked towards a garden, so did Adheesh. They looked at each other. A smell was coming from the sublime, sweet-smelling flower garden. Senses alert, they stopped and sniffed, there was no stench now, only the sweet smell of the roses and jasmine and petunias. But their noses had not fooled them at all. They knew that there was something here positively. They had their hands ready on their weapons, but they could not find anything. They also knew that their modus operandi in the next couple of days would be to find the demons, after which the demons may become suspicious of their activities. From tomorrow their retreat in the ashram would begin and they wouldn't have any time for foraging.

Later they met in the large dining hall. The food was totally organic and vegetarian. It was a lavish spread with Indian, Continental, and Chinese cuisines. They ate their food, then settled down for a meeting in the lobby for a small discreet discussion. There were other people around too. They were sure there were security people around though no one gave that impression.

'I could not find anything,' began Uday, 'though there were subtle signs that things are not as hunky dory as they are being portrayed. We do not have much time. From tomorrow we will have a tight schedule. We won't get much time to find the demons and their real den or dens.'

The others concurred with the same conclusion. Aishani recounted her experience of the fetid smell. Only Ruby was quiet. They turned to look at her. She looked sad but there was a victorious expression on her face too.

'I have been able to extricate some valuable information from Swami Muktananda. The demon's den is behind the sermon room, which is very convenient for them. After studying the background of the visitors, during the sermons they call the most vulnerable one outside, overpower him and take him or her to their den. They generally choose someone who does not have a family or who is largely a loner or a very private person. That way that person goes quite late in the missing people's list. Many other methods are also used to cover up a disappeared soul.'

Tejas protested, 'But Didi, we searched everywhere and behind the sermon hall too, we did not see or hear any suspicious sound or activity!'

Aishani turned to Adheesh, 'Wait, we did notice a strange thing, a smell—a familiar but fetid stench. When we paid attention and inhaled deeply, the stench was gone or rather it was replaced by the fragrance of the sweet-smelling flowers.'

Jayant looked a trifle embarrassed. 'I looked for them everywhere, it just did not cross my mind that their den would be so close. I have a lot to learn,' he said sheepishly.

'Precisely,' Ruby agreed, 'Many a times we have lived in identical atmospheres ourselves in our Gurukul, but it didn't cross our minds that these demons could also be using the same method of camouflaging themselves and their real workplace. They have covered their headquarters with invisible walls. Such a simple, effective technique!'

'Which we would have discovered eventually,' Adheesh remarked, 'Ruby you've done a commendable job,' Ruby acknowledged with a faint smile and a nod. Aishani looked at her closely but Ruby wouldn't meet her eyes.

Adheesh turned to the rest of his team, 'We go to work in the afternoon. That is when the demons would get up and search for food in their den. There is no need to catch them red-handed, though it'll be better if we do so. Each of us knows the drill. After we destroy the demons, everyone leaves except Uday and I. We will follow you after we plug all the loopholes. Ruby, your work is over. You and Tejas will go for the medicinal massages. After that wait for us at the reception. The rest will join you there.'

'Wait, Adheesh,' Ruby interjected rather quickly. They all turned to her and waited.

'Swami Muktananda or Tito is just a petty thief, he is not really a criminal. He is mortally scared of the demons and he still rues the day he came in contact with them. He is a good man, and his heart is simple. He really wants to change to a better, honest and God-fearing man for which he never had a chance in his life. He also gave me this to prove his good intentions,' Ruby held up one of the three ancient coins triumphantly and then tried to give it to Adheesh.

Adheesh declined, 'No Ruby, you keep it with yourself for the time being. I don't want even an iota of negative influence on us even though Guruji has made us immune to such effects. Our operation should be over in minutes, though extricating the coins can be quite dicey. We won't have much time to search for the coins in all the chaos.'

'Adheesh,' Ruby uttered hesitatingly, 'I am meeting Muktananda or Tito again after a couple of hours. I'll try to elicit the information from him—that is, if he knows where the coins are hidden.'

'Thanks Ruby, you're a gem, and as you say we will free Tito from the clutches of the demons too,' Ruby smiled. Aishani thought she could see the sadness in Ruby's eyes. Later, she promised herself, she'll ask Ruby later when they return to the Gurukul.

Very early in the morning Aishani heard a soft knock on the door. She knew it was Ruby. She gave them a small piece of crumpled paper with a basic sort of map with just four lines.

'Behind this cabinet is a small insignificant but foolproof safe. The other two coins are there which are taken out sometimes by the senior rakshasa. The other demons are too scared of him to take out the coins.'

Aishani and Ruby hugged each other. Ruby left immediately and was lost in the dim light of dawn.

Their initial classes began in the ashram with early morning yoga. After that there was healthy breakfast, a small break, then to the sermon room for Swami Muktananda's lecture. In the afternoon, they had to select the health massages. That was the time they would slip out and reach the demons' den. Ruby and Tejas would be there to lessen any suspicions.

When the time came, they swiftly followed Jayant, who

now knew exactly where to go. They went through a massive door which they could not see but Jayant could because of his special vision. They had entered a hall which was all marble and shining chrome. There were rooms across the hall. Aishani and Adheesh again got the whiff of blood and putrefying blood, but the others did not notice. The smell disappeared as soon as they sensed it. For a minute Jayant stood in awe of the place. It was veritably a castle in the midst of an ashram! Uday nudged him softly. Jayant shuddered then ran ahead to where his vision was leading him. The other three were ready with their weapons. Aishani had a Kora, a sort of sword in her hand. Instead of tapering at the end, it became broad. It was very heavy and very sharp, not meant for normal human beings. It was one of Aishani's favourite weapons. This deadly weapon coupled with Aishani's high emotions had seen the destruction of many vicious demons. Uday had his Pash with him, his pupils were already turning black in anticipation of the kill. Adheesh had his loyal khukhri with him and a few supernatural detonators. He had to blow up the safe in such a manner that the other two coins would not be destroyed. He knew that Aishani and Uday were more than enough to destroy the four demons who would be feeding at that time. Jayant was also there but they would hardly need him apart from guiding them in this invisible maze. Jayant led them directly to the room where all the four demons were having their feast.

They stopped in their tracks. The hair on their arms rose in revulsion. No matter how many times they had espied the true behaviour of demons, they were always shocked in the beginning. This was a real flesh-eating orgy going on. Some of the victims were still partially alive. It was as if they were deliberately kept alive so that the demons could torture them and then kill them. There were groans and in some cases, screams too. That along with the guttural sounds of gnawing, tearing of flesh and gorging on it produced a macabre sight and a cacophony of ghastly, revolting sounds. For a moment they stood rooted to the spot. The demons were totally oblivious of them. They were probably too confident of their invisible and concealed barriers. Uday was totally out of control now. Picking up his Pash, he hit the demon nearest to him with all his strength. Caught unaware, the demon fell hard on the floor. But he was a demon and that too a strong one. He might have been dazed but he quickly got up and faced his unexpected enemy. The other three demons had also been alerted by this fricassee. After that there was a free-for-all between Aishani, Uday and the four demons. Apart from fighting with the demons, Uday and Aishani had to lead these demons away from the wall where the invisible safe with the coins was. With single-minded focus, they attacked the demons. The demons were no less though they had become just a bit laidback and lazy with everything coming to them so easily.

Adheesh just had a small piece of paper in his hand with a hastily scribbled map to guide him towards the wall where the safe would be. The wall was huge, the safe could be anywhere in it. He thought feverishly. He did not have much time and he did not have too many detonating devices to blow up the whole wall, which was something that nobody wanted. Both the parties would not have wanted any visitor to see a blown-up wall and the gory scenes within. He couldn't have used a heavy-duty detonator for fear of breaking the coins. Who knew what effect the broken pieces of coins would have on the people who chanced upon them?

Hence the detonations had to be small and at the precise place. He tapped the wall. The sound and feel were like any brick-and-mortar wall. Frantically he tapped all over the wall again. He was so fast, almost like a whirlwind, that it was not possible for anybody to notice. Ah! He came across a place where the sound was denser. Adheesh was almost sure that the safe was here. He began his procedure.

On the other side, Aishani and Uday were going strong in their combat with the demons. The demons were also never without their weapons, though Aishani and Uday had the first advantage. Uday was fighting them on the ground whereas Aishani was all over the place, sometimes with her Kora and sometimes with her bow and arrow, sometimes in the air and sometimes on the ground. Suddenly, one demon jumped upwards and attacked Aishani headlong. It happened in an instant. Aishani fell in the altercation and another demon attacked. Aishani was too fast and too fierce for them, nevertheless one of them still managed to nick her in the arm and a bit of blood came out. Uday fighting the other two demons was keeping an eye on both Aishani and Adheesh. He did not see the nick on Aishani's arm, he only saw her blood. Immediately, Uday became very still. He immediately went into a murderous rage. He went into a blood-thirsty attack on the demons who were shocked by his extra bout of energy and force. In any case, they were finding it exceedingly difficult to cope up with Uday, and now this. He was like a whirling dervish hitting the demons with his Pash. He destroyed two demons and then swiftly turned to the other two. Before his eyes, the other two demons vanished.

And that is why, when they left the ashram, they took Tito with them to ensure that he was not harmed by the missing demons. The ashram would no doubt be taken over by his deputies and run successfully.

AMMA

'Amma!'

'Ash!' Mother and daughter hugged each other. They smiled and laughed in each other's arms. 'Let me look at you darling, my baby is looking so beautiful. Marriage suits you, Ash,' Madhu declared.

'Yes Amma, Adheesh is the best. You and Baba couldn't have chosen a better husband for me,' she smiled tremulously, her eyes showing a hint of moisture. Madhu noticed it but didn't say anything.

'Come beta, let's sit and talk. Sit in the aangan (courtyard), I'll make your favourite tea.'

'No Amma, you sit, I'll make our special tea,' so insisting, she made her mother sit in the kitchen. There was so much to talk about that they didn't know where to start.

She saw that Amma had made the special almond biscuits for her and the pakoras were hot and crisp. Ash quickly made a pot of ginger and cinnamon tea and then sat down with her mother at the kitchen table.

'Oh Amma, it's so good to be back here with you, just like old times.' This was the first time she had visited her home after the destruction of the Gurukul. Guruji had told her that her people were safe, and they had shifted to some place in Haridwar because of the micro demon menace. After some time, Madhu had gone to the Gurukul to meet her and she had started meeting Jayant regularly in the Gurukul.

Madhu smiled affectionately. It was nice that the servants were not there, the maid servant Deepa had gone to her village for a few days and the other servant Chhedi had left for the night. Both of them had wanted to stay back because of Aishani, but Madhu did not want to share her daughter with anybody for some time. The house was another matter altogether. Had it any human form, it would have hugged Aishani and never let go. It would have told her about its travails and tribulations repeatedly. Aishani knew all this. The past few months had been so overloaded and bizarre that there had been no time to be with her mother and the newly renovated house. So much water had flown under the bridge. She had so much to tell Amma. In turn even Amma had so many things to tell her. Aishani wasn't sure Amma would like to hear all about her adventures, she would get very worried and may even discourage her to continue with her work—but no, her Amma would never do that.

She did not miss Jayant as he had been with them in so

many stints. Aishani had reassured the house that she would be sitting with it for a long time, but first she would talk to her Amma. 'Fair enough,' the house had acquiesced, but that didn't stop it from eavesdropping on their conversation.

Mother and daughter talked well into the evening, late into the night. Chhedi had insisted on making a special dinner before leaving, most of which went into the refrigerator as neither was hungry. Still, Madhu could make out that Aishani was not telling her everything. Madhu did not mind. She knew that in their line of work, it was better not to speak of many things as that would have only hurt her and make her very tense and apprehensive. But she had to share some of her pain. She told her about the total destruction of the Gurukul, about Guruji too being killed by the demons. Amma took a sharp breath when she heard this. Aishani then told her how Garuda devta had taken them into the past on Kailash with forty almost dead people and how Einar came to be with them.

She stopped when she saw the puzzled look in Madhu's eyes.

'Guruji?' Madhu asked quietly.

'Guruji came back, Amma. I was in Kailash with Devnath and Einar. Adheesh had come down looking for medicines and to find out about all of you. He visited the destroyed Gurukul too. I have a particularly strong feeling that Adheesh with his strong and forceful prayers and meditation, forced Guruji to return to Earth.'

'Yes, that too,' Madhu concurred, 'But Guruji's work was incomplete here. He is Mahabali Hanuman's representative. He has to be here to guide all of you. We know that there is no alternative to him. Guruji too knows this.'

'Yes Amma,' she concurred, 'But now tell me about you and the rest in detail. How did all of you defend yourselves against the micro demons?'

'In a minute, beta, you have to complete your story first. Tell me the main points first. We can fill the minor points later. How was the Gurukul reconstructed so swiftly and how did you get rid of the nano demons?'

'Oh Amma, I can answer the first question easily enough. Everybody worked indefatigably with Guruji periodically throwing his magic bits.'

'And the micro demons?' Madhu enquired, as if she had already guessed the answer.

'Amma, I'd rather you didn't ask me this. It will be painful for you. I just want us to be happy together. Be assured that those demons have been completely destroyed.'

Madhu nodded sadly. She knew that Aishani was saving her more heartache and shock.

'Oh Amma! I've bored you with so many creepy and gruesome stories. This is our life, as you had told me before I joined the Gurukul. Now I cannot think of any other life than this.'

'Yes beta, our destiny has been written by Brahma and Hanuman ji and we are blessed by them.'

Aishani shook her head as if getting rid of her cobwebs. 'Amma,' she said softly, 'what have you been doing? How do you spend your days? I've been jabbering away all this while. Jayant is with us most of the time. What did you do, Amma? I have a faint idea that the demons had come here too. How did you tackle them?'

'Beta, your father had trained me for such exigencies. There was loads of volatile material in the basement. Plus Uday, Jayant and Tejas were here. Uday took control of everything, killed the demons, but in the process, most of this house was destroyed.' The house flapped two windows in scorn as if nobody would have the temerity to destroy it. It wanted to answer this question. A few things fell from the top of an almirah.

'We went and took refuge in Haridwar.'

'Oh, at least there are no demons there.'

Madhu kept quiet. Aishani asked suspiciously, 'Amma, were there demons there too, in that holy city too?'

Madhuji nodded and falteringly told her about the beautiful female demon Prisha with whom Uday fell in love. And later how they returned with Devnath.

'Devnath? What was he doing here?'

The house was really excited now. This was its story, nobody could tell because nobody knew, only Devnath and the house. It made all sorts of desperate noises which only Aishani and Madhu understood.

'Shh!' Aishani gestured to the house to keep quiet. It retreated. Aishani had the feeling that it was trying to tell her something that Madhu may or may not tell her. Maybe Amma didn't even know about it.

'Amma, just a minute. I'll talk to the house for a minute.'

'Yes, do that. I'll make some more tea. It's so happy with you around. It didn't tell me half of the things which it's trying to tell you.'

Madhu went to the kitchen and Aishani turned towards the house. Initially, it just blabbered and even Aishani could not catch on. She made it repeat the story many times and finally the horror of the whole thing struck her. The house was burned and destroyed. Then everybody had to leave it and run away. Only Uday had the presence of mind to hide their new address inside the house. The house had very safely kept the address within itself and gave it to Devnath only when it confirmed that Devnath was sent by Adheesh. Aishani was astounded by these revelations. She wasn't aware of any of these goings on, having been so engrossed in helping Adheesh and Guruji to get rid of the nano demons.

But Adheesh had taken care of everything. He had sent Devnath to find and bring everybody back. Her heart was full, and it sang. Her dearest darling Adheesh, her husband and her lover, who looked after her interests behind her back too. Oh! How lucky she was! And Devnath! Adheesh's best protector and sentinel, who always put his knowledge and magic to the best use. Mentally, she empathised with and praised the house. The house was quiet, now that Aishani applied the soothing balm on its soul.

Another thought came to her mind. The house was lonely! Something was afoot. She would just have to wait for Amma to tell her or she would talk to the house later.

Madhu came back with a fresh pot of herbal tea.

'What have you been doing, Amma, after the house was renovated?'

'Nothing much Ash, just pottering around here and there. There is nothing much to do,' the house banged a window fiercely. Madhu sighed and made a gesture to the house. It retreated for a short while.

'Ash, if I don't tell you, then this silly shack will tell you,' Madhu joked affectionately. The house reciprocated by softly opening a window. Ash waited.

'Your father knew that he wouldn't be around too much with us. We also knew that our two children will continue with the good work that God has sent you in this world for. With both of you away and your Baba no more, life would indeed have been very lonely for me had it not been for Ajitha and Badri Bhaiya.' Madhu was referring to Ruby's parents, 'Their children too had grown up and had to be around you to protect you,' Aishani wanted to protest but Madhu put up her hand.

'We were at a loss. We had too much time on our hands and not enough work. Each of us are warriors, rather were warriors and here we were, time sitting like a heavy stone in our hands. It was then that I remembered that your father had handed me a list of demons and told me to keep it safely. He had also told me that I would open it myself when the time came. This time was probably what he meant. I remembered the list, but I could not have access to it because the house, our house was destroyed,' the house shuddered at the memory. Madhu continued, 'It was when we returned and the house was being renovated by all of you that I came across this list. Our dear house had concealed it in one of his hiding places, God bless it,' the house simpered and almost gave a curtsey, which only Aishani and Madhu ji could make out.

'So what did you'll do, Amma? Don't tell me you killed demons?'

Madhu kept quiet.

'AMMA! You did! Without any experience! What if anything had happened to you? How can I live without you? Baba is also not here!' Aishani was shocked.

Madhu smiled wryly, 'I am a warrior and mother of warriors. Can a human stop breathing? Can a warrior forget her skills? They may become rusted but they are still there. Same is the case with Ajitha and Badri Bhaiya. Between the three of us, we have plenty of experience.'

'Amma what did you do? I know you can sniff out demons, but tell me, how did you pull this off and how many demons have you killed?'

'Only one as yet, Ash,' she laughed at Aishani's incredulous face, 'We are not going to stop there. Your father has made a list of those demons who have not become so ferocious as yet, but given time they may become more harmful than, say, the traditional Rakshasas. In a way, we shall be paving the path for you and your group, making it a bit smoother.'

Aishani was dumbstruck. She was aware that her mother was a warrior, though a passive one. She had never imagined her mother to be an active warrior. Well, life was full of surprises.

'Amma tell me all about this demon which you all executed,' she demanded.

'Well, with all of you away and busy in your lives either on some assignment or in the Gurukul, Ajitha, Badri Bhaiya and I decided to take a vacation of sorts, somewhere near Rishikesh. It's such a beautiful place. We have been there with your Baba so many times.'

'Yes, Amma, I remember,' she said nostalgically.

'While going around, we made friends with many people. In the course of our conversations with them, we came to know of a place where many people went to pay their homage and pray to the live deity there. Apparently, the deity was exceptionally beautiful and ageless. She blessed whoever went to her, with health and long-lasting beauty. We too went to her more out of curiosity than anything else. She was indeed very attractive, alluring and exquisite. She lived slightly away from the main city almost at the periphery of the mountains. The path which led to her abode was so green and captivating that we started going for walks there. The only jarring note was the absence of birds. Such a beautiful green place had to be full of flora and fauna, but it was not so. The stillness and quiet too was one of the reasons that we would go there for walks. The absence of living creatures should have warned us, but we didn't pay heed to this. We would go to Meena Devi's abode along with other devotees, sit there for some time and walk back. Meena Devi would talk about life and how to adjust and improve upon it, nothing special; that's what the other lifestyle gurus teach, but her voice had a mesmerising and reassuring quality to it.'

Madhu continued, 'On the fourth day, Badri Bhaiya was not well but he insisted on accompanying us to Meena Devi's place. He had a slight fever too, I think Ajitha gave him a Crocin for the fever to come down. We told him to lie down and sleep for some time for the medicine to take effect. Badri Bhaiya went to sleep and we sat a little away so that we could chat without disturbing him. It was dusk by then.

All the devotees had left. We were also planning to leave after Badri Bhaiya awakened. We were sitting behind a small grove of trees talking idly of nothing in particular. Suddenly, we saw Meena Devi coming out from her house. We were just getting up to greet her when she furtively looked around and then quickly went to the back of her house. There was absolute silence, no birds, no insects. It was then that our hair rose. We knew for a certainty that there was some mischief afoot. We left Badri Bhaiya sleeping and quietly followed Meena Devi. You know, we never travel anywhere without weapons and a few necessary items just in case we encounter a demon or in this case a Rakshasi.'

Aishani was all agog with curiosity and excitement, which Madhu found amusing as Aishani had annihilated so many ferocious, ruthless and bloodthirsty demons. The list was endless—and here she was showing such childlike curiosity. She patted Aishani's cheek.

'We followed her to the back of her house. She was walking quickly but had started faltering as if she had some trouble or pain in walking. She almost ran for about a mile. We followed her as surreptitiously as possible. Fortunately, it had rained the previous day so the vegetation was still wet and we did not make much sound while following her. After some time, we began getting the fetid stench of rotting flesh. We were alarmed. Something was seriously wrong here. We hid behind some trees and peeped from there. Meena Devi was sitting on the rotting grass eating a dead human child. It was as if she had just killed the child and was now eating it like a wild animal. Ajitha and I knew that it was now or never. We had thin but very strong plastic ropes and our knives with us. Shouting loudly, we rushed to her and caught her unawares. She was so hungry and so engrossed in her eating that she completely failed to notice us. Before she could react, Ajitha had thrown the rope around her like a lasso and before she could do anything we had bound her with the rope.'

Madhu paused for a minute to put her thoughts together and continued, 'She was not fully satiated with her meal, because we had disturbed her. We were shocked when we looked at her. Half of her face was as beautiful as it was earlier, but the other half was all wrinkled like the face of a very old woman and her hair had also become white. But her hand still held a limb of the human child which she desperately tried to eat. When we didn't allow her to do so, she began entreating us piteously to let her eat.'

'We told her that we would not allow her to eat human flesh, no matter what. She began babbling in desperation, telling us a strange story. She told us that she was 500 years old. When young, she was very vain and very arrogant about her beauty. Her father was a Rakshasa and also the land owner of a few villages. He was as good and fair as any Rakshasa can be. They still ate human flesh but in a smaller ratio. They combined it with grains, fruits and vegetables. In such pagan times, when a villager went missing, not too many eyebrows were raised; the simple villagers could not even dream that Meena and her family could be involved in these disappearances. By the time Meena became a teenager she had become so haughty and careless that she would just go out at nights, hunt randomly, eat as much as she could, which was not much and just leave the dead body there itself. Most of her family was in awe of their little princess. One demon was designated by her father to follow her everywhere and hide or destroy the so-called evidence. The fawning and bootlicking reached such levels that her companions, that is the lower level demons, convinced her that in order to maintain her ethereal beauty she had to eat young human children. This way they could tell her father that they had to eat the humans in order to hide the evidence. Things came to such a head that the vain beauty would just kill for the sake of killing to make herself more beautiful. Everything was hunky dory at the lower level. Her father was not aware of what his darling daughter and her schemer friends were doing. Meena began getting bored. The thrill of killing began dissipating. Her flunkies were in a fix now. With their princess not interested in killing, they began killing humans on their own and offered them to their princess. She would eat a little and give the rest to her friends.

Once the demon princess along with her sycophants was on a round of the market, laughing and creating chaos just for the heck of it. A small child was playing there. The princess was not hungry. She barely glanced at the child but her guards were greedy, insatiable. Their mouths watered when they espied the plump and beautiful human child. 'Meena, this is such a beautiful baby, if you eat it you will become more ravishing.' Meena could not resist this temptation. Picking up the child like a rag doll, she pulled it apart right in the middle of the market in front of the horror-struck people. The child's mother was nearby buying something. She looked over her shoulder to see what the commotion was all about.

What she saw blew away her senses. She dashed towards Meena and collected her mutilated baby, cried and crooned to it. There was shock all around. Meena's groveling guards ran away. Gradually, the mother collected her emotions and stood up. Holding her baby, she cursed Meena, 'To retain your beauty you will eat only small children, even your own babies, especially your own children.' There was a collective gasp from the spectators who had gathered there. As Meena retreated, many stayed with the young mother to help and console her.

Meena did not give much credence to the woman's curse but there was something in the woman's tone which stayed in her subconscious. Soon she forgot about the incident. But the curse came into effect when she got married and became pregnant. Her husband was also a Rakshasa, very much in love with his wife and proud of her beauty. Everybody was overjoyed by her pregnancy. When the baby was born, Meena was overwhelmed by her love for him. She looked after him lovingly, fed him and took great pleasure in looking after him. After a week or so, she was holding her baby and crooning to him, when something came over her and she became the old Meena who would eat babies. She became a split personality; one wanted to love and protect her baby and the other personality wanted to kill and eat the baby. After a tussle of two hours, the demon side won. She tore the baby in her arms and ate a part of it. The baby died immediately. When Meena came to her senses, her baby, her life was gone. She told her husband that some animal took their baby while she was asleep. They searched for the baby everywhere in vain.

The second time, she was carrying twins. She devoured

them one by one when they were one and two months old. This time her husband became suspicious. The third time he caught her in the act and threw her out of the house. Her father got her married again, and again the same thing happened. This time her father drove her to the outskirts of his kingdom. Though they were demons, they ate other people, not their own. Outside her father's kingdom, she managed to survive and lead a precarious existence. Men and demons were equally attracted to her extreme beauty and quite a few of them married her, with disastrous results. She was thrown out of every home. She had to change her location many times because people would eventually become suspicious of her activities. Finally, she came here to the edge of Rishikesh. Once in a while, she did manage to catch hold of a child and eat it. That kept her and her beauty alive. She lived alone and kept to herself. A rumour spread among the women that she was a deity and anyone who went and prayed to her was blessed by beauty and attraction. She came to be known by the appellate Sadhvi Meena.

'She was very clever and cunning. While she was recounting her sob story, she had broken the cord with which we had bound her. Both of us were caught unawares. We pounced on her with our knives and stabbed her multiple times. She was extraordinarily strong for such a frail woman, mainly because she was a demon. But, you know, we too had special knives, forged specially to kill demons. She began ageing right in front of our eyes and gradually turned into dust at our feet. We were shocked, but we felt good because we had done a good deed for humanity.'

Aishani was listening spellbound. It took her two minutes to realise that the story was over.

She hugged her mother, 'Amma, I'm so proud of you. I would have never imagined you slapping a person, leave alone wielding a knife.'

Mother and daughter talked some more then went to bed. Aishani slept in her mother's room. Who knew when she would have a chance to be with Amma again?

TEJAS AND JARA

'We are getting reports that quite a number of demons have surfaced in the jungles of Bihar and Jharkhand,' Guruji told them. 'These are male as well as female demons. The government's thinking as of now is that the disappearances and some gruesome murders are the result of tribal groups fighting each other. A probe has been ordered but ever since two policemen were captured and parts of their half-eaten bodies were found strewn in the jungles, even the police are scared. There is now only a half-hearted attempt to search for the killer or the group of killers. The superstitious villagers are convinced that a prate atma is doing all the murders. For once they are right.'

'All of us will go to Bihar. We will begin from West Champaran, get rid of the demons there and then go to other adjoining areas to continue with our work,' Guruji looked at his attentive set of warriors. 'Champaran at one time was the seat of spirituality. In fact, some of you may be aware that the Ramayana was written by the great sage Valmiki here, much before the birth of Shri Ram, who is the avatar of Bhagwan Vishnu. Champaran was named thus by joining Champa and Aranya. Champa is the fragrant plumeria and Aranya means forest. The place was full of Champa trees.'

They nodded respectfully but were surprised too. Guruji never accompanied them in their exercises, only in dire emergencies. So, this was a dangerous operation! They straightened up automatically.

'There are many things which even I have to witness and learn. Probably, this will be one of those times. It is embedded in us that all demons are bad and all devtas are good. We human beings are an amalgamation of good and bad. But it is not always so. There are exceptions to the rule, though rare. Once in a while, there can be offshoots of the central theme. A devta can turn rogue or a demon can have good qualities.'

'Guruji, will we encounter good demons there?' Aishani queried.

'We don't know, Aishani. We may or may not,' Guruji answered enigmatically. 'I want my core team to be there so that you can learn to sift the good from the bad. Though rare, there is kindness in negative creatures and wickedness in upright people too.'

Guruji had said what he had to say. They had to be

satisfied with that.

Next day, they started for Bettiah by train. From there they took a taxi to Champaran. Guruji did not accompany them. They knew that Guruji would teleport there when the need arose. It was the holy eleventh month of Magh, which is sometime in January-February according to the Gregorian calendar. A huge mela was being held in the historical district of Champaran to commemorate the birth of Mahaprabhu Vallabhacharya, the great reformer of the Vallabh community. It was cold, green and extremely scenic. There was quite a lot of hustle-bustle at the fair, with happy faces all around. The fair was an eagerly awaited annual event in this otherwise quiet town.

They checked into a hotel and spent a day acclimatising themselves to the surroundings. They discovered that there were quite a few temples in Champaran. The outer city was covered by deciduous forests of mainly huge Sal trees, with their rather large leaves. These leaves were collected and used for making plates and bowls. Its branches and leaves are also used as kitchen fuel. They foraged some more in the jungle. Tejas couldn't stop himself. For two days, he had been cramped, first in the train and then the bus and then the hotel. Now here was a place of his liking. Clean surroundings with tall trees and lush foliage in the nearby jungles. The fair was also to his liking. Tejas found delight in even the smallest things in life. Though he was a warrior, he was innocence personified, laughing and chuckling at the inanest things. Nobody could resist his harmless pranks. He was like a child and would remain so forever.

Tejas looked at his elder brother and sister furtively and impatiently, skipping from one leg to another, waiting for their permission. He swiped a fruit from a nearby vendor who just smiled indulgently, for who could resist sweet Tejas. A woman from a sweet shop offered him a sweet. Tejas laughingly went to her to take the sweet. She also smiled back at him, gave him a laddu and then kept holding his hand. Tejas flushed, slightly embarrassed. He was used to people wanting to hold and touch him. But this woman held his hand for more than a minute. She was looking up at him adoringly. Slowly she let go of his hand, but not before giving it a kiss.

'Coo,' she said and then gave him a crooked smile.

Heaving a sigh of relief, Tejas swiftly ran away. His group watched indulgently. They were amused. Tejas had a huge fan following as he brought out motherly feelings in all females. It seemed to be a bit more in this sweet shop owner. Maybe Tejas resembled her long lost child or her grandson. On the contrary, Jayant seemed a bit worried about this overt display of emotion by this old woman. Alarm bells went off in his head the moment he first lay eyes on her.

Customers, particularly children were coming to buy sweetmeats from the old woman. Apparently, whatever she was selling was delectable enough for customers to flock to her stand. She eagerly sold her sweets and savouries to her customers, always smiling but not talking. The only sound that emanated from her when she handed over the items was a happy 'Coo, coo.'

Jayant had x-ray vision. He could see through all animate objects but he was not a mind reader. So why did he tense up as soon as he saw the woman? He pushed the thought at the back of his mind and joined the others. They split into two groups and walked towards the Sal jungles. Because of the government's stringent policies on tree cutting and strict vigilance, the jungles were covered with lush trees, mainly Sal with a sprinkling of other trees like Khair, Simal, etc. They went some more inside as if they were interested in the flora and fauna of the place, which indeed they were. But mainly they were on the lookout for the more dangerous kind of fauna: the demons. They were in no doubt that there were demons in these jungles. They were experienced warriors and their instincts were honed to smell out the demons, even if Guruji had not told them. They were on red alert.

This time Guruji's instructions had been a bit ambiguous, with the proviso that there were good demons too in this world. They decided to wait and watch.

One fact which all of them noticed was that the sweet shop old woman seemed to be following Tejas around. However, this was not the first time such an incident had happened. In fact, Tejas was quite used to older women following and mothering him.

In the two days that they were there in the small town of Champaran, they made a few friends in the market. To be on the safe side, Ruby made friends with a few female vendors there and began chit chatting with them. Deftly, Ruby maneuvered the topic towards the old woman who had taken a fancy to Tejas.

'Oh, that's old Cuckoo. We call her Cuckoo because that is the only sound she utters. Her real name is Shara. She is everybody's grandmother,' one giggly girl who had an eye on Uday told her breathlessly. 'Tell me Ruby, who is that man standing near the tea stall?' she asked gesturing towards Uday.

'Oh, him? He is my brother,' Ruby's friendly tone suggested that more information could be exchanged.

'Tell me more about this mela,' Ruby asked the girl, 'Does Shara come to the mela regularly? Does she stay with her children here?'

The girl was a little perplexed. 'No, she stays alone at the end of the village, towards the jungle.'

'Oh, poor woman! What about her husband and children?'

'Don't know. I've seen her like this ever since I can remember. She's deaf and dumb too,' the girl informed her importantly.

'Oh, she must be eating alone then,' Ruby came straight to the point, though the girl didn't know it.

'Yes I suppose so, though I've never seen her eating. She keeps on feeding the other children but she does go to the jungle to collect twigs and leaves of the Sakhua trees for fuel,' the girl was eying Uday again.

Ruby sighed. Shara showed all the signs of being a demon. She was seen near Tejas at the most unusual places. Tejas would catch a glimpse of Shara even when he was jumping from tree to tree. Probably his friskiness attracted her all the more. He knew that she was following him because every once in a while, she would mouth a 'Coo'. Mulling over these facts, Ruby went and sat beside Aishani who had made friends with some more villagers.

'She might be a demon or maybe not, we just have to be

very careful Ruby,' Aishani mused. 'We don't have any clear instructions on where and how to find the demons. We'll anyway just keep on looking for them.'

'When is Guruji coming, Ash? If Guruji himself has decided to come, then the demon must be the most dangerous kind.'

'Let's wait and watch, Ruby. Let us wait for the drama which is going to unfold here,' Aishani sighed.

The following morning, they started off early for the outskirts of the town towards the Sal and the Sakhua jungles. They knew they were being followed by the dumb Shara. They ignored her as long as she did not cause any problems. They looked around. The lushness of the trees still surprised them. They were relieved that the government had taken such stringent measures to stop deforestation. They were discussing all this when suddenly they came across a large patch of bare land. It was like an island surrounded by the huge trees. There were two-tree mechanical saws and a large generator standing there. They stared amazed at the scene in front of them. There were about fifty-odd logs of wood neatly stacked on the periphery of the clearing ready to be transported to their destination. So poaching was indeed going on. It was too far inside for the local people to have heard or noticed anything amiss.

They sat down on the stumps of trees that had been sawed off. It was indeed very sad that such large-scale deforestation was going on. The whole operation could not have gone on without the connivance of the local police.

'It's atrocious!' Jayant fumed, 'We must do something about it. We'll go to the local administration and tell them to take strict action against these thieves.'

'Careful, Jayant,' Adheesh warned him. 'We are not here to catch smugglers; we are here to catch and annihilate demons, though it wouldn't be wrong to catch these thieves too. But we need to completely focus on finding demons. We cannot divert our attention to these mundane activities,' he smiled at his own choice of words.

At an unconscious level, they could hear Shara's periodic cooing. Tejas must be somewhere around, Aishani mused. The sun was now up in the sky and it was broad daylight. Uday suggested that they go behind some trees so that if any poacher arrived, they would not be easily spotted. It was a thick jungle; it was not too arduous to camouflage themselves. Sure enough, a raggedy band of people did start coming to the clearing. They went about their work in a very confident manner, not really furtive. One person seemed to be keeping an eye on the workers, he seemed to be a supervisor of sorts. From a short distance came the familiar 'Coo coo' of Shara. The supervisor smiled and the workers continued with their work. They were obviously friendly with Shara, who they must be considering a harmless old lady. But the nature of Aishani's group was to suspect everybody. Jayant already had reservations about her. Very soon, Shara came into the clearing where the poachers were cutting trees with their huge electric saws. The saws had handles on their outer edges. Two people guided the saw to the exact place from where they had to cut the tree, then switched on the current. It took them almost half an hour to cut one tree and then a couple of hours to cut off its branches and foliage.

'They may not be demons in the real sense, but they are sure doing demoniac work without any real fear. Chopping trees has such cascading long-term effect on ecology and the flora and fauna of a place. The administration must be hand-in-glove with these people. For their immediate gains, such people are slowly but surely destroying our beautiful Earth,' Aishani commented sadly. Shara cooed as if in assent, though she was a bit far away. They sat there unhappily, mulling over the whole matter. It was getting hot and the workers decided to take a break. They put their saws between two tree trunks in a way that the cutting sharp edge was facing up. They knew that the saws could not be put facing down, because that could blunt their sharp blades.

More than a couple of huge trees had been cut. Tejas was still flitting on the tree tops nearby. The workers were sitting around in a group eating their lunch. One young boy got up, maybe to drink water. His hand accidentally touched the switch of one of the electric saws. With nobody to hold the handles of the saw, it started whirring uncontrollably against the two tree trunks against which it was put up almost vertically. Tejas was jumping on the same trees. He lost his balance, fell on top of the saw and was neatly cut in half.

They watched horrified. One moment Tejas was jumping around, the next moment he was dead, his body cut in two parts.

Crying loudly, they rushed towards him. Even the labourers ran towards the accident, but Tejas was gone, he was dead. Ruby was the first one to reach him. She gave a shriek of horror. Tejas' body had been sliced vertically. Ruby tried to hold him in her arms. To her horror, only half of his body came in her arms, the other half remained on the ground where it had fallen over the saw. She looked at Uday and Aishani piteously. For the first time, Uday was shell-shocked, no words came from his mouth. He sat down heavily on the ground beside Tejas. By this time, the workers had also run up to them.

Seeing such a horrific accident, that too by their own tool, they panicked. Cowards that they were, they swiftly collected their tools and ran away. Adheesh and Aishani came to their senses soon enough. Their sweet Tejas, the life of their group, was no more! Felled by a freak accident! Adheesh covered him with a towel. Too bewildered at the drastic turn of events, they sat down and cried. By this time, Shara had also come near them. She began keening tragically and cooing too.

Their sunshine who always shone even at night, who brought happiness and laughter wherever he went, who should always be on tree tops, was now lying crumpled, sliced in two parts on the ground. They were afraid to touch him, lest some more bones break. Too shocked for words or actions, they just sat beside him uncomprehendingly, not knowing what to do. Soon Aishani got up in a daze and tottered under a tree. Without waiting a moment, she immediately went into a trance and began meditating. She was trying to reach Guruji. She knew that she had to be completely calm and collected for her thoughts to reach Guruji. Her body was shaking, she could not think, nor could the others. Years of practice again came to the fore and all sounds and thoughts receded. She began sending thought waves to Guruji.

Guruji arrived in a matter of minutes. They were still sitting around Tejas' body. The old woman Shara was crying loudly now. In their shock and misery, they completely ignored her. Her presence was more like a sad backdrop for them. As they stepped aside for Guruji to approach Tejas, he sized up the situation in a flash. Ruby looked at him helplessly, tears in her eyes. Guruji sat down beside Tejas' body, looked at him and then looked around. He espied Shara who was standing a bit away from them whimpering. Guruji turned gravely towards them. 'Tejas has left us, we cannot take him back in this condition. As bitter as this sounds, we will have to cremate him here in Champaran itself. His body has sustained such a huge injury that it cannot be moved anywhere else.'

There was shocked silence all around. They could not believe it! Tejas, their youngest, was the first to die that even in such a freak accident! Ruby moaned, they were all sobbing. Even in this haze of pain, at the back of his mind, Adheesh was just a bit puzzled. He knew that Guruji was above all human emotions. Guruji had not shown any emotion when he saw Tejas' body but it almost seemed to him that Guruji was expecting it. Adheesh could not explain it to himself. Guruji spoke again, 'We will have to take him to the cremation ground which is on the bank of the Ram Rekha river. We will have to make a makeshift stretcher to carry him,' Guruji looked at the others. Uday and Ruby had turned to stone. Guruji's words had fallen on deaf ears. Finally, Jayant and Adheesh began to gather some logs to make a makeshift bed to carry Tejas.

By the time they reached the crematorium ground, it was evening. The sky was overcast and it started drizzling, not much but enough to postpone the cremation for some time. Shara, the old woman, followed them to the cremation ground. It seemed she wanted to say something but nobody paid any attention to her nor did they understand her sign language. Guruji looked at her pensively then decided to let her follow them. A man in charge of the crematorium gestured to a shed nearby to keep Tejas' body there and wait for the drizzle to stop. Since the body was to be burned in the open, they had to wait. Adheesh, Uday and Jayant laid his body carefully on the ground inside the shed, came out and sat on some wooden stumps which were scattered there. They were still too stunned, but grief had begun seeping in now.

It was getting dark. They had nothing to do except wait. They dreaded the cremation. Contrarily, they also wanted it to be over as soon as possible. Bittersweet memories were flooding their brains. Guruji was also sitting along with them. They could hear the soft falling of the rain as if the heavens too were continuously crying with them. Shara had stopped keening and cooing. From the corner of his eye, Guruji saw her slowly inching towards the shed. Once Uday made up to go towards the shed but Guruji stopped him by diverting his attention towards the river. It was less of a river and more like a dirty drain now.

To divert their attention, Guruji told them about the story of the Ram Rekha River. 'When Bhagwan Ram was returning with Devi Sita from Lanka, they sat down here to relax for some time. Sita ji was very thirsty, so Bhagwan Ram drew a straight line on the Earth with his bow and arrow and pure water came out from the ground. It became a river and was known as the Ram Rekha river from then on. Sadly, we have not cared for it and now it has become little more than a drain.'

Nobody knew whether they were listening to Guruji or not. But Guruji was satisfied. He had managed to divert their attention from the shed. The rain did not show any signs of dissipating. They were very tired. Night had set in. At around 10 pm the crematorium in-charge left, informing them that he would come early the next morning. 'Guruji,' he folded his hands in respect, 'The cremation cannot take place tonight, I suggest all of you go inside the shed and wait. The rain will surely stop in the morning.'

They didn't answer. Nobody could have eaten anything. Nobody went inside the shed either. It would have been too painful to sit beside a lifeless Tejas. So they waited outside, sometimes sleeping, sometimes awake, reliving their moments with Tejas. At around 2 am, everybody slept. Only Guruji was awake, gazing at the horizon and at his unhappy brood of warriors. They were all soaking wet but the rain had finally stopped. At 3 am, Guruji heard a soft sound from inside the shed. He got up with alacrity. This was the signal Guruji was waiting for. He heard the sound again, so soft that the others didn't hear it; they were fast asleep after the long grueling day. Guruji got up warily and went inside the shed. An earthen lamp was burning on the ground beside Tejas and Shara was sitting beside him. She turned towards Guruji and cooed softly. Guruji looked at Tejas and then looked at Shara. He folded his hands in respect to her. Had the others been awake, they would have been shocked to see Guruji bowing his head before someone. They had never met a person higher in the hierarchy than Guruji. As such, everybody bowed to Guruji, not vice versa.

Shara did not even look at Guruji's folded hands; she was much more excited about something else. The sounds of her cooing were raised a few decibels now. Guruji carefully followed the direction of her eyes. He knew what he was going to witness; even then Guruji's heart also missed a beat. Tejas was lying on the makeshift bed, apparently asleep. There were no signs of any injuries on his body. The two parts of his body were joined together and healed and Shara was clucking and fussing around him like a proud hen. Tejas seemed to be in deep sleep. He was not disturbed by Shara's excited cooing.

The group of warriors was back at the ashram, sitting at the back of their library. Guruji had told them to assemble there. Ruby and Uday were keeping a sharp eye on Tejas, who was somehow less fidgety these last few days, though he didn't really know what he had undergone. He knew it must be something big since they were not telling him anything. Moreover, everyone made sure that he was within arm's length from any one of them. He must have done something really bad, Tejas mused, but try as much he could not remember what he had done. He just remembered waking up in a crematorium and the rest of the team surrounding him. Ruby and Aishani were holding him gingerly and crying and the boys were also sniffing. The old woman Shara was jumping up and down and Guruji had folded his hands in obeisance to that woman. What a strange sight. Maybe today Guruji was going to punish him in front of everyone. This thought put a dampener on his spirits and friskiness too.

For once in his life, Tejas was tense. When Guruji didn't come for some time, he couldn't stop himself. He turned towards Ruby, the only one who would answer him, if at all. The others were still too tense and were looking at him as if he was the most delicate thing in the world. 'Ruby Didi, please tell me what I did,' he whispered. 'I don't remember anything, is this ceremony going to be my purging ceremony? I must have done something so bad that I cannot remember anything,' Tejas was scared, frantic to know the truth.

'Shh…Tejas, you haven't done anything bad. In fact, you have been the precursor of the discovery that there is something good in the very bad also,' she smiled at him affectionately. 'But you did give us a scare.'

Tejas was more confused now. He opened his mouth to ask some more questions, then saw Guruji being escorted towards their table by an almost fawning Vashisht ji. Guruji looked at him and he retreated hurriedly. Guruji came to the point immediately. 'When I sent you to find some demons in the historical Champaran, it was with this purpose. We know that demons per se are wicked and immoral. But sometimes, though rarely, some of them are good. As they are already so powerful, when they are good, they become all the more powerful. In ancient times, Champaran was the seat of religion and spirituality where great sages would meditate and perform their havans. And where there are sages, there are demons. Evil and good go hand in hand. There is this story of the great King Brihadratha of Magadh who had two wives. He loved them equally and promised that he will always love them equally. The king had everything except a progeny. Years went by, the king became old and morose. He had no desires left. He had achieved whatever he had to achieve but his greatest desire was not being fulfilled. So he handed over the reins of his kingdom to his trusted ministers and went to the jungles with his two wives to spend the rest of their days there.

'In the jungle, the king met the sage Chandakaushika and divulged to him about his greatest wish not being fulfilled. The sage, happy with the king, gave him a mango to give to his queens. The king was very fair to his wives. He cut the mango in equal halves and gave each half to his wives. Soon the queens delivered babies. The king watched in consternation as each queen delivered only half a baby. These were just a mass of flesh; they had only one arm, one leg, one eye, and no life. The shocked and grievous king ordered these two parts of flesh to be thrown out. In the jungle, a Rakshasi named Jara who was also called Van Durga and Barmata, was roaming around when she came across these two parts of baby flesh. She was happy that she got food without fighting for it. She took the two small pieces of flesh in her hands and went home happily. At home she playfully put the two halves together. To her utter shock and surprise, the two halves stuck to each other and became a whole and turned into a proper human baby with life. Jara's maternal instincts came to the fore. She could not kill or eat the baby. Instead, she decided to return the baby. King Brihadratha was so happy and grateful to the demoness Jara that he named his son Jarasandh, meaning a child who has been joined by Jara.'

Guruji looked at the faces of his audience who were listening to him with rapt attention, 'This old woman Shara who you met in Champaran and who joined Tejas is a descendent of the same Jara who joined Jarasandh, who later became a great king. I had some idea that one of Jara's descendants was around, that is why I sent you all there to find her. There are some good demons also though rare.'

Tejas gasped, 'I was divided in two parts and then joined? How did this happen?'

'I'll tell you later,' Ruby reassured him.

'Why don't we bring her here Guruji?' Jayant asked, 'We can request her to help us. God knows we get enough cut and mutilated bodies who do not deserve their fate.'

The others also perked up. Guruji didn't answer but looked at Adheesh, who cleared his throat and sat up. 'That cannot happen, Jayant.' Though he addressed Jayant, his assessment and reflections were meant for all of them. 'Shara is first and foremost a demon. She might develop maternal feelings for a few children, but not for all. We cannot infuse empathy in her. It will be disastrous for us to be associated with her. She helped us in this situation but we cannot depend on her to revive others too. Plus on learning about her association with us, other demons may follow her here. That, we know, would be a disaster. She is happy in her village. Though she has joined Tejas, the villagers are not aware of her powers. They love her and in their own way care for her too. We will forever remain grateful to her and we will periodically visit her and see that she is comfortable. For the time being, we have to leave it there.

'The killings have stopped, we don't know for what reason, but we cannot rule out the presence of demons just because Shara lives there. You may have to go there again if we get more reports,' Guruji informed them.

THE MANTIS

'We are getting reports of some strange killings or murders in the eastern regions of the country. It is being said that these killings are done by very thin, almost impoverished females. They devour the head of their partners or husbands.' They looked at each other puzzled and would have laughed if it wasn't so gory. Guruji looked at them somberly as if he had guessed their thoughts, 'Well, take it seriously. Go to your respective libraries and find out more about these women and their ilk.' 'Yes, Guruji,' they said obediently, a bit chastened. They knew that Guruji had not approved of their thoughts. A killing was a killing; a person was dead by wrongful means. They touched Guruji's feet and hurried towards the library.

As usual, Tejas was the first to reach as he swung through the trees. Adheesh, Aishani and Uday went to the senior library while Ruby, Jayant and Tejas went to the general library.

They discovered that it was not a very difficult or rare creature to find. This demon was actually an insect grown quite large, almost like a petite human, mainly female. It had all the traits of a Preying Mantis, a grasshopper-like insect with its long arms folded in such a way that it seemed to be praying. The female demons of this kind are always frail and are so thin that they resemble sticks; they are always hungry and deprived of nutrition. They are femme fatales who lure unsuspecting males in their so-called boudoirs and when the male is totally engrossed with them, they begin by first eating their heads because they feel it has the most nutrition and then the other parts. The rest of the time, they behave like human beings. One human head and some other parts last them for about three to four months, in which time they slowly eat the rest of the body. They generally become pregnant in their first encounter with a male. Instead of producing a human baby the normal way, they lay innumerable small eggs in the tropical jungles of the country. Not much had been written in the library books about how they rear up their children after they hatch. Many eggs get spoiled by the travails of nature, many are eaten up by animals in the jungle and some are eaten by the mothers themselves for sustenance.

Armed with this knowledge and with the notes that he had jotted down, Adheesh went to Guruji. He instructed the rest of them to do some more research just in case they could discover other facts. Guruji was in his sadhana. Adheesh waited, utilising the time to think about how to kill this insect demon. They would have to go to the North-East part of the country where the tropical forests were hot and humid, perfect for breeding insects. They would have to find out if any human males were missing—if so, then from where.

Guruji's sadhana was complete by now and he opened his eyes. Adheesh touched Guruji's feet, then recounted all they had learnt from the ancient books.

'The survival instinct is so strong in all living beings that they will go to any extent to exist in this world. But insects and animals are much better off than humans and demons. The animals kill and eat only to survive whereas humans and demons kill unnecessarily for the sake of it, for their enjoyment, demons much more so. This Praying Mantis who takes the form of a human and kills and eats her partners has become a demon, but it is still more of an insect than a human or a demon in the sense that it kills and eats only for its survival, not for any other ulterior motive,' Guruji explained to Adheesh.

'Yes Guruji, it's such a sad travesty, some of these insects have jumped the scale of evolution and become human beings, but they haven't been able to overcome this killer trait of theirs.'

'Adheesh, this is what happens when for some inexplicable reason the evolution scale is jumped. The body changes are a huge modification. When evolution does not happen gradually, many traits of a living being remain the same, in this case the insect Mantis has become half human. Its survival instincts are still of an emaciated insect, hence the killing and eating of its partners,' Guruji looked up. 'Prabhu has his own plans, maybe it is to teach not to jump the evolution train, maybe some other reason. Maybe it's a freak of nature, who knows.'

Adheesh nodded. 'Obviously such creatures have to be destroyed. Where should we begin, Guruji?'

'You will have to go to the North-East where reports have come of men being killed. Their heads have been pulled off from their necks. Earlier there were very few reports of such incidents, very few and far between but lately they have increased substantially. We can guess that the creatures have produced more of their own who in turn will produce more. You will have to move fast, dig as much information as you can and annihilate them. Ashutosh and Divyansh will also accompany you and your team. These insect demons are multiplying at a fast pace. You will need more warriors to destroy them. And Adheesh, take extra mosquito repellants.' Adheesh was puzzled, Guruji was instructing him to take mosquito repellants! Well, whatever, Guruji's instructions were never taken lightly by anyone; he would follow them to a T.

'Yes, Guruji,' Adheesh touched Guruji's feet and left. Ashutosh and Divyansh had just completed their course in the Gurukul. They were serious focused pupils and were among the top five in their batch. Adheesh did not have much interaction with them, mainly because he was busy and secondly, he was a loner who mixed only with a certain set of people. They had responded very well to their training in the Gurukul but whether they had extra abilities or were blessed, only Guruji knew. Divyansh was just a bit more outgoing, or so Tejas said.

That was about a month ago. They had first gone to Guwahati, where they stayed for a day as Guruji had told them to visit Mata Kamakhya temple and take her blessings. As is the ritual, they took a bath in the Kund in the Kamakhya temple and then went to the inner sanctorum to pay their respects to Ma Kamakhya. The legend is that when Lord Shiva's wife Sati died, in his grief he carried her body with him everywhere. The world's balance began tilting. Bhagwan Vishnu had to cut Mata Sati's body with his Sudarshan Chakra. The middle part of Mata Sati's body fell here in Guwahati and it became famous as Kamakhya and became a Shaktipeeth.

The next morning, they boarded a bus and crossed the mighty Brahmaputra river, regarded as the largest male river in India. It was like the sea in its breadth, for one couldn't see one end of the river from the other. It flowed furiously and roared as it went past. Their bus seemed to flail and cower in fear but it rattled away anyhow on the strong bridge. The topography had begun changing from Guwahati itself. There was lush green vegetation and the very air seemed to be moist but not humid. They got down at Tezpur and booked into a mid-level hotel. Tezpur at one time was known as the City of Blood.

'An appropriate name,' Aishani remarked to Adheesh.

Adheesh smiled 'It was also known as the City of Love.'

'Both names are so apt, you love and then you kill. Many incidents must have happened here for this place to acquire these names.'

They were tired after their long, arduous journey. After dinner, they retired to their respective rooms. Three rooms had been booked: one for Adheesh and Aishani, one for Uday and

Tejas and the third one for Jayant, Ashutosh and Divyansh. Ruby was not really required so she opted out. This time too Aishani had the feeling that Ruby was hiding something and she had deliberately chosen to stay back.

'I must talk with Ruby as soon as I return after this mission,' she made a note to herself.

It seemed as if they had just gone to sleep when the birds started chirping. So soon! Tejas opened one eye and looked at his watch. It was 2.45 am. Ok, so he must have dreamt the birds' chatter. He pulled up his covers, turned and went off to sleep again. There was the sound again, this time louder, as if more birds had joined the chorus. He crinkled his eyes and peeked at the thin curtain. It was light outside, dawn had broken. That meant his watch had stopped. He turned to look at Uday, who was also fully awake now.

'This is the East, Tejas, the more East you go, the earlier the day begins. Remember, this is why Japan is called the Land of the Rising Sun.'

Tejas groaned. There was still so much of sleep left in him.

'Come on now,' Uday ordered, 'Go wash yourself, we have a long day ahead.'

The brothers freshened up and went down. The other four were already there, looking refreshed, having their cups of fragrant Assam tea. After a light breakfast, they left the hotel with their rucksacks. To any other person they looked like tourists with their paraphernalia of cameras, tripods, phones, water in their backpacks. These things were there and so were their weapons.

The Gurukul intelligence experts had reported a happening

in one of the villages on the outskirts of the city. They took a bus again, disembarked halfway through and walked the rest of the way. They were surrounded by lush greenery, freshly washed and shining with raindrops. There were huge litchi trees all around, groaning under the weight of their fruits. It was such a beautiful sight: miles and miles of overgrown green litchi trees with their luscious red juicy fruits. One would have thought that Tejas would become delirious with excitement at such a sight but it was the other two warriors Ashutosh and Divyansh who laughingly rushed from one tree to another to pluck the litchis and eat them. As for Tejas, he was just flying from one litchi tree to another. Giving him company were a troop of monkeys who recognised a leader when they met one. They chittered-chattered, following Tejas with full equanimity.

'Careful,' Uday warned the others. 'These are jungle litchis, they may be infected. Peel and examine them before you put them in your mouths.'

Jayant quipped, 'I'll see through them and tell you which ones to eat.' They all laughed and Jayant did exactly that, saving them a lot of trouble, otherwise they would have spat out half the litchis.

It was a dampish walk. As they walked more towards the village, mosquitoes began hovering over them and biting them. Adheesh now remembered that Guruji had told him to take extra mosquito repellents. The mosquitoes here were huge, almost like small flitting birds. They hovered over the group and bit them constantly. The mosquitoes were so huge that they could see their colours and designs, their eyes and the long thin proboscis which they inserted in their flesh to drink their blood. Soon the members of the team were itching all over. Their progress had slowed down considerably.

Adheesh motioned all of them to stop, 'Here, rub these on the exposed parts of your bodies, it should help in repelling the mosquitoes and lessen your itching too,' he handed over tubes of cream to each of them.

'Adheesh,' Aishani exclaimed, 'So many tubes! You've really packed them; good.'

Adheesh gave her a smile. Later he would tell her about Guruji's instructions.

Very soon, it would be dark. They knew that nights in the North-East begin at around 4.30 or 5 in the evening. There would not be much time for research and to get to know the people of this place. Fortunately, a former student of the Gurukul lived here. His name was Gouranga. He could not complete the course at the Gurukul because his father had died in an accident and he had returned to look after his mother and siblings. He was a very keen student and he had kept in touch with a couple of his teachers and Guruji too. Adheesh and Aishani knew that Gouranga had some knowledge of the gory murders which were taking place in these villages. They reached the village. Gouranga was waiting for them on the outskirts itself. They greeted each other and he took them to a nearby tea shop. He was a small built man with a thin, fair and slightly yellowish face with eyes like slits, like most Assamese people.

Gouranga came straight to the point. 'There is not one but many such females going around who are ready to kill. Though most of them have not struck as yet, they will very soon. Till now they are not very hungry, but they are reaching that stage very soon, maybe in a day or two.'

'How many do you think are there?' Aishani asked.

'See, in the beginning there was only one huge insect which resembled the Praying Mantis. It had the power to change into a woman. It lured a man and became pregnant, then ate its head to give it immediate sustenance. It hid the body and ate parts of it regularly. The villagers thought that the man had run away or left the village. They didn't give the incident much importance; such incidents had taken place earlier also. In the meantime, this woman turned back into her original form and laid her eggs. Her children too had the same power of turning into human females. The males somehow didn't survive or were killed by them. I guess there must be ten of them at least by now,' Gouranga ended his narrative.

'How do we place them, I mean how do we recognise them?' queried Uday.

'Well, coming from the North it may be difficult for you to recognize them. You'll catch up eventually, but by that time it will be too late. I have identified a few of them. You can get rid of them in the next couple of days. After that you will catch on,' Gouranga assured them.

'Don't stare now,' he suddenly whispered. 'One of them is actually sitting here near that broken table. She is wearing a brown skirt with a green top. This could be a good time to catch one,' Gouranga looked at them questioningly and then admiringly. They were age-old warriors, nothing had changed in their demeanour, but with his experiences of the Gurukul he knew that they were completely alert and that each of them had thoroughly scrutinised the woman.

She was a thin scrawny woman on the verge of collapse, a miserable expression on her face. She had half a cup of tea in her hand which for some strange reason she was not drinking. She turned to look at them; a smile lit her face which changed everything. She saw a group of young men sitting in front of her. She seemed to turn beautiful in an instant.

After a few minutes, she seemed to have come to a decision. She had begun eying Ashutosh. All of them noticed this. Gouranga gestured to them to leave the place. They all got up to leave while Ashutosh lingered behind. She went to Ashutosh as soon as the others were out of sight. Gone was the gauntness and the dark circles under the eyes. This was displaced by a chirpy, earthy sensuousness. Her whole body was shining. Her perfume was of the rain washing the Earth after a long-parched day. She was totally irresistible. They saw her talking to Ashutosh to which he smilingly replied. They talked some more and then decided to leave the tea shop for a better place which would provide them more privacy. They passed the other members who were nonchalantly taking photographs of the flora and fauna surrounding them. Adheesh looked at Uday, who gave an imperceptible nod. His bag contained his Pash also. Their eyes were closely monitoring Ashutosh and the girl. Suddenly they disappeared from view. Puzzled, they looked around but could not locate them.

They knew that the girl or the creature had turned invisible. If she could do so, then she could mesmerise Ashutosh too. Everybody looked at Jayant, who was quietly walking in the opposite direction behind the tea shop. Jayant was using his x-ray eyes. He was following Ashutosh and the girl and the rest of them followed at a distance. The girl or the Mantis was taking him inside some thick and lush shrubbery. Inside the shrubbery was a beautiful room made of leaves and fragrant flowers. Attached to one wall of shrubs, was a bed. It was here that she led Ashutosh. Uday's hand tightened on his Pash. Adheesh gestured to him to wait. Ashutosh lay down on the bed, it seemed that he was under the spell of the creature. She lay down on top of Ashutosh, took his face between her hands and began kissing him. Ashutosh became a docile partner. Suddenly the creature began changing before their very eyes. It was scrawny to begin with, it became scrawnier. Its head became huge and the body began looking like a large grasshopper's. Ashutosh's eyes were closed now, they couldn't make out whether it was in pleasure or he was goading the demon to come nearer to him. Suddenly the demon or the Praying Mantis opened its mouth huge enough to snap off Ashutosh's head in one bite. But Ashutosh was faster. With one stroke of his hatchet he struck off the creature's head. The demon's head went back even as it bared its teeth. But its head remained attached to its undernourished, skeletal frame. It got up swiftly even with its slashed throat and lunged at Ashutosh to bite off his head, but its speed had diminished considerably. Ashutosh jumped up from the bed and struck the creature's throat again. This time the creature's head was completely severed from its body. The huge head fell down beside the bed. The creature's scrawny limbs flailed for some time and then slowly started fading away. Even the head turned into powder. Finally, what was left of the creature was just a minuscule amount of very fine powder which blended with the air which came inside when the others rushed in.

'Well done, Ashutosh,' Adheesh patted him on the back. Ashutosh smiled a little self-consciously. He didn't reveal this to the others but he was feeling a bit regretful about not having killed the demon with his first strike. The others were full of praise for him. There was a feeling of relief that they wouldn't have to dispose of the body, hence no explanation would be required to be given to the villagers.

It was time for them to go back to their hotel. As they were walking towards the bus stand, Adheesh asked Gouranga, 'How many such creatures do you think are here?'

'This is their breeding season. The Mantises grow berserk in this season, searching for mates to reproduce with. The demons have a very tough time finding human beings to prey upon. Sometimes they just starve and wither away for want of a human prey. Hence these are desperate times for them. At this time of the year, they are generally found in markets looking for a partner. I would say that there are approximately ten of these female Preying Mantis who can change into human form. I think you will have to come and stay here.'

They nodded. Their bus would come after one hour. Adheesh, Aishani and the others sat on the benches at the bus stand and discussed their strategy for the next day.

They returned early the next day. This time they were better prepared to face any contingencies. Gouranga took them straight to the market which was just beginning to prepare for the day. Not many people were around. It was a small village, but people from the other villages too came to this market because it offered more variety of goods and better quality.

Customers began trickling in. Many men went and sat in the tea stalls while some women began bargaining for clothes and cosmetics, while others bought grocery and vegetables. Suddenly, Gouranga stiffened: He had spotted one creature. Following his gaze, they all spotted her. She was a skinny yellow female standing near a paan and betel shop scrutinising the crowd. Soon another famished woman joined her. Adheesh gestured to Uday and Divyansh. Both these warriors sauntered towards the shop and asked for a paan. They gave a casual glance to the women who were eyeing them greedily.

'Would you like to have a paan?' Divyansh asked one of them. She nodded. Very soon, Uday and Divyansh strolled away with the two women. Gouranga pointed to two other women. This time Jayant and Ashutosh went with them.

'Four of these creatures have been taken care of. Now six are left. Tejas and I will go with the next two. I hope they come soon so that we can come back and take care of the rest.' 'Don't hurry, Adheesh,' Aishani said sotto voce so that the others don't hear them. 'You have to take care of Tejas too, he has not been given active work as yet. Gouranga is here with me. We will take care of the others.'

Adheesh nodded. Nobody ever doubted Aishani's capabilities. She was more accomplished than ten warriors put together. Nor did he ever doubt her ingenuity. When Gouranga pointed to the next two creatures, he went with Tejas without any qualms.

Now only Aishani and Gouranga were left behind and there were four more creatures. They didn't have anything to do but wait for these demons to lure other men. Gouranga was not a full-fledged warrior, though he had been a great help in giving them all the intelligence which they required and pointing out to the Preying Mantis demons. On their own, they would have also found out but this saved so much of time and effort. They waited for a long time for the last four creatures to appear but they did not show up. Aishani and Gouranga went around the market window shopping and Aishani ended up buying a few things. Gouranga had told some of the villagers that this was a group of people from Mumbai who were making a documentary on the villages of Assam.

'Don't look now, keep on buying, the last four have come and they are tying up with two men. Probably they cannot wait any more so all four of them will use these two men', Gouranga said. Aishani slowly turned around. The women had pulled on all their charm. They looked ravishing. They wore modern clothes though their mouths were full of betel nuts. This was what gave them away. When they morphed into humans, they would chew on betel nuts to stave off their hunger till they found a human male. Aishani and Gouranga followed them from the corner of their eyes. The two men were enraptured by the beauty and boldness of these women. That and the musky smell that they were throwing at the men totally captivated them. They began moving out of the market.

Aishani and Gouranga followed them at a discreet distance. The two men and the creatures did not pay any attention to them. They were all engrossed in their own agendas. They finally reached a two-room hut made of mud and grass, went inside and closed the door. There were no windows from which Aishani and Gouranga could peep, but

Gouranga found a kink in one of the walls. His eyes took a minute to adjust to the darkness.

'Didi, fast!' he blurted out, 'They have begun the process!'

Aishani was impatiently waiting for this signal. She rushed inside with her Kora. Two of the women were sitting on top of the men who were totally passive under them. The two females had turned into their original selves, that is they had taken their insect form—huge insects with mouths big enough to pluck a man's head in one go. With a sharp cry, Aishani jumped and slashed their throats in one go. The two demons slumped down on the two men. There was hardly any blood. The men underneath them had their eyes closed and didn't comprehend what was going on. Gouranga had a knife. He slashed his knife at the woman near him, but she was faster, snatched the knife from his hands and bit him hard on his shoulder, taking out a chunk of his muscles. Gouranga staggered, the second woman also joined the first woman and they both opened their mouths wide to chomp his head out of his body. Gouranga was no match for them. But Aishani turned like lightning towards them and hacked their bodies. She could not make a clean cut because Gouranga was entangled with them. Aishani was an expert slayer. Her moves were crystal clear and she struck exactly where she wanted to strike. The other two creatures did not have any time to morph into their original forms. Soon all four of them turned into fine dust and some of it dissipated through the open door.

Aishani helped Gouranga to his feet and took him outside to the outskirts of the market. She made him sit on a tree stump and took out some gauge and antibiotic liquid from her pocket. They all carried small first aid packets with them whenever they were on a mission. She gave a painkiller to Gouranga. Tejas and Adheesh and the others had also returned and Tejas had espied Aishani from a tree top. They rushed towards them and Divyansh began to administer first aid to Gouranga. He had lost a lot of blood, but it was a muscle wound and would heal fast under proper care. He was in pain but could speak almost clearly, 'We have destroyed all the Mantis here, at least for this season. I don't know if any of them could lay any eggs this season. They could not entice and devour any man. But for now, the village has been cleared of this creature.'

Adheesh nodded, 'Okay Gouranga, we will stay here for two more days and wait for any more Praying Mantis and to look after you too. We will leave after that.'

MAHEESH

'His name is Maheesh, and he is a magician, one of the greatest magicians of the world. He is yet to be surpassed by any other magician in this century. His shows are so popular and so much in demand that he does not need to advertise. His fans just adore him. Apart from having such a huge fan following, he is actually good. His legendary act is where he can change into so many creatures without any props. He stands alone on the stage—a huge stage, mind you—with nothing and nobody there and poof! he suddenly changes into an elephant. He then changes into a huge bird while the audiences is still gasping. As their eyes follow the flight of the bird, he changes into a massive bull and charges at the audience.

Before the mayhem can really begin, he again transforms into his original form of a human being. He does all this while being in the midst of an audience.'

He looked around at his less than receptive listeners. Uday was looking out of the window, Tejas was busy with his calisthenics, Ruby was filing her nails and Aishani had just stifled a yawn. Only Devnath, who was sitting near the door, was listening in rapt attention. But then that was expected from Devnath.

'Oh! Come on guys, wake up! We are talking about a demon here!'

'Is that so, Bhaiya?' Tejas slipped down to the ground with a thud. 'I thought you were talking about a magician and his shows.'

Ruby butted in, 'Tejas, Adheesh never talks lightly about anything.'

Aishani, sitting across from them, smiled at them with glazed eyes. She and Ruby had gone with Jayant to the jungle where Jayant had shown them so many wonders with his x-ray vision that they were awestruck. They spent more than half the night admiring and exploring these wonders. It was a night picnic for them. Jayant was still sleeping, but Ruby was fresh and Aishani was sitting languidly on a cane chair with lots of cushions.

'Of late, he has stopped giving these stage shows for reasons of his own. He allows his selected crew members to perform in his shows. Nevertheless, the maximum applause and adulation comes when he is performing.'

'So how is he a demon, Bhaiya?' It was Tejas again.

'Well, for one, wherever his troupe goes they leave behind a trail of murders and unexplained deaths—plenty of them. Sometimes these killings have directly pointed out to him but intelligence reports say that he is so rich that he just buys off the officials.'

'Then why do it only? The purpose of any such show is to make money and live comfortably. If he has made so much money that he easily buys off people, then he should quit and disband his troupe,' Aishani commented.

Adheesh kept quiet. Clearly, they were not in the right frame of mind. Some other time, he thought then quickly corrected himself: In their line of work, there can be no other time. It had to be now if any life had to be saved. But yes, they would have to wait for more information from their sources.

Uday chipped in, 'Why do we all do what we do? Do we do it for money? Do we do it to command praise from others? No, we simply do it because that is why we are born, that is our destiny. In the same context, Maheesh might be doing something which is stamped in his genetic code.'

The others sat up. Coming from Uday, that was a long speech. Uday was usually so taciturn that they had stopped expecting to hear his views. They knew that he had very strong opinions, it was just that he never expressed them. His iterating Adheesh's thoughts now alerted them. They knew that Adheesh and Uday were on the same wavelength most of the time and this was no exception. They also knew that Uday would not mince words if it came to rebuking them. In lighter moments, they could take a chance with Adheesh but never with Uday.

Aishani began, 'Let us gather some more intelligence, make a plan and then go to Guruji.'

'That's it, Ash, Guruji wants us to meet him now,' Adheesh informed them.

'Oh, okay, let's go,' they perked up and began filing out. Ruby and Tejas were clearly uncomfortable after last night's romp. Even Aishani was not feeling up to the mark but she was slightly better off than the others. Tejas and Devnath stayed outside Guruji's cottage—Tejas because he couldn't sit still and would have distracted others and Devnath because he never felt comfortable sitting with the others.

If Guruji noticed Jayant's absence, he gave no sign of it. They always had a niggling feeling that Guruji favored Jayant just a little bit, though there was no obvious reason for it. Aishani and Adheesh had discussed it too but had found no explanation for it.

'Maybe they are related through some past birth, though Guruji cannot be related to anybody,' Adheesh shrugged. 'Either way, it's good; Guruji will always keep an extra eye on him, he does keep on getting into scrapes and is just a bit careless too.'

Aishani nodded, she was also of the same opinion.

Guruji came straight to the point, 'The demon Maheesh goes back a long way. You can go to the library and discover his antecedents. At one time, his ancestor was the king of the universe who plundered and ravaged human beings and devtas too. The universe was in turmoil till Ma Durga annihilated it. The magician Maheesh who has been reported now is believed to be distantly related to the Rakshasa Mahishasur.

His powers are greatly watered down but he can still change form and all the gory demon lusts remain the same. Earlier it was difficult to catch him and his cohorts as they were a veritable army. Circus was a huge mode of entertainment and people flocked to see them. Now there are so many kinds of entertainment and people hardly go to the circus anymore. Therefore, this so-called magician Maheesh is in a fix. Earlier, killing one person from the spectators or killing one worker from his own setup did not raise too many eyebrows. Bribing the police also greatly helped. All this is not possible now. He has to close his shop, the circus. This has made him desperate but vulnerable and weak too. The killings happen more often now. Since there is a limited audience and less performers, the killings have been noticed by the police and they have not been very successful in hushing up the matter even with huge amounts of bribe. Our intelligence got a whiff of this, and they discovered this demon and his army. He still has the powers to change many forms, each one as powerful as the other. His powers heighten, especially during Navratri, and it is during this period that he gets killed by Ma Durga. Nobody else can destroy him,' Guruji stated and looked out of the window unseeingly. Everybody knew who he was talking about, even Aishani. They nodded in understanding.

'Yes Guruji, we'll go to the library and find out some more about this Rakshasa,' Adheesh acknowledged. Guruji nodded. He turned towards Aishani and Adheesh and motioned for them to stay back. The others left.

Guruji took out a bottle of liquid from one of the shelves, 'This is an elixir known as Madhu which Ma Durga used to drink during the destruction of demons. Guruji told Aishani to put her hands over the bottle for a minute while he chanted some mantras. Then he placed the bottle again on the shelf. 'I will keep on activating the Madhu till the time you leave.'

Turning to Adheesh, he said, 'You will have to give her half a bowl of this liquid when she faces Maheesh and his army. This will give her extra momentum to kill the demons.' They nodded, then touched his feet and went outside.

Tejas bombarded them with his questions and curiosity. They heaved a sigh of relief when they saw a sheepish Jayant coming towards them.

'Let us go to the library,' Uday almost admonished them. 'I'll brief both of you there.' Turning to Adheesh and Aishani he said, 'Both of you go, I'll join you in the senior library after settling down these people.' These days even Devnath was allowed to use the library, though he still trusted his instincts more.

As they reached the senior library, Aishani quipped, 'Adhee, Guruji told us that this demon Maheesh becomes enormously powerful during Navratri, and he gets killed in the Navratris too. The festival is just fifteen days away. We'll have to prepare ourselves in these fifteen days to destroy him.'

'Yes, Ash, we'll pave the way for you, but only you have the power to actually kill him,' he iterated.

She sighed, 'I pray to Maa to give me the energy to kill him.'

Adheesh pressed her hand as they entered the library.

A few days later, they were in a dusty town near Uttar Pradesh. Guruji had sent Ashutosh and Divyansh along, as more warriors were needed to counter Maheesh's demons. The circus had been set up here. It was a huge affair. Rumour was that since the circus business was not doing well, its owner the magician Maheesh had decided to close it. The coming week was going to be a spectacular extravaganza after which the circus would sadly close. Some of the crew members had already left, looking for better pastures. Still, there were more than a hundred members of the circus troupe left, along with the animals. The whole scenario was more like a mela (fair) than a circus. There were colourful streamers and balloons everywhere, games of many kinds, shops selling clothes and jewelry, food stalls, merry-go-rounds, and many other modes of entertainment. There was so much of fun going around that Aishani and her team too got embroiled in the infectious happy chaos. But Adheesh and Uday remained serious and alert. He could see the circus tent beyond the fair. Their immediate mission was getting inside the curtain. Tejas had already been briefed and Adheesh knew that he would take his work very seriously. Adheesh and his whole team were dressed as poor villagers out to have a good time at the fair. Adheesh and Tejas went to the back of the circus and tried to enter the tent. They were immediately stopped by a ferocious-looking guard. Adheesh could deduce that this fellow was a demon.

Addressing the guard, Adheesh folded his hands and said, 'Sir, I am a poor man, and this is my younger brother Dhincha. He is the world's best acrobat. Test him, Sir, and give him a chance.'

The guard scowled at Tejas' diminutive form and smirked, 'This pipsqueak? Acrobatics is no joke. Just because this Dhincha can jump around doesn't mean he can perform on the net. Go away! Shoo!' the guard raised his stick, but Adheesh implored, 'Please Sir, please give my brother one small chance!' Adheesh knew that a number of acrobats had left the circus and that they desperately needed a couple of replacements. The guard hesitated for a minute, then took them to the manager. Tejas was asked to perform a few of his stunts. Tejas climbed on the ceiling, wriggled under the table, and then stopped. Adheesh had told him not to show his best powers, lest the demon became suspicious.

The manager hired Dhincha. So many acrobats had left, and they had to put up a show somehow. This boy Dhincha did have some skills, though he was not up to the mark. Polish was what the child required and that needed time, the manager rued. Time was something they did not have. His lord and master Maheesh, the magician, was in the throes of despair. The closing of the circus was affecting him in more ways than one. The circus was just a façade for his other nefarious activities and businesses. Maheesh was a magician par excellence, he would always remain a star, but what about his army in the circus, how could he keep them now that the circus was closing? Plus, it was that time of the year when he would be his most powerful, creating havoc and chaos in the whole world. Nothing gave him more happiness and satisfaction than killing and torturing people, usurping their powers, money and women.

The manager, who was himself a demon, knew that there was no greater Rakshasa in the world than Maheesh. Yet the manager also knew that in this time period itself Maheesh became the weakest, it was almost as if he was dead. The manager whose name was Chawar knew all about his master's cycles, knew all about this time of the year, because along with his master, he too became very severely affected by this phenomenon.

Adheesh heaved a sigh of relief when Tejas was hired. The manage Chawar had immediately put Tejas on duty, which was excellent as that would allow Tejas to go around and see what was happening backstage. Adheesh begged the manager to fix a higher wage for Tejas, which was of course promptly denied—Adheesh had negotiated only for effect.

It had been advertised that there was going to be a light and sound show at the fair and people were looking forward to it. He left Tejas in the backyard of the circus, promising to come back after midnight.

The others were having a good time, as far as he could tell. He hoped that each of them was fully alert for any sign of trouble. Aishani and Ruby were standing in front of a cosmetic and jewelry shop while Uday, Ashutosh and Divyansh were taking part in some game. Jayant was nowhere to be seen. Adheesh knew that Jayant with his special vision had gone to find about the hidden lairs of the demons and weak spots. If Jayant comes back with a proper report then tonight would be the night, otherwise tomorrow night. When Jayant did come back it was quite late and the crowd had begun trickling away. No untoward incident had been reported so far. Around midnight, Adheesh went to meet Tejas.

They had not come to this place to witness unpleasant incidents, nor had they come to catch the culprits. They were warriors and their orders were clear: 'Kill and destroy.' There would be no mercy shown, just killing of the demons who had kept themselves so well hidden these past centuries and continued with their gory bloodshed and carnage.

Aishani had shifted into destructive mode. The others had already paved the way for her by killing the smaller demons. She drank the elixir that Adheesh gave her, the drink that Guruji had provided. Her human frame needed every iota of energy and intensity to counter the ferocious demons. The conflict started the next night. A young man went missing. Nobody paid much attention to it as he had come alone to the fair, easy prey. Adheesh and his team were waiting for just this kind of news. Tejas had also given them some tips from the time he was in the circus: There were some tents which nobody was allowed to enter. These tents were heavily guarded. When circus manager Chawar saw Tejas hovering near the tents, he not only hollered at him but gave him a wallop. Tejas had to hurriedly go back to his practice.

Furthermore, Tejas said that there was an aura of fear and dread in the camp. Even the animals seemed to be fearful. It was not the fear of being shouted at or being hit, it was the raw fear of death, of torture, so strong that he could smell the fear all around.

The warriors barged inside the circus from the back, but they had not expected so many demons to come out of nowhere to confront them. A bloody battle ensued behind the circus tents. There was so much noise outside that even if anybody heard the sounds of the clamour inside, they did not pay any attention to it. The magician or the demon Maheesh was in the ring entertaining the audience by changing into different living beings. He rampaged in the ring first as a boar, then as an elephant. The audience and the children were suitably impressed and there was a lot of genuine clapping. It was when he became a huge bird with huge wings and was flapping around the ceiling of the huge tent that he noticed the bloodbath behind the tents. Shocked, he fell down in the ring itself. Maheesh quickly changed into his human form, made his bows and quickly ran inside. Some acrobats took his place along with jokers and animals. The audience was lapping it up happily thinking it was all part of the circus itinerary.

Maheesh rushed out of the ring, his anger breaking all bounds. He threw his hands in the air. Immediately a few huge weapons materialised in his hands. He turned to look who had fought and caused such havoc in his army of trusted and fierce generals. All he saw was a woman with weapons standing in front of him. Dimly, he could register that his people were being massacred behind the woman's back. He looked at the woman. She was beautiful and she seemed to have more than two hands and she was looking at him angrily. When he looked closely, he saw only two hands which held two weapons. She was drinking some kind of wine which was making her cheeks red and her eyes glow. Though Maheesh was a direct descendant of the demon Mahishasur, his powers had also diminished through the ages. His power of changing into different forms had remained more or less intact, so was the lust for killing. Here there was a woman standing in front of him, the feeblest of all living creatures challenging him. He would have laughed had he not seen the dead bodies of his soldiers behind her. Maheesh charged at her with his sword, which Aishani promptly cut in two parts along with his other weapons. Shocked, he stared at his hands, then at the woman unbelievingly. Without waiting for even a moment, she rushed at him with her weapons. He could see the anger on her face now that she was near him.

Behind them, a terrible battle was raging between Adheesh's warriors and Maheesh's demons. Maheesh was aware of the boon which his ascendants had attained from Brahma. The boon was that nobody could kill the great demon Mahishasur, only a woman could kill him. Mahishasur had not asked for any protection against women, because he felt that women were frail, the weaker sex, hence there was no chance that they could counter a great Rakshasa like him, let alone kill him. Though he was personally not blessed with this boon, nevertheless he knew he could tackle any woman, especially in the present century when the effectiveness of a woman was at its lowest zenith on the battlefield.

Initially, when Aishani attacked him, Maheesh was not scared but rather surprised. When he was without weapons, it was easier for him to change into another entity. He had become famous as a magician because he could change himself into any creature that he wished. Simple human beings thought that it was his magic, they thought that he could mesmerise them into thinking that he had changed his looks. But in reality Maheesh was able to change form because he was the demon Mahishasur's descendant and had been endowed with this trait. He immediately changed into a ferocious buffalo and started running around the woods behind the circus crushing and felling the huge trees as he ran around in fury.

He had not reckoned with an opponent like Aishani. She was a warrior par excellence who had been personally blessed by Ma Durga. The buffalo ran around bellowing his destruction. It then entered the circus ring itself. The audience had been waiting for his reappearance, as they were quite disappointed when the magician left the ring so abruptly. They happily lapped it up as part of the show. The fair was held during Navratri, and they presumed that the circus was enacting the killing of the Mahishasur by Ma Durga.

Among the many weapons that Aishani was carrying was a Pash, a kind of thick rope which had the capacity of binding anything or anyone. Maheesh then changed himself into a lion and began roaring his displeasure. The audience clapped excitedly in fearful anticipation. But as soon as Aishani ran towards the lion with her powerful sword, the lion turned into its original form, that of the magician Maheesh. He had several weapons with him including a huge shield. The audience was thrilled. Quite a few in the audience were familiar with the story of the annihilation of Rakshasa Mahishasur by Ma Durga. Aishani was in her element now. She swiftly slashed at his weapons and broke his shield in two. Now the demon and magician Maheesh knew that he had a formidable enemy in this woman. But undaunted by this fact, he quickly turned himself into an elephant. The audience was thrilled.

From the back, Adheesh was monitoring the fight. He hastily poured the elixir in a goblet and gave it to Ruby while he fought off attacking demons. Ruby rushed to Aishani and gave the elixir to Aishani to drink. The Madhu began showing its effect, giving Aishani an immediate extra boost of strength and energy. She forgot who she was. She roared in anger and slashed off the elephant's trunk. Maheesh immediately turned into a buffalo again and began stomping his foot on the ground, snorting, and bellowing and then turned towards the audience. The audience screamed en masse. They were hysterical with thrill and fear and anticipation. Not aware that this was the real thing, they by and large kept sitting and cheering, though a few did make a hasty retreat.

Suddenly, Adheesh and Uday jumped in the fray. Between them, they held the huge bull by its hind legs so Aishani could have a clear shot at his neck. The audience was not too familiar with this part of the story, nevertheless they watched the whole scene with bated breath. The ground of the circus was covered with blood. Since its legs were held in a vice-like grip by Adheesh and Uday, the demon could not change its shape. The audience watched as if hypnotised. They knew what was going to happen, they had seen too many idols of the same scene during Navratri, though they were not prepared to watch its enactment which looked as if it was really happening.

When it could not immediately change its shape, Maheesh nevertheless changed into his original shape, that of a demon and began coming out of the buffalo's huge mouth. Aishani was waiting for it. With one stroke of her sword, she slashed its head. The head was severed from the body in one clean stroke. It fell with a thud on the blood-soaked ground of the circus ring. Aishani stood near its body, chest heaving and breathing noisily. Everybody stayed frozen in the same posture for some time. Then the audience stood up. Nobody thought of clapping. There was pin drop silence in the circus. It all looked so real, as if Ma Durga herself had killed Mahishasur. Then after a few minutes, the whole place erupted into massive clapping and cheering. The sound was deafening.

Adheesh was the first one to come to his senses. Gathering his wits, he gestured to Uday who let go of the buffalo's legs. Uday quickly went outside the circus tent where the Gurukul's warriors were sitting or lying down, nursing their wounds. He scanned the area. All the demons seemed to have been exterminated. He gestured to his warriors to come inside the circus ring. They were a bit surprised, but they followed him.

By now, Adheesh had somewhat taken control of Aishani and her heaving body. As soon as everybody was in the ring, they turned to the audience, bowed down and put their hands together in a Namaste. It seemed as if this act was their daily routine. This gesture gave the impression that the whole act was indeed a melodrama which was successfully accomplished.

The audience slowly came out of its reverie. Then began a thunderous round of applause which refused to die down.

Postscript

In the third book of the series, *The Kumbh Conspiracy,* the next generation comes into spotlight. Aishani and her partner, Adheesh, now have twins. Will the twins have their parents' powers? Will they be warriors or killers, just for the sake of it? What about the other children? Will they have powers too? Aishani and others are still going strong fighting the demons of this and another world. Coming from the same bloodline but so young in age, who knows what the future holds for them; for the ones fighting and the ones learning to fight.